"Tell me, Rebecca. Did your escort behave like a gentleman around you?"

"Of course he did!" Rebecca gritted her teeth. "He's a minister for goodness sake! He treated me like a lady—"

"Oh?" A hint of a smile played on Grady's lips. "I dare say he must have stolen a kiss from you, then."

"He did not steal a kiss," Rebecca denied. "He asked permission for one."

"Ah, the true gentleman." He edged forward, lifted his hand, and brushed his fingers through her untamed strands. "Did his kiss leave you breathless and dizzy and begging for more?" he challenged. "Did he kiss you like this?"

He bent his head and brushed his lips across hers ever so softly.

But in the next instant, everything changed. Grady whipped his arms around her and crushed her against the broad expanse of his chest. "Or did he kiss you the way a woman should be kissed, like this . . ."

Courting Rebecca

Susan Sawyer

AVON BOOKS ◆ NEW YORK

COURTING REBECCA is an original publication of Avon Books. This work has never before appeared in book form. This work is a novel. Any similarity to actual persons or events is purely coincidental.

AVON BOOKS
A division of
The Hearst Corporation
1350 Avenue of the Americas
New York, New York 10019

Copyright © 1995 by Susan Sawyer
Inside back cover author photo by Mary Schamehorn
Published by arrangement with the author
Library of Congress Catalog Card Number: 95-94510
ISBN: 0-380-77892-0

First Avon Books Printing: December 1995

AVON TRADEMARK REG. U.S. PAT. OFF. AND IN OTHER COUNTRIES, MARCA REGISTRADA, HECHO EN U.S.A.

Printed in the U.S.A.

RA   10   9   8   7   6   5   4   3   2   1

With much love to my aunts,
Evelyn Long and Winnie Scates,
two wonderful ladies
who hold a special place in my heart

Chapter 1

August 1871
Hope, Kansas

"For cripes' sake, Carl! Why did you have to stir up trouble on our first night in town?" Grady Cunningham stomped out of the Red Dog Saloon and scowled at the paunchy man beside him.

"Damn if I know." Carl unknotted the red bandanna around his neck and wiped off the blood dribbling down his face. "All I did was ask that purty little gal to dance. How was I to know the bartender was her damn beau?"

Grady narrowed his eyes, studying the jagged cut near the top of the man's receding hairline. "At least you had the good sense to duck when whiskey glasses started flying through the air. Hell, if that glass had landed a few inches lower, it would've hit you right between the eyes."

"Yeah, I'm damn lucky, ain't I?" Carl muttered sarcastically.

"Luckier than you have the sense to admit." Chuckling, Grady clapped his friend

1

on the back. "Be grateful the bartender took a shot at you with a whiskey glass instead of a loaded pistol."

Carl winced as he pressed the bandanna against the wound. "You musta been too busy to see that he got me with a whiskey bottle, too. Pounded my head right into the damn bar, he did, right on top of a freakin' whiskey bottle."

"Then you must be the luckiest son of a bitch in all of Kansas tonight." Grady's smile disappeared as he jammed a white Stetson over his dark hair. Carl's condition was no laughing matter, he knew, but he hoped his friend didn't sense his alarm. "Let's get moving, Carl. The gals in the saloon told me where we can find a doctor who can stitch you up like new."

Carl blinked in confusion. "Hope, Kansas, has a doctor now?"

"That's what the ladies said, my friend." Grady pointed to a row of stores across the way, just beyond the railroad tracks that ran through the center of Hope. "He lives on the south end, they said, about a half mile from the edge of town. So let's get saddled up and—"

"Ain't no use in gettin' our horses out of the livery," Carl insisted, stepping down from the planked walkway. "We can get there faster by walkin'."

"Sure you can manage?"

"For Christ's sake, Grady! I ain't feelin' too great, but I ain't gettin' ready to kick the bucket yet."

"And that's the way I want to keep it. I

sure as hell don't want to lose my right-hand man." Grady stole another look at the slash in Carl's head and grimaced. "Let's don't waste any more time arguing, bud. If you want to walk, let's hit the road."

The two men fell into step beside each other, their boots kicking up clouds of dust as they crossed the wide street. A half moon and an August sky full of twinkling stars yielded enough light to guide them across the railroad tracks without any difficulty.

Walking through town, Grady gazed at the familiar surroundings with interest. He hadn't set foot in this place for almost three years. Hadn't wanted to. When he'd stormed out of Hope in 1868, he'd sworn he'd never come back. He'd been sick of living in a two-bit town full of angry people who had nothing better to do than to condemn his every action, every move. So he'd damned them all to hell and set off on his own.

He'd carved out a new life for himself on the plains as a buffalo hunter. And he'd discovered an exhilarating sense of freedom on the open range. Roaming the plains, he'd found there were no standards of conduct to follow, no expectations to meet, no rules of propriety to obey. No one judged him by his past or condemned him without just cause.

As an added bonus, the huge demand for buffalo had swelled his coffers until they were overflowing with more money than he could ever hope to spend. After landing a contract with the Union Pacific to provide railroad construction crews with buffalo meat, Grady discovered profitable markets back East for the massive creatures' hides. Every few months, he shipped out carloads of buffalo skins from railroad terminals in Abilene and Ellsworth.

Until this week, he'd never considered using the railroad facilities in Hope. But preparing to haul his goods to market, he'd been gripped by a wild, reckless yearning that he couldn't explain. Restless and bored with his life on the plains in recent days, he'd felt the need to do something daring, to try something new.

Guided by sheer impulse, he'd set off in the direction of the cattle town that had once been his home. Though Carl and the rest of his crew hadn't balked at the change in scenery, Grady sensed they'd been surprised by his decision to come here.

He was glad they hadn't asked any questions. Grady couldn't explain his reasons for coming here, didn't even understand them himself.

He wasn't welcome in Hope, and he knew it. Very few people in this town had believed in his innocence when a murder charge had been hanging around his neck three years ago. Though a judge from Kansas City had cleared him of all charges, most of the people in Hope had not been convinced that Grady Cunningham was truly blameless in the sordid murder of Ned Sikes.

Worse yet, no one had bothered to believe in him. A stab of pain shot through him, just thinking about the people who had turned their backs on him. Priscilla had called off the wedding, and his own damn father, the cattle king of Kansas, had disowned him. . . .

Grady shrugged. None of it mattered anymore. Since leaving Hope, he'd stopped seeking the approval of other people. He'd learned not to give a damn about anyone's opinion of him. People would believe what they wanted, no matter what he did or said. So he lived his life just the way he wanted to.

And why should he care what other people thought about him? He'd never lived up to anybody's expectations, anyway. Hell, he had never met with his own damn father's approval. All of his life, he'd longed for the old man to look at him with a glimmer of pride, to voice a kind word about his accomplishments. But he'd never been able to do anything good enough to win a scrap of praise from the stalwart, rigid mayor of Hope, Kansas.

An old, gnawing ache twisted inside his gut. Once—just once—he wished the old coot could find something about him to like. . . .

Forget it, Cunningham. Grady clenched his jaw in determination. He had no intention of coming into contact with Malcolm Cunningham while he was in town. He'd only come back to Hope to load up his goods on the train. Now all he wanted from his visit was a few days of fun, the chance to raise a little hell, drink a little whiskey, find a little excitement. He wasn't looking for anything more.

Still, he'd never expected to run across so many changes. Gazing around the cattle town for the first time in years, Grady was amazed by what he saw. Respectable-looking houses had cropped up all over the place. New businesses, shops, and restaurants now stood on spots that had once yielded nothing but prairie grass.

Crossing into the south side of Hope, Grady suddenly realized that Carl's pace had slowed considerably. Turning, he glanced over at his friend.

All color had drained from Carl's face. Fresh blood oozed from his wound, and he was staggering like a drunken sailor. Alarmed, Grady reached out and draped the man's arm over his shoulder. "Keep those boots shufflin', bud," he urged.

Grunting, Carl gave a weak nod. Grady clamped a steadying arm around the man's thick torso as they turned the corner. Carl leaned heavily against him and moaned.

Leaving the business district of Hope, they trudged over the dirt road. Nothing but empty, barren fields, parched dry by the summer heat, was visible until Grady spotted the jagged outline of a two-story, frame house in the distance. Relief swamped through him as his gaze locked on the soft glow of a lantern spilling through the windows of the building.

Someone was home, someone who could help Carl. Fearing his friend might pass out at any moment, Grady tightened his grip around the man and guided him toward the doctor's house.

A warm August breeze floated through the small kitchen, rustling the eyelet curtains that framed the open window. Rebecca Summers inhaled a deep breath and smiled, enjoying the aroma of baked apples and cinnamon wafting through the evening air. She had just placed a freshly baked apple pie on the table when her father-in-law entered the room.

"Don't wait up on me, Rebecca." Heaving a weary sigh, Jacob Summers placed a black leather bag on the table. "I may not get home until morning. Henry Littleton is a very sick man, I fear. When his son came by a few minutes ago, he said the old man's fever was getting worse."

"Maybe it won't be as bad as it sounds," Rebecca said, trying to offer a bit of encouragement to her father-in-law. "I'm certain some of your medicine will help him rest more comfortably."

"I hope you're right." Jacob ran a weathered hand through his thinning, gray hair. "Looks like I won't be here to tuck Jessica into bed again tonight, I'm afraid."

"She's as disappointed as you are. She's upstairs in her room right now, pouting about it." Shaking her head, Rebecca grinned as she inserted a knife into the pie. "I think you've spoiled your granddaughter, Jacob."

"Granddaughters are meant to be spoiled." Jacob peered at the pie and frowned. "You saving that for somebody?"

"You." Rebecca's smile widened. "That is, if you have time to eat some pie before you leave for the Littletons."

Just as she'd hoped, the sight of the golden-crusted pastry was too tempting for Jacob to resist. "I've always got time for a piece of your pie, 'Becca," he conceded, pulling up a chair to the table.

As soon as Jacob tasted the first bite of the dessert, his head bobbed with approval. "Emma taught you well, my dear. I can't say she made a pie any tastier than this in all of our thirty-four years together."

"Thanks, Jacob." Touched by the unexpected praise, Rebecca smiled as she slipped into a chair beside him at the round oak table. "I wish all my dishes could be as tasty as Emma's. She was a wonderful cook."

"A wonderful woman, too. You know, sometimes it seems like she's been gone forever . . ." Jacob's voice faltered, and an expression of sadness shadowed his lined face. ". . . And sometimes it seems like only yesterday when all of us—you and Jessica, and Emma and me—were living together back on the homestead."

Rebecca placed a linen napkin in her lap, thinking about the dear, sweet woman who'd been like a mother to her. "I wish Emma could have moved here with us."

"She would have liked Hope," Jacob agreed with a somber nod. "And I'm sure she would have agreed that moving here was right for all of us . . . especially for you."

"Everything is so different for me now, sometimes I have to pinch myself to make sure I'm not dreaming," she admitted.

And it was true. The changes in her life were so profound that Rebecca often wondered if she were the same person who'd bid good-bye to the Kansas prairie less than a year ago. Since that wondrous day when she'd pulled into the Kansas cattle town with her daughter in her arms and Jacob at her side, Rebecca had been able to hold up her head with pride for the first time in her life. Here in Hope, no one knew except Jacob about the shameful secrets that Rebecca McRae had left behind on a Tennessee farm and the Kansas prairie.

In the eyes of the people here, she was Rebecca Summers, widowed mother and daughter-in-law of the town's sole physician. And she fully intended to keep it that way, not only for herself . . . but for the sake of her six-year-old daughter.

As if sensing her thoughts, Jacob placed a weathered hand over hers. "It's not a dream, 'Becca. You're one of the most respectable ladies in this town. And nothing is going to change that."

"I hope you're right." Seeing the affection and concern glistening from Jacob's eyes, Rebecca felt her heart swell with love for the elderly gentleman. Never in a thousand years could she repay him for all of the support and encouragement he'd given to her. He'd believed in her when no one else would; he'd stood beside her when she didn't have the strength to stand alone. And along the way, he'd become the father that she'd always dreamed of having.

"I know I'm right," Jacob continued. "You've already earned the respect of everyone in this town. Why, the ladies for miles around don't want anyone except you tending to their female problems or delivering their babies or taking care of their little ones."

"Yes, but . . ." Rebecca hedged, wondering if everyone would be so trusting if they knew about her past. "But sometimes I almost expect to hear all those horrid whispers again," she admitted in a shaky tone.

"No one here knows what happened to your father back in Tennessee, Rebecca," Jacob reminded her solemnly. "And we left behind all the gossip on the prairie when we moved away from those blasted Breckinridges, too."

Rebecca forced a smile onto her lips. "It's almost like I have a new identity, isn't it?"

"Yes, but you haven't changed at all, as far as I'm concerned. You're the same, caring young woman who came to live with Emma and me seven years ago." Grinning, he patted her hand affectionately. "Except for your cooking skills, of course. You've greatly improved your talents in the kitchen, my dear."

As Jacob delved into the remainder of his dessert, Rebecca tried to concentrate on enjoying the slice of pie on her plate as well. But discussing the events leading up to her arrival in Hope sparked a flame of fiery memories in her mind that she couldn't seem to shake, no matter how hard she tried.

Her thoughts skittered back to her childhood at the tender age of four, when she'd been forced to live with a cruel family who'd treated her like a slave. From the moment Rebecca had moved into the Breckinridge household back in Tennessee, the family had never allowed her to forget that she was a murderer's daughter, nor that her father had actually sold her to them before he was hanged for his crime. Alfred, the oldest of the four boys, was the worst of the lot; and none of the family had ever bothered to offer a shred of affection or a snippet of love to her.

And they never settled down long enough for Rebecca to make any friends of her own. Certain their pot of gold was waiting for them just beyond the horizon, the Breckinridge clan packed up and moved more times than Rebecca cared to remember. After leaving Tennessee, they'd ventured to Arkansas, then on to Missouri. As the years passed, Rebecca lost all hope of ever finding Tyler, her older brother.

In 1864, they'd finally settled in Kansas, filing a homestead claim for one hundred and sixty acres of free land. There, on the Kansas prairie, David Summers had ridden into Rebecca's life like a knight in shining armor. On leave from the Union Army to visit his parents, the handsome, dark-haired soldier had swept Rebecca off her feet and into his arms.

But sharing her life with David Summers was not meant to be. Soon after returning to his brigade, David had been killed on the battlefield. To Rebecca's sorrow, he died without knowing the union of their love had created a child.

Though grieving for the loss of their only son, Jacob and Emma Summers invited Rebecca and their unborn grandchild to share their home with them. Anxious to escape from the clutches of the cruel Breckinridge family, Rebecca readily agreed. And while living with the kindly physician and his wife, Rebecca learned about the true meaning of kindness and love.

Soon after Emma's death, Jacob learned about the need for a physician in the growing cattle town of Hope. When he suggested they leave behind the painful memories of the Kansas prairie, Rebecca quickly agreed. Grateful for the opportunity to start afresh, she continued to appreciate Jacob's concern and thoughtfulness for arranging the move. "What would I do without you, Jacob?"

Finishing the last bite of pie, Jacob looked up and grinned. "You don't have to do without me, 'Becca. You and Miss Jessica are stuck with me for the rest of my days."

"Nothing could please me more."

Jacob's smile faded, and his eyes clouded with concern. "But I'm not going to be around forever, you know." Leaning back in his chair, he stroked the thick, gray mustache sprouting over his upper lip. "And you need to be thinking about the future. You need to be thinking about finding a nice man to settle down with. A man who would be a fine father for my granddaughter, a good husband for you."

Rebecca floundered for a moment, not knowing how to respond. Since David's death, she'd often dreamed about the possibility of falling in love again. Though she'd never voiced her secret longings to Jacob, she'd always sensed her father-in-law wouldn't object to the prospect of suitors calling on her. Now, hearing his words of encouragement, she confessed her private yearnings aloud.

"I've often thought about the possibilities of sharing my life with someone," she admitted.

"Then why haven't you allowed anyone to call on you since we've been here?"

"Because a decent man is hard to find in a town full of cowboys and drifters." She dropped her gaze to her plate. "And besides, I haven't met anyone who interests me."

There was another reason, too, one that she didn't care to divulge to anyone. She'd worked too hard to earn the respect of her neighbors to risk the chance of allowing anyone—especially a man of questionable integrity—to wreak havoc on her reputation. She was terrified of losing her honorable standing in the community by consorting with any man who possessed less than an impeccable character.

"What sort of man might interest you?" Jacob pressed on.

She propped her chin in her hand, narrowing her eyes, searching for the right words to describe the elusive man of her dreams. "Whoever comes calling on me doesn't have to be wealthy or particularly handsome. But he must be decent, honorable, respectable. The type of man who would never be prone to scandal or embarrassment. The kind of man who would love Jessica as much as I do. The sort of man who would overlook my past . . . and share my dreams for the future."

Rebecca supposed her standards were high. But she knew they weren't impossible to meet. She refused to settle for anything less than a deep, abiding love for a lifetime. Witnessing the bonds of devotion between Jacob and Emma Summers had proven to her that true love could exist between a man and a woman who were right for each other. And someday, she hoped to find that special brand of happiness for herself.

"Seems we've been having a shortage in town of the sort of fella you've been looking for," Jacob assessed. "Of course, our new minister might be a good possibility. From what I've seen of Pastor O'Leary, he seems like a decent young man. And he's a bachelor, too."

Embarrassed to admit the auburn-haired pastor had already caught her eye, Rebecca felt a heated flush rise to her cheeks. "Timothy O'Leary appears to be a very nice gentleman," she said as lightly as she could.

"I'm certain you'll be getting to know each other better soon." Chuckling, he reached out and brushed a finger across her flushed cheek. "But it appears you've already been considering that possibility."

Rebecca grinned sheepishly. "You know me too well, I fear."

"That I do, my dear." Rising, he reached for his hat. "As much as I hate to leave, I suppose I'd better get over to the Littletons' place. Give Jessica a good-night kiss for me, won't you?" he asked, picking up his black leather bag.

"Of course, Jacob," Rebecca agreed.

On the way to the door, Jacob affectionately patted the German shepherd that had been quietly sitting at the foot of the stairs. "Take good care of my girls while I'm gone, Uly."

The dog thumped his tail, then leaped to his feet and hobbled across the room. After Rebecca closed the door behind Jacob, she

called out to the animal. "Let's lock up for
the night, you three-legged wonder."

Uly scrambled up beside her, watching intently as she secured the latch on the front
door. A sense of security flowed through Rebecca, knowing the dog was close at hand.
Uly's presence always made her feel safe and
secure during Jacob's frequent absences—and
especially on dark, lonely evenings like this
one.

The dog had become her faithful friend and
guardian since she and Jacob had retrieved
the injured animal from the side of the trail
during their move to Hope. His left hind leg
had been badly mangled, and Jacob had no
choice except to amputate the injured limb.
Miraculously, the dog had survived the ordeal and adjusted to his condition quite
admirably.

Now, Uly trotted behind her as she checked
the house for the night. Peering into the large
room that served as Jacob's office, she smiled
with satisfaction. Everything was neat and orderly, just as she liked it.

Pleased that the front parlor was also tidy
and clean, Rebecca retreated into the kitchen.
After clearing the dessert dishes from the
table, she located a stale biscuit for Uly. Satisfied, the dog settled down in his customary
resting place at the foot of the steps.

With her chores completed for the day, Rebecca straightened her narrow shoulders and
lifted her chin. As she climbed the stairs to
tuck Jessica into bed for the night, she resolved not to dwell on the long, lonely evening ahead of her.

When she swept into Jessica's room, she found her daughter playing contentedly, putting her doll to sleep for the night in a small wooden cradle. "Time to get to bed, Jessica," she announced.

"I don't want to go to sleep yet! I want to wait until Grandpa gets home!"

"But it's already past your bedtime, Jessica." Rebecca picked up a hairbrush from the dresser, then sat down on the edge of the bed. "Now, no more arguing. Hop up here beside me, and let's get all those tangles out of your hair before you go to sleep."

With a sigh of resignation, the child trudged across the bedroom, hiked up her white muslin nightgown to her knees, and crawled up onto the mattress. "I don't like going to bed without kissing Grandpa goodnight," she grumbled.

"And Grandpa doesn't like having to miss your good-night kisses, either," Rebecca said, running the bristles through the dark, thick waves streaming over the child's small shoulders. "But Mr. Littleton is very, very sick, and Grandpa might have to stay with him for most of the night."

Jessica's brow crinkled with worry. "Is Mr. Littleton going to . . . die?"

Rebecca hedged, groping to find the right words to ease the child's concerns. "I hope not, sweetheart. Nobody—except God, of course—knows for certain. But I'm sure he's getting the best possible care if Grandpa is taking care of him."

"Grandpa is the best doctor in the whole wide world," Jessica agreed, smiling. "And he's the best grandpa in the whole wide world, too!"

"He thinks you're pretty special, too, young lady." Setting the brush aside, Rebecca pulled the little girl into her arms. "And so does your mother."

Jessica curled her arms around her mother's neck. "Do you think Grandpa will be home in time for breakfast in the morning?"

"I hope so. And I bet he'll be real hungry after staying up all night. Do you think you can help me fix breakfast for him?"

Nodding, Jessica grinned. "Can we make flapjacks? And eat them with lots of butter and syrup?"

"Sounds delicious to me." Rebecca laughed. "And I'm sure Grandpa will be pleased, too."

"As long as we don't burn the flapjacks like we did last time." Jessica wrinkled her nose at the memory, then scrambled out of her mother's lap. "Since we've got so much work to do in the morning, I guess I'd better say my prayers and get to sleep."

Bedtime prayers were a ritual for Jessica, and Rebecca was grateful that she never had to remind her daughter about giving thanks for her blessings. But as she quietly listened to Jessica's petitions each evening, the sweet innocence of the child's heavenly requests never failed to tug at her heartstrings.

Now, following her established routine, Jessica dropped to her knees beside the bed, folded her hands together, and squeezed her eyes shut.

"Dear God, it's me again, Jessica Summers. Mama says this Mr. Littleton is a real sick

man. So please take care of him tonight while
I'm sleeping, and let Grandpa get back in time
to eat flapjacks with Mama and me in the
morning. And please, please, *please* don't let
Mama and me burn Grandpa's flapjacks. He
hates burned flapjacks, you know. And they
stink up the house somethin' terrible."

She paused for a brief moment. "Well, I
guess that's all for tonight, God. Just remember to give my daddy a big hug for me the
next time you see him up there in heaven,
and don't forget to tell him that I love him.
Amen."

Yawning, Jessica rubbed her eyes with the
back of her hand and crawled into bed. Rebecca leaned over and tucked the quilts up to her
chin. "Sweet dreams, my Jessica. And here's
two good-night kisses—one from Grandpa
and one from me," she whispered, brushing
her lips across the child's forehead.

"I love you, Mama. And Grandpa, too,"
Jessica murmured in a sleepy tone. Closing
her eyes, she burrowed her head into the
pillow.

Rebecca picked up the lantern, intending to
leave the room. But she'd taken only two
steps toward the door when a small, drowsy
voice called out to her.

"Mama?"

She paused. "Yes, Jess. What is it?"

"Will you stay here with me . . . for just a
little while?"

Since Jessica usually drifted off to sleep
without any problems, Rebecca was somewhat surprised by the request. Jacob's absence
must be bothering her, she thought.

"I'm right here, sweetheart," she assured the child, retracing her steps across the room. After returning the lantern to the table, she added, "And I'm here as long as you need me."

"Good," Jessica murmured, her pink lips curling into a sleepy smile. "Knowing you're here makes me feel all warm inside."

With that revelation, her thick, dark lashes fluttered and closed. A few errant strands of hair tumbled across one rosy cheek as she snuggled her head against the pillow.

Gazing down at her daughter, Rebecca couldn't resist the maternal urge to brush back the silky curls from her face. Jessica breathed a soft sigh of contentment, and Rebecca felt her heart swell with emotion.

Nothing in the world could compare to the intensity and strength of her love for her daughter. From the moment she'd felt the first stirrings of life in her womb, Rebecca had resolved to surround her child with all the love and affection that she could offer. And she'd never forgotten that silent vow.

Making Jessica feel safe and secure, wanted and loved, was the primary focus of Rebecca's life. She was determined the child would never experience the pain and heartaches, the scorn and ridicule, that had shadowed most of her twenty-five years.

All too well, she could remember the shameful hurt of being branded as a murderer's daughter. And Rebecca didn't want her child to know the pain and heartache of being condemned for her parents' wanton ways.

Jessica. Rebecca glanced over at the sleeping

child and smiled. Satisfied she was resting comfortably for the night, Rebecca quietly retreated into the privacy of her own room.

Sitting down at her dressing table, she uncoiled the tight chignon at the nape of her neck. Then she brushed the dark waves of hair streaming down over her shoulders until they felt as soft as black velvet beneath her fingers.

Sometimes she wished she had the nerve to wear her hair down in public, without the restrictions of hair nets or pins. But deep in her heart, she knew she would never do so. Drawing attention to herself was the last thing she wanted. Especially if her behavior or appearance provoked raised eyebrows or scornful disapproval.

Sighing, she separated the length of her hair into three parts. As she coiled the long strands into a thick, single braid for the night, she heard a loud thud on the door. A tiny pulse of fear pounded through her veins. Who could be calling at this time of night?

Alarmed, she glanced at the clock on the wall. *Ten o'clock.* Jacob had been gone less than an hour. What reason would he have for returning home so soon? Had he forgotten something?

She rushed down the steps. On her way to the door, she paused to run a hand over the German shepherd who was still resting, undisturbed, at the foot of the stairs. "Stay here until Grandpa gets into the house, Uly," she cautioned.

Picking up her skirts, she crossed the room. Then she unfastened the latch and hurled open the door. "Jacob, I'm so glad you're home!" she exclaimed.

Then she froze in shock, staring in disbelief at the stranger standing in front of her.

He was tall, so very tall that her eyes were barely level with his wide chest. His broad shoulders filled the doorway, and the white Stetson angled over his dark hair added several more inches to his imposing height. Rebecca surmised he was at least six feet tall.

It appeared as though he hadn't changed clothes in days. Dust and grime covered every inch of him. The filth spanned the width of his deep-pocketed vest and blue cotton shirt and trailed down the long length of his buff-colored pants. Even the pointed toes of his boots were marred by scratches and scuffs.

His skin was deeply bronzed from the wind and the sun, and he smelled of whiskey and leather. Images of smoke-filled saloons and wild, open spaces filled Rebecca's mind. She noticed a stubble of whiskers sprouting along the line of his jaw. And his gunmetal-gray eyes were staring back at her with such piercing intensity that a cold shiver of fear crawled down her spine.

Something tight and restricting gripped her chest as she looked at him. The man was rugged and wild, dark and dangerous; as raw and untamed as the western frontier.

The kind of man that Rebecca Summers avoided at all costs.

She placed one hand behind her back, concealing it from the stranger's view. And then she did what any respectable woman would do when confronted by a stranger at her door in the middle of the night.

Snapping her fingers, Rebecca signaled her dog to attack.

Chapter 2

The lady standing in front of him was a little wisp of a woman, wearing a prudish blue dress and a stunned expression on her face. One dark, thick braid fell over the pristine white collar of her gown. Her eyes were wide and incredibly blue, and she was staring at him with as much astonishment as if the devil himself had knocked at her door.

A faint clicking noise penetrated the silence, followed by thumps sounding across the wood floor behind her. Then something huge and furry whizzed past the woman and leaped into the air, barreling straight through the open door and heading straight toward Grady.

He bolted to his left, but not fast enough. The creature rammed its front paws into his chest, hurling its full weight against him. The force of the impact knocked his hat off his head and his boots off the porch.

Thump. Grady hit the dirt, flat on his back. The animal clamored over him, growling menacingly, and clamped a huge set of white, pointed teeth into his vest.

"Call him off, lady!" he demanded. "I'm not out to hurt anybody! I'm just looking to find Doc Summers."

The commotion roused Carl's attention. Slumped over a wooden bench on the porch, he struggled to lift his wounded head. "What's goin' on here?"

The woman peered around the corner of the door. Her eyebrows rose at the sight of the wounded man sitting on her porch with a blood-soaked bandanna in his hand.

"Can't you see the man needs some help?" Grady bellowed, still grappling to free himself as the dog nipped on his vest. He clamped a hand around the creature's neck and tried to hold him at bay.

Straightening, the woman clapped her hands. "That's enough, Uly."

Suddenly, the dog let go of his vest, lifted his head, and let out a bark of triumph. Wagging his tail, the animal bounded over his conquest and trotted back to the door.

Grady pulled up, wiping the dust from his sleeves and staring in disbelief at his attacker. The dog was a fine-looking German shepherd, but there was something odd about the creature's gait. The animal was hobbling back to the house.

And then he saw the reason why. One of the dog's hind legs was only a stubble. The blasted animal was limping around on three legs!

Furious that he'd been knocked to the ground by a mangled mutt, Grady snapped

to his feet. He retrieved his hat from the
ground and slapped it across his thigh. Bil-
lows of dust clouded his vision.

When the air cleared, he could see that the
little woman was frowning. "So what's the
problem, gentlemen?" Her voice was as cold
as a Kansas ice storm.

"Your damn dog, for one," Grady bit out,
glaring at her.

She glowered right back. "Be grateful I
didn't reach for my gun."

"For Christ's sake, quit the hollerin'," Carl
muttered, staggering across the porch, holding his head in his hands.

Grady bolted to Carl's side and wrapped
his arm around him for support, then he
turned to the woman at the door. "We're
looking for Doc Summers. Some of the gals
down at Red Dog Saloon said we could find
him here."

She bristled. "Then you've wasted your
time this evening, I'm afraid. You shouldn't
have bothered to leave your lady friends all
alone down at the saloon. Doc Summers isn't
here at the moment."

Grady glanced over her shoulder, peering
into the house. The only visible sign of life
was the German shepherd, standing alert and
ready to leap to the aid of his mistress at
any second.

A sudden flash of understanding assaulted
him. The woman was telling the truth, he realized. She was alone, unaccustomed to
strangers knocking at her door during the
night, and had called upon her dog to protect her.

He supposed he should be furious that she'd used the blasted mutt to try and scare him away. But instead he felt a grudging respect for her. Siccing her dog on him had been a damn good idea.

Too bad it hadn't worked.

"We'll wait, then." Grady nudged Carl closer to the door.

She lifed her chin and crossed her arms over her chest. "I'm not about to allow you to bring your drunken friend into my house in the middle of the night."

Hot waves of anger stormed through Grady. "Carl isn't drunk, lady. He might have had a few drinks at the saloon, but whiskey isn't the cause of his problems. Take a good look at him, will you? The man is bleeding to death!"

Her eyes swept over the streams of crimson trickling over Carl's forehead, and the rigid lines of her face softened. "He must be hurting ... very badly," she admitted, her voice tainted with compassion and sudden understanding.

Seizing the moment, Grady barreled past the woman and dragged Carl into the house. After a quick survey of the two rooms on either side of him, he veered to his right and guided the man over to a cot beneath the window.

All the while, the tiny lady was hard on his heels, still protesting. "Haven't you heard anything I've said? I've already told you that Doc Summers isn't here!"

He snapped around. "And I told you we'd

wait. We're not going anywhere until Carl gets his head stitched up."

One had to admire the man's persistence, Rebecca thought, though she could find little else about him that was admirable. He was insufferably rude, and obviously hot-tempered. From the filth of his clothes to the gruffness in his voice, everything about him said he was far from respectable.

At that moment, the man on the cot emitted a low, guttural moan. Rebecca gazed down at him, alarmed by the amount of blood gushing from his wound. The cut was deep and jagged, full of tiny shards of glass. There was no doubt in her mind that the wound should be cleansed and bandaged as quickly as possible.

She sighed. She didn't want these men in her house, especially while Jacob was away. But she wouldn't be able to live with herself if she refused to help someone who was hurting. What other choice did she have except to tend to the injured man's wounds?

Besides, keeping her hands busy would take her mind off the other man who'd brought him here. Something—or everything—about him had left her shaken to the core. Even now, she could feel his eyes boring through her, studying her intently.

She was silently vowing to ignore him as best she could when she felt something warm and fuzzy brushing against her skirt. She reached down, patting Uly's thick coat of fur. "Everything's all right now," she said, grateful for the creature's protective nature. "These men aren't threats to us anymore."

As the German shepherd trotted back to his

usual resting place at the foot of the stairs, Rebecca positioned a chair for herself beside the cot. "I suppose I can clean him up while we're waiting for Jacob to come home," she announced, praying they wouldn't have to wait for long.

She placed a washcloth, a basin of water, an empty jar, and a small, tweezerlike tool on a wooden tray. Then she settled down beside the cot, dipped the cloth into the water, and placed the wet fabric over the bloody wound.

Grady peered over her shoulder, watching as she cleansed the injury. Her hands were dainty and delicate, her nails clean and groomed, her fingers slender and agile. But she wasn't wearing any jewelry, he noticed in surprise. Where was her wedding ring?

"Aren't you the doc's wife?" he wondered aloud.

"No." Her hands stilled. "I'm his daughter-in-law."

"And your husband?"

She turned, gazing up at him. "He was killed several years ago ... in the War."

Seeing a hint of sadness in her eyes, hearing a slight tremor in her voice, Grady felt as though she'd twisted a knife into his gut. Shame coursed through him for being so short with her. He tipped the brim of his hat in an awkward attempt to atone for both his gruffness and her losses. "I'm sorry to hear that, ma'am."

Her lips curved into a weak smile. "Thank you, but ..." She paused, shrugging. "It all happened a very long time ago."

She resumed caring for her patient. Grady

noticed her hands worked quickly and efficiently. After a few moments, she picked up the metal instrument from the tray.

"This won't be comfortable for you, Carl, but we have to remove the glass from your wound," she said in a soothing tone. "I'll try to be as gentle as possible."

Carl gave a weak nod and closed his eyes. She pinched the instrument between her thumb and forefinger and guided the tip of the device into the laceration. Within seconds, she extracted a tiny shard of glass. After dropping the crystal fragment into the empty jar, she repeated the procedure.

Wincing at the sight, Grady decided to focus his attention elsewhere. He swung his gaze around the room, studying his surroundings with interest.

Everything was neat, tidy, orderly. A massive rolltop desk and leather chair were positioned in one corner. Several cabinets with glass fronts, similar to china cupboards, were lined up against the walls. Rows of brown bottles in various shapes and sizes filled the shelves, along with stacks of fresh bandages and an assortment of other medical supplies.

Beneath one window was a long, narrow worktable covered with a tray of surgical instruments, various apothecary gadgets, and several thick, leather-bound reference books.

His gaze shifted into the adjoining room. The area was obviously a parlor, containing several wooden tables and upholstered chairs, a matching sofa, and two bookcases. A fringed floral-print rug covered the wood floor and lace curtains adorned a pair of long, narrow windows.

There was nothing ornate about the parlor or its furnishings. Yet there was something about it, something indefinable, that roused Grady's curiosity. He edged forward, narrowing his eyes, scrutinizing the room and its contents.

Like the physician's office, everything here was immaculately clean. The furniture glistened with a fresh coat of polish, and nothing seemed unkempt or out of place. There was a certain order about the room, a neat precision to the arrangement of every chair and table.

And then it hit him. Everything was too tidy and neat, like a fancy showroom of sorts. Not one item in the room revealed anything about the people who lived here. There were no sentimental displays, no framed photographs, no treasured mementos. Nothing of any value hinted about the personal lives of the town physician and his widowed daughter-in-law.

He was still mulling over the puzzling situation when the woman called out to him. "May I speak with you for a moment, please?"

Startled, he crossed the room. "Anything wrong?"

Her brow furrowed with concern as she pulled a brown bottle from one of the cabinets. "I've removed all the fragments of glass, I believe, but we can't wait any longer for Jacob to get home. Your friend has lost a lot of blood, and he needs to be stitched up . . . before he loses anymore."

As she doused a cloth with some liquid from the bottle, Grady scowled at the strong odor. "What in the hell is that stuff?"

"Ether. Once it gets into his system, he won't feel a thing." She returned the bottle on the shelf. "While I'm stitching up his wound, I'll need you to hold this cloth over his nose and mouth."

It sounded simple enough. Grady reached for the cloth. To his surprise, she snatched it away, refusing to give it to him.

"First, take off your hat," she ordered. "I don't want it to block my light while I'm working. And wash your hands, too."

Grady waited a full ten seconds before complying with her requests, if for no other reason than to irritate her. He didn't like taking orders from anyone. Especially short, bossy women who barked out directions like army sergeants.

Still, as much as he hated to admit it, he was getting the distinct impression that this woman knew precisely what she was doing. "You a nurse?" he finally asked, placing the cloth over Carl's face as she'd instructed.

She nodded crisply. "And a midwife. I take care of most of the women and children in town, but I also assist Jacob during surgeries. He's the one who usually tends to the serious injuries and accidents among the men around here."

"I see," he murmured, absently wondering if she was always so focused, so intent. Unable to resist poking a little fun at her, he grinned. "So men aren't your primary interest?"

The curve of her back went rigid. "How observant of you."

Ignoring him, she returned to her chair and threaded a needle. Then she inhaled a deep breath, leaned over the edge of the cot, and inserted the sharp point into Carl's forehead.

Grady grimaced, finding the sight too gruesome for his tastes. Shifting his gaze to the woman beside him, he decided she was much more interesting to observe than a bloody operation. While she concentrated on her work, he took the opportunity to scrutinize her, unnoticed.

His gaze wandered over her face, studying each delicate feature. Her complexion was creamy and flawless, and nature had tinted the sensuous curves of her mouth with a rosy hue. Her nose was small and perfectly formed, her brow narrow and smooth. At the moment, her high cheekbones were tinged with a slight blush, and there was a stubborn thrust in her well-defined chin. Thick, dark lashes and brows framed a pair of sky-blue eyes.

A true beauty, she was. Grady had seen enough women in his thirty-one years to know when he'd run across a genuine gem. And this one sparkled with a natural loveliness that was as rare as a rose blossom in January.

Too bad she was such a prude.

Loose 'n' easy was the way Grady liked his women. He didn't care for uptight, nervous, snippy little females who got their kicks out of bossing other people around. He liked the kind of woman who could kiss like crazy, laugh on a whim, say good-bye with a smile. The sort who didn't expect anything except an occasional night of passion. The type who didn't demand or want anything else.

The sound of her voice shattered his thoughts. "All done." She rose from the chair and wiped her hands on a clean rag. "You can remove the cloth from his face now."

She scurried to her worktable and measured out an assortment of ingredients from various bottles and jars. Grady stepped up behind her, watching with interest as she pounded the mixture together with a mortar and pestle. "What are you doing now?" he asked.

"I'm preparing a poultice."

He peered into the mortar bowl. "From a bunch of dead weeds?"

Turning, she glared at him. "These are not weeds. They're herbs."

"Herbs?" He laughed. "You don't seem like the type who believes in all that hocus-pocus stuff, lady."

"This is not hocus-pocus." The line of her jaw tightened. "The Shakers have been using herbal poultices like this for years, and—"

"The Shakers?"

She nodded toward the rows of bottles and jars stored in the surrounding cabinets. "Most of these bottles contain medicinal herbs that we order from the Shakers' colonies in New York and Ohio. I also buy seeds from the Shakers' catalogues so I can grow some of my own herbs right here."

"Well, ain't that fascinatin'." Grady stole another look at the concoction and shuddered. It still looked like dead weeds to him. "What's this stuff for?"

"To reduce swelling and scarring. Considering the position of your friend's wound on his face, I'm sure he would appreciate anything that could make his scar less noticeable."

"I'm sure he would, too." He paused. "If he believed in such nonsense."

Dropping the pestle with a clatter, she whirled on him. Her eyes crackled like blue fire, and he could feel the stormy heat of her gaze scorching through him.

She thrust out her chin with defiance. "I'll have you know that I take my work very seriously, and I would never do anything to jeopardize the health of my patients. As long as your friend is under my care, he's my responsibility, and I fully intend to treat him with this poultice. Besides, the practice of botanical medicine is quite common and has been highly regarded as an effective form of treatment for years." She paused, raking her eyes over the length of him with obvious disdain. "Of course, people who live in the wild like primitive savages aren't always aware of such civilized practices."

No sooner had she voiced the last remark, regret and anger sliced through her. She despised him for questioning her judgment, hated herself for allowing him to provoke her. Certain he would retaliate, she dragged her eyes back up to his face and steeled herself for his scathing reply.

To her astonishment, she saw none of the anger that she'd expected to find. His lips were twitching with the hint of a smile, and she detected a glint of humor shining from his eyes. Rebecca felt a surge of relief rushing through her until his hand reached for the thick braid dangling over her shoulder.

"Nice speech, lady. Quite effective. Very informative, too." Stroking the soft coil of hair beneath his fingers, he dropped his voice to a low, husky tone. "Just take care not to poison the man with that concoction of yours, darlin'. Because if you do, I'll wring your pretty little neck with my savage, uncivilized hands."

Trying to ignore the frantic beat of her heart, she lifted her chin. "Threatening me isn't necessary. Your friend isn't in any danger of getting poisoned, I can assure you."

"You'd better hope you're right, darlin'," he warned, his fingers still lingering on her hair.

A strange tingling sensation assuaged her as she felt the warmth of his hand brushing across her shoulder, the heat of his gaze sweeping over her face. Looking up at him, she was startled to discover that he was much more handsome than she cared to admit.

There was a reckless, abandoned air about him. His hair looked as if it had been brushed by nothing other than his fingers and the wind. The dark waves were a rich, deep shade of brown, thick and luxurious. A few errant strands tumbled over his forehead, and the long length skimmed his ears and curled over the collar at the back of his shirt.

Her gaze traveled across his face. His

cheekbones were high and broad, his nose straight and strong, the line of his jaw hard and unyielding. But it was his mouth that mesmerized her. The slight curve of his lips was sensuous, intriguing, almost as if beckoning to her.

Studying him, Rebecca felt as if someone had knocked the wind from her lungs. An unfamiliar, dizzying sensation swarmed through her, and she struggled to catch her breath. Troubled and shaken, she pulled away from him with a start. Grasping the pestle, she prayed he wouldn't notice that her hands were trembling. She closed her eyes, wishing he would go away and leave her alone.

The rapid beat of her heart didn't return to normal until she heard the sound of his boots clattering into the parlor. Regaining her composure, she returned her attention to the herbal mixture in front of her.

After packing the ingredients into the tight folds of a cloth, she placed the poultice over the injured man's wound. Then she drew in a deep, steadying breath and marched into the parlor.

"Your friend is resting comfortably now," she announced as she stepped into the room.

She stopped cold, horrified by what she saw. The man was sitting in her favorite wing back chair, his long legs stretched out in front of him. Uly was resting contentedly beside him, licking his front paws and obviously enjoying the brush of the man's hands through the thick coat of fur along his spine.

Stunned, Rebecca reeled in confusion. She'd always trusted the dog's judgment about people. The animal seemed to possess some sort of sixth sense, a kind of internal warning system that seemed to know whether or not someone could not be trusted. She would have never imagined the animal would take a liking to someone like this man.

Realizing her only form of protection was consorting with the enemy only made matters worse. A knot coiled in her stomach at the revelation. And the lazy, arrogant grin sprouting on the man's lips heated her blood to a raging boil.

"Looks like I've found me a friend," he noted with undisguised glee.

She wanted nothing more than to slap that impudent grin off his face. "Uly has never been a good judge of character," she lied through gritted teeth.

"Uly," he mused aloud. "What kind of name is that for a dog?"

"It's a nickname." She offered nothing more.

He contemplated the matter for a moment, then snapped his fingers together. "Ulysses. That's it, isn't it? Uly is short for Ulysses."

She concocted a grim smile. "How astute."

Chuckling, he brushed his hands over the dog's back. "Bet you didn't know you were named after the president of the United States, did you, boy?"

Uly wagged his tail and looked up at the man as though he adored him.

Irritated by the amiable companionship that seemed to be growing by the second, Rebecca pursed her lips together. Unable to endure the disturbing sight for another moment, she whirled around and marched over to one of the bookcases in the room.

Not knowing what else to do, she concentrated on straightening the neat rows of books lined up along the shelves. Though not one volume was out of place, she knew she had to keep her hands busy. Otherwise, they might wander over to the man's neck and choke him to death.

"Are you always like this?"

She jumped. "Like . . . what?"

"Nervous, tense. Snippy, even."

She snapped around. "I am not nervous."

"Don't try to fool yourself, lady." He grinned. "You're wound up tighter than an eight-day clock with a bad spring."

The knot in her stomach tightened. She whirled back around, squeezing her eyes shut, despising herself, hating him even more. How much longer did she have to put up with this torture?

Grady didn't think it was possible for her to stand any straighter. But as he'd voiced his observations, her back went ramrod stiff. Even now, raking his eyes over the length of her petite frame, every muscle in her body was taut with tension.

From head to toe, she was perfectly groomed. Her crisply pressed gown flattered her nicely rounded figure, emphasizing the full swell of her breasts, the tiny span of her waist, the gentle flare of her hips. The wide starched collar that circled her neck and covered her shoulders was as white as new fallen snow, and a pair of ribboned slippers peeked out beneath the full hem of her skirt.

Grady couldn't even find one hair out of place in that tightly coiled braid of hers. He had the sudden urge to plunge his fingers through those carefully-woven strands and scatter them around her shoulders, free and unrestricted, if for no other reason than to see how she would react.

He figured it would be fun to loosen her up a bit. Life was too short to be wound up in knots all of the time. "What's wrong, dar-lin'?" he taunted, his voice smooth and easy. "Scared of me?"

She whirled on him. "Men like you don't scare me at all."

"That's good to know. I'd hate for you to be frightened." He stretched out his legs in front of him, unintentionally clicking his boots together as he put the heel of one on top of the pointed toe of the other. Bits of dust and grime that had been clinging to the scuffed leather showered down onto the floral rug.

She glowered at the mess. "Men like you merely disgust and irritate me," she muttered.

Ah, now they were getting somewhere. She was opening up to him, expressing all those bottled-up feelings.

For some strange reason, he sort of liked making her twitch and squirm. He clicked his boots together again, spreading a little more dust over the rug, just as the front door rat-tled open.

A stocky man with graying hair and a thick mustache stepped inside the house. The woman flew across the room and hurled her-self at him. "Jacob, I'm so glad you're home!"

He patted her on the back and planted a

kiss on her forehead. "You didn't have to wait up on me, 'Becca."

"It wasn't intentional, believe me," she murmured just as Grady stepped up to join them.

"What's all this, now?" the physician asked. A puzzled frown wrinkled his thick, gray brows as he peered at the strange man beside him.

"Your daughter-in-law was kind enough to tend to my friend's injury during your absence this evening," Grady explained, motioning toward the injured man.

Concern furrowed Jacob's brow as he walked over to the cot and removed the poultice from the man's forehead. After studying the tiny lines of neat stitches for a few moments, he stepped back and smiled. "Nice work, 'Becca, I couldn't have done a better job myself."

"Thanks." Rebecca felt a flush of heat rising along her neck and cheekbones. "I wanted to wait for you to get here, but he was bleeding so badly . . ." A shudder coursed through her at the memory.

"You did the right thing," he assured her. Heaving a weary sigh, he slumped down into the chair beside the cot. "I couldn't get away until just now. Old man Littleton put up quite a fight . . . and I'm glad to say he won. His fever broke a while ago, and he's out of the woods now."

"I'm glad to hear that, Jacob." Rebecca breathed a sigh of relief.

"Me, too. It's been a long night." Conjuring up a smile, he turned to the stranger beside him and held out his hand. "I'm Jacob Summers, son. Sorry I didn't introduce myself earlier."

"No apologies necessary." The man gripped Jacob's hand. "I'm Grady Cunningham."

"Cunningham, you say?" Jacob's eyebrows rose a notch.

The line of his jaw hardened. "I'm afraid so."

The doctor studied Grady for a moment. "Malcolm's boy?"

He shrugged. "Guilty as charged, as they say."

An uneasy feeling rolled through Rebecca as she quietly observed the exchange. Everyone knew that Malcolm Cunningham was the founder and patriarch of Hope, Kansas. Malcolm Cunningham had put the town on the map by persuading the president of the Union Pacific that cattle could be moved by rail from the Midwest to packing houses in New York and Chicago. He'd built holding pens beside the railroad yards and made a fortune from his ingenuity.

And he'd recently become one of Jacob's patients. Since he'd suffered a stroke in late spring, Jacob and Rebecca checked on him frequently, calling at the Cunningham ranch three or four times a week.

Now she combed the recesses of her mind, struggling to remember what she had heard about Mayor Cunningham's younger son. There had been some sort of trouble between them, she thought, but she couldn't recall the details.

Not that it mattered, of course. She had no intention of crossing paths with Grady Cunningham again.

"Go on upstairs now, 'Becca," Jacob urged. "I'll stay here with your patient for a little while. I think he'll probably rest comfortably until morning. I'm too wound up to get to sleep at the moment, anyway, so I'll bandage up his head before I turn in for the night."

Grateful for the reprieve, Rebecca nodded in agreement. "Thanks, Jacob."

Grady picked up his hat to leave as she whirled around and headed for the stairs. When she reached the first step, she heard the man call out to her.

"Mrs. Summers?"

Her hand tightened around the banister. "Yes?"

"Thanks for all your help this evening."

She slowly turned her head, stunned by the genuine sincerity in his voice. "I'm glad everything ... worked out," she managed to say.

A smile lit up his face, a smile so warm and genuine that Rebecca found herself reeling from its dazzling effect until he spoke again. "Yeah, it's been kinda fun, wouldn't you say?"

Fun? She stared at him in disbelief. Irritated by the outrageous twinkle glinting from his eyes, exhausted from contending with the most aggravating, irritating man she'd ever encountered, she spun around and marched up the stairs. "It's been interesting, to say the least," she murmured, praying she would never experience anything like it again.

Chapter 3

Shortly before one o'clock, Grady entered the Red Dog Saloon. He felt much too restless to be confined to his room at the hotel, and he intended to have one more drink before turning in for the night.

In spite of the late hour, dozens of patrons were milling through the saloon. Several men tipped their hats to Grady as he worked his way through the smoke-filled haze and stepped up to the bar. He ordered a shot of whiskey, noting that a new bartender was serving up drinks. He chuckled, wondering if the man who'd attacked Carl had been fired.

Within seconds after placing his order, he found himself surrounded by a crowd of familiar faces. All of the men clamoring around him had witnessed the clash of glasses and fists earlier in the evening. Most had been regular patrons of the Red Dog for years. Some were drifters and cattlemen who stopped by the saloon each time they passed through town; others were permanent residents who frequented the Red Dog each night.

"Tell us about Carl," one of the men urged. "Is he doin' all right now?"

"At the moment, he's sleeping like a baby over at Doc Summers's place," Grady said.

"So the doc got him all fixed up?" another man asked.

"Not exactly." Grady guzzled down the drink in one gulp. "Doc Summers wasn't home when we got there, so the little lady took care of him. Stitched up his head prettier than a quilt."

"The Widow Summers?" The man behind the bar nearly dropped the glass in his hand.

"Well, I'll be damned," another man mumbled in disbelief.

Grady frowned, confused by the surprise swarming around him. "She seemed competent enough to me. Doesn't she help out a lot with the doc's practice?"

"Yeah, but I ain't never heard of her tendin' to a cowpoke all by herself," a skinny man claimed.

"She usually just tends to the womenfolk and the children around here," another explained.

"She wasn't exactly receptive to the idea of letting us into the house," Grady admitted, choosing not to elaborate on the details.

"She ain't exactly receptive to lettin' any man inside her house," a tall man muttered.

"But it ain't for a lack of tryin'," another moaned. "Lord knows, every man in this town who ain't already hitched has tried to court her—includin' me—but nobody can get a foot in the door."

"She ain't uppity or snobbish about it, mind you," a third man said. "When she turned me down, she was real sweet 'n' nice about the whole thing. I couldn't even get mad at her 'bout it."

Grady ordered another drink, mulling over the information buzzing around him, remembering the woman's prim and proper ways. "I'd wager the right man could turn the little lady's head," he mused aloud.

A wave of chuckles rippled through the saloon. "Don't bet your boots on it, Cunningham," one man warned with a laugh.

"I'd work a month of Sundays for the fella who could pull that off," another said.

"And I'd wager a whole year's pay," a third man claimed.

"I might know of a man who'd take you up on the challenge of romancing the lady." Grady pushed back the brim of his hat and looked around the bar. "Anyone interested in wagering some bets?"

One of the older men twisted his mouth into a frown. "I don't mean no disrespect or nothin', Cunningham. But you ain't gotta a chance of wooing the Widder Summers. She's a *church* lady, for Pete's sake! She ain't gonna let a buffalo hunter court her!"

"And she won't have nothin' to do with you at all if she knows about ..." The bartender paused, wincing. "You know what I'm talkin' about, don't you, Cunningham?"

Grady nodded, but refused to think about the scandal that had driven him out of town.

What did he care? "With everything considered, aren't the odds in your favor?" he challenged.

"It would be kinda interestin' to see if you could turn her head," one man mused.

"What kinda odds are you considerin', Cunningham?" another asked.

Grady pulled out a wad of bills from his pocket. "I've got five dollars for every one of yours that says I can persuade the Widow Summers to allow me to call on her within the next two weeks." He stole a glance at the stunned bartender. "Mind keeping track of the wagers?"

"No, but . . ." The bartender scratched his head, confused. "But what makes you think you can convince her to court you?"

"Not a damn thing. Actually, I'm not sure if I can," he admitted honestly. "But tryin' sure sounds like a helluva lot of fun to me."

A moment of stunned silence swept through the bar. And then all hell broke loose.

Men scrambled to slap down their money faster than the bartender could count it. Glasses clinked, voices cheered, hands pumped.

"We're all gonna be rich!" one man shouted with glee.

"And in just two weeks!" another yelled.

Looking around at the commotion, Grady grinned. Romancing the prudish widow was just the kind of challenge he'd been looking for.

This was gonna be fun.

Rebecca stepped onto the planked boardwalk lining the main thoroughfare of Hope the next morning, squinting from the glare of the August sun. A few feet away, a wagon rolled past her, showering bits of powder-fine dirt over everything along the way—including her new coral gown.

Sighing, she shook off the dust from her skirt, wondering if she would ever become accustomed to the clouds of dust billowing through Hope. The dry spell had been lingering over the region for weeks, and Rebecca longed for a few days of steady rain to wash away the dusty haze from the Kansas sky.

But it seemed, as Rebecca observed the activity surrounding her, the drought wasn't affecting the town's economy. The boardwalk was clogged with crowds of pedestrians, and dozens of wagons and horses were lining the main street. Shopkeepers were greeting their first customers of the day, offering bargains to lure shoppers into the stores. Across the way, hundreds of longhorns were rumbling through the stockyards beside the railroad tracks.

Scurrying through the bustling business district, Rebecca headed toward the simple frame building at the end of the street, anxious to arrive at Hope Congregational Church for the weekly meeting of the Women's Missionary Auxiliary. Though she always enjoyed the companionship of the ladies in the group, she was particularly eager to attend this morning's meeting. After last night's unsettling encounter with the stranger at her door, she was looking forward to focusing her thoughts on the auxiliary's latest mission project.

Cunningham didn't care what anyone—
his own father—thought about him.

Determined not to waste any
mulling over the man and his
traits, Rebecca pulled back her
ders with resolve as she
church. A few moments
small assembly room
where several wom
for the auxiliary

"There you
lins, a thin,
rushed a
yards
"Lo

wh ... was well enough to go on his way. Since she'd seen vast improvements in the injured man's condition that morning, she felt certain he would be gone by the time she returned home from her meeting. Which meant the possibilities of crossing paths with Grady Cunningham again were practically nonexistent.

Still, she had to admit she was mystified by the man who'd haunted her dreams for most of the night. He seemed like the type who enjoyed roaming from place to place, a drifter of sorts with a reckless, devil-may-care philosophy about life. Rebecca sensed he didn't care about his own reputation, even though he was the son of one of the most prominent men in the state. In fact, she suspected Grady

-even

more time
nredeemable
narrow shoul-
approached the
ater, she entered the
next to the sanctuary,
en were already gathered
meeting.

are, Rebecca!" Charlotte Col-
wiry woman with frizzy red hair,
cross the room, dangling several
of dainty lace trim from her hand.
k what Agnes Millsaps has donated for
r mission project!"

"How beautiful! This will be the perfect touch for the infant gowns we're making." Genuinely impressed by the donation from the wife of Hope's most prominent attorney, Rebecca nodded with approval as she examined the fine lace. "And it will look wonderful on the fabric that you and Virgil contributed from your store."

Charlotte's smile vanished, replaced with a pensive expression. "It was the least we could do, especially after you told us about those poor homesteaders who don't have a stitch of clothes for their new babies to wear." She shook her head in dismay. "It's a shame this dreadful drought is causing such problems for them."

"With no sign of rain in sight, I'm afraid conditions won't be improving for them anytime soon." Rebecca sighed. "And two more of my patients are expecting new additions to their families around the end of the month."

"Two new babies . . . this month?" As Rebecca nodded, Charlotte's eyes widened in alarm. "We need to get busy on these gowns, my dear."

Whirling around, Charlotte scurried to spread the news about the upcoming births to the rest of the women. Last week, the group had cut out the gowns from the bolt of fine lawn that Charlotte had contributed for the project. Now, hearing about the immediate need for a pair of the tiny frocks, the women scurried to sort out the fabric pieces and distribute needles and thread.

Pleased to see the enthusiasm generated by her suggestion to make gowns for the homesteaders' infants, Rebecca felt her throat tighten with emotion. Being accepted by this clan of decent, honorable ladies still seemed too good to be true, even though she'd been part of the group for almost a year.

And she especially cherished the friendship of Charlotte Collins. Charlotte and her husband Virgil, a member of the town council, owned and operated a thriving general store in the heart of town. Rebecca often depended upon their teenage daughter, Samantha, to take care of Jessica on days when she was checking up on her patients.

At that moment, a short, plump woman rushed into the room, catching Rebecca's attention. The feathered hat perched atop the woman's curly brown hair was slightly askew, and her round cheeks were flushed with dots of crimson. "We have a problem, ladies." Her voice cracked with emotion. "A very serious problem, I fear."

The auxiliary president's announcement sliced through the buzz of conversation like the sharp edge of a butcher knife, cutting off the lively chatter among the women. Puzzled and concerned, Rebecca broke away from the circle of stunned ladies. "Whatever is wrong, Mrs. Davenport?" she asked.

"It's dreadful, dear. It's—it's simply the worst thing that could possibly happen!" Lydia Davenport wailed.

"Lots of people have been feeling the effects of this ghastly August heat wave in recent days," Rebecca remarked, noting the woman's shortness of breath and flushed face. "Are you feeling faint?"

"No, no, it's nothing like that!" Lydia dabbed her forehead with a dainty, lace-trimmed hanky.

"For heaven's sake, Lydia!" Charlotte frowned. "Don't keep us in suspense. Get to the point!"

"All right." Lydia clutched her throat and shuddered. "It was *him*. That dreadful man is back in town."

"Oh, my." Charlotte's hand flew to her mouth, stifling her gasp. "Are you certain?"

"As certain as I've ever been about anything in my life. I saw him walking down the street just a few minutes ago. He was carrying some packages and heading into the Grand Central Hotel." The dark feather in her hat fluttered as she shook her head in dismay. "It was almost like witnessing the arrival of the devil himself."

"None of us will be safe as long as *he* is lurking around Hope, Kansas," Agnes Millsaps proclaimed.

"I won't sleep a wink as long as *he* is in town," another lady predicted.

"I can't believe *he* has the nerve to show his face around here again!" exclaimed a third woman. "After all the trouble he caused. . . ."

One by one, the ladies slumped into their chairs. After Rebecca slipped into a vacant seat between Lydia and Charlotte, the conversation resumed its frantic pace.

"I'd say he's the most notorious man this town has ever seen." Agnes stabbed a needle into the fabric with quick, angry strokes. "I'll never forget that big brawl he started down at the Red Dog Saloon over some woman a few years ago. Half the men in town were sporting black eyes and broken noses the next morning. Sheriff Emerson locked him up for a couple of days for disturbing the peace, but the damage had already been done to most of the menfolk in Hope."

"And don't forget about his fondness for whiskey," Lydia reminded the group. "I'm telling you, the man drinks like a fish! I'll never forget the night he got lost on his way home from the Red Dog, wandered into my house, and passed out in front of my fireplace. Why, he didn't even wake up while Sheriff Emerson was hauling him off to jail! Mark my word, ladies, I'll be latching my doors while that scoundrel is around."

"And we'll have to keep a close eye on our daughters, too. Remember the time Pastor Bartlett caught him in the barn with his daughter?" Charlotte heaved a troubled sigh. "After the way he disgraced that girl—refusing to marry her and all—it's no wonder Pastor Bartlett left Hope for a church in Ellsworth. I would've moved my daughter away from that man, too."

"I still don't believe he was merely trying to defend himself when he killed Ned Sikes," Lydia said with a shake of her head. "To my dying day, I'll never know why the jury didn't convict him of murder. Ned's aunt—that dear little Fanny Otten—told me it was obvious he wanted Ned's wife all to himself. Said he'd been sniffing around the woman's skirts for months in Kansas City. And then he killed the poor woman's husband and got off scot-free!"

"My husband figures he's become one of the richest men in Kansas since he got that big contract with the Union Pacific to supply the railroad construction crews with buffalo meat," Agnes announced. "And we've heard he's doubled his fortune by shipping buffalo skins back East."

Lydia snorted her disgust. "Gambling is what has made the man rich. I've heard nobody can beat him at the poker table. Why, the man nearly wiped out Homer Dixon at the Red Dog a few years ago. Poor Homer had to borrow money from my husband to make ends meet for the rest of the summer after that scoundrel got through with him at the poker table."

Interesting, Rebecca thought, mentally sorting out the information. The man was obviously a murderer, an adulterer, and a gambler. But nobody had mentioned his name.

"Pardon me, ladies," she interrupted in a quiet tone. "But who is this man?"

"Why, Grady Cunningham, dear." Lydia lowered her voice to a whisper and shuddered. "No one wants to be associated with him, not even his own father! Malcolm doesn't even acknowledge the boy as his son any longer, you know. He disowned him after that dreadful scandal, and ..."

But Rebecca didn't hear another word. The room started to spin. Her stomach churned; her mouth went dry. The murmur of voices became nulled and distant, and for a brief instant, she actually thought she was going to get sick.

Grady Cunningham. Dear heavens, what had she done?

She lowered her head, pretending to concentrate on her needlework. But the churning in her stomach intensified. *Please, God,* she pleaded silently. *Don't let them find out that I let him into my house last night. They'll never forgive me. I'll be an outcast again. And everything I've worked for will be gone.*

"I hope no one considers that we're gossiping about the man," Charlotte mused aloud, working her needle into the fabric with quick, efficient strokes.

"We're not gossiping!" Lydia denied. "It's our Christian duty to keep each other informed about the perils facing us. Why, our own dear Rebecca wasn't even aware that Grady Cunningham presented such a distressing threat to the respectability of our town!"

Now, however, no one was more acutely aware of Grady Cunningham's threatening presence than Rebecca Summers. She was grateful when the conversation turned into a discussion about the recent soar in attendance at Sunday morning worship services. The disturbing news about the newest arrival in town had left her shaken beyond words, and she didn't dare risk the chance of exposing all her emotions to anyone.

Still, she couldn't ignore the sickening feelings rolling through her. How could this have happened? Since the day she'd arrived in Hope, she'd taken care not to expose herself to anything—or anyone—that could tarnish her good name. She'd tried to avoid situations that could threaten to destroy the respectable life that she'd worked so hard to establish for her daughter.

But now everything she'd worked to achieve was on the verge of collapsing. All because she'd made the dreadful mistake of consorting with the most notorious man in Hope during the middle of the night.

Trying to quell the frantic thundering of her heart, she stabbed her needle into the soft fabric. *It doesn't matter*, she told herself repeatedly. *No one will ever know about your encounter with Grady Cunningham if you don't tell them about it. Besides, it isn't likely that he'll stay in Hope for very long. Chances are, you'll never see him again.*

She pursed her lips together with renewed determination, refusing to succumb to the panic in her heart. She would not, could not, allow a scoundrel like Grady Cunningham to destroy the life of respectability that she'd built for Jessica.

She bowed her head, pretending to concentrate on her needlework once again, praying she had seen the last of Grady Cunningham.

Standing in his rented room on the second floor of the Grand Central Hotel, Grady Cunningham grinned as he studied his reflection in the mirror. "Not too bad for an uncivilized savage, even if I say so myself," he assessed aloud.

In all of his thirty-one years, he couldn't remember the last time when he'd felt—or looked—so squeaky clean. By damn, he almost looked *wholesome*.

The ever-present stubble of whiskers along his jaw and chin had vanished beneath the blade of a razor, revealing the smooth, clean-shaven lines of his tanned face. And the neatly trimmed waves of dark hair, once jagged and tangled, were now shiny clean, still slightly damp and bearing the marks of the barber's comb.

His clothes—purchased at a well-stocked clothing store that morning—hugged the length of his long frame as though they had been tailored especially for him. He tugged at the hem of his new vest, then straightened the crisp collar of his hunter-green shirt. Dropping his gaze to the floor, he was pleased to see that his boots, peeking out beneath the hem of his snug-fitting, dark trousers, were sparkling from a fresh coat of polish.

He nodded with approval, satisfied with the results of his morning efforts. The remarkable transformation in his appearance, after all, had not been the result of rash impulsiveness. Everything about his new image—the clean-shaven face, the neatly-trimmed hair, the crisply pressed clothes—was part of his master plan to court the prim and proper Rebecca Summers.

Last night, as soon as he'd left the Red Dog Saloon, he'd wracked his brain, trying to come up with a creative strategy to win his reckless, impulsive wager. How could he possibly attain the affections of the most unattainable woman in town?

Surprisingly, the answer had hit him like a thunderbolt as soon as he'd awakened that morning, nearly jolting him out of bed by its sheer simplicity.

He would simply act like a gentleman, treating her the way a respectable lady should be treated.

In spite of all the stories he'd heard about Rebecca Summers, Grady figured the woman had good reasons for declining the invitations of every man in town. And the most likely explanation for her refusals, he'd assessed, had to be centered around the lack of respectable men who'd tried to call on her. It was no secret that the majority of males in Hope, Kansas, were uncouth, foul-mouthed weasels, ignorant about the time-proven, gentlemanly art of pursuing the affections of a respectable lady.

But he, of course, was different than the other men in Hope, Kansas. He was much

more likely to be a successful candidate in the
contest to win the heart of a prim and proper
lady like Rebecca Summers. Grady Cunningham was well-versed in the art of knowing
how to please a respectable woman. His own
mother, raised in the heart of Boston society,
had trained her two sons in a manner be-
fitting of proper gentlemen, supervising their
instruction in everything from proper table
manners to the acceptable rules of social
etiquette.

Along the way, experience had taught
Grady even more about the preferences of respectable ladies. Women of good breeding,
he'd learned, placed utmost importance on
the appearances of both themselves and their
male companions. They would rather die a
slow, lingering death than endure a moment
of shameful disgrace, like accidentally displaying their bare ankles in public or being
seen in the company of a man who hadn't
bathed in days.

Honorable women settled for nothing less
than smartly groomed men with clean clothes
and impeccable manners. They adored males
who were lavish with their compliments.
They loved to be showered with flowers and
trinkets. And they couldn't resist a bit of po-
liteness, a dash of charm, or a snippet of
flattery.

Every instinct Grady possessed warned him
that Rebecca Summers wasn't different than
any other woman who was concerned about
her social standing in the community. The
way to her heart, he was certain, was to act
like a gentleman while treating her like a

lady. What woman could resist the charms of a gentleman who catered to her every whim?

Of course, he was fully aware that he wasn't a bona fide gentleman. And the challenge of courting Rebecca Summers was simply a little diversion to occupy his time for the next week or two, nothing more. But his charade might result in a sizeable deposit to his bank account, and he was sure to have a helluva good time along the way.

More importantly, no harm would come from his brief spree of fun. It was just a game, after all. Grady was certain there would be no emotional attachments to untangle, no bitter feelings to resolve, no broken fences to mend. In the end, when all was said and done, he'd simply head back to the plains where he belonged, and resume his old way of life.

Anxious to set his plan into motion, Grady grabbed his new Stetson from the dresser and bolted for the door. Checking on Carl was the perfect excuse to return to the Summers' residence, he sensed, and the ideal way to initiate another encounter with the prissy little lady who resided there.

His brisk, long strides carried him down the steps to the first floor of the hotel, across the lobby, through the door, and over the planked boardwalk. He maintained his quick pace, crossing over the main thoroughfare and the railroad tracks that cut through the center of town, until he reached his destination.

When he stepped onto the porch and knocked on the door, he was confident that he was prepared to launch the first portion of his game plan. But a jolt of surprise shot through him, overshadowing his boldness, when a little girl answered the door.

The child couldn't be more than five or six years old, Grady surmised, yet her delicate features were already blossoming with the promise of beauty. Her wide, blue eyes were peering up at him through thick, dark lashes, and her diminutive, heart-shaped mouth was slightly agape. Dark waves of hair curled around her narrow shoulders.

Who was this enchanting waif? Taken aback by the child's unexpected appearance, Grady was assuming he'd arrived at the wrong house until a familiar-looking German shepherd scrambled up beside the girl and greeted him with a friendly bark.

"Uly acts like he knows you," the child observed candidly. Her eyes narrowed as she tilted back her head and gazed up at him in confusion. "Who are you?"

"Grady Cunningham." He hunkered down and brushed his hand over the dog's thick mane of fur. "Uly and I became acquainted with each other last night."

"Last night?" Her frown deepened. "Did you come here with . . . Carl?"

Grady nodded just as Jacob stepped up to the door. "Good morning, son. I see you and my granddaughter are already becoming acquainted."

"Good morning," Grady choked out, springing to his feet, feeling as bewildered as if someone had smashed a rock over his head. If the child was Jacob's granddaughter, then that meant her mother was the Widow Summers.

He dropped his gaze, studying the child who was still peering up at him. With her dark hair and bright blue eyes, she looked like a tiny replica of her mother.

Her mother. The realization stunned him to the core. No one at the Red Dog Saloon had mentioned anything about the widow having a daughter.

"Come on inside," Jacob urged, opening the door wider and motioning for him to enter.

Grady stepped into the house, trying to ignore the stab of uneasiness pricking away at his conscience. When he'd agreed to the challenge of courting the Widow Summers, he'd simply been amused by the idea of breaking through the barriers that the prim and proper lady had erected around herself. He hadn't known she was a *mother*, and never dreamed she was the sole parent of a child.

He trailed behind the physician, following him into his office, where Carl was sitting on the cot beside the window. A white bandage was wrapped around his forehead.

"You look like hell, my friend." Grady grinned. "But, then, I have to admit that you look a helluva lot better than you did last night."

"I'm feelin' better, too. 'Course, I've had plenty of good doctorin' since you've been gone." Carl winked at the little girl standing beside Grady. "And Miss Jessica here is the best nurse I've ever had."

Grady looked down at the child. "Is this scoundrel telling the truth?"

Jessica's nod was accompanied by a girlish giggle. "Of course he is!"

"Then you must be an angel to put up with

the likes of this rascal." Peering behind her back, he feigned confusion. "But if you're an angel . . . where are your wings? Did you lose them when you flew across the room to answer my knock at the door?"

"I've never had any wings!" She laughed again. "Besides, I only answered the door 'cuz I thought you were Sam."

"Sam? Is he your husband?"

"Of course not! I'm not old enough to be married to anybody!" she insisted, launching into a fit of giggles.

Something about the innocence, the purity, the genuineness of her laughter pierced the depths of Grady's heart. He couldn't deny the child was the most pleasant surprise he'd encountered in a long time. In fact, she was downright adorable. Grady had the strange feeling she could wrap him around her little finger in the space of a heartbeat.

Of course, little tykes had always been his weakness. He couldn't remember a time when he didn't adore them. He and Priscilla had even talked about having a dozen or so of their own. But that was before . . .

He shrugged aside the disturbing memories, making way for a surge of optimistic thoughts. No, he'd never courted anyone with a child. . . . But what difference should it make? He'd always gotten along with kids, hadn't he? Couldn't he use the situation to his advantage now?

Seized by the sudden urge to get to know the child better, he kneeled down to meet her at eye level. "So who is this Sam you were expecting? Your beau?"

She threw her head back and laughed. "No, no, no! Sam is my friend Samantha. She visits us almost every day. Sometimes she stays here with me when Grandpa and Mama are away, taking care of sick people."

"I see." He paused, looking around the room, wondering why he hadn't seen Rebecca anywhere. "Where is your mother, by the way?"

"She's not here right now," she explained. "She's gone to a meeting at church. And I'm not sure when she'll be back."

Unable to explain the disappointment reeling through him, Grady steeled himself. Why should it matter? This was only a game, after all. He could always drop by the house on another day, put his plan into action at some other time.

"Your mother should be home in time for lunch, Jess." Jacob shifted his gaze toward Grady. "Care to join us for a bite, son?"

Before Grady could decline, Jessica curled her fingers around the wide expanse of his hand. "Won't you please stay?" she asked, her eyes and voice pleading with him.

He didn't have the heart to turn down the invitation, couldn't even think of a single reason why he should refuse. "Thanks," he said with genuine sincerity. "I'd like to stay for—"

The door knob clattered, cutting off the rest of his thought. Grady swung his gaze toward the entrance just as Rebecca hurled open the front door and stopped cold.

Chapter 4

Waves of panic swept through Rebecca. What would the Women's Missionary Auxiliary say about one of their own consorting with Grady Cunningham? Worse yet, how would they react if they knew he'd been to her home *twice* in the course of the last twelve hours?

The thoughts were too horrible to fathom. True, her home was isolated from the heart of town, and it was unlikely that her closest neighbors—who lived a good half-mile down the road—would have noticed him entering the house. But Rebecca wanted to get rid of him before anyone discovered he was here.

Why hadn't God answered her prayer? Didn't He realize she never wanted to see this man again? Jarred by the sudden realization that the unwelcome intruder was holding her daughter's hand, she glowered at the man. She was wondering how long he had been here, trying to think of some way to make him leave, just as Jessica broke away from his hold and scrambled up beside her.

"Look, Mama! We have company!"

"So I see." Rebecca grimaced, closing the door behind her.

"He's a friend of Carl's," Jessica babbled on. "Grandpa and I asked him to stay and eat lunch with us. And he said he could stay!"

"As long as it's not too much of a bother," Grady interjected smoothly. "I wouldn't want to cause any trouble."

"As a matter of fact . . ." She paused, groping for an excuse that would encourage him to leave. Couldn't he sense she didn't want him here? Didn't he realize she never wanted to see him again?

"It's no bother at all, Grady," Jacob insisted, shuffling toward the kitchen. "We've got quite a bit of ham left from last night's supper. Corn bread, too."

"And don't forget the apple pie Mama made yesterday!" Jessica added merrily.

Rebecca cringed. As much as she adored her daughter and father-in-law, she wanted nothing more than to strangle both of them at that moment. Opening their home to the most despicable man in Hope was *not* the way to maintain an honorable reputation, after all.

Yet, what could she do? Jacob was already placing food on the table and motioning for the little group to take their seats. Arguing with her father-in-law about his decision to invite these men to stay for lunch was hardly the thing to do.

A sinking feeling rolled through her as Jessica tugged at her hand, leading her into the kitchen and guiding her toward the table. She sighed, silently conceding defeat in the matter, just as Grady stepped up beside her. He was standing close to her, so very close that the masculine scents of bay rum and shaving soap assaulted her senses.

Gazing up at him, she couldn't ignore the changes in his appearance since last night. The man had cleaned up nicely, she had to admit. Too nicely, in fact. His clothes seemed crisp, clean, new. The dark waves of his hair, now stylishly cut, shimmered with a fresh-washed glow. And last night's stubble of whiskers had disappeared, unveiling a clean-shaven face that was even more arresting and intriguing than she remembered.

For a fleeting instant, she struggled to remember all the reasons why she didn't want him here, fought to remind herself that she wanted nothing to do with the likes of him. If she hadn't known better, she might have thought the man was *respectable*.

Her confusion intensified when he pulled out a chair from the table and motioned for her to sit down. Rebecca sank into the seat with a polite nod, too flustered and surprised to acknowledge his display of gentlemanly behavior with anything more. Was there more to this man than she'd thought? Was it possible that the members of the Women's Missionary Auxiliary had misjudged him?

Nonsense. After all the horrid things she'd heard about him, how could she contemplate such ridiculous ideas? She silently vowed to banish the outrageous thoughts from her mind. Rebecca placed a white linen napkin into her lap, anxious to finish with the meal as soon as possible. The sooner Grady Cunningham was out of her house, the sooner she would be able to think logically—and breathe normally—again.

The sound of Jessica's voice broke into her thoughts. "What are you doing, Mr. Cunn'ham?"

Rebecca looked up, startled by what she saw. Once again, Grady was pulling a chair from the table. Only this time, it was Jessica who was being seated.

"I'm seating you for lunch, Miss Jessica," he explained.

Nothing could have pleased Jessica any more than being treated like a grown-up lady. After scrambling into place, the child peered up at Grady, her face awash with pure adoration. "Mama says only gentleman help ladies to their seats. Are you a gentleman?"

"I try to be a gentleman when I'm around ladies like you and your mother."

A frown of confusion wrinkled her brow. "Then why are you dressed like a cowboy?"

"Cowboys can't be gentlemen, too?"

"Oh, no. Mama says cowboys aren't gentlemen at all. She says they don't have good manners, and they're always loud and rude."

Rebecca shifted uncomfortably. "Jessica, I don't believe our guests are interested in hearing about my opinion of—"

"But you're always saying that you don't like cowboys, Mama!" Her gaze shifted back to Grady. "Mama doesn't allow me to talk to cowboys, you know. She doesn't go out of her way to talk to them, either."

"Then I'm glad I'm not a cowboy." A grin sprouted on his lips. "I'd hate not to be able to talk to you and your mother."

"I wouldn't like that, either. Mama doesn't let me talk to cowboys because she says they aren't used to being around little girls, and they might burn my ears if I get too close to them." Clamping her hands over her ears, she shuddered. "And I don't want anyone setting fire to me."

Jessica's literal interpretation of her mother's warning caused Jacob to choke on his coffee; Carl launched into a coughing spasm, and Grady looked as if he might strangle on his laughter. Biting back a smile, Rebecca reached over and gently grasped her daughter's hands. "I'm afraid you've misunderstood, Jessica. I never intended for you to think that cowboys might actually burn your ears! It's their language that concerned me. I didn't want you to hear them using bad words."

Jessica breathed a sigh of relief. "That's good to know. I was afraid cowboys might try to put marks on my ears with a branding iron, like the way they mark cattle."

"Jessica Summers!" Jacob scolded playfully. "Do you think I'd let anyone get away with that?"

The child looked across the table at her grandfather and grinned. "I guess not, Grandpa. But do you think—"

"Enough questions for now, Jess. It's not polite to monopolize the conversation at the dinner table," Rebecca interrupted in a firm voice. She placed a slice of ham on the child's plate. "Eat your lunch, and let the men have a chance to discuss some things they want to talk about."

Jessica picked up her fork. "I'm just glad to know that Mr. Cunn'ham isn't a cowpoke."

As Rebecca passed the platter of ham to Carl, she became acutely aware of her daughter's regard for Grady Cunningham. And she fully understood why Jessica had become fascinated with the man so quickly. How many men were considerate enough to treat a six-year-old girl like royalty?

Rebecca dropped her gaze to her plate, uneasy with the realization that she *liked* the way Grady Cunningham was treating her daughter.

"So what brought you into town, gentlemen?" Jacob probed.

"Business." Grady stabbed a fork into a thick slice of ham. "But we've already taken care of all our transactions. We shipped out four carloads of buffalo skins on the train to Chicago yesterday morning."

"This is the first time we've used the railroad facilities in Hope," Carl added. "Most of the time, we take our skins to Abilene or Ellsworth."

"Skin hunters, eh?" Jacob nodded approvingly as he buttered his cornbread. "From what I hear, the market for buffalo has never been better."

"The demand for hides has become just as strong as the run on buffalo meat," Grady said. "In fact, one of my contacts back East says he can't fill orders fast enough. Seems that buffalo coats have become all the rage in Europe."

"Sounds like you've got a profitable operation," Jacob remarked, reaching for another piece of ham. "Of course, I shouldn't be too surprised, knowing your father's sharp eye for business. You must have inherited Malcolm's Midas touch."

For a long, awkward moment, Grady didn't respond. Rebecca noticed a tight clench in his jaw, a sudden hardness in his eyes. When he finally spoke, his voice was harsh and strained. "My father and I have nothing in common, I'm afraid. His business dealings and my affairs are completely independent of each other."

"I see." Jacob munched on the last bite of his cornbread. "So you haven't been in contact with Malcolm recently?"

"No. And I don't anticipate that I'll be seeing him while I'm here." He lifted a fork to his lips. "Quite frankly, I don't think either of us care to associate with each other any longer."

He resumed eating, promptly closing the discussion. Rebecca sensed he was attempting to appear indifferent about the strained relationship with his father. But everything about him—the tight set of his jaw, the stiffness in his shoulders, the crisp tone in his voice—left her with a far different impression about his true feelings for Malcolm Cunningham.

Did Grady realize his father's health was failing? She suspected he didn't want to hear anything—good or bad—about Malcolm. But if he was aware of the elderly man's condition, why was his heart so cold and hardened toward him?

It's none of your business, she scolded herself, suddenly coming to her senses. Why should she concern herself about Grady Cunningham's relationship with his father? Instead of worrying about his personal life, she should be concentrating on getting the man out of her house.

She flashed a smile in Grady's direction. "So now that you've taken care of your affairs here in Hope . . . you'll be leaving soon?" she asked sweetly, unable to mask the hopefulness in her voice.

"Actually, it's time for my crew to enjoy themselves for a while. I suspect we'll probably be staying in town for a couple of weeks."

Rebecca's smile vanished. "A couple of . . . weeks?" she choked out.

Subdued amusement sparkled from the depth of his gray eyes. "Do you have an objection to that, Mrs. Summers?"

"Of course not," she denied, feeling a heated flush rise to her cheeks. "I'm merely surprised, that's all. I assumed you would be anxious to return to the plains and get back to work, considering the high demand for your goods."

He shrugged. "We'll get back to work soon enough. Besides, I've run across several things here in Hope that have intrigued me, things I'd like to investigate before leaving town."

Rebecca shifted uncomfortably, unable to explain why she felt as if she were one of the items that he intended to investigate during his visit. To make matters worse, she wasn't able to shrug aside the unpleasant feelings until the meal was finished and the men retreated into the parlor.

As Jessica scrambled down from her chair and trailed after the men, Rebecca whipped an apron over her dress and cleared the dishes from the table. Relieved the ordeal was finally over, she picked up a knife to carve the remaining morsels of ham from the bone. The leftovers, she thought, would lend a nice flavor to the soup that she intended to prepare for the evening meal.

She was almost finished when she sensed the presence of someone standing behind her. A tingling feeling swept through her; the hairs on the back of her neck prickled.

"I'd be glad to give you a hand," Grady whispered into her ear.

Rebecca's fingers tightened around the handle of the knife. "Thank you for the offer, Mr. Cunningham, but I have everything under control here. I'm sure you have better things to do with your time. Besides, I wouldn't want to be guilty of delaying your departure any longer than necessary."

"Tryin' to get rid of me?"

His voice was taunting, tantalizing, teasing. As the warmth of his breath whispered across her neck, Rebecca struggled to hold on to her composure. Steeling herself, she dropped the knife with a clatter and whirled around to face him. "Yes, Mr. Cunningham. That's precisely what I'm trying to do."

Without a second glance in his direction, she deposited the ham bone on a plate, darted past him, and hurled open the back door. "Good day, Mr. Cunningham," she said crisply.

Uly trotted up to greet her as soon as she stepped onto the small porch that overlooked the rear yard. While the dog contentedly gnawed and crunched on the ham bone, she sauntered across the yard to check on her herb garden, hoping Grady Cunningham and his friend would leave before she returned to the house.

Located at the corner of the property, Rebecca's herb garden was her pride and joy. In spite of the drought, her plants were thriving, she noticed. Pleased with the results of her daily efforts to water each plant, she smiled with satisfaction. Then she whirled around, intending to return to the house.

But she'd taken only three steps across the yard when she looked up and stopped cold. Grady was leaning against the porch in a lazy stance, one lean hip propped against a wooden railing, arms crossed nonchalantly over the width of his chest. Though the brim of his white Stetson was cocked low over his forehead, Rebecca could see amusement glinting from his unreasonably beautiful gray eyes and the trace of a smirk forming on the sensuous line of his lips.

Stiffening, she glared at him. "I thought you were leaving!"

"Obviously." He had the audacity to chuckle. "But you can't get rid of me so easily, Mrs. Summers."

Exasperated, Rebecca crossed her arms over her chest and frowned. "I wasn't aware this was a social call, Mr. Cunningham. I thought Carl was the reason for your visit. I thought you'd returned here to check on him, with the intent of getting him settled elsewhere, now that he's—"

"Carl is only *one* of the reasons why I'm here." His long strides bridged the distance between them. He halted directly in front of her, standing so close that she could practically count every thick lash framing his eyes. "To be honest, I wanted to see you again."

"Me?" A sliver of fear pulsed through her. "But . . . why?"

His bluish-gray eyes raked over her face with such intensity that her breath snared in her throat. "You intrigue me, Mrs. Summers. I can't recall ever meeting another woman who has fascinated me more than you."

Hearing the husky timbre of his voice, seeing the passion glinting from his eyes, Rebecca almost wished she wasn't aware of his sinful past. She suspected she could actually enjoy being pursued by a man as handsome and charming as Grady Cunningham.

But that, of course, could never be, she reminded herself sternly. She took a step back, hoping he couldn't hear the frantic thundering of her heart. "You're wasting your breath, Mr. Cunningham, along with your time. Sweet talk doesn't work on me. Save your flattery for someone who will appreciate it."

His brows narrowed. "You don't like being told that you're a beautiful, attractive woman?"

She lifted her chin. "Of course I do . . . as

long as the words are being spoken with genuine sincerity."

"And you think I'm not being sincere?"

A shadow of darkness crossed his face, and Rebecca reeled in confusion. Common sense warned her to ignore his seductive charm, walk away from him, forget he had ever been here. But another part, the softer, more vulnerable side of her, wanted to know more about the man with a penchant for little girls and a sensitivity for being accused of lying. Until this moment, she had been quite certain he was nothing but a silver-tongued devil. But that was before she caught a glimpse of the wounded, distraught expression marring his handsome features.

She inhaled a shaky breath. "Quite frankly, I'm not certain what to think about you," she admitted truthfully.

"Well, I don't want to give you the impression that I'm the type of man who expects something for nothing, darlin'." His long, lean fingers dipped into the pocket of his vest and pulled out a roll of bills. "I always take care of my crew—even when they get into scuffles. So this is for you, for all you did for Carl last night."

Rebecca stared in disbelief at the thick wad of bills in Grady's hand. None of her patients had ever offered such a hefty sum for her services. But it was more money than she had rightfully earned, more than she could possibly accept with good conscience.

She shook her head. "I don't want your money."

"You deserve to be paid for your services. If this isn't enough—"

"It's more than sufficient," she assured him. "But it's not what I want."

"Fine, then. I'll play your little game." Scowling, he shoved the money back into his pocket. "What kind of payment do you want? Credit at the Collinses' store? Some fancy new dresses? Or how about—"

"All I want from you is a promise," she interrupted in a quiet tone.

He stilled. "A promise?"

Nodding, she pursed her lips together. "Promise me you'll forget you were here last night. Disregard the fact that Jacob and Jessica invited you for lunch today. Pretend you were never here, that we've never met, that none of this ever happened."

Taken aback, Grady felt as stunned as if she'd slapped him across the face. Though he hadn't expected her to be the easiest conquest in the world, he'd never dreamed she would put up such fierce resistance to him. Obviously, he'd underestimated the little lady's resilience.

Worse yet, his ego was smarting from her scathing rejection. Unaccustomed to the sting of feminine rebuff, Grady bristled. "What's wrong, darlin'?" he goaded. "Afraid of what people might say if they find out you've been entertainin' a gentleman?"

She boldly met his gaze. "If I'd been entertaining a gentleman, I wouldn't have any reason to worry about what people might say."

"Then you must have some serious vision problems, lady," he snapped, unable to conceal the anger searing through him from the insulting remark. "Apparently, you aren't capable of recognizing a gentleman when you see one."

She lifted her chin a notch. "A gentleman can't be identified by sight alone, Mr. Cunningham. Looks can be deceiving at times. It takes more than donning a new set of clothes or spending a few moments in a barber's chair to transform a man into a bona fide gentleman. A man's actions speak louder than his appearance."

"Open your eyes, darlin'. You're blindin' yourself to the truth," he scoffed, dropping his voice to a low, menacing keel. "I've been nothing but a gentleman to you—and to your family—since I've been here. You can't deny it, and you know it."

"Your manners have been impeccable during your visits to my home," she admitted. "But in spite of all your charming ways, Mr. Cunningham, I can't ignore the fact that your standing in this community is far from honorable."

He narrowed his eyes, studying her in disbelief. "So you form your opinions about people based on what others have to say about them?"

"Not always." She dipped her head, feigning a sudden interest in the dust clinging to the toes of her slippers. "But people usually are deserving of their reputations, in one way or another."

"Even if those reputations have been tainted by gossip and hearsay?"

She lifted one shoulder in an airy shrug. "Gossip usually has some basis to it."

"Don't believe everything you hear, Mrs. Summers. If you trusted your own instincts instead of putting stock into everyone else's opinions, you'd see a person's true colors much more clearly," he advised gruffly, tipping up her chin with a callused finger, forcing her to meet his gaze. "If I believed everything I heard, I would be assuming it's impossible for any man in this town to snare your affections. But I'm not foolish enough to believe the hearsay. I suspect all the talk is nothing more than idle gossip."

"Then you must be a very perceptive man," she countered, the line of her jaw tightening.

"Just a realistic one. Something tells me you have a good reason for avoiding the men in Hope." His fingers drifted over the curve of her cheek, and a tingling sensation rippled through him at the soft feel of her skin even beneath his callused hand. "Maybe you're tryin' to hide something. Perhaps you're scared someone might uncover a secret or two if you let down your guard. Or maybe you're—"

"My private life is none of your concern, Mr. Cunningham." Her voice was as stiff and rigid as the curve of her back.

Still, he pressed on. "Afraid of losin' your heart? Scared a man might take advantage of you if you drop your guard?"

Anger glinted from her eyes and spotted her cheeks with dots of crimson. "I'm not an innocent young girl, Mr. Cunningham. I'm perfectly capable of watching out for myself.

I've worked very hard to merit the respect of this community. And I can't afford to risk my good name by consorting with the likes of you."

She jerked away from him just as the back door slammed. As Grady's gaze shifted in the direction of the noise, a young girl with long, blond hair rushed out of the house.

"Oh, Rebecca, you won't believe what happened to me this morning!" the girl cried.

Rebecca picked up her skirts and scurried across the yard. "Whatever is wrong, Samantha?"

Moisture swelled in the girl's eyes. "It's horrible, simply horrible!" Noticing Grady for the first time, the girl paled. "Oh, I'm sorry. I didn't realize . . . I didn't know . . ."

"You're not interrupting anything," Rebecca quickly assured the girl. After introducing her to Grady, she added, "Mr. Cunningham was just getting ready to leave, I believe."

Taking the hint, Grady politely tipped the brim of his hat. "Good day, ladies."

As soon as Grady disappeared into the house, Rebecca turned her attention to the distraught girl. "Tell me, Samantha," she urged, draping a comforting arm around her shoulders, guiding her over to the small porch. "What's disturbing you so?"

"It's Hank." Samantha plopped down into a rocking chair and sighed. "He left town this morning. Joined up with a cattle drive, so I hear. And he won't be back for months!"

"Oh, my." Rebecca grimaced, knowing how much Samantha adored Hank Murdock, the young man who had been courting her for several months. "I know you must be terribly disappointed that you won't be seeing him for a while," she offered sympathetically.

"But that's not the worst of it!" Samantha wailed. "He didn't even tell me that he was leaving! His father was the one who broke the news to me." Tears swelled in her eyes. "I just know he's jilted me, Rebecca, I just know it. He left town without a word, leaving me here—"

"Was he troubled about something?" Rebecca probed, genuinely concerned. "Or did the two of you have a disagreement, perhaps?"

"We don't always agree on everything," Samantha admitted reluctantly. Rebecca sensed she wanted to say more about their differences until she burst into tears. "I thought he loved me! I had no idea he would leave me like this."

Rebecca plucked a handkerchief from her pocket and dabbed at the girl's tear-stained cheeks. "I know you're hurting, Samantha. But tomorrow will seem brighter, I'm sure of it."

Samantha sniffed. "That's easy for you to say."

"What do you mean?" Rebecca asked.

"Well, it's not hard to comfort someone who's just been jilted when you've got somebody of your own to love." A trembling smile formed on her lips. "That Mr. Cunningham is quite a catch, Rebecca. He's just about the most handsome man I've ever seen in my entire life."

"Mr. Cunningham is not a catch, Samantha." Rebecca cringed. "I hardly know the man. He came here seeking medical care for an injured friend, and nothing more."

But Samantha didn't seem to be listening. Her eyes were clouded with a distant, dreamy look. "Cunningham," she murmured. "I've heard that name before. But I know I've never met Mr. Cunningham. I'd never forget a man as handsome as he is."

A wave of uneasiness swept through Rebecca. A highly emotional sixteen year old, Samantha possessed a dramatic flair with the tendency to exaggerate the truth at times. Obviously, she'd been captivated by Grady Cunningham, awed to the point that she'd conjured up the crazy notion of romantically linking him to Rebecca.

Which was precisely what Rebecca was trying to avoid. Determined to clear up the confusion, she said, "You've heard Mr. Cunningham's name because he is the son of our mayor, Samantha. But his reputation is far from honorable, I fear. Not many people in Hope care to be associated with him."

A look of bewilderment crossed Samantha's face. "But . . . why?"

"He was involved in some sort of scandal a few years back. Apparently, the incident permanently tarnished his name, and I'm afraid people don't forget scandalous situations easily." She winced, remembering the shame, the ridicule, the gossip, that had once clouded her own life. "I think it would be best—for you and for me—if you didn't tell anyone about meeting Mr. Cunningham here."

"Not even my parents?"

"I'm not in favor of being deceitful to anyone, Samantha, especially your mother and father. But I'm certain your mother would be quite dismayed if she discovered that you had any contact with Mr. Cunningham. And we don't want to needlessly upset her, do we?"

"Of course not." Samantha slowly rose from the chair. "I won't tell anyone about Mr. Cunningham's visit here. It'll be a secret, just between you and me."

"I'd appreciate that, Samantha."

She trudged across the porch. "You don't have to worry about anyone gossiping about Mr. Cunningham while he's in town, either, I suppose. Everyone will be too busy talking about the way Hank Murdock jilted Samantha Collins."

"Then give them something else to talk about," Rebecca challenged.

Samantha stopped in her tracks. "Like what?"

"Like the way you're recovering from your broken heart. Show everyone that you're not sitting at home, crying into your pillow. Prove to them that you're moving on with your life, that you're not going to let a scoundrel like Hank Murdock shatter your heart for long."

"You know something, Rebecca?" A tiny smile sprouted on her lips. "Maybe it isn't the end of the world for me, after all."

Samantha turned and disappeared around the corner of the house. Rebecca lingered on the porch, hoping the girl would remember how to keep a secret in the midst of mending a broken heart.

Chapter 5

"You did *what*?" Carl gaped at Grady in disbelief as they trudged down the street, heading back to the Hope business district.

Grady bit back a smile. "Close your mouth, Carl, before you swallow a bug."

Carl clamped his lips together in a tight line. "You musta been outa your mind—or rip-roarin' drunk—to make a crazy wager like that, Cunningham."

"I was sober and sane, my friend," Grady insisted. "When the guys at the Red Dog claimed no one could turn the widow's head, I couldn't resist the challenge of courting her. Besides, it seemed like an amusing way to pass the time and have a little fun before we head back to the plains."

"Havin' a little fun can get a man into a helluva lot of trouble," Carl warned with a grimace, fingering the bandage on his head. "Believe me, I know."

"For cripes' sake, Carl, it's just a damn bet!

No one is going to get hurt by a harmless wager." Grady snarled, unable to dispel the bitter taste lingering in his mouth from the tartness of Rebecca's rejection. "But it's not a wager I intend to lose, mind you."

"A lot of money at stake, huh?"

"The money is insignificant, whether or not I win or lose." Grady pulled back his shoulders with determination. "No, something more valuable than money is the real issue at stake in this wager. Miss Prim and Proper needs to be taught a lesson. Someone— namely, me—needs to teach the woman that she can't go around condemning an innocent man without just cause."

Carl scratched his head in confusion. "What do you mean?"

"The little lady insists she can't be associated with me because my standing in the community is far from honorable." Grady scowled at the thought. "Apparently, some of the old biddies in town have been dredging up the past, gossiping about my involvement in Ned Sikes's murder. God knows, they've probably distorted the truth so much that they've convinced the Widow Summers—and everyone else who wasn't living here three years ago—that I'm a blood-thirsty, axe-wielding murderer."

"But you ain't gonna let them get away with that, are you?"

"Of course not." Grady set his mouth into a hard line. "Nobody is going to get away with unjustly condemning me again."

"So what are you gonna do?"

A sly smile curled at the corners of Grady's

lips. "Why, I'm gonna court the widow, my friend. I'm gonna woo her and charm her and romance her until she admits she made a mistake about me. Nothing could give me more satisfaction than hearing her admit that she listened to the town gossips, formed an opinion about me without knowing all the facts, and judged me on nothing but hearsay." His smile widened. "Of course, it's not such a bad way to spend my time. In fact, I think I'm gonna enjoy every single minute of putting the woman in her place. She's not exactly the kind of lady who's hard to look at."

Carl grinned. "Can't say I blame you, Cunningham. I don't know of anyone who wouldn't enjoy courtin' the purtiest lady in Hope."

Approaching the center of the business district, Grady nodded toward the tallest building in town, a three-story structure that loomed over the other pitch-roofed stores and businesses on the main thoroughfare. "Come on, Carl. Let's get you a room for the night before the Grand Central fills up."

"The Grand Central?" Carl frowned in confusion. "Why not Hope Cottage, instead? That's where the rest of the crew is stayin'. The rooms are cheaper, and—"

"I don't care for Hope Cottage," Grady snapped. "The owner and I don't get along, in case you've forgotten."

"But . . ." Carl slowed his pace. "I guess you didn't hear the news last night at the Red Dog. A real nice married couple is runnin' Hope Cottage now. Your old man sold the place to them back in the winter."

"Now, why in the hell would he do that?" Grady stopped cold, glaring at his friend in disbelief. "King Cunningham has never sold off anything that was turning a handsome profit for him."

"The guys down at the Red Dog said the cattle king has been feelin' a mite poorly of late. Maybe that's got somethin' to do with it."

"That's ridiculous, Carl. You know as well as I do that King Cunningham never been sick a day in his life," Grady balked, unable to imagine his stalwart, imposing father in poor health. The man had always been as sturdy— and as stubborn—as an ox.

Carl shrugged. "Believe what you want, then. I'm just tellin' you what I heard."

"Don't always believe what you hear, my friend."

As they resumed their walk into town, Carl regarded the hotel with interest. "You know, I ain't got no objections to stayin' at the Grand Central. Looks like a mighty fine place to me. But I reckon it's too rich for my blood."

"Tell you what." Grady clapped a hand on his friend's shoulder. "If you'd like to stay at the Grand Central, I'll foot the bill while we're in town. Consider it a bonus, of sorts. After all, I couldn't have shipped out four carloads of buffalo skins without you."

Carl grinned. "My mama didn't raise no fool, Cunningham. I sure as hell ain't gonna turn down an offer like that."

Chuckling, the two men resumed their walk toward the Grand Central. Located one block west of the stockyard, the hotel fronted the railroad tracks. Green louvered shutters framed the windows, and the clapboards had been painted a delicate beige. As Grady and Carl approached the building, several patrons were relaxing along the hotel's lengthy veranda, enjoying the shade and comfort as they watched the activity at the railroad depot across the street.

A bar, restaurant, and billiard room were located on the first floor of the hotel. As Carl surveyed the luxurious setting, he nudged Grady with his elbow. "What's goin' on over there?" he asked, pointing to a group of men huddled around a large desk.

"It's a stock register," Grady explained. "Sellers can list their livestock, and buyers can check the register to find herds to purchase."

"Well, I'll be damned," Carl mumbled. "I'll bet Hope Cottage ain't never had nothin' like that."

How true, Grady agreed silently. Malcolm Cunningham had probably kicked himself a hundred times for not thinking of the idea himself. The old coot had always considered Hope Cottage an important link to the cattle trade.

Which was precisely why the news about the sale of the place was so puzzling to Grady. Why would the cattle king of Kansas sell one of his most profitable connections to the cattle industry? It was hard to believe his father's health had prompted him to sell the business. King Cunningham, robust and hearty, had always been the picture of perfect health. Whatever was ailing him, it couldn't be too serious ... could it?

There could be dozens of other reasons that had motivated the man to sell the place, Grady told himself. Maybe he'd gotten an offer he couldn't refuse. Perhaps he was focusing his attention on other ventures. It was possible that his kingdom of businesses had grown so vast that Hope Cottage no longer held any challenge for him.

An outbreak of laughter from the men gathered around the cattle register resounded through the hotel lobby, jarring Grady back into reality. Good God, why was he worrying about Malcolm Cunningham? Not one word had been exchanged between them since the murder trial. The old geezer had no interest in a son who'd brought shame to the illustrious Cunningham name.

Besides, he had more important things to think about. Things like getting Carl settled for the night, paying a visit to the bar ... and charting the next step of his course to win the challenge of courting Rebecca Summers.

Late in the afternoon, Jessica bounded into the kitchen. "Dinner smells good, Mama! When are we going to eat?"

Stirring the ham and potato soup with a wooden spoon, Rebecca smiled down at her daughter as she dashed up to the stove. "We'll eat dinner as soon as Grandpa gets home."

"Has he gone to see somebody who's sick?"

Nodding, Rebecca set aside the spoon and

wiped her hands on the skirt of her apron.
"Mr. Littleton had a rough night, and
Grandpa wanted to check on him this afternoon. But he should be home any minute."
She motioned toward the wash basin. "Wash
up for dinner now so you'll be ready to eat
when Grandpa gets here."

As Jessica scampered up to the basin to
wash her hands, Rebecca stepped back from
the stove and sighed. Her shoulders ached,
her back hurt, and her head was throbbing.
But she had no one to blame for her frazzled
state except herself. Throughout the afternoon, she'd tackled her chores with the frenzy
of a woman gone mad.

She'd been delighted to discover that Carl
and Grady had left the house during her conversation with Samantha. Jacob departed for
the Littleton home a few moments later, wanting to check on the progress of his patient.

Assuming she could forget about the disturbing events of the day by keeping her
hands busy, Rebecca had plunged into her
household tasks. After weeding the herb garden and dusting every piece of furniture in
the house, she'd laundered two tubs of
clothes and hung each garment to dry. Then
she'd mixed the ingredients for a fresh cherry
cobbler and prepared soup for the evening
meal. While the cobbler was baking, she'd
peeled and sliced potatoes, then placed them
into a large pot of boiling water. Later, as the
potatoes simmered, she'd added the leftover
ham for flavor to the soup.

Despite her efforts, however, Rebecca's
frenzied attempts to ward off all thoughts of

Grady Cunningham had been a dismal fail-
ure. At odd moments, bits and pieces of conversation from the auxiliary meeting had
crept into her thoughts, reminding her that
any affiliation with Mayor Cunningham's son
could only result in disaster. At other times,
her mind whirled with doubts about trusting
Samantha with the secret about Grady's visit.

But most of all, Rebecca had been plagued
with unsettling thoughts of the man himself.
Her face still burned from the brush of his
finger across her chin, her skin still scorched
from the heat of his gaze raking over her, her
mind still blazed with memories of his rugged, chiseled features.

By dinnertime, Rebecca was weary from
battling with her wayward thoughts. Still, she
made every attempt to be pleasant and cheerful during the meal. She attended to Jessica's
chatter with the patience of a saint, smiled
through Jacob's report on Mr. Littleton's progress, and even managed to laugh at herself
for spilling some soup on her dress.

But after listening to Jessica's prayers and
tucking the child into bed for the night, she
could no longer hide her exhaustion. Yawning, she trudged into the parlor.

Jacob was settled comfortably on the settee,
absorbed in the pages of a book, smoking his
pipe. As Rebecca entered the room and
slumped into a wing chair, he glanced over
at her. Concern glimmered from his eyes.
"What's on your mind, 'Becca?"

She stifled another yawn with the palm of
her hand. "Sleep," she murmured, grinning

halfheartedly. "It appears I didn't get enough rest last night, I fear."

"It was an eventful evening," Jacob agreed, setting aside his book. "And an eventful day, too."

"Too eventful for me." Massaging the bridge of her nose, she grimaced. "You don't think we'll be seeing any more of Grady Cunningham . . . do you?"

"I suspect we might run across him in town from time to time, considering that he's planning to stay here a few weeks."

"I was afraid of that," Rebecca admitted, too weary to conceal her fears from Jacob any longer. "At the auxiliary meeting this morning, Lydia Davenport reported that Grady was back in town. The news sent everyone into a tizzy."

After Rebecca recounted the ladies' dismal discussion about the town's latest arrival, Jacob frowned. "I noticed you weren't overly enthusiastic about inviting guests for lunch," he said. "And now I know why."

"To make matters worse, Samantha was smitten by the man." Rebecca sighed. "I asked her not to tell anyone that she met him here. But if Lydia ever gets wind of this . . ." She shuddered at the unspoken thought. Unable to contain the anxiety searing through her, she sprang up from the chair and paced the room. "Being associated with someone like Grady Cunningham is the last thing I need."

Jacob scowled. "Sit down here a minute, 'Becca."

With a sigh, she returned to the chair. Jacob

reached over and patted her hand. "Listen to me, child. Nobody in this town is perfect—not you, not Grady Cunningham, not me. I dare say most of the folks around here aren't proud of something from their past. The West is brimming with people who are trying to get a fresh start in life, men and women who are running away from their mistakes."

"But not everyone is trying to hide the fact that she's the daughter of a murderer," Rebecca countered in a shaky voice.

"That nightmare is behind you now, and you don't have to answer to anyone about your past any longer," Jacob reminded her. He squeezed her hand tighter. "You know, sometimes things happen in our lives that are beyond our control. You weren't—and still aren't responsible for your father's mistakes. And you couldn't have prevented him from murdering his brother anymore than you could have prevented . . ." He paused, gulping before continuing. ". . . David's death on the battlefield."

Tears swelled in Rebecca's eyes at the memory of her beloved David, for the lasting love that might have been. "Yes, but . . ."

"My son would have married you, 'Becca, if he'd had the chance. We both know that. But his death was beyond our control, just like so many other things in life that we can't predict or foresee. We especially can't control what other people think, how other people will react to situations. All we can control in life are our own emotions, our reactions to the circumstances in our lives."

"I've been trying to control my emotions and reactions to circumstances." Rebecca heaved a weary sigh. "But sometimes it's difficult. I live in constant fear that Jessica might bear the brunt of gossip about me if I associate with the wrong people or if I say or do the wrong thing. And I can't bear the thought of her suffering for my mistakes, the way I suffered for my own father's crimes as a child."

"There's a big difference between mistakes and crimes, 'Becca. Everyone makes errors, but not everyone commits crimes. You've made a few mistakes in life, just like the rest of us. But you're runnin' yourself ragged tryin' to hide things about yourself that nobody even knows about. You're pretty near perfect, if I say so myself, and anybody who's got a lick of sense will know that as soon as they get to know you."

Rebecca managed a smile. Soothed by Jacob's calming words of encouragement and assurance, she felt her doubts and fears subsiding. Sometimes it was difficult to remember that those storms of scandal were no longer casting shadows of gloom over her life, and she was grateful to Jacob for boosting her spirits with the reminder that she was now leading an exemplary life in Hope. "Thanks, Jacob," she whispered, planting a kiss on the man's cheek as she quietly left the parlor.

She slipped up the stairs and retreated into the privacy of her room. After opening the window, hoping a few cool breezes would bring some relief to the stifling heat, she quickly donned her gown and slipped between the sheets.

She felt as though she'd just closed her eyes when a thunderous noise split through the air. Startled, she shot up in bed, listening intently. Had she been awakened by thunder?

At that instant, a series of harsh pops crackled through the dead of night. With a start, Rebecca recognized the sudden, sharp sounds coming from the direction of the business district. *Gunfire.*

With her heart pounding in her chest, she leaped out of bed. She dashed down the hall to check on Jessica, praying the disturbance had not frightened her. She was relieved to find the child sleeping peacefully, undisturbed by the commotion.

But as Rebecca returned to her room, the disruption weighed heavily on her mind. Violence had always been the exception rather than the rule in Hope, Kansas. Open gunfire was a rare occurrence in the business district of town. Briggs Emerson, Hope's sheriff, kept a close watch on potential troublemakers, often preventing problems before they could escalate into more serious calamities. Tonight, however, something had gotten out of hand, Rebecca was thinking as she finally drifted off to sleep.

She was still mulling over the situation when she awakened the next morning, hoping no one had been seriously injured during the disturbance. After slipping into one of her better gowns, a teal dress with a lacy inset around the neck, Rebecca scurried down the stairs.

The aroma of freshly brewed coffee greeted her as she entered the kitchen. Jacob was sitting at the table, sipping the hot, steaming liquid from a large mug.

"Must have been some trouble in town last night," Jacob mumbled as she swept into the room. "Did you hear all the ruckus?"

"Unfortunately." Rebecca poured a cup of coffee for herself. "I got up to check on Jessica because I was afraid the noise might have frightened her. Thankfully, she slept through it all."

"I wish I could be such a sound sleeper." Jacob took another sip of coffee.

"When I first heard all the commotion, I thought I was having a nightmare. Then I thought the sound of thunder had awakened me. And then I realized it was ... gunfire."

"The noise startled me, too. And then I couldn't get back to sleep because I kept expecting someone to knock on the door."

"But no one came." Rebecca pursed her lips together. "What do you think that means?"

"Either no one was hurt or ..." Jacob grimaced. "Or it was useless to call for a doctor."

A tiny pulse of fear throbbed through her veins. "I don't like the sounds of this, Jacob. I'd hate for Hope to become the type of place that's known for violence. And I certainly don't want Jessica to be exposed to any sort of danger."

"Lots of people in Hope share your feelings, Rebecca, including me. But the railroad terminal and stockyard are luring new faces into town every week, especially men from cattle drives. And after months on the trail, cowboys are ready to spend their money and have a good time when they pull into town. They've become a dependable source of income for the town's businesses. I suspect most folks couldn't survive without the business brought here by the cattle industry."

Rebecca's brow creased with worry. "But if the violence continues, how can we build decent homes for our families here?"

"Sheriff Emerson won't allow anything to get out of hand," Jacob said with confidence. "He's been doing a good job up until now, and I imagined he intervened in the commotion last night. Besides, the cattle season will be over in October, and Hope will quiet down until spring."

"I hope so," Rebecca remarked just as Jessica darted into the room.

"Look, Mama!" she cried in distress.

Whirling around, Rebecca saw the reason for her daughter's dismay. The child was struggling to shove her arms into her favorite summer dress, a powder-blue frock in the same exact shade as her eyes. Normally, Jessica took great pride in dressing by herself, only asking for her mother's assistance with buttons or sashes that were beyond her reach.

But this morning, pure frustration was etched into her face. At the moment, she was tugging and yanking at the dress with such vigor that Rebecca feared she might rip the garment in two. Rushing to Jessica's side, she remarked, "Looks like you're having some problems this morning."

Nodding glumly, Jessica moaned. "I can hardly breathe!"

"Let me show you why." Rebecca grasped the girl's hand and guided her over to a mirror mounted on the parlor wall. "Look at yourself, Miss Jessica! You've sprouted up faster than a weed this summer, and you're growing out of your clothes."

Jessica's eyes widened in disbelief as she studied the taut seams of her gown. "No wonder it was so hard to get my arms into the sleeves! And look how short the skirt is!"

Rebecca met her daughter's gaze in the mirror. "I'd say you're past due for some new clothes, young lady. While I'm in town this morning, I'll stop by the store and get some fabric to make you some new dresses."

"Some pink fabric?" Jessica's face lit up with a smile. "I'd love to have a pink gown."

"I'll see if Charlotte has a bolt of pink in the store," Rebecca promised. She grasped the child by the shoulders and whirled her around. "Run along, now. I'll be making breakfast, while you're putting on another dress that isn't so tight on you."

Before Jessica scampered back to her room, she darted into the kitchen. Hurling her arms around her grandfather's thick neck, she planted a wet kiss on his cheek. "Guess what, Grandpa? I'm growing out of all my clothes, and Mama is going to buy some material this morning to make me some new dresses!"

"Is she, now?" Jacob chuckled as Jessica nodded. "Well, then, I don't suppose you want to stay here with your old grandpa this morning, do you?"

"Of course I do, Grandpa!"

"That would work out nicely for me, Jacob," Rebecca chimed in.

"It will work out good for me, too. I'm planning to ride out to the Cunningham ranch and check on the mayor, but I don't intend to leave until after lunch."

"I'll be back by then," Rebecca assured him.

A half hour later, Rebecca headed into town. On the surface, it seemed like an ordinary day in Hope, Kansas. Dust was flying through the air, wagons were rolling down the street, and the main thoroughfare was bustling with activity. Still, walking across the railroad tracks, Rebecca sensed an imperceptible tension crackling through the August morning, as if danger were lurking around every corner.

Wary, she looked over her shoulder. Was someone following her? Was that the reason for the uneasiness churning inside of her?

Nonsense. Dismissing the thought, she marched across the tracks. Stepping into the Collinses' store, she was surprised to see a group of the town's most prominent citizens huddled by the counter, deep in conversation.

"We can't tolerate this, I'm telling you! If we don't end all this carousing and drinking, these cowboys are going to put an end to our town!" exclaimed Zeke Gallagher, the outspoken editor of the *Hope Gazette*, the town's weekly newspaper.

"But what in the hell are we going to do about it?" challenged Virgil Collins, the store's owner. "I don't like the idea of anyone

gettin' killed around here, mind you, but cattlemen are the bulk of my business!"

"Apparently, they're the bulk of my business, too," quipped Parker Simpson, the
bearded undertaker, "considering the two
bodies brought into my place last night are
the only customers I've had all month."

"But you'll be having more, I'm certain,
now that Sheriff Emerson has walked out on
us. Can't say I blame the man for quitting in
disgust, though. Controlling the violence in
this town is getting to be too much for one
man to handle. Next month is the height of
the shipping season, and it's going to get
worse before it gets better around here,"
Zeke predicted.

Quietly listening to the discussion, Rebecca
felt a surge of fear course through her. Two
men were dead, and Sheriff Emerson had
quit. What more was going to happen?

"A shame, isn't it?"

Startled, she nearly jumped out of her skin.
She jerked around, horrified to find Grady
Cunningham standing beside her. She'd been
listening to the discussion so intently that she
hadn't even realized he had approached her.

"What are you doing here?" she demanded
in a hoarse whisper.

"Shopping." A lazy grin curled over his
lips. "What are you doing here? Other than
catching up on the latest news in town, that
is."

"I'm here to pick up a few supplies and to
buy several yards of material to make Jessica
some new dresses. So if you'll excuse me . . ."

Whirling around, she darted into a narrow

aisle in the store, praying she could disappear from sight among the high, well-stocked shelves of goods. After threading her way through a maze of merchandise, she paused at the end of an aisle to catch her breath. Noticing a leather-bound set of books displayed beside her, she plucked one of the volumes from the shelf. If she stood here long enough, she thought, maybe Grady Cunningham would grow weary of looking for her in the store . . . and leave her alone.

She opened the book to the first page, hoping she could distract herself from her worries for a few moments. But she'd only scanned the first sentence when she heard the sound of boots shuffling toward her.

"So you like . . . poetry?"

Irritated, she snapped the volume shut. "I wasn't aware you could read," she muttered, returning the book to the shelf.

"There's a lot of things you don't know about me, Mrs. Summers. Of course, if you'd care to find out more . . ."

She snapped around, intending to retort with a scathing reply. But hearing the provocative tone of his voice, seeing the passion shimmering from the depths of his eyes, feeling the delicious shivers of excitement coursing through her, Rebecca was incapable of uttering a sound. What was it about this man that mesmerized her so?

She lunged forward, intending to flee from his unsettling presence. But she'd taken only one step when his hand caught her arm. "Is Jacob with you?" he demanded.

Her skin sizzled from the heat of his touch. "No, he's at home with Jessica."

"Then you're alone?"

She jerked her arm away from him. "What does it matter to you?" she blurted out.

"Your safety matters a great deal to me, Mrs. Summers. Tempers are short and tensions are high around here. Two men are dead and the sheriff has resigned. Unescorted ladies can't be too cautious, even if they've just ventured into town to shop."

Rebecca paled, recalling the uncanny sensation of being scrutinized by an unknown source as she'd walked to the store. Had someone truly been pursuing her? Worse yet, could that someone have been Grady?

"Rebecca, I didn't realize you were here!"

Hearing Charlotte's voice, Rebecca cringed with alarm. Spinning on her heels, she darted away from Grady's side, praying the high stacks of merchandise had blocked Charlotte's view of the man who had been standing beside her.

Charlotte was working behind the long, narrow counter, unpacking an assortment of merchandise from a wooden crate. "Good morning," Rebecca said brightly, rushing up to the woman. "There were so many people in here, I didn't get a chance to speak to you when I first arrived."

"Everybody in town has dropped by here this morning." Charlotte picked up her skirts and stepped around the counter. "I guess you've heard the news?"

"I'm afraid so. It's unfortunate Sheriff Emerson walked out on us during the height of the cattle season," Rebecca mused.

"Indeed it is," Charlotte agreed sorrowfully. Her frizzy curls bounced around her thin face as she shook her head in dismay. "We need him now more than ever, especially while that man is in town. I won't feel safe as long as Grady Cunningham is roaming our streets. Why, I've heard the man is . . ."

As Charlotte babbled on, a tall figure quietly came up behind her. Rebecca peered over her friend's shoulder and froze. *Grady*.

For one, heart-stopping second, panic ripped through Rebecca. Would he call her name and expose their acquaintance to Charlotte?

She shifted her attention back to her friend. Maybe if she ignored him, he would go away and leave her alone. But she couldn't disregard the heat of his gaze scorching through her, no matter how hard she tried to concentrate on what Charlotte was saying.

She felt a flame rise to her cheeks from the fiery intensity of his blatant stare. Distracted from the conversation by his intent scrutiny, her eyes wandered back to his arresting face. And what she saw made the beat of her heart accelerate wildly.

Those silvery eyes were darkening with passion, sending unspoken messages to her. Though he voiced not a word, the intent of his thoughts was unmistakable. Desire, raw and flaming, was glinting from the depths of his heated gaze.

Dear heavens, the man was seducing her with his eyes.

Rebecca's knees went weak. She was leaning against the counter for support just as Charlotte's voice caught her attention. "Now, what can I get for you today, dear?"

"Why, I need ..." Rebecca fumbled for words, still reeling from the unsettling force of his gaze. Grinning wolfishly, Grady winked and tipped the brim of his hat before heading for the door.

Flustered, Rebecca stared blankly at her friend, unable to recall the reason for her trip to the store. She sighed, irritated that a scoundrel like Grady Cunningham was capable of driving her to distraction.

Chapter 6

Someone was following her.

Within seconds after leaving the Collinses' store, Rebecca sensed the weight of a heavy gaze pressing down on her. The fine hairs on the back of her neck prickled; goosebumps popped out along her arms. Tightening her hold on the heavy parcel of yard goods that she'd just purchased, she darted through the throng of pedestrians on the boardwalk.

As she crossed the wide thoroughfare, she glanced to her left, then her right, desperately searching for a familiar face—or even a curious stare—amid the sea of people swirling around her. Finding nothing, she peered over her shoulder. Who was following her?

Unable to identify the source of her uneasiness, she picked up her pace as she crossed the railroad tracks. Was her imagination running wild? Was the news about the shootings taking a toll on her nerves? Worse yet, was Grady Cunningham the root cause of all her worries?

She paused for a moment, juggling the

weight of her purchases from one arm to the other, just as the sound of her name sliced through the morning air. "Mrs. Summers!"

Rebecca whirled around. Across the street, a bearded man hurled his arm into the air and waved in her direction. Relief and joy flooded through her when she recognized the auburn-haired, handsome gentleman wearing a black suit and a white clerical collar.

"Good morning, Pastor," she called out, feeling a bit foolish for allowing her suspicions to soar out of control. All the while, rushing through town, she'd suspected someone had been trailing after her. But she'd never dreamed that someone was Timothy O'Leary.

He stepped up beside her, smiling warmly. His dark, neatly trimmed beard contrasted sharply against the whiteness of his smile, she noticed. And the sincerity in his expression told Rebecca that he was genuinely delighted to see her.

"Allow me." He removed the cumbersome parcel from her hands. "Your shopping trip appears to have been quite successful," he noted, his grin broadening with amusement.

"I purchased more fabric than I had planned. Unfortunately, it never occurred to me that I might be buying more than I could carry home at one time," she admitted. "Thanks for your help. I don't know how much longer I could have managed by myself."

"It's my pleasure, I can assure you." He fell into step beside her as they resumed walking down the street. "As a matter of fact, I've been searching for you all over Hope this morning. I stopped by your house earlier today, but Jacob said you had gone into town to pick up a few things."

"You've been looking . . . for me?"

He nodded. "Quite frankly, I need some assistance, Mrs. Summers. And the ladies of the church tell me that you're the only person in town who can give me the kind of help I need." His face tightened with concern. "Last night, a young couple arrived in town without any money or food. I've given them shelter at the church. But their baby is quite sick, I fear. If you would be so kind as to take a look at the child—"

"I'll be glad to help in any way I can," Rebecca offered.

Relief washed over his face. "I'm certain the baby's parents would be most grateful, Mrs. Summers."

When they arrived at the house, Rebecca ushered the minister into the parlor. "I won't take long," she assured him. "We'll leave as soon as I gather up a few supplies to take with me."

At that moment, Jessica scampered into the room. "Did you find some pink fabric at the store, Mama?"

"I certainly did. And you can help me decide on the pattern for your new dress this afternoon." She nodded toward the bearded gentleman standing beside her. "But right now, Pastor O'Leary and I are getting ready to leave."

Jessica whirled around to face the minister. "Where are you going?" she demanded, peering up at him inquisitively.

"Your mother and I are returning to the church for a little while."

"The church?" Jessica wrinkled her nose. "What's happening at church today?"

"We're just taking care of some business. Your mother has agreed to help a sick child," he was explaining just as Samantha and Jacob stepped into the room.

"Samantha!" Surprised, Rebecca hugged the girl warmly. "I didn't realize you were here!"

"I just dropped by for a visit," she explained. "But Dr. Summers asked me to stay with Jessica for a while."

"I haven't paid a call on the mayor in several days," Jacob interjected, "and it's past time for me to check on him."

"I haven't had the privilege of meeting Mayor Cunningham yet," Timothy said. "In fact, I didn't even realize he was ill."

While Jacob described the mayor's condition to the young minister, Rebecca seized the opportunity to collect an assortment of herbal mixtures from the cabinets in the physician's office. Not knowing the exact nature of the baby's illness, she hoped one of the remedies would bring relief to the suffering child.

She'd just finished packing the herbs into a basket when Jacob announced he was leaving for the Cunningham ranch. A few moments later, after bidding good-bye to Jessica and Samantha, Rebecca left for the church with Timothy.

When she entered the church's small assembly room, Rebecca's heart wrenched at the sight of the distraught young couple. Trying to soothe the cries of their child, the pair appeared troubled and weary. Judging by their soiled, tattered clothing and their haggard, drawn expressions, Rebecca suspected they hadn't eaten a decent meal or slept in a comfortable bed for days.

Timothy quickly introduced Rebecca as a skilled nurse who was anxious to offer her assistance. Without a moment's hesitation, the frazzled young mother handed the baby to Rebecca. "This is Caleb, ma'am. He's three months old, and he's mighty sick. Sicker than I've ever seen him."

Rebecca gently placed the fretful infant on a quilt that had been draped over a low table. He appeared small for his age, and she wondered if he had lost weight during his bout of illness. Whiny and irritable, the baby seemed malnourished and slightly congested. "Has he been able to keep anything on his stomach?"

The woman shook her head in dismay. "My milk dried up a few days ago, so we started giving him milk from our cow. But it doesn't agree with him. Everytime I feed him, the milk just comes right back up. And since last night, he has refused to drink anything."

"I see." Rebecca examined the infant more closely. Considering his lack of appetite and upset stomach, she suspected the baby was on the verge of dehydration.

"What do you think is wrong with him, ma'am?" The child's father stepped forward, worried and concerned.

"The sudden switch from breast to cow's milk has upset Caleb's stomach," she assessed. "Since babies have an instinctive way of knowing what isn't good for them, I'm not too surprised he has refused to take any more of the cow's milk."

"So what can we do?" the mother asked.

"We'll have to find another source of nour-
ishment for him, something that will agree with
him, as soon as possible." Rebecca hoisted the
baby into her arms, patting him tenderly on the
back as he whimpered against her breast.
"Goat's milk should be a good alternative, I
believe."

"I can take care of getting the milk for him,"
Timothy offered. "Farmers from the outlying
homesteads come into town every day to sell
their products. I'm sure one of them will have
some goat's milk for sale."

"But what if goat's milk upsets his stomach,
too?" Lines of apprehension were etched into
the mother's face.

"I truly believe he'll tolerate it." Trying to
ease the woman's worries, Rebecca gently returned the baby to her. "If not, we'll see if we
can find a wet nurse. But I don't think that will
be necessary. After a few days of drinking
goat's milk, I think Caleb will be feeling much
better."

"I'll get started on finding that milk for him
right now," Timothy volunteered.

"And I'll go with you," Rebecca offered.

"Thank you," the woman whispered in a
choked tone, cradling the baby in her arms.

As the concerned father draped a comforting
arm around his wife's shoulders, Rebecca quietly slipped out of the assembly room, leaving
the church through the sanctuary. She was halfway down the aisle, heading toward the door,
when Timothy fell into step beside her. "I appreciate your willingness to lend a hand to
some weary travelers, Mrs. Summers. Your

kindness and concern will not be forgotten, I'm certain."

"It's your kindness and concern that brought me here," Rebecca declared. "You're the one who was considerate enough to seek help for a troubled family in the first place."

She detected a slight flush of embarrassment sweeping over him. "Helping those in need is part of my calling," he insisted in a humble tone. "It doesn't merit any praise, Mrs. Summers."

Rebecca paused at the door, gazing up into Timothy's handsome bearded face, liking what she saw. This was a man who was truly concerned about the plight of others. A decent, honorable gentleman, worthy of a woman's love and devotion. "You're a rare breed of man, Pastor O'Leary," she admitted aloud.

He reached for her hand. "And you, Mrs. Summers, are one of the most delightful women I've ever encountered." His fingers tightened over hers. "I sincerely hope we can get to know each other better in the coming weeks."

"I hope so, too."

Sauntering down the street beside Timothy a few moments later, Rebecca couldn't deny the man was making quite an impression on her. Obviously, he possessed qualities and values that she admired and cherished. Throughout the morning, he'd displayed the traits of a perfect gentleman. Timothy O'Leary was the type of man she'd dreamed of meeting for years. Not only was he well-respected, but charming and compassionate.

She suspected he could be passionate, too,

remembering the way he'd clasped her hand at the church door, the tender look glimmering from his eyes. And she'd been pleased and flattered when he'd taken her hand into his.

But the extent of her emotions had been nothing more than a mere snippet of pleasure, she realized, startled by a disturbing notion. If Timothy O'Leary was the perfect man for her, why hadn't her pulse raced uncontrollably from the pleasure of his touch? Why hadn't she struggled to catch her breath, fought to control the frantic beat of her heart?

Timothy's voice cut into her thoughts. "Let's see if this gent is selling what we need today," he suggested, motioning toward a farmer who was offering fresh produce and eggs for sale from a wooden cart.

The farmer had positioned his cart near the entrance to the Grand Central, attracting a steady stream of customers from the traffic flowing to and from the hotel. While Timothy approached the farmer to inquire about a supply of goat's milk, Rebecca's gaze drifted toward the Grand Central's long verandah.

She stopped cold, startled by what she saw. Grady was leaning against the verandah railing in a lazy stance, watching her intently. The brim of his hat, cocked low over his forehead, shadowed much of his face. But Rebecca didn't have to see his eyes to know that they were focused on her. She could tell by the tingling sensations rushing through her like tiny shockwaves.

Her mouth went dry as their gazes collided, locked, held. For one heart-stopping moment, the rest of the world seemed distant and far away. Grady Cunningham mesmerized her like no other man ever had, causing her heart to pound so loudly that the thundering in her chest almost obliterated the sound of Timothy's voice. "Look, Rebecca!"

She whipped around. "What?" she asked blankly.

"God was watching out for us today." Apparently oblivious to Rebecca's momentary distraction in the direction of the Grand Central, Timothy proudly held up two pints of milk. "Caleb won't be going hungry tonight."

"How wonderful!" Rebecca breathed a sigh of relief. "Let's get back to the church. I'm anxious to see how well the baby responds to goat's milk this afternoon."

She slipped a hand around Timothy's arm, genuinely pleased he had located a supply of fresh milk for the baby so quickly. But as they retraced their steps through town, Rebecca couldn't forget the unsettling encounter with Grady Cunningham. Stabs of irritation lanced through her. Why couldn't Timothy O'Leary elicit all those tumultuous, turbulent feelings that Grady Cunningham provoked within her?

A heavy weight filled her chest as she trudged down the street. In time, maybe the mere touch of Timothy's hand would send that wondrous, tingling sensation rushing through her.

And maybe she could forget the scorching memory of Grady Cunningham's heated gaze burning through her, arousing all those hidden, secret longings that she had buried within her heart long ago.

*   *   *

"Anything else for you this morning, Mr. Cunningham?"

Seated at a table beside the window at the Grand Central, Grady gulped down the last bite of his fried eggs. "I could handle a little more coffee, darlin'."

The waitress reached across the table, thrusting her hefty chest within inches of Grady's face. Refilling the empty coffee cup, she flashed a beguiling smile and fluttered her lashes. "Anything more?"

Grady lifted the cup of coffee to his lips. "Nope, darlin'. I've had my fill for this mornin'."

The woman's smile vanished. Ignoring her seething glare, Grady turned to gaze through the window. The main street of Hope, he noticed, was bustling with Friday morning activity.

Friday. He cringed. *Day five.* Only nine more days to win his wager.

His lack of progress was disconcerting. Apparently, a new set of clothes and a clean-shaven face hadn't impressed Rebecca Summers in the least. And with each passing day, she seemed more and more determined to avoid him.

After their encounter at the Collinses' store on Tuesday morning, he'd snatched a glimpse of her later that afternoon. He'd been lounging on the verandah of the Grand Central, resting after a leisurely lunch in the hotel's restaurant, when she'd emerged from the church and began sauntering down the street. Accompanied by a bearded gentleman wearing a clerical collar, she appeared to be enjoying herself immensely, laughing, smiling, and amiably chatting with her escort.

But seeing her in the company of another man had been no laughing matter to Grady. A stab of jealousy, as piercing and sharp as the blade of a knife, had penetrated through him. Determined to divert her attention away from the minister, he'd focused his gaze on her with as much intensity as he could muster.

Devouring her with his eyes, Grady had felt a brief surge of triumph racing through him when their gazes met and held. A delicious moment of tension hovered between them. Though she didn't verbally acknowledge his presence, everything else about her said she was acutely aware of the desire radiating from the heat of his gaze. And his success with the calculated, seductive maneuver momentarily convinced him that he was making progress in winning the wager to court the woman.

Or so he'd thought.

On Wednesday afternoon, he'd stumbled into her at the railroad depot. She'd mumbled something about picking up a parcel of supplies that she'd ordered from the Shakers. Then she'd scurried away from him, scrambling through the depot like a frightened rabbit trying to escape from the threatening clutches of a menacing predator.

And yesterday, he hadn't seen her at all.

But today was gonna be different, Grady vowed. Time was running out, and he couldn't afford to waste another minute. Leaving the hotel, he set off in the direction of the Summerses' residence.

As he neared the house, he heard the murmur of voices coming from the direction of the small barn located to the side of the two-story dwelling. When he rounded the corner, he saw Jacob harnessing a fine-looking gelding to a four-wheeled buggy. Rebecca was standing beside him.

She was dressed for an outing. Blue satin ribbons dangled from a bonnet perched over her head. Her gown, a stunning shade of royal blue, highlighted the vivid hue of her eyes. A lace inset adorned the bodice of the dress, spanning the narrow width of her shoulders and ending in a pointed vee between the swell of her breasts.

Mesmerized by her beauty, Grady struggled to tear his gaze away from her. Uninvited yearnings bolted through him, igniting flames of desire so powerful and strong that his loins burned from the intensity of them.

"I don't like the idea of you goin' off by yourself, 'Becca," Jacob was saying as Grady approached. "Too much trouble has been brewin' around here lately."

"I'm sure I'll manage just fine," she said, though the furrows in her brow told Grady that she wasn't as confident as she claimed. "Besides, I have to think about Hattie Ford and her husband waiting for me at their homestead. Their baby is due to arrive at any moment, and I—" She halted abruptly, her eyes widening in surprise as Grady stepped forward.

With an outstretched finger, he tilted the brim of his new Stetson. "Pardon me for eavesdropping, but I couldn't help overhearing your conversation. If you need an escort this morning, I'd be happy to oblige."

"I'm afraid you've misunderstood the situation." She stiffened noticeably. "I'm only traveling a short distance, and—"

"Don't be so hasty to refuse the man's offer, 'Becca," Jacob cautioned. Turning to Grady, he added, "I'd certainly feel much better if she didn't have to travel alone. I'd go with her myself, mind you, but I've got a couple of patients who need my attention today."

"Pardon us for a moment, Mr. Cunningham," Rebecca interrupted hastily. She linked her hand around her father-in-law's arm. "May I speak with you privately, Jacob?" Without waiting for an answer, she nudged the older man in the direction of the barn.

As they stepped inside the building, Jacob's brow furrowed with concern. "Now, what's this all about?"

Her lips formed a tight line. "I'm perfectly aware of the reasons for your concern over my safety, Jacob. But traveling across the plains with a man like Grady Cunningham won't make me feel safe and secure. Why, he's probably more dangerous than any of the drifters roaming through Kansas!"

Jacob brushed his fingers over the thick, gray mustache sprouting over his upper lip. "I think you're being a bit hasty in your judgment of the man, 'Becca."

Her eyes widened incredulously. "After all we've heard about him?"

"It's hearsay, nothing more." He grimaced. "Something tells me the man hasn't been judged fairly by this town. I can't put my finger on it, but my gut instincts tell me that he's not the scoundrel everyone wants him to be."

Rebecca flinched, not wanting to admit her instincts had been sending the same, subtle messages to her.

"I know you'd rather not be associated with him, considering his reputation," Jacob continued, "but I'd rest much easier today, knowing you weren't traveling alone through the prairie."

"But if anyone should see us . . ." She shuddered at the thought.

"You won't be running into any familiar faces, believe me," Jacob pointed out. "It's not your friends who'll be roaming the plains. You're much more likely to run across strangers, drifters, troublemakers—the ones who've been causing all the ruckus in this part of the state. They're the reasons why you need the company of a man today."

Jacob's logic was sound, his arguments persuasive. But it was the anxiety glistening from his eyes, the concern vibrating from his voice, that melted all of Rebecca's resolve. Unable to bear the thought of causing her father-in-law so much worry, she forced herself to set aside her doubts and fears about traveling with Grady Cunningham.

"Considering the circumstances, I suppose it wouldn't hurt for Mr. Cunningham to accompany me today," she conceded, shrugging with resignation. "I just hope he understands that this isn't a social outing."

"I'm sure you'll make that point perfectly clear to him, my dear." Chuckling, Jacob wrapped an arm around Rebecca's shoulders as they walked back to the buggy.

Grady was standing beside the vehicle, one

boot propped over the spoke of a wheel, one elbow resting over an updrawn knee. Emerging from the barn, Rebecca felt a strange fluttering in the pit of her stomach as her gaze traveled over the length of his long, powerful frame. She admired the width of his shoulders and the muscles rippling beneath the fabric of his shirt. She admitted with reluctance that the man possessed a commanding presence.

As Jacob checked the harnesses, Rebecca inhaled a deep, steadying breath as she pulled back her narrow shoulders and marched up to Grady. "If you're still willing to accompany me to the Fords' homestead this morning, I'd like to accept your offer, Mr. Cunningham."

He pushed back the brim of his hat, studying her intently. "Are you certain about this?"

"Of course." She retrieved some money from the pocket of her gown. "Will five dollars be sufficient for your services?"

Stunned beyond words, Grady stared at her in disbelief. He'd never expected to be paid for accompanying her, never dreamed of asking for a dime.

How ironic, he thought. Rebecca Summers, the innocent victim of his wager—a wager that should net a sizable sum to his bank account— was attempting to pay *him* for his services! The idea was so absurd that he clamped his lower lip between his teeth to keep from laughing out loud.

But as his gaze swept over the rigid angle of her shoulders, the tight line of her mouth, Grady realized the situation was no laughing matter to Rebecca.

"I won't take your money, Mrs. Summers,"

he finally said. "As I recall, you refused to accept any payment for your services from me on Carl's behalf."

At that moment, a door slammed at the back of the house. "Don't leave yet, Mama! You haven't kissed me good-bye!" Jessica cried, vaulting across the porch and running toward her mother.

A smile as bright as the Kansas sun illuminated Rebecca's face as the child scampered up to her. Kneeling, she opened her arms, capturing her daughter in a warm embrace. "I wouldn't leave without saying good-bye to you, Jess," she insisted.

"I didn't think so." Jessica threw back her head and laughed. "You wanted a good-bye kiss from me, too, didn't you?"

"Of course I did!" Rebecca returned, giggling along with her daughter, raining showers of kisses over her neck and face.

Observing the scene, Grady felt a strange stirring in the depths of his chest. No doubt, this was love in its purest form, love so strong and unyielding that it could never be broken by time or space. Seeing the love that flowed so easily, so openly, between them, Grady suddenly felt as though he'd been plunged into the midst of an intimate family gathering.

Still, he couldn't tear his gaze away from the laughing, joyful pair. He'd never seen a mother so devoted to her child, never known a child who admired her mother more. Fascinated by the strength of the bonds between them, he stood motionless, gawking, until Jessica squirmed away from her mother's hold.

"Are you leaving soon, Mama?"

"In a few minutes, dear." Straightening, Rebecca smoothed down the folds of her skirt. "Mr. Cunningham is going with me. And we'll be leaving as soon as I can get the rest of my supplies out of Jacob's office."

As Rebecca swept across the yard, returning to the house, Jessica peered up at Grady. "Mama says you're going with her today."

"Well, if that's what your mama says, it must be true." He hunkered down beside her, playfully pinching the tip of her nose.

She swiped his hand away from her face, giggling. "Don't make me laugh, Mr. Cunn'- ham. I have a very important question to ask you." The smile on her lips vanished, and her narrow brow crinkled with concern. "Will you please take good care of my mama while you're gone?"

The question hit him with full force. Grady suddenly felt as dizzy as if she'd smashed a brick over his head. The innocence, the goodness, the sweetness, of her simple request rendered him speechless for a long moment.

"Of course I'll take good care of your ma, angel," he finally choked out. "You have my word on it."

"You'll take care of her, just like Samantha takes care of me when Mama and Grandpa are away?"

"Even better," he vowed solemnly.

"That's good to know." She breathed a sigh of relief. "I miss Mama a lot when she goes away to deliver a baby. But I'll feel better this time, knowing you're taking care of her."

"I don't suspect we'll be gone too long," Grady mused, trying to ease the child's worries. "Who knows, Jess? Your ma may be home before you've had time to miss her!"

"Sometimes she's only gone for a few hours," she admitted. "And sometimes she's gone for days and days! But Mama says it isn't her fault. She says only God knows when it's time for a baby to come into the world."

Astounded by the child's candor, Grady had no idea what to say or how to react. He was still groping for an intelligent reply when Jessica peered up at him, wide-eyed and curious.

"While you and Mama are waiting on God to make up his mind about Mrs. Ford's baby, what are you going to do?"

Grady hedged, seriously contemplating the question. Until this moment, he hadn't stopped to consider that the trip might involve more than a day's journey. But Jessica had made a strong point. Since it wasn't possible to predict the exact time of a child's birth, he and Rebecca could be waiting together at the homestead for several days. And how would they pass the time, waiting for the birth of a stranger's child?

Forbidden images flashed through his mind, images so provocative and tantalizing that a smile curled over his lips. "I'm sure we'll think of something, Jess," he finally answered, chuckling at the prospect.

At that moment, Rebecca stepped down from the porch, traveling bag in hand. "I believe we're ready to leave now, Mr. Cunningham."

Leaping to his feet, Grady placed her bag into the buggy. As she stretched out a gloved hand to hoist herself into the seat, Grady clamped his hands around the small expanse of her waist. Beneath the gentle pressure of his fingers, he felt her muscles tighten with tension as he boosted her into the vehicle.

While she adjusted her skirts around her legs, Grady settled down beside her and grasped the reins between his hands. Rebecca waved to her daughter and father-in-law as they began their journey.

"The back road leading out of town is shorter than the main route," Rebecca advised as soon as the buggy rolled into the street. "And if you turn at the next corner, we'll avoid running into any traffic along the main thoroughfare, too."

Grady complied with her request without argument, though he knew that traffic was not her primary reason for wanting to avoid the main street of Hope. In truth, she wanted to avoid being seen with him.

Ignoring the sting to his pride, he tried to focus on their journey. "How long before we reach the Ford homestead?" he asked conversationally.

"A little more than two hours. Three, at the most."

"So you've visited there before?"

She nodded crisply. "Several times."

"By yourself?"

"On one occasion."

"Were you uncomfortable traveling alone?"

"Not any more uncomfortable than I am traveling with you."

Her honesty was refreshing, he thought. "So how do I make you feel uncomfortable?"

She shifted uneasily, turning her head away from him, gazing into the distance. "It's just that ..." She faltered for words. "It's just that I don't know you very well, Mr. Cunningham."

Vowing to resolve that problem before the end of the day, Grady bit back a smile as the buggy rattled down the road.

Chapter 7

⌒∽◯◯∽⌒

"I don't want you to feel uncomfortable
around me, darlin'." Grady flashed a
disarming grin in Rebecca's direction. "Since
we're gonna be travelin' together for a while,
we might as well learn how to get along with
each other and enjoy ourselves for the next
few days."

"This isn't a social outing, Mr. Cunningham." Rebecca stiffened her spine in a vain
attempt to maintain an air of propriety between them. "Need I remind you of the reason for this journey?"

"I'm not tryin' to make light of your devotion to your patients, Mrs. Summers. Delivering babies is a serious matter, I know. But
that doesn't mean we can't have a little fun
along the way." His grin widened. "Besides,
if you got to know me a little better, you'd
realize what a charming fellow I can be. You
might even discover that I'm not the incorrigible scoundrel everyone insists I am."

Far more mindful of the man's beguiling

ways than she was willing to admit, Rebecca struggled to ignore the unsettling effects of his devastating smile on her nervous system. "Maybe I've already learned everything I need to know about you," she countered primly.

"And, then, maybe you haven't. Not everything about me is as scandalous and sinful as the gossips in town would like for you to believe."

"But perhaps I don't care to find out anything else about you," she muttered, acutely aware of the teasing warmth in his voice. She had the sinking feeling that the potency of his charm was powerful enough to destroy every defensive instinct she possessed.

"Then perhaps you should," he argued smoothly. "I'm sure you'd find lots of things about me to like if you'd give yourself—and me—a chance."

Which was precisely Rebecca's greatest fear. She'd already discovered more appealing traits about the man than she cared to remember, and she didn't want to risk the chance of learning anything more.

But the warmth and humor encompassing his chiseled features—from the devilish gleam twinkling from his eyes to the arrogant smirk forming on his lips—suddenly crumbled her last vestiges of resolve. Keeping her distance from the man would be impossible during their trek across the plains, she conceded. Surely she could set aside her doubts and fears about him for a few hours without endangering her heart.

"You're making this journey quite difficult

for me, I'll admit." A shy smile blossomed on her lips. "I assumed you agreed to accompany me to the homestead simply to assure my safety across the plains. I didn't realize that becoming better acquainted with you was part of our bargain."

"I'll make it easy for you, I promise." An irreverent wink accompanied his solemn vow. "In fact, I've already thought of lots of ways for us to get to know each other better."

Before Rebecca could respond to his suggestive implications, the buggy hit a rut in the road. The force of the impact hurled her across the wooden seat and slammed her into Grady. Crushed against the hard length of his body, Rebecca struggled to catch her breath.

His arm shot out, wrapping around her protectively. But the sizzling contact between them jolted her to the core. She jerked away from his hold and scooted across the seat, placing as much distance between them as possible. "I hope that wasn't one of your ideas for becoming better acquainted," she quipped weakly.

"You all right?" he asked on impulse.

"Just a bit jostled." A quick, tight-lipped smile flashed across her lips. Then she pulled back her shoulders and adjusted the bonnet perched over her head, as if trying to regain her composure.

"Not many trails are as rough as this one," he said, leaping at the chance to strike up a conversation again, hoping to divert his thoughts from the kissable little dimple in her left cheek.

Rebecca nodded absently, her gaze sweeping across the desolate landscape. Once green and thriving, the surrounding sea of prairie grass had been parched to a crisp by the relentless summer rays. "Without any rain, all this heat is burning up everything in sight. It's no wonder so many homesteaders are packing up and abandoning their claims."

Following her gaze, Grady winced as a deserted homestead came into view. Acres of wheat, as crumpled and lifeless as broken skeletons, encompassed the barren dwelling.

It was the second forsaken shanty they'd encountered since leaving Hope. But Grady wasn't surprised to discover that the sites had been abandoned by their former owners. Between the miserable heat and infertile soil, who could survive in this strip of hell?

He jammed his hat lower over his head, squeezing his eyes shut for an instant as a gust of dry wind whipped a cloud of dust into his face. "Do you take this route very often?"

"About once or twice a month. More often when an expectant mother's time draws nigh."

"Looks like it would be a lot easier if your patients were the ones who traveled to you." Grady veered the buggy to the right, hoping to dodge another deep rut in the trail. "Instead of venturing across the plains in this blasted heat, you could be tending to the womenfolk and children back in town."

"But if I stayed at home, many of these homesteaders wouldn't get any medical care at all. Jacob is the only physician within fifty miles of Hope, and he has more patients than he can handle at the moment." She lifted her chin a notch, and Grady discerned sparks of determination glimmering from her eyes. "Visiting the homesteaders, delivering their babies, is the least I can do. Traveling into town is almost impossible for most of my patients, especially when they're swollen with child. And most women prefer the security of familiar surroundings, the comfort of their own homes, when they're giving birth."

"Still, you're the one who has to leave your home, your family, never knowing exactly how long you'll be gone or when you'll return," he pointed out.

"It isn't easy for me to leave Jessica, I'll admit. But if I can make life a little easier for the people who live on these homesteads, I'm willing to endure a few inconveniences from time to time."

Hearing the concern resonating from her voice, seeing the compassion glinting from her eyes, Grady felt a grudging admiration for her. But he was still puzzled by the reasons for her generous, giving spirit. "Sounds like you're making a helluva lot of sacrifices for a bunch of women who are practically strangers to you. Why should you care about their lot in life?"

For a long moment, she didn't respond. When she finally turned to face him, her eyes sparkled. "Most of the people out here are down on their luck, and I'm just trying to show them that someone truly cares. I know what it's like to live without hope, Mr. Cunningham. And when you're living in a world that seems dark and dreary, it means a great deal when someone steps into your life—even for just a moment—and offers some encouragement."

Grady shifted uncomfortably, wishing someone had cared enough to lend a few words of support to him; wondering what kind of tragedy had cast clouds of despair over her.

"Take the Fords, for instance," she continued. "Nature hasn't been kind to Owen and Hattie, I'm afraid. The heat wave has destroyed their crops this summer."

"So why haven't they left?" Grady swept his gaze over the parched terrain. "Most of their neighbors have pulled up stakes, it appears."

"Owen didn't want to uproot Hattie in her condition. Last year . . ." A shadow of darkness crossed her face. "Last year, they lost their baby. Hattie had some complications during labor. No one was there to help them, and they didn't know what to do . . ." Her voice trailed off.

"But this time will be different," Grady heard himself saying. "You're here now. And this time, nothing will go wrong."

A trace of surprise swept across her face. "Thanks for the vote of confidence," she said, her voice just above a whisper.

At that moment, the jagged roofline of a low-lying structure jutted over the horizon. Approaching the building, Grady noticed it was similar to the other abandoned shanties along the trail. He was assuming the dwelling was deserted until Rebecca breathed a sigh of relief. "Thank goodness we're finally here!" she exclaimed.

"This place belongs to ... the Fords?"

She nodded, the ribbons from her bonnet bobbing around her shoulders. "Follow these wagon tracks," she said, pointing toward a narrow trail that veered off the main road, "and they'll take us straight to the Fords' front door."

As Grady guided the buggy over the rugged, seldom-used trail, he scrutinized the building with interest. Dried clumps of sod, fashioned into rectangular shapes about a foot in length, had been stacked like bricks to form the walls of the structure. A chimney pipe poked up through the roof, which appeared to be constructed of more layers of sod. Nearing the structure, Grady was surprised to see panes of glass sparkling from the windows.

More than likely, the windows were the couple's one extravagant purchase for their home, Grady was thinking just as the buggy rolled to a stop in front of the shanty and a bearded, heavyset man hurled open the front door.

"Praise be!" A broad smile erupted on the man's face. "If you ain't the most welcome sight I ever did see!"

In spite of the man's warm greeting, Rebecca tensed. "I'm not too late, am I?"

"No, no!" The man bounded toward the buggy, offering his arm to Rebecca as she stepped down from the vehicle. "But you and your friend ain't a minute too soon, neither. My Hattie is feelin' a bit poorly this mornin'."

"That's not too unusual, Owen, considering

her condition." She retrieved her basket of medicines from the back of the buggy. After pausing for a moment to introduce the two men, she whirled around and scurried toward the house.

As Rebecca disappeared inside the shanty, Owen turned to Grady, who was unharnessing the black gelding. "Mighty nice of you to come out here with the lady, Mr. Cunningham," he said, lending a hand.

"Her father-in-law and I thought it would be best if she didn't make the trip by herself." Noting a fine sheen of sweat glistening from the horse's hide, he added, "Looks like he could use some water."

Owen nodded in agreement, leading the horse to a crude trough at the side of the house. Grady trailed behind the tall man, deciding he bore a striking resemblance to a grizzly bear. A dark beard coated his face, and bushy brows framed his flashing dark eyes. Thick and square and tall, he moved with a lumbering gait.

After guiding the horse into a sod barn located behind the shanty, Owen motioned toward the house. "Come on inside and meet the missus," he invited.

When Grady entered the dwelling, his boots shuffled across an earthen floor. He noticed simple, sparse furnishings were scattered throughout the one-room shanty, and faded lace curtains framed the two windows. A woman with chestnut-brown hair sat in a rocking chair beside one of the windows.

Owen rushed to the woman's side, brushing his lips across her forehead and affectionately patting her bulging tummy. Observing the woman's swollen abdomen, Grady suddenly understood why she couldn't possibly make the trip into town. At the moment, she looked incapable of even waddling across the room.

"This here is Mr. Grady Cunningham, Hattie," Owen told his wife. "He was nice enough to come all the way out here from Hope, just so Mrs. Summers wouldn't have to make the trip by herself."

"How thoughtful of you, Mr. Cunningham." Hattie smiled shyly.

Fully aware that his motives for making the journey were not as honorable as they appeared, Grady quickly changed the subject. "Do you mind if we drop the formalities?" He smiled. "I'd prefer Grady, if you don't mind."

"And I'd rather not be called 'Mrs. Summers' anymore," Rebecca chimed in, stepping up to join them. "Rebecca is more to my liking."

"Then Grady and Rebecca it is," Owen agreed.

"As long as you call us Hattie and Owen," Hattie added. Gripping the arms of the rocking chair, she struggled to pull herself up from the seat. "After making that long drive from Hope this morning, I'd wager you two must be famished. I'll just get—"

"You're not getting anything," Rebecca insisted, darting to the woman's side, nudging her back down into the chair. "I can take care of lunch for all of us."

Collapsing into the chair without argument,

Hattie nodded wearily. "There's some beans simmering on the stove. And I've already made some salt pork and corn bread. It's not much, but—"

"It's more than enough, Hattie," Rebecca assured the woman.

Skirts rustling around her slender ankles, Rebecca turned and headed for the cookstove. As she swept across the room, Grady admired the gentle sway of her hips, the supple grace of her limbs, the fluid rhythm of her movements.

Since arriving at the homestead, Rebecca had removed her hat and gloves. But Grady was noticing other, more subtle changes about her, too. Her carefully controlled expressions were giving way to more spontaneous ones. She was smiling more frequently, laughing more easily, chattering more freely.

Why was she dropping her guard? Though he couldn't be certain, Grady suspected that absconding from the watchful eyes of Hope's citizens, fleeing into the wild, open prairie, had something to do with her abrupt change in behavior. He was still mulling over the puzzling situation when she arrived at the table, carrying a steaming pot of beans, and announced that lunch was ready to be served.

Just as Grady approached the table, Owen bounded over to Hattie. Gently wrapping his arms around the woman, he tenderly pulled up her hefty frame from the rocking chair, then guided her over to a straight-back chair at the table.

Throughout the meal, Owen kept a close eye on his wife, gauging her movements and

actions with the watchfulness and protec-
tiveness of a fussy mother hen. And judging
by Hattie's puffy face and swollen fingers,
Grady sensed Owen had good reason for his
concern. With each passing moment, she
looked more and more uncomfortable.

By the time they'd finished eating, Hattie
had lapsed into silence. Just as Owen helped
her from the chair, she grimaced in pain. "Oh,
my," she whispered in a choked tone, placing
her hands over her bulging abdomen.

Owen paled. "What's wrong, Hattie?"

"I think . . ." Shuddering, she gazed down
at the water seeping through the folds of her
skirt. "I think my water has just broken."

"Don't be alarmed, Hattie," Rebecca
soothed. "It's just Baby Ford's way of telling
us that he's anxious to make his appearance
to the world." Rounding the table, she
wrapped a steadying arm around the woman's thick waist. "I believe it's time you got
off your feet, Mama Ford."

Grady bounded up from his chair. Trying
to squelch the urge to run as far and fast as
his legs could carry him, he stalked to the
window and gazed aimlessly through the glass
panes. He shoved his hands into the deep
pockets of his vest, not daring to turn around
until he could be certain that Hattie was comfortably settled in bed.

By the time Rebecca and Owen came up
behind him, every muscle in his body was
tight with tension. "Is everything all right?"
he asked.

"Hattie isn't very comfortable at the moment," Rebecca revealed, "but that isn't too unusual at this stage of labor."

"Is there anything you can do for her?" Owen's voice was choked, strained.

"In a little while, I'll be preparing some ergot to stimulate her contractions. In the meantime . . ." She paused, her eyes glimmering with compassion and understanding. ". . . we'll simply have to wait for nature to take its course."

"So it's gonna be a long day for all of us," Owen surmised.

"Maybe a long night, too," Rebecca cautioned. "We can't rush these things, you know. Do you think the time would pass more quickly if you occupied yourself outdoors for the afternoon?"

"Probably so." Owen's grimace was replaced with a grin. "And I reckon I can pace the length of the wheat field just as well as I can pace the length of this room."

Rebecca laughed. "While you're pacing back and forth, you can make yourself useful. We'll be needing lots of fresh water from the creek, and—"

"We're already on our way," Grady announced, snatching up his Stetson and jamming it over his head.

"Just holler if you need me for anything, Miz Rebecca," Owen called out over his shoulder, picking up a pair of water buckets on his way out the door.

Anxious to escape from the confines of the shanty, Grady fell into step beside Owen. Though he'd never witnessed the birth of a child, he had the strange feeling that he didn't want to start now.

But he couldn't ignore Owen's mounting excitement as they stomped over acres of parched wheat and rows of singed corn, trudging toward the grove of towering cottonwood trees beside the creek. "Just think!" Owen kicked the heels of his boots together. "By the end of the day, I'll be a father!"

Grady couldn't keep from smiling, amused by the boyish antics of the stalwart male. "Got some names picked out?"

"Olivia, if it's a girl. That's in honor of Hattie's mother. If it's a boy, we'll call him Blake, after my father. We wanted to use family names, you see ..."

Owen rambled on, but Grady suddenly realized that he didn't want to hear anything more. Clenching his jaw, he stalked across the field, determined not to listen to another word. He didn't want to get caught up in the anxieties and thrills that were certain to transpire throughout the day. Hattie and Owen Ford seemed like nice people, but he had to remember that they were practically strangers to him. Why should he be concerned about the arrival of their first child?

From bitter experience, he'd discovered that caring about anyone—or anything—only resulted in heartache and pain. First, he'd made the grave mistake of caring about his father's opinion of him. Then he'd been foolish enough to care about the welfare of a childhood friend whose husband thought he could beat on his wife whenever he wanted to. And he'd cared enough about a woman to ask her to marry him.

But all of it had been useless. In the end, his father had disowned him. Priscilla had walked away from him. And the people of Hope had rejected him, even though he'd been found innocent by a court of law.

Over the years, Grady had learned to stay away from situations that threatened to tug at his heartstrings. He'd mastered the art of disguising his true emotions by pretending not to care, by using shrugs of indifference and devilish grins as shields of protection.

Determined to summon all those apathetic feelings once again, Grady pulled back his shoulders as he continued marching toward the grove of cottonwood trees. Distracted by his thoughts, he didn't even notice the huge mountain of white beside the trees until he reached the edge of the creek.

Stumbling to a halt, he gaped, amazed by what he saw. Hundreds upon hundreds of bones were stacked on top of each other, heaped into a pile that towered at least a couple of feet above his head. Nearing the white mound, Grady had no doubt about the kind of bones accumulated here. He'd seen enough buffalo carcasses to recognize the creature's bones when he saw them. But he'd never seen such a gigantic mass of bison skeletons in one place.

Owen's voice interrupted his thoughts. "Like my little collection?"

Grady shook his head in disbelief. "Never seen anything like it," he admitted.

"Took me nigh onto a month to gather 'em

off my claim. All hundred and sixty acres were full of 'em."

Narrowing his eyes, Grady studied the remains for a long moment. "You know, there's a demand for every other part of the buffalo—hides, meat, even tongues. But no one has come up with a way to make use of all these bones."

"If I could find someone who wanted to buy this hill of skeletons, I'd be a rich man." Owen chuckled at the thought, then added in a more serious tone, " 'Course, I'm rich, anyway."

Grady's gaze wandered over the dry, parched land, then lingered on the sod shanty that lay across the barren field. Try as he might, he could find no evidence of wealth or riches here. All he saw was a fruitless, desolate claim that held nothing but a family's pitiful excuse for a home.

He made a weak attempt at humor. "Got some buried treasure around here that you're hiding?"

"If I do, I haven't found it yet." Owen's smile faded into a pensive expression. "No, I'm not rich in terms of money or possessions. But I got my Hattie, and that's all that matters to me."

The poignant admission, uttered with such genuine sincerity, was so unexpected, so startling, that it almost knocked Grady to his knees. Stunned beyond words, he stared at Owen in disbelief.

From the top of his head to the soles of his boots, Owen Ford was the epitome of masculinity. He was brawny, huge, robust, a man's

man in every sense of the word. Yet Grady
had never encountered a male as candid and
open about his love for a woman, never heard
one admit his wife was the center of his
world. Obviously, Owen cared deeply for
Hattie, and he wasn't ashamed to declare
his feelings.

Would he ever be able to feel so intensely,
love a woman so completely, express his emotions so freely?

A gust of wind whipped into his face,
bringing him back to reality with the brutality
of its sting. Good God, was he going daft? All
he'd wanted from this trip was the chance to
steal away with Rebecca for the day, the opportunity to increase the odds of winning
his wager.

He'd never fathomed that he might lose
control of his emotions. Never considered that
a little girl's request might tug at his heartstrings. Never dreamed the closeness of a
woman during a two-hour ride could ignite
longings that were in danger of bursting into
flames. And he'd never imagined a man's
simple admission of love for his wife could
make him question his own sanity.

Frustrated, he stalked to the edge of the
creek, regretting that he'd insisted on coming
here, wishing he'd never set foot in this god-
forsaken place.

Chapter 8

Rebecca closely monitored Hattie's progress throughout the afternoon, never
leaving her side. By early evening, the woman's contractions had become steady and
regular.

Dousing a washcloth in a basin of cool
water, Rebecca offered an encouraging smile.
"It won't be much longer now, Hattie."

"I hope you're right," she murmured, grimacing. "I don't know how much more pain
I can endure."

"You'll be able to endure just as much as
it takes, I'm certain," Rebecca assured her.

"But I heard tell you can cut the pain by
putting an axe under the bed." Her eyes reflected her physical anguish as she peered up
at Rebecca. "Think it would work for me?"

"If I thought an axe could relieve some of
your suffering, I would have brought a
wagon load of them with me." Rebecca
dabbed the cool, damp cloth over Hattie's
flushed face. "Besides, you'll forget all about

the pain as soon as you see that beautiful new baby of yours."

Hattie nodded wearily, closing her eyes. She had just buried her head into the pillow when the shanty door swung open. Grady gingerly stepped into the house, water bucket in hand.

"I thought you could use some more water." Avoiding Rebecca's gaze, he placed the bucket beside the cookstove. "Do you need anything else?"

"Thanks, but I believe we have everything we need for the moment."

Something akin to relief flickered across his face. He quietly edged back to the door. "Then I guess I'll get back to the barn and help Owen finish up with the chores for the night." Pausing, he looked over at Hattie. "How's she doing?"

"As well as can be expected. Her contractions are coming at regular intervals now, so her pain is intensifying. But I don't think she'll be suffering much longer. I suspect she'll be delivering within a few hours. By midnight, at the latest."

"Just knowing you're here with her should ease some of her worries." His gaze drifted over her face, studying each delicate feature with such intensity that Rebecca quivered inside. "And I can see why. If I ever needed a nurse, I—"

He stopped abruptly, as if catching himself saying something he shouldn't. "If you need anything else, I'll be in the barn with Owen."

Rebecca reeled with confusion as Grady bolted through the door. Dear heavens, what was going on? Heaving a troubled sigh, she crossed the room and quietly sank into a chair beside Hattie's bed.

Grady Cunningham puzzled her, intrigued her, like no other man ever had. She had no idea why he'd volunteered to accompany her to the homestead, couldn't fathom his reasons for wanting to undertake the journey in the first place.

Ever since they'd arrived, he seemed edgy, troubled by something Rebecca couldn't define. Though she'd only caught brief glimpses of him throughout the afternoon, she'd detected that something was weighing heavily on his mind. The casual, nonchalant air about him had disappeared, she'd noticed. Was he full of regrets for having made this journey? Or was the anticipation of the upcoming birth causing his distress?

She sighed, unable to explain his obvious dismay anymore than she could explain the tension that had sizzled between them during their journey through the plains, tension as hot and scorching as the heat of the August day. Throughout the jarring ride, Rebecca had constantly reminded herself that she could never be attracted to a man like Grady Cunningham. But when the buggy had hit a rut in the road, hurling her against him, Rebecca had felt as weak as if a bolt of lightning had seared through her.

Even now, her face burned from the memory of his scorching gaze before he'd retreated to the barn. She had the strange feeling that he'd wanted to kiss her. A sudden flash of desire had glimmered from his eyes, she was

certain, recalling the delicious shiver of anticipation that had coursed through her from the
heat of his gaze.

At that moment, Hattie moaned, jarring Rebecca from her memories. Determined to set
aside her wayward thoughts, she picked up
her skirts and scurried to the woman's side.

A bone-chilling scream sliced through the
tranquility of the prairie night, jolting Grady
from a peaceful slumber. Snapping up from
the hay, he propped up on his elbows just
as another high-pitched wail reverberated
through the barn.

Hattie. Heart thundering in his chest, Grady
leaped to his feet. Good God, was the
woman dying?

Terrorized beyond words, Grady stormed
through the barn. But as he blindly raced
toward the shanty, the anguished cries subsided. He paused to catch his breath, not
knowing whether he should be elated or
horrified.

Had the baby arrived, safe and sound? Was
the worst over for Hattie? Or did the silence
mean something awful had happened?

At that instant, another cry sounded from
the shanty. But this time it wasn't the distressed cry of a woman in pain, Grady realized. It was the cry of a baby.

Relief swamped through him. Still, he shuffled over the patch of ground between the
house and the barn, impatiently waiting for
admission to the house.

God help him, he didn't want to care anything about this home, this family. But how

could he not? He couldn't ignore the tension, the excitement, the anticipation, sizzling through the air.

He was still pacing across the yard when Rebecca appeared at the door a few moments later, cradling a tiny baby in her arms.

"Look, Grady." Her voice was hushed, choked with emotion. "Have you ever seen anything so wondrous in all of your life?"

As Grady peered down at the little creature nestled against Rebecca's breast, he understood why her voice was trembling with emotion. Even he found it hard to believe that this squirming, red-faced infant had been safely cocooned within his mother's womb before making his entry into the world a few moments ago. Awed by the sight of the wee babe, perfectly formed from head to toe, Grady felt his throat tighten with emotion.

He was still admiring the baby when Owen stepped up to the door. A grin as wide and broad as the Kansas prairie sprouted across the man's face. "Fine lookin' boy, wouldn't you say?"

Nodding, Grady clapped the man on his shoulder. "Congratulations, Owen."

At that moment, the baby opened his mouth and howled furiously. "I believe your son is hungry, Hattie," Rebecca said, sweeping across the room. After gently placing the baby in his mother's arms, she returned to the door. "I'll be back in a little while, Owen. I'm sure you and Hattie would like a few minutes of privacy with your new son," she said, quietly slipping outside.

She closed the door behind her and looked

up at Grady, a slow smile spreading across
her lips. "When you volunteered to come
with me this morning, did you realize what
you were getting into?"

"Hardly." He managed a weak chuckle.
"It's the first time I've been exposed to child-
birth. And I have to admit, it's quite an
experience."

"Nothing can compare to it." Rebecca
heaved a sigh of contentment, tilting back her
head and gazing up into the starry sky. "Isn't
Blake a beautiful baby?"

"I'm not sure I'd describe him as 'beautiful,'" Grady admitted. "He seems kinda
prune-faced and awfully red. Of course, I've
never seen a newborn until now."

"Most of them are prune-faced and red, but
no one ever admits that." Rebecca laughed.
"Still, he's hearty and healthy, and his vocal
cords sound like they're working pretty good,
too. And that's all that matters."

She whirled around, looking as though she
wanted to dance for joy. Watching her, Grady
sucked in a shuddering breath. Still caught
up in the excitement of the evening, she was
radiating with a beauty so mind-boggling that
he could barely breathe, beaming with a joy
so deep and moving that he couldn't take his
eyes off her. "So, were you like this when
Jessica was born?" he couldn't resist asking.

"In a way." Her eyes filled with distant
memories, and a wistful little smile touched
her lips. "I remember I couldn't stop touching
her. I couldn't believe she was real."

"And what about your husband? Was he
as excited as you?"

Her smile vanished, replaced with an expression of sorrow. "Unfortunately, David never saw Jessica. He died before . . . before she was born."

A knot coiled tight in Grady's stomach. "I'm truly sorry, Rebecca. I didn't know . . ."

"You couldn't have known. And I'm sorry, too, especially for Jessica's sake. David would have been a wonderful father, and I wish Jess could have had the chance to know him."

"But you're doing a wonderful job with her, Rebecca. She's quite a charming young lady."

"Do you really think so?"

He nodded. "She's already stolen my heart. And she's especially crazy about you. Just before we left, she made me promise I'd take good care of you while we're gone."

"That sounds like my Jess." She laughed, shaking her head. Hair pins loosened by the day's work slipped from their hold, threatening to uncoil the chignon at her nape. Grady's mouth went dry, and he wondered what she would say if he reached out and tugged the last of the anchors free.

"Still, I haven't raised her all by myself, you know," she continued on. "Jacob has been a major influence in Jessica's life."

"And yours, too, it seems," Grady observed candidly.

A warm breeze whispered across her face, rustling the wispy curls around her temples, her cheeks. "I owe a great deal to Jacob Summers," she admitted. "He's the one who encouraged me to believe in myself. And he's the one who has given me confidence in my own abilities. If it hadn't been for Jacob's encouragement, I don't think I would have ever become a midwife."

"It must be wonderful to have someone believe in you like that." He regarded her, silent for a moment. "It must make you feel like you can conquer the world, at times."

A rueful smile crossed her lips. "And sometimes, it gives you the strength to make it through one more day."

Were there clouds of remembrance haunting those sky-blue eyes? Pain cutting into the tender corners of her mouth?

Surely not, he thought. Surely this beautiful, enchanting woman had never been exposed to the kind of pain and scorn that made a person want to crawl into a hole and die. The kind of pain he'd known, that he never wanted to experience again.

"You're fortunate, you know." Memories clawed away at him, pressing down with a heavy weight, clogging his throat until his voice became hoarse and strained. "Not everyone is lucky enough to have someone like Jacob."

"I've never forgotten what my life was like before I met him." A pensive expression shadowed her face. "Everything might have been so different if my natural father had been more like him. . . ." She gave her head a shake, as if promptly dismissing the thought.

"Apparently, some men are better fathers than others," Grady mumbled irritably, thinking of the man who'd fathered him.

"You and your father don't get along, do

you?" Rebecca whispered, as if reading his thoughts.

His laughter sounded harsh, even to his own ears. "That's the understatement of the century, darlin'."

"Have you considered some sort of reconciliation?"

"And what good would it do?" He was snapping at her, he knew, but he couldn't seem to help himself. The subject of Malcolm Cunningham was a tender point with him. "Never once have I done anything that was right in his eyes. My old man and I, we . . ." He paused, wincing as memories, rough and raw, seared through him. "We haven't associated with each other in several years. He hasn't acknowledged me as his son since . . ."

"Since the trial?" she finished.

"I should've known my sordid past wasn't a secret to anyone in Hope." He grimaced, trying to ignore the pain, wondering why it should matter. "Nothing I've ever done is good enough for that old miser. He's never believed in me. I won't deny that I've made my share of mistakes in life, especially when I was young and foolish and sowing my wild oats. But my old man should have had faith in me. He is my father, after all." He clenched his jaw. "No, the only person who has ever believed in me was a judge in Kansas City. Everyone else—even the woman who was supposed to become my wife—believed I was guilty of cold-blooded murder."

"Even your . . . fiancée?"

An old ache gnawed at his chest. "Priscilla wasn't different from anyone else in Hope—

including my own damn father—when she learned I had a murder charge hanging over me." His laughter was forced, strained. "None of them—not a single, solitary soul—believed in my innocence. And they still don't, it appears."

"I can imagine how you must have felt." Her eyes were blue pools of compassion and understanding, and her voice reflected the pain in his heart. "And I know what you must be going through now. It isn't easy to hold up your head with pride when you're the object of ridicule and shame."

Confusion reeled through Grady. "What could you know about rejection and scandal?" he scoffed. "You couldn't possibly fathom what it's like to be the focus of malicious whispers and haughty stares. You couldn't understand what it's like for no one in the world to believe in you."

Rebecca pursed her lips together, quietly studying the man beside her, trying to look beyond all the sordid stories about him, struggling to see him clearly for the first time.

And what she saw made her melt inside. There was more, much more, to this man than she could have ever imagined. Every instinct she possessed warned her that he wasn't the cruel, heartless man that everyone wanted him to be. She could tell by the pain glimmering from those wolf-gray eyes, the anguish reverberating in his voice, the distress lining the pinched lines of his face.

All along, he'd been hiding that pain behind a mask of indifference, Rebecca suddenly realized. Those crooked grins and careless shrugs had been flimsy disguises, covering up his true emotions.

Until this moment, she hadn't wanted to consider the possibility that Grady Cunningham was anything more than a scoundrel who was deserving of his reputation. Like the rest of the town, she'd condemned him by his past.

But seeing the pain in his eyes, hearing the husky timbre of his voice, Rebecca sensed he wasn't as guilty as everyone claimed. All too well, she could identify with the inadequacies he'd described, the brutal sting of rejection that he'd felt.

"Maybe I understand more than you realize, Grady Cunningham," she finally said.

With that, she whirled on her heel, intending to return to the house. But she'd taken only two steps when Grady placed a hand on her arm. He spun her around, forcing her to meet a gaze so ardent that she trembled from the intensity of it.

"I don't know how you could possibly understand what I've gone through, Rebecca." His voice dropped so low she could barely hear the words as he whispered, "But God help me, something tells me you do."

He reached up and tucked a wispy curl behind her ear. Then one callused thumb skimmed the pulse-beat at her throat, circling it so slowly, so seductively, that her breath snared in her throat.

Rebecca's heart slammed against her ribs. She wanted to deny everything she was feeling, wanted to escape from the tumultuous emotions raging through her. But as he cupped her chin in his hand and tilted back her head ever so slightly, all of her resistance melted away. Consumed by the hunger exploding from those silvery eyes, absorbed by the heat of his passionate gaze, Rebecca could no longer deny the rush of longing searing through her.

Still, she wasn't certain what she should expect when he leaned forward and bent his head to kiss her. It had been years since she'd been kissed by any man. But that first, exquisitely tender, soul-jarring contact jolted her to the core. The instant she felt the agonizing softness of his mouth claiming hers, the tip of his tongue sweeping along the seam of her lips, she knew something magical, something wondrous, was taking place.

The warmth of his kiss billowed through her, thick and sweet, filling her with a heady, dizzying sensation that left her longing for more. The deepening pressure of his mouth bedazzled her with its seductive power. Staggering against him, she felt the magic of his touch seeping into her veins, rushing through her, possessing her very soul.

She wanted to plunge deeper, explore the passion he was offering, until she heard the cry of a baby in the distance. Suddenly jolted back into reality, she pulled away from him with a start.

"I suppose I should be getting back to Hattie," she choked out, acutely aware of the shakiness in her voice.

"Yes, I suppose you should," he admitted with reluctance as the baby's cries intensified. "But I wish you didn't have to go."

She managed a tremulous smile before she whirled around and headed back to the shanty, not daring to admit that leaving the warmth of his embrace was one of the most difficult things she'd ever had to do.

Rebecca kneeled beside the bank of the creek the next morning just as dawn burst over the horizon, splashing hues of mauve and gold across the sky.

She inhaled a deep breath, hoping the tranquility of her surroundings would ease the ache in her heart. Part of her wished she'd never come here with Grady Cunningham. But another part wished they didn't have to leave.

As soon as she'd awakened, an overwhelming sense of sadness had suffused her. She dreaded bidding good-bye to this place, leaving behind all the magic that had sprung so wondrously between them.

But her work was accomplished here, and Rebecca knew it was time to leave. Hattie's milk was flowing freely now, and Rebecca didn't anticipate any complications for either the mother or her babe. The energetic child had been wide awake until the wee hours of the morning, demanding everyone's full attention until he'd drifted off to sleep.

With a heavy heart, she trudged back to the shanty. Reaching the entrance, she stumbled to a halt, amazed by what she saw through the open door.

Grady was sitting in Hattie's rocking chair. He was leaning forward, elbows propped on his knees, holding Blake in his hands, peering down at the child. A sense of wonder and awe filled his face.

A warmth permeated her as she observed the scene unnoticed. Had she not already realized that he was someone other than the legendary Grady Cunningham of notorious fame, this single glimpse of him would have driven all doubts from her mind. Those were not the hands of a vicious murderer, she knew. And the tenderness in his expression validated her belief that he was a caring, compassionate man. She only wished he didn't have to live with the injustice of his reputation for the rest of his life.

Trying to set aside the unsettling thoughts, she pursed her lips together and stepped into the house. She retrieved a small package from her traveling bag, then approached the bed where Hattie was resting peacefully.

"This is for you, Hattie." Rebecca presented the parcel to her.

"For . . . me?" As Rebecca nodded, Hattie struggled to sit upright. Tearing into the package, she gaped at the dainty infant gown nestled beneath the brown paper. "It's beautiful," she whispered.

"I'm glad you like it," Rebecca said. "It's from the Women's Missionary Auxiliary."

"Please convey my thanks to them." The woman patted Rebecca's hand. "I wish I could pay you properly for everything you've done, Rebecca. But money has been tight this year, with the drought and all, and I—"

"It's all right, Hattie. I didn't come here expecting to be paid."

"But I do have something I made especially

for you." Hattie nodded toward a neatly folded quilt draped across the foot of the bed.

Rebecca brushed the tips of her fingers across the dainty piecework, admiring the fine stitches, reveling at the countless number of hours that Hattie must have devoted to the gift. "Thank you, Hattie. I will treasure it, always."

At that moment, Owen stepped up to join them. "Are you sure you and Grady can't stay with us a few more days?"

"I wish we could," Rebecca admitted with all honesty. "But I need to get home to my daughter."

After bidding good-bye to the Fords and their newborn son, Rebecca left the homestead with Grady around mid-morning. While the buggy rattled over the trail, she quietly observed the skillful touch of his hands on the reins, the endearing way his hair curled over his neck and skimmed the collar of his shirt, the laugh lines crinkling at the corners of his eyes.

Her gaze swept over his ruggedly handsome features, then lingered on the sensuous curves of his mouth. A tingling sensation rippled through her at the poignant memory of those hungry lips caressing hers during that all too brief, fiery moment of passion on the prairie.

Turning, Grady stole a glance at her and grinned. "See somethin' you like, darlin'?" he teased.

Horrified she'd been caught gawking at him, she felt her cheeks burn with embarrassment. Gulping uneasily, she admitted, "I was just thinking about last night . . . and everything that happened . . . between us."

"A night worth rememberin', I'd say." There was a trace of glibness in his voice she hadn't expected to hear, a touch of devilish arrogance in that naughty grin of his. "Of course, as I recall, we were just gettin' warmed up when the baby started squallin'. But now that we're alone again without anyone disturbing us . . ."

He slipped an arm around her shoulder and drew her closer to his side. Then he dipped his head and planted a hot, smoldering kiss on the curve of her neck. Though shivers of desire were coursing through her from his fiery touch, Rebecca sensed something wasn't quite right. His memories of their magical time together seemed much too casual and nonchalant to be especially meaningful. Where was the compassionate, caring man who'd moved her so deeply at the homestead?

Sliding his lips over her throat and the sweep of her jaw, he rained showers of wet, open-mouthed kisses over her tender flesh. But just as he began to nibble on her ear, she pulled away from him.

Confusion shimmered from his eyes. "What's wrong, darlin'? Already wanting more than what you're getting from me?"

Fury raced through her. Outraged by his audacity, Rebecca instinctively hurled back her hand, intending to seek revenge with physical force. But a flash of common sense shot through her at the last moment, warning her that some carefully chosen words could be far more wounding than a smack across the face.

She lowered her hand to her lap and quietly scooted to the far side of the seat. "I'm surprised at you, Grady. Last night, I thought something very special transpired between us. But now, you're acting as though I'm nothing more to you than a dance-hall girl. What in heaven's name are you trying to prove?"

"I'm not trying to prove a damn thing," he snapped, focusing his gaze straight ahead, clenching his jaw.

But even as he voiced the denial, Grady felt a knot of guilt coiling in the pit of his gut.

Chapter 9

❧

Things weren't exactly working out like he'd planned. Cursing under his breath, Grady tightened his grip on the reins. How in the hell had he lost his focus so easily? How had his innocent little wager gotten so out of hand?

Somewhere along the way, somewhere in the wilds of the prairie, he'd forgotten any other world existed other than one revolving around Rebecca Summers, forgotten why he'd insisted on making this journey in the first place. Good God, was he going daft?

But even as the question plunged through his mind, he was acutely aware that the reason for his turmoil was sitting right next to him. Though he couldn't see her face, he didn't have to. Every delicate ivory curve, every dimpled smile, every twinkle of delight that had once sparkled in those summer-sky eyes, had been branded into his very soul.

An uneasy feeling rolled through him. From the beginning, he'd assumed Rebecca

Summers wasn't the type of woman who could arouse his passions, the kind who could heat his blood to a raging boil. And he'd presumed he could control his emotions during their trek across the plains.

Never in a million years would he have imagined that he would lose control of his own emotions just by looking at Rebecca Summers. Never had he anticipated such a tremendous surge of attraction for the woman, an attraction so powerful it nearly knocked the wind from his lungs.

And he'd never expected she could make him feel so vulnerable. Last night, he'd told her things about himself that he'd never told another living soul. Now, in the full light of day, being callous about those passion-drenched moments at the homestead, pretending to be heartless about his soaring desire for her, had been the only ways he'd known how to cope with all the unwanted emotions reeling through him.

How could he have known this woman would enchant him, bewitch him, intrigue him, like no other female ever had? Her smile, her goodness, her compassion had brightened every corner of that desolate little shanty, every dark corner of his heart.

Shame, stark and raw, coursed through him. He'd never known a woman so unworthy of being treated like a pawn in a game of chance. Remorse consumed him with such intensity that his gut was churning and his head was throbbing by the time he guided the buggy to a stop at the Summerses' residence.

No sooner had they stepped down from the

buggy, Jessica darted out of the house, waving and squealing with delight. As the child bounded across the yard, Rebecca opened her arms, greeting her with a warm embrace.

Within a few moments, Jacob came up to join them. As the physician expressed his thanks to Grady for making the trip with Rebecca, Jessica launched into a barrage of questions. "Did Mrs. Ford have a baby girl or a baby boy? Does the baby have a lot of hair? And do you know if—"

"Hold on, Jess." Rebecca laughed. "Let's unload the buggy, and then I'll answer all of your questions."

Jessica's narrow shoulders sagged with disappointment. She peered up at Grady, wiggling an outstretched finger, gesturing for him to bend over and meet her at eye-level. "I need to tell you something, Mr. Cunn'ham."

Taken aback by the child's serious expression, Grady hunkered down beside her. "Is something wrong, Miss Jess?"

"Oh, no!" She snuggled close, coiling her arms around his neck. "I just wanted to thank you for keeping your promise to take care of Mama," she whispered into his ear. "And for bringing her home so soon, too."

"Taking care of your ma wasn't too hard, darlin'," Grady said, mindful of the love that flowed so easily between Rebecca and her daughter. "And we were lucky, too. We didn't have to wait very long before Mrs. Ford's baby arrived."

Rebecca, standing beside the buggy, retrieved a basket of herbs from the back of the vehicle. "How about taking this into the house for me, Jess?" she called out.

Jessica darted to her mother's side. As the pair retreated into the house, Grady and Jacob unharnessed the black gelding, unhitched the buggy, and rolled the vehicle into the barn. Knowing what he had to do, Grady wasted no time in bidding good-bye to Jacob and wheeling in the direction of Hope.

As Grady headed into the business district, he clenched his jaw with steely resolve. He'd made a grave mistake when he'd centered his wager around Rebecca Summers. And putting a stop to all this nonsense was the least he could do.

Stalking into Hope Savings Bank, Grady approached the thin, spectacled banker who was standing behind a counter shielded with iron bars. After withdrawing a substantial sum from his account, he tucked the thick roll of bills into his vest pocket and headed across the street to the Red Dog Saloon.

Business was booming when Grady entered the establishment. A smoky haze hovered over the crowd of patrons who were wagering bets, guzzling drinks, and ogling ladies dressed in low-cut gowns. But as Grady stepped up to the bar and ordered a shot of whiskey, the laughter faded into a dull roar; the lively conversation dropped to a hushed murmur.

A man with a droopy mustache eyed Grady with a glare of suspicion. "I'm gonna be one unhappy man if you're here to collect your winnings, Cunningham. I got a lot of money wagered against you."

"You got at least another week to get the Widder Summers's attention, don't you?" another man asked, his voice wavering with uncertainty.

Grady picked up his drink from the bar and held it high in the air. "I believe congratulations are in order, gentlemen."

"And just what are we celebratin', Cunningham?" the bartender asked.

"Victory for the winner." As a stunned silence swept through the saloon, Grady's gaze traveled over the crowd. "The gamble regarding my courtship of Rebecca Summers is over," he announced.

"Guess we owe you some congratulations, then," one man mumbled, shaking his head in dismay. "Ain't no man in this town ever got to court the Widder Summers till you came along."

"Can't imagine how you did it," a second remarked. "The woman is sweeter 'n sin, but—"

"I'm afraid you've misunderstood, my friends," Grady interrupted. "In all honesty, our little game of chance wasn't as enjoyable as I expected it would be. As of this moment, I'm officially withdrawing from my wager. And a withdrawal, of course, means I'm conceding defeat."

"You mean you're . . . givin' up?"

For a long moment, Grady didn't respond to the stranger's question. He really didn't care what these men thought about him. If they wanted to believe he'd backed down from this challenge like a yellow-bellied coward who couldn't bear the sting of a woman's rejection, so be it.

"Yep, I'm givin' up," he announced flatly. Swallowing his last vestiges of pride, Grady reached into his vest pocket and tossed a roll of bills across the polished surface of the bar. "Enjoy your winnings, gentlemen."

With that, he wheeled and exited the saloon. Shouts of glee erupted behind him as patrons stampeded toward the bar to claim their share of the winnings.

Just as Grady stepped onto the boardwalk, Carl came up behind him. "What's goin' on with you, Cunningham? I heard what you said in there, but—"

"I said what I came to say, Carl." He lifted one shoulder in a careless shrug. "The gamble just wasn't as much fun as I thought it would be."

"But that don't sound like you. I wasn't in favor of this little wager in the first place, mind you, but it ain't like you to walk away from somethin' you've agreed to do." Carl's eyes narrowed with suspicion. "What's the real reason behind this sudden change of plans?"

Irritated by his friend's perceptiveness, Grady scowled. "It was a ridiculous wager in the first place, Carl. Besides, I don't want to take the chance of publicly embarrassing Rebecca Summers. She's too nice of a lady for the likes of me. I'd rather not waste my time—and hers—playing a foolish game of chance."

But even as he voiced the words, Grady silently acknowledged that he wasn't being completely honest with Carl. There was much more involved with his withdrawal from the wager, more than he cared to admit to anyone at the moment.

Wheeling, Grady clamped his mouth shut before he could say anything else to Carl. True, the possibilities of humiliating Rebecca with his foolish gamble had been more than his conscience could bear. The woman didn't deserve to be the innocent victim of deceit and trickery.

But could he win her affections on a more honorable—and permanent—basis?

Lapsing into silence, Grady stomped over the boardwalk, contemplating the possibilities.

Rebecca rose early the next morning, anxious to attend Sunday worship services. Sometime during the night, reliving those stolen moments with Grady on the prairie, she'd realized she needed to fall back into a normal routine as quickly as possible. Being surrounded by the familiar faces of neighbors and friends seemed like the best way to put her memories into the proper prospective.

She had no choice except to forget about the last few days, she reminded herself sternly as she slipped into one of her best Sunday gowns. Nothing more could ever result from a relationship with Grady Cunningham, she knew.

She was still smarting from his callous manner toward her during the ride back to Hope, still stinging from his devil-may-care attitude about the sparks of magic that had been ignited between them at the homestead. Was he trying to pretend he didn't care for her?

"It doesn't matter," she reminded herself aloud. Common sense said she couldn't afford to have her name associated with his, even though she was certain he wasn't deserving of his notorious reputation. But, unfortunately, most people in Hope were so blinded by inaccurate perceptions of the man that they couldn't look beyond his reputation and see his true character. And she had to pretend their brief time together had been nothing more than a distant dream.

Even so, forgetting about those too-brief, fiery moments was proving to be much more difficult than she could have ever fathomed. Her cheeks burned with shame for the way she'd practically thrown herself at the man.

Resolving never to let such madness overtake her again, Rebecca pulled back her shoulders with renewed determination. Then she perched a bonnet on her head and marched down the stairs, eager to begin the new day.

The church bell was pealing, calling out to worshippers across the town, by the time Rebecca set out for morning services with Jessica and Jacob. Approaching the simple frame building, Rebecca saw that many members of the congregation had already arrived. Awaiting for services to begin, the crowd was scattered through the church grounds, quietly socializing in groups of threes and fours.

Rebecca chatted briefly with Charlotte and Lydia, relaying Hattie's appreciation for the auxiliary's gift, before advancing toward the sanctuary.

Just before she reached the wide, double doors of the building, she paused, observing the handsome minister as he greeted each arriving parishioner with a handshake and a smile. The morning sunlight cast a golden glow over him, highlighting the auburn hues of his hair and beard. Without a doubt, Rebecca thought, Timothy O'Leary was a handsome man.

At that instant, Jessica tugged on her gown. "Ready to go inside, Mama?"

"I'll be along just as soon as I say hello to Pastor O'Leary," she said. "Can you and Grandpa save me a spot by the aisle?"

Nodding amiably, Jessica darted to her grandfather's side. While the pair entered the church hand-in-hand, Rebecca lingered beside the door, waiting to approach Timothy after everyone else had gone inside.

When their gazes met and locked, Timothy smiled warmly. "You look lovely this morning, Rebecca." His eyes swept over her dress, sparkling with approval. "Is this a new gown?"

"Why, yes, it is." Flattered by the compliment, Rebecca felt a heated flush rise to her cheeks. "It took me several weeks to complete all the stitching, but—"

"It's stunning," he interrupted, a mixture of surprise and admiration lacing his voice. "Mrs. Davenport has been raving about your work on the auxiliary's latest mission project, but I wasn't aware that your talents were so extensive."

"Lots of women are handy with a needle and thread," Rebecca insisted. "And all of our auxiliary members have been enthusiastic about making gowns for the homesteaders' newborns."

At that moment, the church bell chimed for a final time, calling for worship services to begin. Timothy nervously straightened his white clerical collar, then grasped Rebecca's hand. "I'd like to continue our discussion, Rebecca. Would you consider resuming our conversation over dinner this evening?"

"I would like that very much, Timothy."

"Wonderful!" A smile lit up his face. "I'll call for you around seven, then."

Rebecca picked up her skirts and turned to enter the church. "And I'll be looking forward to seeing you, Timothy."

Shortly before seven o'clock, Jessica burst into her mother's room without warning. "Pastor O'Leary is downstairs, and he says he's here to take you to dinner at the Grand Central!"

Securing the final hairpin into the tightly coiled chignon at her nape, Rebecca smiled. "Thanks, Jess." But her smile vanished when she saw the crinkles of worry along her daughter's brow. "What's wrong, sweetheart?"

Jessica's lips twisted into a frown. "I don't understand why Pastor O'Leary can't stay here and have dinner with us tonight. Why does he have to take you out to a restaurant?"

Rebecca sank down on the edge of the bed, pulling her daughter into her arms. "Because that's what men do when they want to get to know someone better."

"Do you like Pastor O'Leary?"

"He seems like a very nice man, although I don't know him very well. But I think I could like him very much."

"Enough to marry him?"

Rebecca smiled. "You're moving too fast for me, young lady. At the moment, I've merely agreed to have dinner with him."

"But do you think you'll get married again someday?"

"If the right man comes along." Rebecca couldn't resist running her fingers through her daughter's silky-fine hair. "Why do you ask, Jess?"

"Because I'd like to have a real daddy, just like Samantha and the other girls in town. I know I already have the best grandpa in the world, but I wouldn't mind having a daddy, too."

An ache swelled in Rebecca's chest. "But not just any man will do, sweetheart. He has to be a very special man, someone who will love us and take care of us and—"

"I know of someone!" Jessica's blue eyes danced with excitement. "Mr. Cunn'ham would be perfect! He took care of you when you went away together, didn't he? And he's so funny! I bet he'd make a great daddy!"

Not knowing whether to laugh or cry, Rebecca wrapped her arms around the child more tightly. Life could be so unfair, she thought. David's death had left a void in this precious child's life, an emptiness that could only be filled by a loving, caring man. She winced, knowing that man could never be Grady Cunningham.

"I'm sure Mr. Cunningham would be flattered to know that you'd like for him to be your daddy someday," Rebecca explained as gently as she could. "But I don't think he's the man we're looking for."

At that moment, Jacob's voice bellowed through the house. " 'Becca, you have company waiting for you!"

Rebecca lurched. "Good heavens, I almost forgot!" Laughing, she helped Jessica down from her lap, then rose from the edge of the bed.

"Coming, Jacob!" she called out, nervously patting her chignon. Taking a deep, steadying breath, Rebecca swept down the stairs.

Timothy, who was sitting in the parlor, chatting amiably with Jacob, sprang to his feet when Rebecca came into the room. "I believe I'm going to be the envy of every man in Hope tonight," he assessed, his gaze traveling over her with approval.

Rebecca flushed, jarred by the sudden realization that this was the first gentleman who had ever truly called upon her. All she'd ever had with David were stolen moments and clandestine meetings when she could escape from the watchful eyes of the Breckinridge clan.

But now, a true gentleman was actually calling on her. He was charming, handsome, and highly respected in the community. And he was gazing at her with admiration and lavishing compliments on her. What woman could ask for anything more?

When Timothy extended his arm, she looped her arm over the crook of his elbow. But she was acutely aware that the beat of her heart was steady and calm, her breathing, level and even. Sauntering toward the Grand Central, Rebecca tightened her fingers around the sleeve of Timothy's jacket, certain that sparks would fly between them as soon as they became better acquainted with each other.

Though Rebecca had heard about the plush interior of the Grand Central's restaurant, the lavish decor was unlike any other she'd ever seen. Entering the dining room with Timothy, she tried not to gawk at the rich velvet draperies framing the windows, the lush rugs covering the floors, the fine china and crystal adorning the linen-covered tables.

Unaccustomed to such lavish surroundings, she struggled to compose herself after the waiter escorted them to a table beside the window. "I've never dined in a place as elegant as this," she admitted frankly.

"I've heard this is the nicest place for miles around." Timothy surveyed the restaurant with one, sweeping glance. "It appears inviting, but I'm afraid some of the restaurants back in Virginia could put this one to shame."

Rebecca's gaze traveled over the other diners as Timothy ordered the restaurant's specialty—beefsteak and potatoes—for both of them. Though she didn't recognize any familiar faces, she was impressed by the clientele who were patronizing the establishment. Most appeared to be neatly dressed businessmen.

As soon as the waiter had taken their orders, Rebecca turned to her companion and smiled. "Are you a native of Virginia?" she asked, picking up the conversation again.

He nodded. "I was born and raised in the Tidewater area. Most of my family still resides there. My oldest brother is a waterman who spends most of his time on the Chesapeake Bay. And then there's my sister and her family, who live on the Eastern Shore of Virginia . . ."

An hour later, Rebecca regretted she'd ever asked Timothy about his native state. The question had prompted a detailed account of the man's life history. Along the way, she'd learned about the occupations of every member of his large family, and heard about his ancestral background. She'd even listened to stories about his rather uneventful journey from Virginia to Kansas, and learned the names of several professors from the Virginia seminary that Timothy had attended.

As he rambled, Rebecca made every effort to keep a smile on her lips and appear intrigued by the lengthy recourse about his life. She even refrained from mentioning that her steak was tough and tasteless, covering up her disappointment in the meal by insisting she wasn't as hungry as she'd thought.

But as they lingered at the table over coffee and pie, Rebecca became increasingly disheartened. On the surface, Timothy O'Leary appeared to be the man of her dreams. But if he was so perfect for her, why were her thoughts drifting away from their conversation? Why was she struggling not to yawn?

And where was the breathless sense of wonder that should be glimmering so brightly between them? Rebecca longed to recapture the feelings that had soared through her when she and Grady—

No. She squeezed her eyes shut, grimacing, trying to block the memories of Grady Cunningham from her mind. This was neither the time nor the place to be conjuring up thoughts of that man, she was reminding herself just as she felt Timothy's hand covering hers.

"Is something wrong, Rebecca?"

Her eyes shot open. She hadn't even considered that Timothy might be alarmed by her sudden frown of displeasure. Embarrassed as if she'd been caught doing something naughty, she felt a heated flush rise to her cheeks. "It's nothing," she insisted.

A shadow of darkness crossed his face. "I hope I wasn't the cause of your dismay."

"Oh, no, Timothy." She forced a strained smile. "An unpleasant thought just popped into my head from out of the blue. And it had nothing to do with you."

He breathed a sigh of relief. "That's good to know."

By the time they left the restaurant, stars were twinkling in the August sky. A halfmoon shone down over them, brightening their way back to the house. Approaching her home, Rebecca noticed the dwelling was dark except for a single lantern glowing from the parlor window. She assumed Jacob had retired for the evening, but had been thoughtful enough to leave a lantern burning for her.

"I had a wonderful time this evening, Rebecca," Timothy said as they stepped onto the porch. "May I call on you again, perhaps next week?"

Though her instincts automatically responded with a resounding *no*, Rebecca's logic warned her not to reject this man so hastily. She couldn't afford for her disappointments in the evening to dampen her hopes for the future. If she refused to spend any more time with Timothy, how could her feelings for him blossom and grow?

Besides, she desperately wanted to care for this wonderful man. And surely she would learn to care deeply for him after they became better acquainted with each other. Nodding, she finally said, "I would like that very much, Timothy."

Turning, she grasped the knob on the door. But before she could step into the house, she felt Timothy's arm slipping around her waist, gently spinning her around to face him. "I have one more request, Rebecca. May I take the liberty of kissing you good-night?"

"Why . . ."

It all happened so quickly that Rebecca didn't have time to protest. His kiss was so brief, so polite and simple, that it was practically over before it had begun. By the time Rebecca could comprehend what was happening, Timothy had already brushed his lips over hers and was backing off the porch.

"Good night, Rebecca," he whispered, grinning sheepishly. Whistling merrily, he disappeared into the darkness, heading back into town.

Rebecca heaved a weary sigh as she hurled open the door and stepped inside the house. "What an evening," she mumbled.

She impulsively yanked the pins from her hair and shook her head. Just as the dark waves tumbled around her shoulders, a husky, low voice sounded from the parlor.

"So how was your evening with the good reverend?"

Rebecca froze in shock for a brief instant, then whirled around and stared at Grady in disbelief. He was sprawled out in Jacob's favorite chair, long legs stretched out in front of him, hands clasped behind his head. He appeared relaxed, confident, and slightly amused.

"What are you doing here?" Rebecca snapped.

"I've been waiting for you. Jacob said you were out with the reverend."

"Then why didn't you leave?"

His mouth twitched. "Because Jacob told me I could wait."

"Let me get this straight." Rebecca frowned. "You came by to visit me while I'm having dinner in town with a gentleman. And my father-in-law invites you to stay until I get home?"

"Well, it didn't exactly happen like that. Actually, I asked Jacob if I could wait for you because I wanted to talk to you about something."

"Whatever you wanted to discuss could have waited until tomorrow, I'm certain."

"Possibly." He rose from the chair, edging toward her. "But when Jacob told me where

you were—and who you were with—I
couldn't resist sticking around. I was anxious
to hear about your evening with the good
reverend."

Appalled, Rebecca stiffened. "I had a lovely
evening, thank you," she said crisply.

"Tell me, Rebecca." Grady's voice dropped
to a low, husky keel. "I'm curious. Did you
enjoy your meal?"

"Yes," she lied.

"And the stimulating conversation?"

"Yes."

"And did your escort behave like a gentleman around you?"

"Of course he did!" Rebecca gritted her
teeth. "He's a minister, for goodness sake!"

"But how did he make you feel?" he
challenged.

"He treated me like a lady," she began.
"He was cordial, polite, pleasant—"

"That's not what I'm asking, Rebecca. I
want to know how he made you *feel*. Did he
make you feel . . . desirable?"

Rebecca's heart thundered in her chest.
"My feelings for Pastor O'Leary shouldn't be
any concern of yours," she snapped. "In fact,
it's none of your business at all."

"Oh?" A hint of a smile played on his lips.
"I dare say he must have stolen a kiss from
you, then."

"He did not steal a kiss," Rebecca denied.
Lifting her chin, she crossed her arms over
her chest. "He asked permission for one."

"Ah, the true gentleman." He edged forward, slowly bridging the distance between
them until they were standing only a breath

away from each other. All traces of amusement vanished from his face, and his eyes darkened with a desire so intense that Rebecca's breath lodged in her throat.

His gaze darted to the streams of dark hair, tousled and wild, tumbling over her shoulders. He lifted his hand and brushed his fingers through the untamed strands. "Did he run his fingers through your hair and make you tremble from his touch? Did his kiss leave you breathless and dizzy and begging for more?" he challenged, his voice as soft as black satin. "Did he kiss you like this . . ."

He bent his head and brushed his lips across hers ever so softly, careful to prevent any other contact between them. Rebecca was acutely aware that his kiss was much like the one that Timothy had given her. It was brief, simple, undemanding.

But in the next instant, everything changed. Grady whipped his arms around her and crushed her against the broad expanse of his chest. "Or did he kiss you the way a woman should be kissed, like this . . ."

His mouth swooped down to capture hers, burning with a heat so fiery and intense that Rebecca melted on impact. His tongue plunged between her lips and thrust inside her mouth, scorching like a sizzling flame.

She instinctively flattened her palms over his chest, intending to push him away, but the heated pressure of his mouth grinding into hers sapped the strength from her limbs. Overwhelmed by the giddy, dizzying sensations swarming through her, she struggled to keep from staggering against him. Her fingers curled over the folds of his vest in a desperate attempt to maintain her balance.

All the while, the urgency of the kiss intensified as his hands roamed over the sweep of her back, the curve of her waist. Just when Rebecca thought she could stand no more of the sweet agony, his hands gripped her trembling shoulders. To her surprise and dismay, he pulled back his head and tore his lips away from hers.

Suddenly breaking the spell, he brushed the tip of her nose with an outstretched finger. "Tell me, Rebecca." His lips curled into a smile. "Did your minister kiss you the way you should be kissed?"

All those passionate feelings, soaring through her only seconds ago, vanished into thin air like a wisp of smoke. She jerked away from him with a start. "Proper ladies don't compare kisses from different gentlemen."

His grin broadened. "Then which kiss will you be thinking about tonight after I'm gone, when you're all alone?"

A stab of irritation lanced through Rebecca. He was perfectly aware he'd kissed the daylights out of her. But she'd never give him the satisfaction of hearing her admit his kisses were more intoxicating and potent than any she'd ever known. She nodded toward the door. "You'd best be leaving now, Grady. It's getting late, and—"

"But I don't want to leave. I want to stay." He reached out and threaded his fingers through her hair. "I want to hear your laughter, Rebecca. I want to see the dimple in your cheek when you smile. And I want to tell you how much I regret behaving like such a pompous ass on the way back to Hope yesterday."

She paled. "You're . . . apologizing?"

"Don't make this any harder on me than it already is, darlin'." His fingers tightened over a silky strand of her hair. "I wasn't certain how to deal with all the unexpected feelings running through me, all the surprising thoughts whirling through my head. So I tried to deny that you were driving me out of my mind, tried to pretend you weren't affecting me like no other woman ever has." He heaved a weary sigh. "I was wrong to have treated you like you were one of the gals from the Red Dog. And I want nothing more than for us to recapture that wonderful moment we spent together on the prairie—"

"Please don't, Grady." She squeezed her eyes shut, trying to block the pain. "It's impossible for us to recapture that moment."

"And why not?" Anger and frustration laced his voice. "You can't deny you felt the magic that night, Rebecca. It was there for both of us."

Her lashes fluttered open. "But I can't allow it to happen again. It just isn't right . . . for me." She pursed her lips together. "I'm sure you understand."

"Oh, I understand." Sarcasm tainted his voice, and the line of his jaw hardened. "My sinful past—and all the gossip about it—is the real issue here. You don't want to be associated with me, do you?"

"Personally, I don't think you're deserving of your reputation in Hope. I believe you're much more of a man than anyone can fathom." The slightest hint of a smile played on her lips. "Besides, any man who wins over Uly's heart must have a few redeeming qualities about him."

"Not a bad point in my favor." Subdued amusement twinkled from his eyes. "And don't forget, I'm richer 'n sin, too."

Her smile faded. "But money can't buy everything, Grady."

"It can buy a helluva lot." He stretched out his arms with a wide, sweeping gesture. "Hell, Rebecca, I can buy you the world on a silver platter."

"But all the money in the world can't give me what I want most in life." She slowly sank onto the settee, heaving a sigh of frustration. "All I want in life is an honorable name. It's all I can leave my daughter. I have nothing else to give her."

Grady sat down beside her, puzzled and confused, wondering why she wanted something she already had. "You're one of the most respected women in this town, Rebecca. You're already giving your daughter a respectable name."

"But I can't afford to jeopardize that respect in any way. I've worked too hard to earn it, and I can't risk losing it. It's much more difficult to overcome a tarnished reputation than to maintain an unblemished one."

His confusion intensified. "And how would you know?"

Pain shimmered from her eyes as she gazed up at him. "Unfortunately, my past isn't as respectable as my life is today. Until I moved

here, I never had the chance to be accepted
for who I was." He heard the catch in her
voice. "No matter what I said or did, I
couldn't overcome the disgrace of being
known as the daughter of a murderer."

Grady felt the blood draining from his face.
"Your . . . father?"

Her eyes clouded with sorrow. "My father
murdered his own brother—my uncle. And
my brother and I witnessed it all, every gruesome minute."

"Oh, God."

"Something inside my father snapped
when he discovered Ma had been having an
affair with my uncle. At the time, I was only
four or five, but I still remember the noise,
the horrible noise, and the screams . . ."

She was shivering now, and Grady slipped
his arm around her trembling shoulders, hoping he could offer a bit of comfort to her,
wishing he could erase the brutal sting of her
memories. Collapsing into the warmth of his
embrace, she snuggled her cheek against his
chest. "I'm sorry you had to witness such a
tragedy, Rebecca."

"But that's not the worst of it. There's
more." Her voice quivered with emotion.
"For some reason, my father decided he
needed some money. Before he was hanged,
he sold off my brother and me."

"He . . . *sold* you?" Grady echoed in
stunned disbelief.

Her head dipped lower into his chest.
"Tyler—my brother—ran off before anyone
could catch him. But I was too young to understand what was happening. When I went

to live with the Breckinridges, I assumed they were taking me into their home out of the goodness of their hearts. But as it turned out, they never let me forget I was nothing more than a piece of merchandise to them."

Absorbing the horror of it all, Grady tightened his grip around her shoulders.

"The oldest boy, Alfred, was the worst of them all," she continued. "He constantly tormented me, ordering me around, trying to make me into his personal slave. By the time I reached my teens, I was terrified of him. And when he cornered me in the barn one afternoon . . ." She drew in a shaky breath. "I knew I had to get away from him. Thankfully, I managed to escape just in time that afternoon. He only managed to rip my dress. But I've never forgotten that glazed look in his eyes, that feeling of horror . . ."

A choked sob drowned out the rest of her thought. Grady squeezed his eyes shut, the brunt of her pain searing through him. "God, I'm so sorry, Rebecca."

She tilted back her head, peering up at him. Tears shimmered on the tips of her thick, dark lashes. "I don't want your pity, Grady. I simply want your understanding," she said quietly. "I've never told another soul in this town about my life before I came here. It's a part of the past that I don't care to remember. And I certainly don't care for anyone else to know. But I wanted you to understand why a life of respectability is so important to me. All of my life, I've been embarrassed and shunned because of my father's sins, and I can't bear . . ."

Her voice faded away. Her brows puckered

across her forehead, as if she'd suddenly been assaulted by another disturbing thought. Grady sensed she was teetering on the brink of revealing something else, but she couldn't summon up the strength to discuss the matter with him.

An ache squeezed his heart. Good God, what else could have happened in this woman's past? Wasn't being sold off like a slave enough for any human to endure?

"I don't want to make mistakes that can effect Jessica's life," she continued. "I won't have my daughter struggling to hold up her head with pride, feeling the agony of all those cruel words and ugly stares and lewd whispers, because of something I've done. I don't feel you deserve your reputation, Grady, but I can't take the chance of consorting with you. I don't want Jessica to suffer the way I have."

He supposed he should be furious, outraged. After all, this woman's rejection of him was a bitter blow to his pride. But for some reason, Grady couldn't dredge up a snippet of anger toward her. All too well, he understood her unbearable pain. And he couldn't blame her for wanting to steer clear of a man with a reputation like his.

Still, he couldn't stop wanting her, couldn't bear the thought of this woman slipping through his fingers. A sudden burst of inspiration seized him. "But what if—?"

He clamped his mouth shut before he could fully voice the crazy thoughts ricocheting through his mind. The idea of trying to redeem himself in the eyes of this town was the most insane notion he'd ever had. Why should he care about everyone else's opinion of him?

At that instant, his gaze collided with Rebecca's. Grady's heart nearly lurched from his chest. He clenched his jaw tightly, unable to admit he was beginning to care about what other people thought of him. Especially one woman, in particular.

Chapter 10

$\sim\!\!\mathcal{O}\!\!\mathcal{Q}\!\!\sim$

The house was quiet when Rebecca awoke the next morning. Struggling to dispel her grogginess, she stretched her arms over her head and yawned.

But as she hurled back the covers and planted her bare feet on the floor, a gnawing sense of uneasiness clawed away at her. Frowning, she padded across the room, unable to pinpoint the cause for her apprehension.

Hazy thoughts came into clearer focus as she hurled open the door to the wardrobe. Hadn't she heard some noises during the night? She'd been sleeping too deeply for the sounds to fully awaken her, but she vaguely recalled hearing some sort of disturbance. At the time, she'd assumed she'd been dreaming. But now . . .

She pulled a lavender gown from the wardrobe, troubled by yet another disturbing thought. Wasn't the house too quiet? Most mornings, she could hear Jacob stirring in the kitchen, fixing coffee, opening a drawer, shuffling a chair.

But this morning, all was silent. Was Jacob still asleep?

Surely not, Rebecca thought. Jacob rarely slept later than six o'clock. Had he left early this morning to call on a patient? And did the distant noises during the night have something to do with his absence?

Not wanting to jump to hasty conclusions, Rebecca tried to remain calm as she dressed for the day. But as soon as she'd slipped into her lavender gown and peered into the hall, she knew something was wrong. The door to Jacob's room was wide open, and her father-in-law was nowhere to be found.

She swept down the stairs. The kitchen was empty, just as she'd suspected, but she spied a note bearing Jacob's scrawl on the table. She picked up the paper, hurriedly reading the message.

My dear Rebecca,

It's three A.M., and I've been called into town to tend to some gunshot wounds. Don't be alarmed if I'm not home by the time you get up.

I do need your help, however. Mayor Cunningham is expecting me to call on him at ten o'clock this morning. Will you please go to the ranch in my place?

Jacob

A sinking feeling swept through Rebecca. Gunfire was becoming a nightly occurrence in

Hope, it seemed. Would the violence never end? And what more was going to happen before someone put a stop to all the senseless killings? Troubled and concerned, Rebecca was pondering the gravity of the situation when a rap sounded at the door.

"Are you home, Rebecca?"

Recognizing Samantha's voice, Rebecca scurried across the room to open the door. She greeted the young girl with a warm hug. "You're up early this morning," she observed.

"Doc Summers dropped by the store and asked me to come over," Samantha explained as she stepped into the house. "And he asked me to tell you that he probably wouldn't be home until late afternoon."

Rebecca grimaced. "Then the situation in town must be worse than I thought."

"Some cowboy went on a rampage last night. Pa said nobody was killed, but a couple of men were wounded pretty bad." Samantha slumped into a chair at the table. "Doc Summers said you might want me to stay with Jessica today while you're taking care of his calls."

"That would work out nicely for me." Rebecca placed a cast-iron skillet on the cookstove. "I appreciate your willingness to help me out with Jessica so much, Samantha."

"It's no bother at all. I like staying with her."

"She loves having you here, too." Rebecca set a basket of eggs on the table. "And I'm sure she'd love for you to have breakfast with her this morning. Have you eaten yet?"

Samantha's blond hair cascaded over her

shoulders as she shook her head. "Breakfast sounds wonderful. I left in such a hurry this morning that I didn't have time to eat."

Rebecca set a bowl on the table. As she cracked an egg on the rim of the bowl, she asked, "So how have things been going lately?"

Samantha shrugged. "Not too bad. I'm still angry because Hank left town without saying good-bye, but I'm not hurting as much anymore. I don't like the way he treated me, I'll admit. But I don't want to give him the satisfaction of knowing that he hurt me really bad, either."

Glad to hear that Sam's spirits were improving, Rebecca smiled as she prepared the eggs for breakfast. Matters of the heart, she was learning, weren't the easiest problems in the world to solve, not at any age.

"What's going on, Mama?" Jessica called out from the top of the stairs.

"Someone is here to see you," Rebecca answered. "And she's going to stay with you today while Jacob and I are tending to our patients."

Jessica peered through the railings and shrieked with delight. "Samantha! I didn't know you were here!"

As the child bounded down the steps, Rebecca called out to her. "Go back to your room, Miss Jess, and get dressed before you come downstairs and eat breakfast."

Though Jessica moaned with dismay, she trudged back up the stairs and disappeared into her room. By the time she returned to the kitchen, fully dressed for the day, Rebecca

had just placed a platter of bacon and scrambled eggs on the table.

The trio was almost finished with the meal
when Samantha turned to Rebecca. "So where
are you going this morning?"

"The Cunningham ranch," Rebecca explained. "I'm not exactly certain when I'll be
home, though."

"Take all the time you need," Samantha offered. "I'm sure Jessica and I will manage just
fine while you're gone."

Pleased she could rely on Samantha to take
care of her daughter, Rebecca retreated into
Jacob's office. After placing an assortment of
medical supplies into a wooden case, she bid
good-bye to Jessica with a kiss and a hug,
then stepped outside to leave.

She had just placed the wooden box into
the buggy when she heard the sound of boots
shuffling up behind her.

Looking up at Grady, Rebecca almost forgot
how to breathe. His Stetson was cocked low
over his forehead, and his lips were slanted
into a crooked grin. Remembering how those
lips had been crushed against hers, hot and
scorching and burning with desire, Rebecca
felt her knees go weak.

"Headin' out early today, aren't you?"

"I don't like to wait too late in the day to
get started on my calls," she explained, relieved her voice was steadier than her legs.
"It's too hot to travel in the afternoon."

He pushed back the brim of his Stetson. "Is
Jacob going with you?"

"I'm afraid not." She hoisted herself into
the buggy as quickly as she could manage,

not wanting to give him the opportunity to leap to her aid. She wasn't certain how she would react to the touch of his hands around her waist. "Apparently, there was some trouble in town again last night, and—"

"There was a helluva lot of trouble." The line of Grady's jaw tightened. "Some guy called Big Al came out of the Red Dog Saloon firing his gun like a madman, shooting at anything that moved. A couple of guys tried to wrestle the gun away from him, but they ended up getting shot. Big Al put up quite a fight, it appears."

"Oh, my." Rebecca's knuckles turned white from the force of her grip on the reins.

"To make matters worse, Big Al got away." Grady frowned. "With a scoundrel like that on the loose, I'm sure Jacob would feel better if he knew you weren't roaming around the plains by yourself again today." He held out his hand. "If you give me the reins, I'll be glad to ride along with you this morning."

"There isn't any need for you to go with me, Grady," Rebecca insisted, quietly moving the reins beyond his reach. "I can manage by myself."

He grunted. "Seems like we've had this conversation before."

"But circumstances are different this time. I won't be gone for hours and hours, traveling across the plains. I'm only going a few miles out of town to check on one of Jacob's patients."

"Then what's the problem?" Grady scowled. "There isn't any reason why I shouldn't go with you, and every reason in the world why I should! If you're heading out of town, chances are slim that anyone from Hope will see us together."

"But it's not necessary," Rebecca insisted firmly. She suspected Grady didn't know about the severity of his father's health. If he arrived at the ranch without any knowledge about Malcolm's condition, how would he react?

She didn't want to find out. Jerking on the reins, she nodded curtly. "Good day, Grady."

"Dammit, Rebecca, don't be so stubborn!" Grady shouted, hurling a clenched fist into the air.

But his warning fell on deaf ears as the buggy rolled into the street and disappeared from sight.

With his pulse racing furiously, Grady stormed into town and retrieved his horse from the livery stables. Within a few moments, he was galloping over the rugged trail leading out of Hope.

With each passing mile, his anger intensified. Why hadn't she wanted him to accompany her? And why had she been so secretive about her destination?

He didn't understand her reasoning. But he had no intention of stepping aside and letting her ride into the wilds of the prairie without an ounce of protection—especially with a trigger-happy lunatic roaming around Hope. If he was forced to settle for lagging behind her, he'd secretively ensue her damn buggy across the state of Kansas, if he had to. But he'd be damned if he'd allow any harm to come to the woman.

Besides, following the dusty tracks of the buggy along the trail wasn't a difficult task. The rugged path was as familiar to him as the back of his hand. He'd traveled the same route hundreds of times when he'd resided in Hope. The sprawling estate owned by Malcolm Cunningham was located along the trail.

In fact, he was rapidly approaching the vast tract of property that belonged to his father, he realized with a start.

Within a few moments, Grady came to the edge of the Cunningham property. He paused, sweeping his gaze over the immense stretch of acreage surrounding him. As far as his eye could see—and beyond—this land belonged to one of the most powerful men in Kansas. *Malcolm Cunningham.*

Grady had never intended to set foot on the property again, not for the rest of his days. The stalwart cattle king had left no doubt in anyone's mind that he'd washed his hands of his wayward son.

Yet, now he was here once again. And he wasn't even certain why.

His gaze narrowed, drinking in the sight of the extraordinary stone mansion in the distance. Though every detail of the house had been etched into his memory, it was even more magnificent than he'd remembered. Undoubtedly, the Cunningham home was the most opulent in the state. Compared to the Fords' pitiful sod shanty and his own crude living conditions while buffalo hunting on the plains, the place looked like a palace. Built of

gray stone quarried in Kansas, the mansion
had taken two years to construct. And no ex-
pense had been spared for King Cunningham,
who'd insisted on living like royalty, Grady
recalled with a wince.

A dark blur in the distance suddenly
snared his attention. Shifting his gaze to the
road, Grady froze. No doubt, it was Rebecca's buggy. But why was she turning into
the drive leading up to the Cunningham
mansion?

A sickening feeling assaulted him. Hadn't
Carl warned him that Malcolm had taken ill?

Beads of sweat broke out along his brow
and trickled down his face. He guided the
horse toward a black walnut tree located a
few feet away from the trail. He dismounted,
stretched his legs, then sagged against the
trunk of the tree and stared at the mansion
for a long moment. What was taking place
behind those gray stone walls? Was his father
desperately ill, needing constant attention?

But why in the hell should it matter? King
Cunningham didn't give a damn about him.
Why should he care if the old man was sick?

He wasn't certain how much time had
passed when Rebecca emerged from the
house. But in spite of his determination to remain aloof and detached about her reasons
for calling at the Cunningham estate, his heart
was racing in his chest as she pulled the
buggy onto the main road.

He stalked to the edge of the trail to meet
her. When she brought the buggy to a stop,
he tipped the brim of his hat. "Been payin'

your respects to the king this mornin'?" he asked cynically.

A tremulous sigh escaped from her lips. "I told you I had my reasons for not wanting you to come along with me, Grady."

"But you sure as hell didn't tell me what those reasons were."

She met his gaze with a sorrowful expression. "It's your father, Grady. He isn't well."

"I'd heard rumors he'd been sick. But I figured you can't always believe what you hear."

"Unfortunately, the rumors are true. Mayor Cunningham suffered a stroke back in the spring."

Grady's throat tightened. "How . . . bad?"

"He's partially paralyzed on his left side. He's lost the use of his left leg, but Jacob thinks he'll eventually regain some use of his arm."

Grady tried to disregard the breathless feeling pressing through him, tried to ignore the hammering of his heart. He didn't want to care about the man who'd turned his back on him.

Still, he felt as stunned and weak as if the wind had been knocked out of him. Envisioning his father as a helpless cripple jolted him to the core. The man had always been too strong and stubborn to allow anything to defeat him. It was difficult, if not impossible, to imagine King Cunningham as anything less than hardy and hale. "Is he in any danger of . . . dying?" he finally managed to ask.

"Jacob can tell you more about his condition than I can. All I can tell you is that he's not recovering as quickly as we'd hoped. And his attitude concerns me as much as his physical ailments. He's extremely irritable and bitter about his situation."

"He's never been an optimist, believe me." Grady snorted. "He's the most cantankerous, bullheaded, obstinate, unreasonable, narrow-minded—"

"I'll admit he's gruff and rude at times. But it almost seems as if he's given up all hope, like he doesn't have a reason to fight any longer."

Grady lifted one shoulder in a careless shrug. "The old man has a mind of his own. He always does what he pleases, no matter what anyone else says or does. So it doesn't matter much to me what happens to him."

But Rebecca sensed that it did. All along, Grady had claimed that he didn't give a damn about his father. But in that instant, Rebecca knew he cared more than he would ever admit. She could tell by the flicker of fear glimmering from his eyes, the lines of worry creasing his brow.

"I think you do care, Grady," she observed aloud. "Anyone who is concerned enough about a friend to take him to a doctor in the middle of the night must be disturbed by the news of his father's failing health."

"You can't make a comparison like that," he ground out. "Carl works for me."

"So you're more concerned about the health of your employees than your own father?" she challenged.

"You're damn right, lady." Every muscle in his body went whipcord taut. "My employees are loyal to me. And they're not as difficult to get along with as King Cunningham. Nobody is, in fact."

His eyes grew cold and hard. Feeling the tension sizzling through the air, Rebecca sensed it was time to leave. "You've just received some unsettling news, Grady. Why don't we find a quiet place so you can collect your thoughts before we return to town?"

Narrowing his eyes, he swept his gaze over the wide expanse of land that surrounded them. "I know just the spot."

Twenty minutes later, a house came into view, a dwelling that Rebecca had never seen until now. Unlike the sod shanties scattered throughout the prairie, this building had been constructed from real lumber. A wide porch wrapped around all sides of the two-story structure, and bottle-green shutters trimmed the long, narrow windows.

In spite of the beauty of the house, Rebecca sensed an air of loneliness about the place. As Grady dismounted, she stepped down from the buggy, curiously gazing at the dwelling. "Who lives here, Grady?"

"No one." He tied the horse to a fence post. "It belonged to my brother, Paxton, before he was killed in the war."

Rebecca's heart sank. "I'm sorry, Grady. I never realized . . ."

"I'm sorry, too." He forced a tight-lipped smile. "Would you like to look around the place?"

"I'd love to."

Rebecca enjoyed rambling through the house with Grady. The rooms were large and spacious, the decor elegant and charming. Yet, for some unexplainable reason, Rebecca felt a sense of emptiness lurking in every room. It almost seemed as if the place was yearning for someone who would breathe laughter and love into it, longing to wrap its sheltering embrace around a family who would treasure all it had to offer.

"This is a lovely home," Rebecca mused after they'd explored both floors.

Grady ushered her onto the porch. "It's not a home," he corrected in a somber tone. "It's a house. No one lives here."

"But someone could easily live here." Rebecca admired the contrast between the white clapboard and the green shutters. "I wonder why it isn't being rented to anyone."

"Because the owner doesn't want anyone living here." The line of his jaw hardened. "Paxton bequeathed the house to me, Rebecca."

The dismal tone of his voice confused Rebecca. "I don't understand, Grady," she admitted freely. "Most people would treasure a house like this."

"But I'm not most people." He gripped the porch railing and gazed into the distance. "Originally, my father promised me this land—and this house—as payment for my work at his cattle brokerage before the war. Since I never accepted a cent in pay from him, he insisted on compensating me for my work by constructing this house for me."

Rebecca's brow narrowed in confusion. "I thought you said all of this belonged to Paxton before he died."

Clenching the railing more tightly, he sucked in a shuddering breath. "When Paxton joined up with the Union, our father believed he should be rewarded for his heroic efforts. So he decided to present this house and land to my brother instead of me."

"But why would he go back on his word?"

"Because the old man always favored Paxton over me. I've never been able to live up to his expectations. I could never work hard enough, long enough, diligently enough, to please him."

Rebecca winced. All too well, she knew the agony of never meeting anyone's approval, no matter how hard you tried.

"But I didn't see the situation so clearly at the time. Instead of directing my anger at King Cunningham for mistreating me, I condemned Paxton for being the favored son." Grady's voice became choked, strained. "I insisted my brother was encouraging the favoritism, and I accused him of trying to steal my inheritance. And then . . ." He squeezed his eyes shut, grimacing in pain. "Paxton was killed in the war. He died without ever knowing I finally realized he wasn't the one at fault."

Overcome with emotion, Rebecca reached out and placed her hand over his.

"My mother never knew how much I regretted my behavior, either. She'd never been fond of Kansas, so she went back to Boston to visit her sister as soon as the war ended . . . and she never came back. I suspect she was so devastated over losing Paxton—and the bitter feuding between her two sons—that the grief literally broke her heart."

"Losing your mother and brother in such a short period of time must have been difficult for you," Rebecca remarked.

"It was hard to deal with," he admitted. "But my regret for never making amends with either of them has been more difficult to cope with than my grief. I never apologized to my mother for causing her so much heartache for feuding with Paxton. And I never told Paxton how much I regretted blaming him for something he didn't cause."

Rebecca longed to say something, do something, to ease the turmoil rolling through him. She squeezed his hand tightly. "Have you ever considered Paxton may have wanted this house to be returned to the rightful owner after his death? Bequeathing all of this to you might have been his way of letting you know that all has been forgotten and forgiven."

He whipped around to face her. Rebecca detected a trace of sudden understanding in his chiseled features. "I've never looked at the situation from Paxton's point of view. But knowing my brother, I suspect you might be right."

The tightness disappeared from his shoulders, and Rebecca hoped some of his guilt had been eased. Sighing, he jerked off his hat and plunged his fingers through his hair in frustration. "Now, if the old cattle king would just have a change of heart—"

He halted abruptly, shaking his head, as if to ward off all thoughts of Malcolm Cunningham.

"It's not too late to make amends with him, you know," Rebecca offered quietly.

The line of his jaw hardened. "Too much has happened between us."

"Maybe so. But maybe not." She reached out, running the tips of her fingers along the harsh planes of that devastatingly sensual face. "You know something? I think we're more alike than either of us care to admit. We're both struggling to deal with issues from our past. Only I've been trying to hide from mine, and you're running from yours."

"I am not running," he denied hotly. "Only cowards run from their problems."

"Maybe you've been avoiding the issue, then."

"Good God, Rebecca, it's more complicated than that." His voice was gruff, but warm. "I can't just waltz into the Cunningham mansion and announce that I'm ready to wipe the slate clean. If the old man suspected I was anywhere near his blasted estate, he'd be sending a lynch mob after me."

"But maybe something could change his mind," Rebecca pressed on. "Maybe he'd be willing to rebuild a relationship with you if he knew that you had cleared your name in Hope."

"And since when have I cleared my name?" Grady scoffed. "The last I heard, it was dirtier 'n mud."

"But you can change public opinion, Grady. I'm certain of it. If people could only see you through my eyes, they'd see a man who is very different from his image."

His wolf-gray eyes narrowed with skepticism. "And how's that?"

"You're a caring, compassionate man. I've noticed your consideration for my daughter, your worry over my safety, your concern over an injured friend. And when I saw the look on your face when you were holding the Fords' new baby ..." She floundered for words, overcome with emotion.

"I've always been a sap for babies and kids," he admitted, grinning sheepishly. "But I'm not sure if I know how to change my image in this town."

"I'm not always sure how to handle situations, either. But Jacob encourages me to simply live by my conscience. He says if I do what I feel is right, the rest will fall into place." She boldly met his gaze. "I'm sure you'll think of something, Grady. I'm certain of it."

Any doubts Grady might have voiced vanished as he gazed down into Rebecca's face. Moved beyond words, he couldn't utter a sound past the lump swelling in his throat. No one—not a single soul—in his entire life had ever expressed so much faith in him.

For the first time in recent memory, his heart stirred with hope. Something about this woman touched his very soul, evoking emotions he'd sworn not to possess. He'd never known anyone so angelic, never met any woman who could elicit such gut-wrenching emotions from such a weary soul as his own.

A few days ago, Grady might have attributed the tightening of his loins to an overwhelming dose of lust pounding through his veins. But now, intoxicated by the enticing sweetness of her rosewater scent, drinking in her kindness and goodness of her, Grady felt a strange stirring in the depths of his heart, a feeling so powerful and overwhelming that it set his loins aflame.

Unable to contain the emotions reeling through him, he reached out and crushed her into his arms. Then he captured the sweetness of her lips with his own, drowning himself in all she had to offer.

Chapter 11

Trying to calm her racing heart, Rebecca inhaled a shaky breath as she guided the buggy over the bumpy road. But as she followed Grady's lead into town, she discovered her heart had a mind of its own. Each time she looked up and caught a glimpse of Grady, perched high in the saddle, the thundering beat in her breast soared out of control.

To make matters worse, her lips were still scorching from the fiery heat of his mouth clamping over hers, her skin still tingling from the burning touch of his hands. And her mind was still whirling, attempting to absorb all the stunning confessions he'd revealed to her.

She'd been touched beyond words as he'd confided his fears and pains, as she'd learned about the anguish still lingering in his soul. Never in her wildest dreams could she have imagined how much turmoil and guilt had been concealed behind that devilish arrogance of his.

In some ways, she felt his candidness had brought their relationship to a new level of understanding and new heights, which made it difficult to remember the reasons why she wouldn't allow herself to be drawn to the man.

She was still thinking about the events of the day when she pulled to a stop beside her home. Grady dismounted, then scrambled to help her down from the buggy. Rebecca totally forgot that she could be risking the chance of demolishing the well-tended walls of respectability she'd built for herself when he slipped his hands around her waist and hoisted her to the ground. She was too absorbed in the wondrous feelings soaring through her from the tenderness of his touch and the breathless dizziness that accompanied it.

She was still enjoying the lingering touch of his hands around her waist when Samantha's voice split through the air. "Look, Jessica! Your mother is home!"

"And Mr. Cunn'ham is here, too!" Jessica shrieked.

Rebecca reluctantly pulled away from Grady as Jessica ran across the yard to welcome them home. She kneeled beside her daughter, planting a kiss on her cheek. "Were you a good girl for Samantha this morning?"

Jessica's head bobbed up and down. Her thick, dark braids flopped around her narrow shoulders. "I'm always a good girl, Mama! Just ask Samantha. She knows!"

Samantha grinned. "We made cookies

today. Jessica helped mix the dough and cut out the shapes."

"What kind of cookies?" Grady asked.

"Sugar cookies! And they're still warm, too." Jessica twinkled up at him. "Want to come inside and have some cookies and milk with me?"

Observing the conversation, Rebecca suddenly noticed an unusual expression flickering across Samantha's face. The young girl was gazing up at Grady with a mixture of fascination and longing, almost as if she idolized him.

Though Rebecca was acutely aware that Sam had given her word not to mention anything about Grady's presence, she was disturbed by the girl's apparent infatuation. If Samantha became too captivated by Grady, she might forget her vow of silence.

Rebecca hastily spoke up before Grady had the chance to accept the invitation. "I'm sure Mr. Cunningham has other things to do. He was kind enough to accompany me home, but I'm certain he—"

"As a matter of fact," Grady interrupted smoothly, "it's been a while since I've had the chance to enjoy cookies and milk with a group of beautiful ladies. And I'd love to sample your cooking, Miss Jess."

Jessica squealed with delight. "I'll get everything ready for you. It'll be just like having a tea party!"

Grady laughed. "I'll be inside as soon as I unhitch the buggy."

As Rebecca followed Jessica into the house, Samantha fell into step beside her. "I guess I should be getting home now," she said reluctantly.

"You won't be staying for Jessica's tea party?"

"I'm afraid not. My mother has some work for me to do at the store this afternoon." Her mouth curled into an impish grin as they stepped onto the porch. "Besides, I wouldn't want to be intruding."

Rebecca stilled. "Intruding? How could you possibly be intruding?"

Samantha's smile broadened. "With Mr. Cunningham here and all, it looks to me like he's interested in courting you."

"Mr. Cunningham and I are not courting." Feeling her cheeks blossom with color, Rebecca prayed Samantha couldn't detect the guilt flooding through her.

"Well, it looks like he wants to court you."

Rebecca entered the house. "What makes you think that?" she asked as casually as she could.

"The way he was looking at you." Samantha heaved a dramatic sigh. "It seemed like he wanted to eat you up with his eyes. And when he helped you down from the buggy, it looked like he didn't want to let you go. Oh, Rebecca, it was so . . . romantic!" she swooned.

Rebecca cringed. "You must be exaggerating, Sam. I didn't notice anything out of the ordinary."

"Don't worry," Samantha consoled, patting Rebecca's shoulder. "I know you don't care for anyone knowing about Grady being here,

and I haven't told a soul about him. Your secrets are safe with me."

But as Samantha turned to leave, a sinking
feeling swept through Rebecca. She didn't like
the notion of sharing secrets with a girl as
young as Samantha. In fact, she didn't even
like the idea of pretending that Grady Cunningham was a stranger to her, considering
the man was occupying more and more of her
thoughts with each passing day.

Besides, she conceded a few moments later,
it was hard to be disdainful of a man who
elicited giggles from little girls and winked at
their mothers. Even now, the man was difficult to resist, sitting at the table, cramming
sugar cookies into his mouth and wearing a
mustache of milk on his upper lip.

Gazing at him, laughing and teasing, smiling and playing with Jessica, Rebecca felt a
bittersweet longing swell in her heart.

It was sad, she thought, that things couldn't
be different between them. If circumstances
had been different, they might have been
right for each other.

And it was sadder still, knowing they
would never have the chance to find out what
might have been.

It was happening again.

A cold sliver of fear coursed through
Rebecca as she walked into town the next
morning. She paused, inhaling a deep breath,
desperately trying to maintain her composure,
before continuing down the street.

But even as she picked up her pace, heading for the church for the weekly meeting of

the Women's Missionary Auxiliary, Rebecca felt that prickly, tingling feeling crawling over her shoulders and creeping up her neck, the feeling that said someone was watching her intently.

She lifted her chin and looked around. Amid the flurry of activity bustling through town, no one seemed to be paying any attention to her.

Stiffening, she pressed forward, marching like a soldier called into battle. But not being able to identify the source of the attention left her edgy and tense. Was she truly being stalked?

During the remainder of her walk, Rebecca mulled over the situation, trying to examine the possibilities from every angle. Several times in recent weeks, she'd felt as though someone had been following her through town. But hadn't she soon discovered the source of her uneasiness each time those shivers of apprehension had raced through her?

Once, Timothy had been looking for her, she remembered clearly. And on several occasions, Grady had appeared by her side soon after she'd experienced those unsettling feelings.

You're just getting paranoid, Rebecca warned herself sternly. All the gunfire and violence in recent days had simply frazzled her nerves. There was no logical basis for suspecting that anyone could be stalking her. And she could give reasonable explanations—namely, Timothy and Grady—for the feelings of anxiety soaring through her in recent days.

Convinced she no longer had a reason to

be fearful of walking through town, Rebecca pulled back her shoulders as she approached the church. But as soon as she stepped into the assembly room, she became acutely aware that the increasing amount of violence in town was the primary topic of discussion among the ladies.

Several of the women, including Lydia, Charlotte, and Agnes, were already settled in their chairs, piercing their needles into the fine lawn fabric, chatting as they sewed on the infant gowns, when Rebecca joined the group.

"I tell you, we need a sheriff to restore law and order to this town, and we need one now," Lydia was muttering as Rebecca sat down beside her.

"But Virgil says a good sheriff is hard to find these days," Charlotte noted. "The town council may have to resort to hiring a reformed gunslinger, he says."

"So the council has some candidates in mind for sheriff?" Agnes asked.

Rebecca leaned forward, focusing on Charlotte, anxiously waiting for her reply. Since the cattle baron had suffered his stroke, Virgil had assumed many of Malcolm Cunningham's official duties as mayor.

"Yes, but I'm not sure how many of them would be willing to accept the job," Charlotte said. "When they find out about all the frenzy goin' on around here, they may withdraw their names from the list of possible candidates."

"Another ruckus broke out in that horrid Red Dog Saloon last night, they say." Lydia shuddered. "Thankfully, no one resorted to

gunfire, but fists were flying hard and fast,
from what I hear."

"I've been seeing more and more disreputa-
ble characters roaming through town," Agnes
added with a frown. "It almost makes a
woman wonder if she's safe walking down
the street."

Listening to the women's remarks, Rebecca
shifted restlessly in her chair. Should she be
paying closer attention to her instincts instead
of groping for logical explanations about her
uneasy feelings each time she walked through
town? Deep inside, she knew something was
amiss, sensed something awry, and she was
running out of reasons for explaining away
those eerie sensations.

"And that Big Al is still on the loose, too,"
Charlotte continued on. "He's the one who
shot those two poor men who tried to wrestle
his gun away the other night."

"All these fatalities must be keeping Parker
Simpson busy down at the mortuary,"
Agnes mused.

"Jacob has his hands full, too," Rebecca
piped in. "He's been so busy that I haven't
even had the chance to talk with him much
this week."

"But you've been working hard, also,
haven't you?" Setting aside her needlework,
Charlotte swung her gaze toward Rebecca.
"Samantha says you've been taking care of
some of Jacob's regular patients lately, along
with your own."

A shot of fear pulsed through Rebecca. For
a fleeting instant, she was terrified Samantha
might have casually mentioned other things

to her mother, things she had promised not to tell. But as soon as Rebecca summoned up the courage to meet Charlotte's steady gaze, she breathed a sigh of relief. Not a trace of suspicion or accusation glimmered from her eyes. Rebecca found only a sense of warmth and concern shimmering from the woman's gaze.

"Yes, I've been quite busy," Rebecca admitted. "As a matter of fact, I called on Mayor Cunningham this morning."

"Well, you be careful out there, making all those calls by yourself," Lydia warned. "A woman alone can't be too careful these days, especially with all these scoundrels drifting through town."

"I'll remember your advice the next time I'm traveling over the plains," Rebecca solemnly declared.

But even as she said the words, she suspected that any potential problems she might encounter would not be lurking on the plains. The source of her uncertainties, she sensed, was hiding somewhere nearby, somewhere on the streets of Hope.

Late in the afternoon, Rebecca strolled through her herb garden, examining the progress of her plantings. A few feet away, Jessica was skipping across the yard with Uly, chattering to the dog as if he could comprehend every word she was saying

Just as Rebecca leaned forward, tilting the spout of her watering can over a patch of chamomile, Jessica scampered up beside her.

"It's too hot to play out here this afternoon," Jessica grumbled. She pointed to the dog, who was hobbling behind her, gasping for breath, and wagging his tongue. "Uly and I are burning up! Can we go back inside the house now?"

With one glance at her daughter's flushed face, Rebecca nodded toward the house. "Run along," she insisted, "and put some water into Uly's bowl while you're getting a drink for yourself. As soon as I water these plants, I'll come inside, too."

As Jessica and Uly scampered across the yard, Rebecca resumed watering the garden. She couldn't blame Jess for seeking relief from the heat of the August day. It was stifling hot, and even her hardiest plants were wilting beneath the sun's unmerciful rays.

Rebecca had just drained the last drop of water from the can when a loud bark wafted through the air. Recognizing the yelp as the sound of a friendly greeting, Rebecca presumed that Uly and Jessica were welcoming a caller at the door. Picking up her skirts, she returned to the house.

No sooner had she stepped inside, Jessica scurried up to her. "Look, Mama!" she shrieked with delight, holding up her hands. A dozen or more hair ribbons, shimmering in a rainbow of colors, dangled from her fingers. "Aren't they beautiful?"

"Why, they're the prettiest ribbons I've ever seen! But who on earth gave you—?"

Rebecca stumbled to a halt just as Grady came up behind Jessica, grinning like the devil. Laughing, the child whirled around and pointed her finger at Grady. "It was Mr.

Cunn'ham!" she shouted with glee. "He's the one who brought hair ribbons to me!"

"How interesting." Rebecca smiled, relishing the joy radiating from her daughter's face.

"Don't you think the yellow one goes with my dress?" Jessica rushed on, holding the ribbon to the bodice of her gown.

"It's a perfect match," Rebecca agreed. "And if you'll run up to your room and get your hairbrush, I'll tie up your hair with your new ribbons."

Letting out a cry of delight, Jessica spun around. As she darted up the stairs, Grady flashed a disarming grin in Rebecca's direction. "I hope you don't mind, but I ran across the ribbons when I was browsing through the stores in town this morning. I couldn't resist getting them for Jessica."

"They're the perfect gift for her. Nothing could have pleased her more." She boldly met his gaze. "But I have to admit, I'm surprised you've given her a present today. Gifts are rare treats around here, except for special occasions."

"Ah, but this is a special occasion, Rebecca." He reached out and skimmed his knuckles over the sweep of her jaw.

His touch sent shivers through her, distracting her from her thoughts. "And exactly what are we celebrating?" she asked in a shaky voice.

"Today." His breath whispered across her neck. "Just today, just being here with you—and Jessica—is reason enough for me to celebrate."

She twinkled up at him. "But that doesn't give you the right to indulge my daughter with extravagant gifts, Grady Cunningham," she teased.

"Maybe not." His lips twitched with the hint of a smile. "But I'd spoil her mother rotten, too, if she'd give me the chance."

"I don't think you need to be given the chance." Her heart swelled with more happiness than she'd ever imagined possible. "You're already spoiling me ... more than you know."

Rebecca was standing beside the cookstove the next afternoon, frying chicken for the evening meal, when a knock sounded at the door.

"I'll get it, 'Becca," Jacob called out.

Listening attentively, Rebecca frowned, acutely aware of Jacob's heavy footsteps as he left his office and trudged toward the front door. With his hectic schedule in recent days, Jacob had spent little time at home, and Rebecca feared he was becoming exhausted from the increasing demand for his medical skills.

She couldn't remember the last time he'd been able to sleep through the night without interruption. Just this morning, he'd left the house before dawn, called away to set the broken legs of a man who'd been thrown from his horse.

Now, as Jacob answered the door, Rebecca prayed he wasn't responding to the knock of yet another caller asking for medical aid. After a busy week of taking care of everyone else's needs, Jacob desperately needed an afternoon to relax and unwind.

Hearing the rumble of male voices in the parlor, Rebecca hastily covered the skillet of chicken on the cookstove and quietly slipped across the room. Curious about the identity of the caller, she peered around the corner of the wall that divided the kitchen from the parlor.

Grady. Merely gazing at him, she felt her heart lurch uncontrollably. More handsome than ever, he was amiably chatting with Jacob.

"It's a nice surprise to find you here at home this afternoon, Jacob," Grady was saying just as Rebecca peeked around the corner.

"It's nice to be here for a change." Jacob lowered his stocky frame into his favorite chair and motioned for Grady to take a seat across from him. "I've been so busy lately, I haven't had a chance to catch my breath."

"From what I hear, the Red Dog supplies you with a new batch of patients every night."

"And the situation won't improve until we find a sheriff who has the guts to restore law and order to this place," Jacob mused, picking up a pipe from the table.

Grady pulled a small pouch from the pocket of his vest. "Maybe this will help ease your worries for a while." He handed the pouch to the physician. "It's a new blend of tobacco. I picked it up in town this morning, thinking you might enjoy it."

"Why, thank you, son." Opening the pouch, Jacob closed his eyes and took a deep whiff of the fragrant aroma. "A fine blend, I must say," he assessed, nodding with obvious appreciation.

"It's nothing," Grady insisted with a careless shrug.

But Grady had done much more than he could ever fathom, Rebecca thought, still standing just outside the room, silently observing the exchange without the men's knowledge of her presence. Already the pinched lines around Jacob's face were giving way to easy smiles, and the rigid set of his shoulders was becoming more relaxed.

Rebecca slipped back into the kitchen, overwhelmed by Grady's thoughtfulness, touched that a pouch of tobacco and the gift of friendship were the perfect remedies for comforting a weary man's soul.

"Musta been some sort of celebration goin' on in Abilene last night," Jacob mumbled the next morning over breakfast. "I'm certain everybody musta left Hope. I actually got to sleep through the night."

Sitting across the table, Rebecca glanced up at her father-in-law and smiled. The sparkle had returned to his eyes, she noticed, and he appeared refreshed this morning. "If you need me to help with any of your patients for the rest of the week, I'll be glad to do what I can," she volunteered, hoping she could ease some of his workload so he wouldn't become exhausted again.

"As a matter of fact, there is something you can do for me." Jacob pushed back from the table. "I dropped by the Cunningham place yesterday, and Malcolm's spirits were lower than I've ever seen them. Would you mind checking on him tomorrow? Your visits always seem to brighten his day."

"I'll be happy to visit the mayor in the morning," Rebecca agreed just as commotion erupted behind the house. Startled by the excited tone in Uly's barks, she rose and darted over to the kitchen window. "What in heaven's name . . ." she wondered aloud.

Peering outside, she immediately discovered the reason for the ruckus. Grady was standing in the yard, laughing as he brushed his hand over the German shepherd's thick coat of fur.

"What's goin' on?" Jacob asked.

Whirling, she scurried to the back door. "It appears Grady is paying a visit to Uly this morning," she explained, stepping outside.

As Rebecca crossed the yard, she saw why Uly was so ecstatic. Grady was presenting the animal with a huge bone. Fresh bits of meat were still clinging to the bone, and the scent was driving Uly insane.

Grady relinquished his gift to the dog just as Rebecca approached. Gazing up at him, she folded her arms over her chest and grinned. "First, Jessica gets hair ribbons. Then you give a pouch of tobacco to Jacob. Now, Uly gets a bone. Should I expect a gift from you tomorrow?" she teased playfully.

"No."

She expected him to laugh or smile or shoot back a humorous reply. She didn't expect to hear such a somber tone in his voice, nor did she anticipate such a serious expression on the chiseled lines of his face. And she'd never dreamed he would pull a small parcel from the folds of his vest and hand it to her.

"You don't have to wait until tomorrow," he insisted, his voice husky and low.

Stunned beyond words, Rebecca looked down at the wrapped gift in disbelief. Her time with David had been so brief that they'd never even had the chance to exchange gifts, and this was the first present she'd ever received from a man. And though she had no idea what was concealed beneath the brown paper wrappings, she was already certain she would treasure its contents until her dying day.

A knot rose in her throat when she discovered a volume of poetry beneath the paper. Bound in leather, the book looked similar to the ones for sale in the Collinses' store, the ones she'd admired on the day she'd been trying to evade Grady . . .

"I saw you looking at it when you were trying to avoid me at the Collinses' store," he said, as if reading her thoughts. "And I thought it might be something you'd like for yourself."

"It's the most wonderful gift I've ever received," she said quietly, pressing the book close to her breast. "I only wish I had some way of thanking you . . . or something to give you in return."

"I can think of a few ways for you to express your appreciation, darlin'." A lazy, provocative smile curled on his lips. "Would you care to hear some of my suggestions?"

She grinned, suddenly feeling as giddy and

carefree as a schoolgirl. He was teasing her, flirting with her, and she was enjoying every second of it. How could any woman resist being courted by a man like Grady Cunningham?

But as her gaze locked on the sensual curves of his mouth, the lighthearted moment vanished. The searing memory of those lips burning into hers, all flame and passion, made her knees go weak. A sharp, almost painful, stab of longing shafted through her. She strained forward, wanting, needing, yearning. "I think I just had an inspiring thought of my own," she whispered.

One little kiss, she thought, would be sufficient enough to express her gratitude to him. With a boldness she never realized she possessed, she lifted her chin and brushed her lips across his. But as she glided her lips over the smooth contours of his mouth, she couldn't find the willpower to pull away.

Grady slipped his arms around her, deepening the pressure of the kiss. Languishing in the warmth of his embrace, she relished the sensuous feelings swirling through her. She closed her eyes, lost in the breathless wonder of it all, until a sudden bark from Uly sliced through the air.

Her eyes shot open. She jerked away from Grady, whirling just as Uly raced around the corner of the house and disappeared from sight, as if chasing an intruder across the yard. Rebecca cringed in horror. "Someone was watching us, I fear."

"More than likely, Uly caught the scent of an animal roaming around the place." Grady scowled, irritated by the interruption. "Just to be safe, though, I'll take a look around and see what I can find."

He stalked across the yard, Rebecca trailing at his heels. Just as he surveyed the empty, flat stretch of land beside the house, Uly hobbled around the corner of the barn. Barking triumphantly, the dog wagged his tail as he trotted up to greet them.

Rebecca laughed. "I'd say Uly looks quite pleased with himself. He must have scared off our intruder."

Grady affectionately patted the animal. "Tomorrow, I'm gonna find the thickest, juiciest beefsteak in this town for Uly."

"As a reward for being a good watchdog?"

Grinning, Grady hurled open the barn doors. "And for giving me some more time alone with you."

Without giving her the chance to protest, he led her into the confines of the frame building and removed the book from her grasp. Then he slipped his hands around her waist and pulled her close to him, emboldened by the kiss she'd offered so freely only a few moments earlier. "As I recall, you were expressing your appreciation to me before Uly started barking. And I believe we were right about here . . ."

He lowered his head and clamped his lips over hers, eager to resume what she had started, anxious to take more of what she might give. He boldly plunged his tongue inside her mouth, exploring the sweet taste of her. To his surprise, she greeted the invasion by matching his move, hesitantly swirling her tongue around his and coiling her arms around his shoulders.

Fiery trails of desire burned through him, ignited by the feel of her breasts crushed against his chest. He ground his lips over hers with more pressure, surging his tongue deeper into her mouth. Hot waves of passion flooded his hardened loins as he clamped his hands over the gentle swell of her hips. Pressing her against his arousal, he rasped against her lips, "Feel what you're doing to me, darlin'?"

A soft whimper escaped from her throat, and she sagged against him. His hands roamed over her back, then drifted over her ribs. Still kissing her, he cupped his hands over her breasts. Feeling the hardness of her nipples protruding from her bodice, he burned to remove the barriers that were preventing him from running his fingers and tongue over the tips of those swollen mounds.

He dragged his mouth away from hers, intending to unbutton her dress and fulfill his unspoken fantasies. But as his fingers fumbled with the first button, he heard a shuffling noise behind him.

"What in the hell?" He whipped around just as Uly trotted into the barn.

The dog scampered up to them with a friendly bark. Grady edged back from Rebecca, cursing under his breath, knowing the spell of the moment had been shattered.

Rebecca stifled a soft giggle as she smoothed down the wrinkled seams of her dress. "Not much gets past Uly around here, I'm afraid."

Grady managed a wry grin, brushing his hand over the dog's furry coat. "Sorry, old boy. Too bad you'll never know how good that beefsteak might have been."

Chapter 12

Ribbons of lavender and rose were streaming across the Kansas sky as the buggy lurched and swayed over the trail the next morning.

But Rebecca was only vaguely aware of the unfolding beauty and the jarring ride. Approaching the Cunningham estate, she was consumed by thoughts of Grady and his father.

Though she'd never been prone to meddling in the affairs of other people, Rebecca sensed the severed relationship between the Cunningham men could use a gentle nudge in the right direction. Was it possible she could say something to Malcolm Cunningham that might pave the way for a reconciliation?

She sighed, knowing she shouldn't allow herself to become so deeply involved in Grady's life. Logic said she should cut off her budding feelings for the man before they went into full bloom. Common sense made her acutely aware that she shouldn't continue risking the chance of being associated with him.

Yet, her heart refused to listen to anything her mind had to say. Deep inside, she knew her soul wasn't responding to her intellect, but only to her emotions.

Despite all of her misgivings and fears about Grady, she was discovering that she genuinely cared for the man. Each new day was like opening a treasure chest filled with untold riches. She was constantly discovering new things about him, little things that made her heart flutter and her pulse pound.

She adored the way he winked at her when no one else was looking, as if they were sharing a deliciously naughty secret. She loved the way he wore his Stetson, cocked low over his forehead. And she relished the way his deep-throated laughter wrapped around her like a warm blanket on a cold winter's night, filling her with joy to the depths of her soul.

Distracted by her thoughts, Rebecca almost passed the entrance to the magnificent stone mansion. Quickly, she veered the buggy to the left and turned into the Cunningham estate.

A few moments later, Rebecca noticed a man of medium build emerging from the mansion with a tall, thin woman. Longtime employees of the Cunningham family, Frank and Helen Taylor were the primary reasons why operations at the vast estate had continued to run smoothly since the mayor's stroke. A stern, disciplined woman who rarely laughed, Helen directed the mansion's housekeeping staff. Frank, a quiet man with a sun-weathered face, served as the foreman of the cattle ranch.

Rebecca was retrieving her basket of herbs from the buggy when the couple stepped forward to greet her. "I'm mighty glad to see that you're here to check on the mayor, Mrs. Summers," Helen said.

Noticing the woman's worried frown, Rebecca stilled. "Is he displaying any unusual symptoms?"

"He's not running a fever or complaining about any aches or pains. But he refused his breakfast tray this morning, and he's more irritable than normal, I'm afraid. Nothing seems to please him."

Rebecca retrieved a packet of dried chamomile from her wicker basket, grateful she'd remembered to bring an assortment of herbs with her. "Some chamomile tea should improve his appetite," she predicted confidently, handing the packet to Helen.

Pushing back the brim of his hat, Frank peered into the basket. "You got somethin' for his disposition, too?"

"I wish I did," Rebecca admitted, suddenly seized by a flash of inspiration. "Frank, didn't you build a chair with wheels for the mayor?"

The man nodded. "But he hasn't seen it. To be honest, I've never even mentioned it to him. He's never acted like he's interested in leavin' that room of his."

"Well, he's leaving his room today," Rebecca predicted. "He needs some fresh air and sunshine, and riding through the grounds of the estate in his new chair should boost his spirits. Can you bring the chair to his room in a few minutes?"

"Whatever you say, Mrs. Summers."

As Frank ambled toward the barn, Helen ushered Rebecca into the mansion. Though Rebecca had visited the mayor's home on many occasions, she never ceased to be amazed by its opulent splendor. With its elegant furnishings, plush rugs, and oil paintings, the mansion seemed fitting enough for royalty. Now, entering the grand foyer, Rebecca admired the glittering crystal chandelier and the beautiful craftsmanship of the wide, curving staircase.

After escorting Rebecca to the mayor's private quarters, the housekeeper turned to leave. "Good luck, ma'am."

"Thanks, Helen." With a bright smile on her face Rebecca hurled open the door. "Good morning, Mayor Cunningham."

Seated in an overstuffed chair beside a large desk, the man glanced up and scowled. "That's what you think," he muttered.

Ignoring the mayor's gruffness, Rebecca breezed into the room. She paused beside the dark, velvet draperies. "Take a look outside, and you'll see what a good morning it is," she insisted, pulling back the window coverings.

Streams of sunlight poured into the room. Cringing, Malcolm squinted against the glare of the bright rays. "Why in the hell did you do that?" he growled.

"Sitting in this dark, dreary room all the time isn't good for you, Mayor. Sunshine always brightens the spirits."

"I don't need my spirits brightened," he

snapped, turning away from the light flooding through the glass panes.

"I believe that's a matter of opinion," Rebecca retorted with sugary sweetness.

His bushy white brows narrowed, deepening his scowl. Gazing at the disgruntled man, Rebecca suddenly realized why Grady referred to his father as "King" Cunningham. In spite of his irritable temperament and failing health, there was a regal demeanor about the silver-haired cattle baron. His broad shoulders were erect and staunch, his gray eyes stormy and bright, and an air of dignity radiated from the proud tilt of his head and stubborn thrust of his jaw.

At that instant, Frank rapped on the door. "I'm ready whenever you are, Mrs. Summers," he announced.

"You're just in time, Frank." Rebecca signaled for him to enter the room. "We have a surprise for you this morning, Mr. Cunningham."

Malcolm stiffened with disdain as the foreman rolled the chair through the door. "Wheelchairs are for old people," he spat out, glowering at the contraption.

"Try it, just this once," Rebecca urged, "and see how you like it."

"I won't like it."

"How do you know?" she challenged. "Give it a chance, Mr. Cunningham. You might be surprised at how much freedom it gives you. And, besides, Frank spent a lot of time working on this chair. The least you can do is try it out."

His eyes narrowed with suspicion. "Is that true, Frank?"

The foreman dipped his head. "It took me a couple of weeks, workin' nights, to put it together," he admitted.

Malcolm heaved a sigh of resignation. "Very well, then. I'll try it, just this once." He cast a scathing glare in Rebecca's direction. "But I'll hold you responsible if I fall out of this contraption and crack my skull open, young lady. I know you're the one responsible for this insane idea."

Rebecca smiled. "I'll assume complete responsibility for your safety, Mayor."

Drawing his lips into a tight line, Malcolm awkwardly boosted himself from the overstuffed chair. Unable to maintain control of the left side of his body, he was forced to lean against Frank for support. "Let's get this over with," he grumbled as he collapsed into the wheeled chair.

Rebecca grasped the wooden handles of the chair, acutely aware of Malcolm's silence as she steered him through the house. When they came to the front entrance, Frank opened the door, clearing the way for Rebecca to roll the chair outside. "Enjoy yourself, Mayor," he said, tipping his hat.

Malcolm merely grunted, lapsing into silence once again. Following a winding trail through the vast grounds, Rebecca studied her surroundings with interest. Numerous buildings for storing feed and grain were scattered throughout the estate, and a large herd of cattle was grazing in the distance.

She halted beneath the shade of a black

walnut tree, sweeping her gaze over the immense stretch of land. "Your estate is very impressive, Mayor," she remarked quietly.

"I know."

Was there a trace of sadness in his voice? A tinge of regret? Curious, she kneeled down beside him. To her surprise, she discovered that his eyes had taken on a cloudy, distant look.

"You know, my wife never liked it here," he said, gazing across the land. "She was a proper Boston lady, and this untamed frontier was too wild for her."

"Kansas isn't for everyone, I suppose." Rebecca paused. "Sometimes, I think it's hardest on families."

"Ah, yes, families." Malcolm winced. "Life was never easy here for my family. Of course, all of my family is gone now."

"All of them?" Before he could respond, Rebecca rushed on. "But what about your son, Grady?"

The line of his jaw tightened. "Grady is no longer my son, not after the way he shamed the Cunningham name."

"But everyone makes mistakes, Mayor." Rebecca knew she was pushing the matter, but she couldn't seem to stop herself. She desperately wanted this man and his son to be reunited. "Have you ever considered the possibility of reconciling your differences with him?"

His eyes darkened like angry thunderclouds. "I'm not a damn fool, woman. I've got enough sense to know why Grady would want to settle our differences. A great deal of land and money is at stake here. Acknowledging Grady as my sole surviving heir means he could expect a large inheritance."

"But what if Grady didn't need your money or land? Would you consider a reconciliation with him, then?"

"Of course not," Malcolm claimed indignantly. "Besides, he couldn't have amassed a fortune. From what I hear, he's been drifting all over the state for years."

"He's been roaming the plains, hunting bison. And he has developed markets back East, profitable markets, for buffalo hides and meat." Rebecca paused. "Grady has become a wealthy man, Mr. Cunningham. He has no need for your land or money."

"And how do you know all this?" Suspicion laced his words.

"Because I've recently become acquainted with Grady. He shipped out several carloads of buffalo hides from the railroad facilities here last week. We met when he was seeking medical care for one of his crew members."

A sparkle of hope glimmered from the depths of Malcolm's eyes. "Virgil Collins told me the boy was back in Hope. He keeps me informed about council matters and the activities in town. But I never realized ..."

His gaze dropped, then lingered on the useless limp arm and hand lying across his lap; a look of anguish replaced the gleam of optimism in his eyes.

As Malcolm cringed in dismay, Rebecca sensed the reason for the man's sudden stab of pain. Once strong and powerful, the baron king could not tolerate the thought of being

perceived as weak and helpless by anyone—
especially his own son.

Yet, Rebecca was positive this father continued to hold affection in his heart for the child
he had disowned. The ray of hope glinting
from his eyes had told her all she needed to
know.

But would his stubborn pride stand in the
way of a reconciliation between them?

"I've had enough fresh air and sunshine, I
believe," he announced stiffly. "I would like
to return to my room now."

"As you wish, Mayor," Rebecca agreed, rising to depart for the mansion.

Rebecca pulled into town shortly before
noon, anxious to share the news of her visit to
the Cunningham estate with Grady. Gauging
Malcolm's emotions toward his son was a
small step, and nothing more, toward eventually restoring their relationship. Yet, Rebecca
wanted to relay her findings to Grady as soon
as possible.

She was speeding by the church just as
Timothy appeared beside the road. "Rebecca!" he called, waving to catch her attention.

She pulled back the reins and rolled to a
stop. "Good morning, Timothy."

"It's wonderful to see you again." He
paused, appearing hesitant and uncertain.
"May we talk for a moment? If you'd like, we
could simply stroll through the church
grounds."

"Under any other circumstances, I would
be delighted to accompany you for a walk,"
Rebecca said with genuine sincerity. "But I've

been at the Cunningham estate all morning, and I'm anxious to get home and check on Jessica. I'm sure you understand."

"But this will only take a few moments, Rebecca. And I truly need to talk to you."

Hearing the urgency resonating from his voice, seeing the anxiety glimmering from his gaze, Rebecca didn't have the heart to refuse his request. "I've been gone all morning, so I suppose a few more minutes won't matter," she conceded with a smile.

He held out a hand to steady her as she descended from the buggy. Detecting a trace of tension skittering through him, Rebecca wondered if he was nervous about making arrangements to call on her again.

"I'm grateful you could spend a few minutes with me, Rebecca." He fell into step beside her as they sauntered over the well-worn path that circled around the church property. "I've been struggling with a matter for several days now, one that has become quite distressing to me, and I've come to the conclusion that it's my Christian duty to talk with you about it."

Assuming the escalating occurrences of gunfights were weighing heavily on his mind, Rebecca sighed. "The violence has become everyone's major concern, Timothy. And I'm beginning to wonder if we're ever going to get a new sheriff. Who would want to tackle a job like that?"

"All the commotion has been unsettling for everyone," Timothy agreed somberly. "However, the increase of violence in Hope isn't my primary concern at the moment."

Startled, Rebecca stumbled to a halt. "What's wrong, Timothy?" she asked, truly puzzled and concerned.

Sighing, he kneaded the nape of his neck in frustration. "It's a matter that concerns you, Rebecca. I've been hesitant to discuss the issue, fearing you would question my motives or be offended by my interference. But I became convinced I should approach the topic with you when I saw ..."

As he floundered for words, Rebecca's heart lurched with fear. "What did you see?"

He inhaled a sharp breath, then spilled out the words quickly. "I saw you and Grady Cunningham together. You were standing behind your house, locked in an intimate embrace."

She felt the blood draining from her face. "That was ... you?"

Grimacing, he nodded. "I never intended to intrude upon your privacy, Rebecca. My intentions were purely honorable, I can assure you. I merely intended to call on you, unannounced, and pay my respects for a few moments. But I heard some commotion behind the house, and when I went to investigate, I saw you with him ..."

"I knew someone had been watching when Uly started barking." She heaved a tremulous sigh. "I'm just sorry it had to be you."

"I'm sorry, too."

Rebecca studied the toes of her slippers. What more could be said between them?

Timothy finally broke the silence. "I know this should be none of my concern, Rebecca, but I feel compelled to tell you what I've heard about Grady Cunningham. It appears he—"

"I'm well aware of Grady's reputation in Hope." She lifted her chin, boldly meeting his gaze. "In fact, the auxiliary ladies were quite distressed when they learned about his return to town."

"So they've warned you about him?"

"They've told me everything they know about him—and more, I'm afraid." She tilted back her head, gazing up into the sky, despising the injustice of it all. "Strange, isn't it? A court of law proclaimed the man's innocence, yet everyone continues to condemn him."

"It's an unfortunate set of circumstances," Timothy agreed. "But I don't know of any excuses that can justify his most recent behavior. He may not have committed a crime, but I find his conduct to be quite distasteful, as well as inappropriate."

"His most recent behavior?" Confusion reeled through Rebecca. "I don't understand."

"I suppose you haven't heard, then." He sucked in a shuddering breath. "Mr. Cunningham made a wager with his cronies at the Red Dog Saloon ... concerning you. He agreed to the challenge of winning your favor within two weeks. And half the men in town wagered you wouldn't allow him to court you." He grasped her hand tightly. "I hope you haven't become a victim of the man's deceitfulness, Rebecca."

"Of course not, Timothy. Grady Cunningham couldn't fool me." She forced a bright smile on her lips, determined to conceal the havoc reeling through her. "I knew about that silly little wager of his all along. Ridiculous, isn't it?"

"It's downright appalling, if you ask me," he muttered.

"But at least no harm has been done," Rebecca assured him. "Thankfully, I'm well aware of what a scoundrel that man can be." Setting aside the matter as casually as she could, she picked up her skirts to leave. "I would love to chat with you for a while longer, Timothy, but I truly need to get home to Jessica now."

"I understand, Rebecca. Allow me to escort you back to the buggy."

"Certainly." Rebecca slipped her hand around Timothy's outstretched arm. Head held high, she fell into step beside him, praying the shuffle of her footsteps and the rustle of her skirts would conceal the sound of her heart shattering into pieces.

Something was wrong. Dreadfully wrong.

From the moment he saw Rebecca, Grady knew something was disturbing her.

As soon as he'd entered the house, Jessica had hurled her arms around his neck and planted a wet kiss on his cheek. But Rebecca had remained distant, not even meeting his gaze.

Now, ten minutes after his arrival, Grady still had no idea why she was being so aloof and reserved. Standing at the worktable in Jacob's office, she was sorting through her precious herbs, placing dried stems and crushed leaves into glass containers. Her movements were stiff and jerky, and her back was ramrod stiff.

"Can Uly and I go outside to play, Mama?" Jessica called out.

"As long as you stay in the backyard," Rebecca replied.

She resumed working, never once acknowledging Grady's presence. Determined to dispel her worries, Grady slipped up behind her and slid his hands around her waist. Nuzzling the tender skin along the curve of her neck, he whispered, "You look like you need some good lovin', darlin'."

She jerked away from his hold and whirled on him so quickly that he lurched forward, almost losing his balance. "That's the last thing I need from you, Grady Cunningham," she bit out.

"What's gotten into you?" he snapped back, stunned by her abrupt manner.

"I'm tired of playing your little games." Her eyes crackled like blue fire. "And this *is* a game we're playing, isn't it?"

A sickening feeling stormed through him. "What do you mean?"

"I know everything, Grady." Her chin was quivering, her voice trembling. "I heard all about the wager with your friends at the Red Dog Saloon."

"Oh, God." Pain stabbed through him with the intensity of a knife slicing through his soul. "It's not what you think, Rebecca."

"It's not?" Her laughter was harsh, hurting. "I wasn't just a diversion for you during your visit to town?"

His hands were trembling as he grasped her shoulders. "Listen to me, Rebecca. I—"

"Listen to you?" Lines of anguish marred her face. "I've listened to you enough, Grady. I was even beginning to trust you! I thought I saw something in you that no one else could see. I thought you were a decent, honorable man who was being misjudged by everyone else in this town. I thought you were a man who was different than any I'd ever known, a man who could possibly care for me ..." Her voice trembled, then broke into a choked sob. "And now ..."

"And now ... ?"

She tossed back her head, glaring up at him. "And now I know differently."

The anguish trembling in her voice, the pain glistening in her eyes, affected Grady like nothing ever had. Something gripped his chest, something tight and constricting. How could this have happened? How could a harmless wager, conceived in jest and fun, have become such a nightmare of horrors? After all, as soon as he'd realized the error of his ways, he'd tried to right his wrong and call off the wager.

Still, he'd never meant to hurt her, never intended to make those beautiful blue eyes cloud with tears. And he hated himself for inflicting so much pain on her. Confessing his sins was his only option. He sucked in a shuddering breath and began.

"It all started as a harmless game, Rebecca. When the guys down at the Red Dog heard that you stitched up Carl's head, they all talked about how you never allowed any of them to court you. Obtaining the affections of the most beautiful, unattainable woman in town sounded like an intriguing challenge to me. So I gambled I could win your heart within two weeks."

"I see." The pain lining her face was so intense, so raw, that Grady could hardly bear to look at her. "So have you enjoyed your winnings?"

"There were no winnings for me, Rebecca. As soon as we got back from the Fords' homestead, I withdrew from the wager, conceding defeat, because I knew you didn't deserve to be a pawn in my heartless little game." He raked a hand through his hair in frustration. "Can't you see what happened? I made the bet before . . ."

"Before what?"

He couldn't resist reaching out and skimming his fingers across her satin-soft cheek. "Before I fell in love with you, Rebecca."

Her eyes widened incredulously. "You're in love . . . with me?" she whispered in stunned disbelief.

"I suppose I shouldn't be surprised that it's difficult for you to believe me." His gaze darted to her open, parted lips, lingered there. Bolts of desire shot through him. "But you couldn't be any more stunned than I am. I've never truly been in love before, Rebecca. I never realized what it was like to feel so intensely, so deeply, until you came into my life. And I never knew what it was like, wanting to spend every minute of the day—and night—with one woman."

She caught her lip between her teeth, looking as if she were considering his words, appearing as if she desperately wanted to believe them. But tears welled afresh in those cornflower-blue eyes, devastating him more than he could have ever imagined.

"Love encompasses much more than just wanting to be with someone, Grady. Love means you would never risk the chance of publicly embarrassing someone. If you truly love a woman, you'd never want to subject her to scorn and ridicule. You'd never want to smear her name, or even remotely involve her in a scandalous situation. And you wouldn't want to make her the laughingstock of the entire town."

The tears swelling in her eyes threatened to tumble down her cheeks. Grady lifted a trembling hand to her face, swabbing away the moisture clinging to her thick, dark lashes. When she met his gaze again, sparks of anger were flaming from her eyes. "And you claim to love me?" Her laughter was mocking, strangled and low. "That's hard for me to believe, Grady. To be honest, I think you don't even know what love is."

Her scathing rejection cut through him, swift and hard. Nothing—not even the razor-sharp edge of a spear—could have wounded him more deeply.

His fists clenched into tight balls. He should've known she'd never truly believed in him. He'd been a damn fool to think this woman was different from all the rest. No one had ever believed in him, after all. He'd hoped—God, how he'd hoped—that Rebecca was the single exception in his life.

But he'd been wrong. Damned wrong.

He yanked his hat from the table. "I should have known better," he muttered, jamming the Stetson over his head as he stalked to the door.

"You seem awfully sad, Mama." Jessica's dark brows narrowed with concern as her mother tucked her into bed for the night.

"I am sad, Jess," she admitted, managing a weak smile. "But feeling sad isn't wrong. Sometimes, things happen in life that make you hurt inside."

The girl's frown deepened. "But what happened to make you so sad? Did somebody ... die?"

She hadn't realized her emotions were so visible. Wishing she could mask the anguish rolling through her, Rebecca brushed back a stray lock of hair from Jessica's forehead. "No one has died, sweetheart," she finally answered. "I'm just feeling a little blue tonight. That's all."

She tucked the quilt beneath her daughter's chin, then gently brushed her lips across her forehead. "Sweet dreams, my Jessica."

"Good night, Mama," Jessica murmured.

As soon as the child's eyes drifted shut, Rebecca quietly retreated into the privacy of her room. Deciding to retire early for the night, she donned a white cotton gown and crawled into bed.

She tried to forget the events of the day, attempted to clear her mind of the turbulent thoughts that had been whirling through her for hours. But the quiet stillness of the night only intensified the conflicting emotions clashing within her. A battle was raging deep inside her soul, ripping her heart into shreds. She was still stinging from learning about Grady's cruel wager, still stunned from hearing his proclamation of love for her. And she was terrified that her worst fears were becoming reality. Was she already losing the respectability that she longed to retain among the people of Hope?

Sometime during the night, she finally drifted into a restless slumber. Only vaguely conscious of the sharp pops crackling through the darkness, she buried her head deeper into the pillow.

With the dawn of a new day, Rebecca was determined to start life afresh. But her spirits plummeted when she found a note from Jacob on the kitchen table. Once again, he'd been summoned to the aid of another gunshot victim during the night.

In spite of the distressing turn of events, Rebecca attempted to set aside her worries and fears for Jessica's sake. Trying to maintain a degree of normalcy in their lives, she quietly prepared breakfast and called Jessica to the table.

When they were finished with the meal, Rebecca glanced over at her daughter and smiled. "Let's take a walk into town this morning, Jess. I need to get a few supplies at the Collinses' store. And while we're there, you can pick out a piece of candy for yourself."

Thrilled, Jessica shrieked with delight.

Within a few moments, they left the house, setting off for town, hand in hand.

The walk brightened Rebecca's spirits considerably. By the time they arrived at the store, she was actually laughing again, cheered by Jessica's company and chatter. But a tiny pulse of alarm riveted through her when she approached the counter.

"Is something wrong, Charlotte?" she asked, concerned by the lines of worry marring the woman's brow.

"Everything is wrong," Charlotte grumbled. "Another drifter from the Red Dog went on a shootin' spree last night. This time, three men got hit, and somebody shot out the glass from the window in the back room here at the store." She shuddered. "I tell you, Rebecca, I don't know what we're going to do in this town. It's getting worse everyday."

"Has there been any progress on finding a sheriff?"

The frizzy red curls around Charlotte's thin face bobbed up and down as she shook her head in dismay. "Virgil met with the town council last night. After they voted to hire a man from Abilene, they sent a wire to him. But he shot one right back, turning down the offer."

At that moment, Rebecca felt a tug on her gown. "Mama, can I have a piece of red candy in the glass case over there?"

"Sure, Jess." Rebecca smiled down at her daughter. "Just tell Mr. Collins which one you want, and I'll pay for it along with the rest of my bill."

While Jessica selected her candy, Rebecca

turned to Charlotte and placed an order for a small sack of flour and a spool of white thread. After placing her purchases in her shopping basket, Rebecca turned to leave. "I guess we should be getting home now, Charlotte."

"Be careful out there," Charlotte warned.

"We will," Rebecca promised, grateful for her friend's concern.

Grasping Jessica's hand, Rebecca left the store. But they'd taken only a few steps across the planked boardwalk when a disturbance erupted behind them. A thunderous crash split through the air, sounding like something had been hurled against the wall of a building. A chorus of men's angry shouts bellowed above the melee, along with the crunch of splintering wood.

Rebecca picked up her pace, clinging more tightly to Jessica's fingers. But as the commotion intensified, a wave of panic swept through the throng of pedestrians on the boardwalk. Suddenly, boots were clattering over the planked walk at a frantic pace.

The crowd surged forward with the force of a tidal wave. People whizzed by Rebecca so quickly that she staggered, nearly losing her balance. As the crowd thickened, shoving its way to safety, Rebecca struggled to hold on to Jessica's small hand.

But Jessica's fingers suddenly slipped from her grasp. To Rebecca's horror, the child was swept away in the rush of the crowd.

"Jessica!" Rebecca cried, straining to grasp her daughter, unable to reach her through the swarm of people rushing by.

Rebecca shoved her way through the crowd in a frenzied panic, watching helplessly as Jessica tumbled from the edge of the raised boardwalk. The child stumbled into the street just as the blasts of gunfire splintered through the air.

"Wildfire!" a man shouted.

Rebecca lunged for Jessica, horrified as the child's screams sliced through air. "Mama! My leg!" Jessica screamed.

In one, swift movement, Rebecca reached down and scooped the child up into her arms. Seeing the blood oozing through the child's white stockings and streaming down her leg, Rebecca thought she was going to faint.

Her beloved daughter, her precious child, had just been shot.

Chapter 13

The next few minutes consisted of nothing but blurred images and muffled sounds for Rebecca. The buzz of voices and the frenzy of activity swarming around her seemed very distant and far away. Numb with shock, she stood frozen, clinging to Jessica.

She was trying to soothe the child's frantic sobs when Virgil and Charlotte suddenly emerged from the crowd and swept them back into the safety of the store. Cradling Jessica in her arms, Rebecca found herself scurrying toward the back room with Charlotte.

"Jessica will be comfortable here until Jacob arrives," Charlotte said in a comforting tone, motioning to a small cot in the corner of the room. "And there's a wash basin here, too."

As Rebecca gently lowered Jessica to the cot, the child winced in pain. "I need Grandpa now, Mama!" she wailed.

"Where is Jacob, Rebecca?" Charlotte asked. "I can send someone for him."

"He's either at the Grand Central or Hope

Cottage, taking care of the gun shot victims from last night's shootings," Rebecca managed to say.

"Then we'll get him here right away." Without another word, Charlotte spun around and darted back into the store.

Rebecca drew in a shuddering breath and peeled back the blood-stained stocking from Jessica's leg. "I know you're hurting, sweetheart," she soothed, "but let me take a look at your leg before Grandpa gets here."

Jessica's shrieks of horror had subsided to whimpers now, but her face was pale and her eyes bright with tears. "I'm scared, Mama," she said, her voice trembling and weak. "I'm so scared ..."

"You're going to be just fine, Miss Jess," Rebecca assured the frightened child. She pulled back the hem of her own gown, yanked on the tail of her petticoat, and ripped off a wide strip. Then she dipped the fabric into the wash basin and turned back to her daughter. "This won't hurt at all," she explained in a gentle tone. "I'm just going to clean your leg."

Brushing Jessica's petticoats and skirts to one side, Rebecca became acutely aware of the dark, singed patches in the child's clothing, along with the lingering scent of gunpowder. She shuddered, realizing the bullet had ripped through Jessica's gown and undergarments before hitting her leg.

She dabbed the wet rag over the girl's tender skin, gently swabbing away the blood, trying to assess her condition from the viewpoint of a nurse examining a patient. The flow of crimson from the wound was decreasing, it appeared. Encouraged that Jessica was fully conscious and alert, Rebecca suspected the bullet had not penetrated her flesh. "Is your leg hurting a lot, Jess?" she asked softly.

"It's hurting, but not so bad that I want to start screaming again," Jessica tried to explain.

Rebecca had just finished cleansing the wound when Jacob entered the room, flushed and breathless. "What's all this, Miss Jess?" he asked, rushing to the child's side.

"It's my leg, Grandpa!"

Wasting not a moment, Jacob examined the wound. After carefully studying the injured area, he breathed a sigh of relief. "You're a lucky lady, little girl. The bullet just grazed your leg, scraping the skin as it whizzed by you."

"Then everything is going to be all right, just like Mama said?"

"It sure is, darlin'," Jacob said, his voice suddenly clogged with emotion. Blinking rapidly, he turned away from the child and retrieved a cotton bandage from the depths of his black bag. "Just let Grandpa wrap this bandage around your leg, and then we'll go home."

Charlotte and Virgil, along with a dozen or so neighbors and friends, were gathered together in the store, anxiously waiting for news about Jessica when Rebecca finally emerged from the back room.

"How is she, Rebecca?" Charlotte asked.

"Jacob says the bullet didn't enter her leg, but she has a flesh wound," Rebecca was explaining just as Jacob came up behind her, carrying Jessica in his arms. Her head was resting on his shoulder, and her eyes were closed.

Sighs of relief filtered through the crowd as they left the store. Fortunately, Jacob had driven the buggy into town when he'd been summoned to the Red Dog during the wee hours of the morning. Now, exiting the building, Rebecca was relieved to see that Jacob had parked the vehicle in front of the door. She hastily hoisted herself into the buggy so that Jacob could place Jessica into her arms.

As the buggy lurched forward, Rebecca assessed the main street of Hope. An air of tension was still hovering through the town, she detected, but the uproar had subsided. Very few pedestrians were lingering on the boardwalk, and all was quiet near the Red Dog, where the disturbance had originally erupted.

Too weary to inquire about the cause of the commotion, too exhausted to discuss the possibilities of locating the scoundrel responsible for injuring her daughter, Rebecca cuddled Jessica against her more tightly, resting her chin on the soft crown of the child's dark hair. Later, there would be plenty of time for asking questions and investigating the tragedy. For now, all she wanted was to forget the horrid events of the morning.

As soon as they arrived home, Jacob carried his granddaughter to her room. Rebecca removed Jessica's soiled, tattered clothing and slipped a nightgown over her head. Then she turned down the covers and tucked the child into bed. "Get some rest, sweetheart."

Jessica willingly complied with her mother's request, nestling her head into the pillow and closing her eyes. Assured the child was resting comfortably, Rebecca quietly left the room.

If for no other reason than to conceal her alarm from Jessica, Rebecca had tried to remain calm and composed throughout the horrid events of the morning. But now that the crisis was over, she no longer possessed the strength to maintain her brave facade. Retreating to the first floor, she felt the reality of the situation hitting her with full force. Her legs were trembling as she swept across the room toward Jacob.

"Oh, Jacob," she whispered tearfully, collapsing into his arms, nuzzling her head against his chest. "It was so horrible . . ."

"I can imagine." He groaned at the thought. "I'm not certain I could've reacted as calmly as you. Just thank God our Jess wasn't wounded more seriously. I don't believe I could've found the strength to extract a bullet from my own grandchild."

"I'm grateful your strength didn't have to be tested." Tears of relief swelled in Rebecca's eyes and tumbled down her cheeks. "Just knowing she was caught in the line of fire has been horrible enough for both of us to—"

"Rebecca! Jacob!" Grady's voice bellowed from the porch. Without waiting for a response, he stormed through the door, whipping into the house with the force of a tornado. "I just heard . . ."

He stumbled to a halt, his eyes wide with fright, his face pale and drawn. "How is she?" he asked, frantically searching Rebecca's tear-stained face.

"She's resting comfortably now, thank goodness," Rebecca said.

"Fortunately, the bullet only grazed her leg," Jacob added.

Grady sucked in a shuddering breath, his gaze locking on Rebecca once again. "And are you all right?"

"Just shaken. And trying to recover from the shock of it all."

Relief seemed to flood through him, easing the tightness from his rigid stance. "Can I see Jessica for just a moment? I won't disturb her, I promise. I just need to see her."

His eyes were begging, pleading, with her. She was overwhelmed by the depths of emotion shimmering from his gaze. "I understand, Grady," she whispered and led the way up the stairs.

But nothing could have prepared her for the expression that flickered across his face when he peered into Jessica's room. As his gaze lingered on the sleeping child, something soft and warm stirred within the depths of those wolf-gray eyes, something so moving and poignant that Rebecca trembled inside.

How could she harbor resentments against a man who obviously cared so deeply for her daughter? The surge of love flooding his face suddenly washed away the anger and pain that had flared within her during their heated argument of the previous evening. Maybe he truly cared for her as much as he cared for her daughter, she thought.

Grady remained unusually quiet until they

joined Jacob in the parlor. "This is like a nightmare," he muttered. Raking a hand through his hair in frustration, he groaned. "I'm just glad it wasn't any worse for Jessica."

Nodding, Jacob puffed on his pipe, sending the scent of tobacco drifting through the room. "The whole blasted town has gone insane," the physician mumbled.

"Surely somebody will be willing to talk about the commotion at the Red Dog." Grady turned to Rebecca. "Tell me every detail about this morning, Rebecca. Review every second for me. Tell me what you saw, what you heard, what you sensed from the instant you left the store with Jessica."

She sank into the nearest chair, dreading the thought of reviewing the horrid event, moment by moment. Still, hearing the urgency in Grady's voice, she didn't have the heart to refuse his request.

Grady listened intently as she described the outbreak of noises, the frenzied panic, the surge of the crowd along the boardwalk, the blast of gunfire. When she'd finished, his mouth twisted into a frown. "Do you know of anyone who might have seen the sniper?"

"Virgil and Charlotte might have witnessed something, but I don't recall seeing any other familiar faces. When I lost my grip on Jessica in the crowd, nothing else seemed to matter." Rebecca sighed in frustration. "I'm certain the shots were fired from the area around the Red Dog Saloon, but I couldn't see who was firing the gun. Too many people were swarming around me on the boardwalk, blocking my line of vision, when I lunged for Jessica."

"I'll talk to some of the regulars at the Red Dog this afternoon. They should be able to tell me something." The line of Grady's jaw hardened with steely resolve. "Mark my words, whoever is responsible for injuring Jessica will pay dearly. And it'll be the last time he'll ever hurt an innocent child."

He snapped around, turning to leave. As he stalked toward the door, Rebecca called out to him. "What do you intend to do, Grady?"

"Whatever it takes." Every muscle in his body went whipcord taut. "First, I'm gonna find the bastard who went on a shootin' spree this morning. Then I intend to restore some peace and order to this blasted town, if it's the last thing I ever do."

He slammed the door behind him, rattling the window panes. Rebecca winced, grateful she was not standing in the path of his fury.

Grady marched into town, trying to ignore the turmoil raging inside him. Just as he neared the railroad tracks, a whistle screeched through the air. He paused, watching a train pull away from the depot. Puffs of black smoke billowed through the skies as the engine chugged its way along the tracks, heading out of town.

For a fleeting instant, Grady was tempted to hop on board. The idea of leaving this town, riding as far away as he could go, was almost irresistible.

He didn't want to get involved in the problems swarming through this Kansas hellhole. Didn't want to care about what happened here. After all, no one had greeted him with open arms when he'd returned to Hope.

But long after the train had disappeared, Grady was still standing beside the tracks, held at bay by something far stronger than his desire to leave.

And he was painfully, awkwardly, aware of what that something was.

Images of a dark-haired beauty and her enchanting daughter danced through his mind, images so powerful and vivid that he couldn't bear the thought of never seeing them again. And knowing that Jessica's life had come dangerously close to being snatched away from his grasp was almost more than he could fathom.

The mere thought of someone harming the child ripped his heart into shreds. God help the man who'd pulled the trigger outside the Red Dog this morning. As soon as he got his hands on the scoundrel, the man would rue the day he was born.

Fury assaulted him, swift and hard. What was happening to this town?

Something had to be done to protect the innocent, to keep children like Jessica out of harm's way. And something had to be done now, before it was too late.

But what? Without a sheriff, law and order were hard to come by. And Grady suspected a new sheriff wouldn't be arriving any time soon. He'd heard no one had accepted the position, even though several offers had been made.

He narrowed his eyes, sweeping his gaze over the layout of the town. Basically, the railroad tracks divided Hope into two parts. Businesses were located on one side of the tracks, while decent, hardworking folks were struggling to establish homes for their families on the south side of town.

Establishments like the Red Dog catered to the cattle trade, attracting hundreds of strangers and drifters through their doors every week. But those strangers and drifters had become increasingly rowdy in recent weeks. And this morning's violence had gotten out of hand.

Grady cursed, his anger mounting. Lives were at stake here. The residents of Hope needed the assurance that their town was a safe place to live and work. The law needed to be enforced. And men entering Hope for the first time needed to be warned about the consequences of using firearms during their stay here.

But how?

He froze, seized by a jolting thought. Yes, there was a way to restore law and order to Hope, Kansas.

And it could start with a piece of lumber and a bucket of paint.

An hour later, Grady hauled his freshly painted sign into the main street of Hope. Attempting to find the perfect location for posting the warning, he considered several spots before settling on an area that was located a few feet away from the entrance of the Red Dog Saloon. He was hammering the wooden post into the ground when Carl stepped up to join him.

"What in the hell do you think you're doin', Cunningham?"

Grinning, Grady wiped the sweat from his brow with the back of his hand. "What does it look like I'm doin'?"

Carl edged back a few steps to read the crudely painted words splashed across the wood in bright red letters.

WARNING: DEAD LINE
NO FIREARMS
BEYOND THIS POINT

Grimacing, Carl moaned. "It looks to me like you're asking for a helluva lot of trouble."

"We've already got a helluva lot of trouble around here, my friend," Grady replied, continuing to pound the post into the ground.

The clank of the hammer attracted a curious crowd. By the time Grady had securely anchored the sign, dozens of men had drifted out of the Red Dog Saloon and were clamoring around him, asking questions.

"What does this mean, Cunningham?" one man inquired.

"It means just what it says," Grady explained. "Anyone who crosses this line with a firearm is dead."

"Says who?" another man sneered.

"Says me," Grady shot back. "A little girl got hit by a stray bullet this morning, gentlemen. And it's not going to happen again. We may not have a sheriff in this town, but that doesn't mean we can't have some law and order."

Hushed murmurs swept through the crowd. "So you gonna stay out here, night and day, to enforce the warnin' on your sign?" a man shouted.

"If I have to." Grady clenched his fists into angry tight balls. "I'm willing to spend several hours each day standing here to keep violence at bay and to assure the safety of the women and children in Hope. Anyone else willing to help?" His gaze swept over the crowd.

Carl was the first to step forward. "Sign me up, Grady."

"I reckon I could help, too," another man volunteered. "I got a little girl myself, and I'd hate for her to get caught in the line of fire."

"Who's gonna be next?" Grady challenged.

One by one, the men came forward. With the exception of Carl and the rest of his crew, Grady noticed that all of the volunteers were permanent residents of Hope. Which was a good sign, he suspected. The men with the most at stake—homes, families, livelihoods—were the ones who would benefit from clamping down on the violence in town.

Once the roster had been filled for continuous watches, twenty-four hours a day, Grady turned his attention to the matter of finding the sniper whose stray bullet had harmed Jessica.

"Would any of you care to tell me what happened at the Red Dog this morning?" he asked.

A skinny man spoke up. "There were four of 'em, Grady. They were just passin' through town, they said. When they started complainin' that the drinks weren't strong enough for 'em, the bartender kicked 'em out of the Red Dog. The next thing we knew, they were shootin' up a storm, ridin' out of town."

"And no one went after them?" Grady roared.

Silence swept through the crowd. Grady scowled. "Let's make sure nothin' like that happens again, gentlemen."

Rebecca was preparing a breakfast tray for Jessica the next morning when Jacob stepped into the kitchen and frowned. "You're not going to church?"

She shook her head. "I thought I would stay here with Jessica this morning."

"There's no need of that," Jacob insisted. "I can keep an eye on her while you're gone. Besides, she slept well last night, and she isn't complaining of any pain this morning. There's no reason why you should stay home while I'm here to take care of her."

"Are you certain you don't mind?"

"You know I never mind staying with our Jess." Grinning, Jacob turned and headed for the door. "I'll be hitching up the buggy while you're getting ready for church. In light of the circumstances, I think it's best if you didn't walk into town by yourself for a few days."

Appreciative of Jacob's consideration, Rebecca smiled as the physician left for the barn. Not wanting to be late for the start of Sunday worship services, she scurried across the kitchen.

After delivering Jessica's breakfast to her room, she hastily changed into one of her best

Sunday dresses. By the time she'd donned a small-brimmed hat and slipped on a pair of gloves, Jacob was waiting for her, standing beside the buggy, ready to hand over the reins for her short drive to the church.

As soon as Rebecca stepped onto the church grounds, Charlotte snared her attention, waving and motioning for her to join the small group of auxiliary members who were casually chatting together before the start of Sunday services.

As she threaded her way through the throng of early arrivals assembled in front of the sanctuary, several members of the congregation approached her, expressing their dismay over the tragedy involving her daughter and inquiring about Jessica's condition. Touched by their concern, Rebecca patiently answered their questions. Timothy, too, offered his condolences, although he had little else to say before he turned and continued wandering through the crowd, welcoming the rest of the worshipers to church.

When she finally joined the circle of ladies, Charlotte greeted her warmly. "I haven't been able to stop thinking about you and Jessica, dear. How is that sweet child of yours this morning?"

"Thankfully, she's doing much better now," Rebecca said. "Jacob predicts she'll be back to normal within a few days."

"That's nice to hear, dear." Lydia Davenport affectionately patted Rebecca's shoulder. "I was sorry to hear about the whole sordid incident."

"Hopefully, none of our children will ever

become victims of violence in Hope again," Charlotte predicted. "At least someone is doing something about putting a stop to all the ruckus now."

"Do we have a new sheriff?" Rebecca asked.

"I'm afraid not, dear. But thanks to Grady Cunningham, we have a ban on firearms. Ever since he posted a notice in town yesterday afternoon, stating that firearms are prohibited in Hope, there hasn't been one speck of trouble around here. Why, last night was the first quiet Saturday evening this town has seen in weeks!"

Lydia shrugged. "Sheer coincidence, I'm certain."

"I'm not so sure," Charlotte mused. "I'm beginning to think this Cunningham fella has hit upon an idea that will work for us. Banning guns—beyond the point of the Red Dog Saloon—is the best solution I've ever heard for solving the problem of violence around here."

Stunned to hear Charlotte praising Grady Cunningham, Rebecca edged forward, straining to hear every word of the conversation.

"But it's not Cunningham's place to ban guns in our town," Lydia pointed out indignantly. "That's the sheriff's job!"

"We don't have a sheriff, Lydia," Charlotte reminded her, frowning grimly. "The town council can't even find anyone who is willing to accept the position. In fact, no one but Grady Cunningham has had the gumption to stand up to these no-account drifters and cowpokes who've been causing all the ruckus in town."

"I thought Grady Cunningham was one of those no-account drifters," Lydia muttered.

"I thought he was, too," Charlotte admitted. "But I'm beginning to suspect he isn't the scoundrel that everyone says he is. Do you realize the man has lined up a group of volunteers who are enforcing the deadline, twenty-four hours a day?"

"Don't be so hasty to praise the man, Charlotte." Lydia tilted her nose into the air. "Only time will tell if his plan can work."

The conversation among the ladies came to a halt as the church bells tolled, beckoning the congregation into the sanctuary. Rebecca quietly followed the flow of worshipers streaming into the church, unable to forget the startling discussion that was still echoing in her ears.

"You know, it's been an unusually quiet day," Jacob reflected the next evening. Sitting in the parlor with Rebecca, he set aside the latest edition of the *Hope Gazette* and picked up his pipe from the table. "As a matter of fact, yesterday was quiet, too."

Rebecca looked up from her needlework and smiled. "Are you complaining?"

"Hardly." He chuckled. "Why should I complain? I've gotten eight hours of sleep for two nights in a row." The slight curve of his lips vanished as a pensive expression crossed his face. "Actually, I was skeptical about this notion of a deadline when you told me about it yesterday. But now, I'm beginning to be-

lieve the concept has some merit. When I
checked on my patients at Hope Cottage this
afternoon, the business district was more orderly than I've ever seen it."

"And no one has been knocking on the
door, asking for your help, since Grady established the firearms' restriction on Saturday afternoon." Rebecca pierced her needle into the
pink fabric, quietly stitching another seam in
Jessica's new dress. "Personally, I think
Grady should be commended for trying to
put an end to all these senseless shootings."

"I'll have to give the man credit for trying,
that's for certain," Jacob agreed.

But by the next morning, Jacob was no
longer crediting Grady for merely attempting
to restore peace to Hope, Rebecca noticed.
After awakening from his third consecutive
night of uninterrupted sleep, the physician
was praising the man to the high heavens.

"I'm going to personally congratulate him
today for coming up with such an ingenious
idea," Jacob was insisting as Rebecca pulled
a tray of hot biscuits from the oven.

Placing the biscuits on a platter, Rebecca
smiled. Did everyone in town share Jacob's
enthusiasm about Grady's efforts to restore
peace to Hope? Maybe public opinion about
Grady Cunningham was changing.

She hadn't seen him since he'd stopped by
to see Jessica after the shooting. But considering his contributions to improving life in
Hope, Rebecca couldn't begrudge him for his
absence from the house in recent days. Obviously, everyone was already benefiting from
his endeavors—including her own family.

Still, she longed to see him again. She had yet to share the news with him about her visit to the Cunningham estate and her conversation with his father. But there was so much she wanted to tell him, so much she had to say.

Since their angry exchange on Friday evening, she'd been filled with regret for her actions. She wished she hadn't balked at his vow of love for her, wished she hadn't judged him so hastily. If only she'd *believed* in him . . .

Yes, he'd ripped her heart into shreds by admitting that she'd been the center of his cruel wager. But in the midst of her own anger and pain, all reason had deserted her. Still stinging from learning the news about the gamble, she hadn't absorbed all that he'd so desperately tried to explain.

But now, reflecting on those moments, she grasped what he'd been attempting to say. He'd expressed regret for involving her in the wager, admitted his mistakes, and tried to correct his wrongs.

And he'd said he loved her.

Why hadn't she accepted his explanations with more understanding? Why had she been blinded by her own pain? And why hadn't she believed in what he had to say? She'd been vividly reminded of that sensitive, caring side of him, the part of the man that very few people had ever seen, when she'd witnessed his concern for Jessica after the shooting. Now, she only hoped she had the chance to tell him how much she regretted rejecting his vow of love for her.

"Mama!" Jessica's voice rang through the

house, jarring Rebecca from her thoughts. "Can I eat breakfast with you and Grandpa at the table this morning?"

"Just as long as you don't try to come down the stairs by yourself," she called out.

"Stay right there, Miss Jess." Jacob lumbered toward the stairs. "I'm on my way to get you right now."

Rebecca hastily set another plate on the table. She was pleased Jessica was feeling well enough to leave her room for breakfast. The child was recovering from her injuries with remarkable speed, she thought.

As soon as the meal was over, Rebecca politely excused herself. "I'll take care of the dishes as soon as I get back from the auxiliary meeting at church."

"Why, I'd almost forgotten about your meeting, 'Becca!" Jacob sprang up from the chair. "It'll just take me a minute to hitch up the buggy."

"I'd prefer to walk today, if you don't mind. I haven't been out of the house since Sunday morning, and I'm anxious to stretch my legs a bit."

Jacob stroked his mustache for a moment. "I don't know if that's such a good idea, 'Becca."

"Didn't you say that there wasn't any trouble in the business district yesterday?"

"Yes, but—"

"And aren't you usually one of the first to know about any outbreak of violence in town?"

"Yes, but—"

"And haven't you been raving about the peacefulness in the streets?"

Jacob heaved a weary sigh. "I suppose it wouldn't hurt for you to walk to church this morning," he conceded with reluctance.

Flashing a triumphant grin, Rebecca planted a quick kiss on Jacob's forehead. Within a few moments, she left for the church.

For the first time in recent memory, Rebecca actually enjoyed a leisurely stroll into town. Knowing Grady and the other volunteers were keeping a close eye on potential troublemakers gave her a sense of security that she hadn't felt in weeks.

Arriving early for the meeting, Rebecca set to work, arranging the chairs in a circular fashion, preparing the room for the ladies' arrival. She had just placed the last chair in the circle when Timothy appeared at the door.

"Good morning, Rebecca." His voice was quiet, strained. "How's Jessica today?"

"Much better." She smiled. "In fact, Jacob expects she'll be back to normal in a few days."

"Children are quite resilient, it seems." His gaze swept over her face. "And how are you?"

"I'm much better, too."

"I'm glad."

There was a touch of wistfulness in his voice, a mixture of sadness and regret shimmering from his gaze. And Rebecca understood the reasons why. She, too, had hoped their relationship would grow and mature into something more than mere friendship.

But friendship, she knew, was all they could ever hope to have.

She was still pondering the situation when Charlotte swept into the assembly room. The woman's eyes were bright with excitement, she noticed.

"Have you heard what happened in town last night, Rebecca?"

"I'm afraid not. Pastor O'Leary and I were just—"

"You'd be interested in this, too, Pastor," Charlotte interrupted. "Two troublemakers tried to get past the deadline last night—and Grady Cunningham literally kicked them out of town!"

"How courageous of Mr. Cunningham." Timothy forced a stiff smile. "And how fortunate for our town." He nodded politely. "Enjoy your meeting, ladies."

Just as Timothy turned to leave, Agnes and Lydia arrived for the meeting. Charlotte bustled up to greet them, once again spreading the news about the latest developments in town. By the time the entire group of ladies had assembled in the room, everyone was talking about Grady's act of valor.

"One of the men who tried to sneak past the deadline was that Big Al who wounded several men last week." Charlotte shuddered. "I hope we don't see any more of him."

"I don't think we should be too alarmed," Agnes mused. "It sounds like Mr. Cunningham has everything under control."

"He's already done more than anyone else has ever tried to do. My Virgil said the man has been an answer to our prayers." Her gaze shifted to Rebecca. "And Virgil also told me about an incident involving you, my dear."

"Me?" Rebecca's heart thundered in her chest until she noticed the amusement glittering from Charlotte's eyes.

"We heard Mr. Cunningham wagered a hefty sum of money at the Red Dog Saloon, gambling that he could win your permission to call on you." A smile touched the corners of Charlotte's mouth. "But when he discovered that he was dealing with such a fine, outstanding lady, he called off the bet and conceded defeat."

Feeling a heated flush rise to her cheeks, Rebecca floundered for a response. "How interesting," she finally managed to say.

"I think it's very interesting," Charlotte agreed. "In fact, I think all of us are beginning to see a different side of Grady Cunningham."

The rest of the ladies were nodding in agreement just as Lydia spoke up. "Maybe the man isn't as incorrigible as we thought he was," she conceded.

Too overcome with emotion to contribute anything more to the conversation, Rebecca breathed a silent prayer of thanksgiving. The women's change of heart toward Grady was almost too good to be true. She could hardly believe they were praising him for his virtues instead of gossiping about his past.

Walking home after the meeting, Rebecca felt like leaping for joy. At last, the people of Hope were gaining a new respect for Grady.

She was still relishing the thought as she sauntered through the main thoroughfare of town. But just as she reached the corner of her street, that old, unsettling sensation of being watched from a distance assaulted her, fast and hard.

Hearing the shuffle of footsteps behind her, Rebecca glanced over her shoulder just in time to see the blur of a heavyset man dashing into a narrow alley. Though the wide brim of his hat shadowed most of his face, nothing could hide the intensity of his scathing glare before he disappeared from sight.

Ripples of fear shot through Rebecca. Without a doubt, the man intended to harm her, she knew.

Terrorized beyond words, she picked up her skirts and raced toward the safety of her house.

Chapter 14

"I won again!" Jessica shrieked. "That's the second time I've beat you this morning!"

Sprawled out beside the child on the parlor floor, Grady groaned. "Don't remind me."

"But I never knew playing poker could be so much fun, Mr. Cunn'ham!"

"It's always fun when you're winning." Unable to prevent his lips from twitching with a smile, Grady tossed aside his losing hand. He'd only been trying to amuse the child when he'd suggested a game of cards. Never in his wildest dreams could he have imagined that a six-year-old would take such a liking to poker—or catch onto the game so quickly.

"Let's play again!" she pleaded.

Chuckling, Grady deftly scooped up the cards scattered across the floor and shuffled the deck. He had just dealt the next hand when the front door swung open.

He glanced up and froze, alarmed by what

he saw. Rebecca was rushing into the house, breathless and pale. Her eyes were wide with fright, her hands trembling with terror. She slammed the door behind her, then backed up against it, squeezing her eyes shut, gasping for breath.

Grady's heart nearly jumped out of his chest. Just as he leaped to his feet, Jessica dropped her playing cards to her lap. "What's wrong, Mama?"

Rebecca's eyes flew open, and her head snapped around. Seeing Jessica, she blinked rapidly and forced a stiff smile. "I'm just a little winded, that's all. I was in a hurry to get home to you."

"I've been having fun!" Jessica held up a playing card in her hand. "Mr. Cunn'ham has been teaching me how to play poker!"

Rebecca shifted her gaze toward Grady. The natural arch of her brows rose higher. "Oh, he has?"

"What can I say?" He shrugged, grinning. "The child needed a challenge. How could I have known that she's a natural cardsharp?"

"And it's so much fun, Mama!" Jessica laughed. "Want to play a hand with me and Mr. Cunn'ham?"

"Maybe some other time, Jess," she answered, distracted by other, more worrisome, thoughts. She peered into the physician's empty office. "Where's Jacob?"

"He's out in the barn, taking a look at the buggy," Grady explained. "He said one of the wheels needed tightening, so I volunteered to entertain Jessica for a few minutes."

"I see." She looked down at her daughter,

a slight frown wrinkling the smooth line of her brow. "I don't want you to exert yourself too much, Jessica. While I'm fixing lunch, I think you should go back to your room and rest for a little while."

Jessica's lower lip protruded. "But Mr. Cunn'ham and I were getting ready to play another hand!"

"Maybe you can ask him to play cards with you some other time," Rebecca suggested.

"Tell you what, Miss Jess. If you'll get your rest, we'll play two more hands right after lunch," Grady bargained.

"Promise?"

"Promise." He reached down and pulled the child into his arms, glancing over at Rebecca. "I'll take her upstairs, if you'd like," he offered.

"I'd appreciate that," she murmured, nervously peering through the parlor window.

Troubled by Rebecca's frightened state, Grady hastily carried Jessica to her room. By the time he returned to the parlor, Rebecca was slumped into a chair, massaging her temples. Her fingers were shaking, he noticed, and her face was still devoid of color.

"What happened out there, Rebecca?"

Her lashes fluttered open. "Someone was following me." Her voice was choked, strained.

"Are you certain?"

"As certain as I've ever been about anything in my life." She heaved a troubled sigh. "The first time it happened, I thought—"

"The first time?" Grady narrowed his eyes

in confusion. "You mean this has happened before?"

"I'm afraid so." She lifted her chin a notch. In spite of her brave front, her bottom lip was trembling, he noticed. "In the beginning, I thought I was imagining things. Once, when I felt I was being followed, it turned out that Timothy O'Leary had been looking for me. On another occasion, I ran into you after I got the strange feeling that someone had been watching me. But now . . ."

Her voice faltered. Grady clenched his fists into tight balls. The thought of someone stalking her was almost more than he could bear. "What happened today, Rebecca?" he repeated, lowering his long frame to the settee.

When she lifted her gaze to his face, the fear glimmering from the depths of those beautiful blue eyes jolted him to the core. "I saw him," she whispered, her voice so low that Grady could scarcely hear it. "He was following me home from church. When I turned around, he was glaring at me just before he took off and disappeared into an alley." She swallowed with difficulty. "But I saw something in his expression that was frightening, Grady. It almost seemed as if he were angry, furious I'd noticed him before he could sneak up behind me."

"Have you ever seen this man before today?"

"He didn't seem familiar. But, then, I didn't get a close look at him." Her brow knitted with worry. "What I saw was enough to make me realize that I didn't want to see any more."

Anger seared through him. Who in the hell could be stalking her? And why?

"I suppose I shouldn't have ventured out by myself this morning," she rambled on. "Jacob wanted me to take the buggy to church, but I insisted on walking since everything has been so quiet in town the last few days." She shifted her gaze toward him, her eyes brimming with sudden admiration. "And the peace and quiet is all because of you, from what I hear. Everyone in town has been raving about your idea of banning weapons."

He shrugged, uncomfortable with the praise that he considered unmerited. "I was so damn furious about Jessica getting shot, I couldn't stand by and watch the violence escalate any longer. But I don't deserve all the credit for restoring peace to Hope. It's a joint effort, believe me. It takes more than a single man to put the idea into practice."

"Still, people are realizing they can't base their opinions of you on events that happened a long time ago. Everyone is beginning to see you as you are, not for what they think you might have done or the mistakes you might have made in the past." A hint of shame tinted her sculpted cheeks. "Everyone ... including me."

He leaned forward, confused. "What do you mean?"

"When I learned about your wager, I was so angry and hurt that I couldn't comprehend what you were telling me. I felt you should've realized that I've been subjected to enough humiliation and embarrassment to last a lifetime, and I was devastated that you'd centered a public wager around me."

"It was a pretty rotten thing to do," he said, his eyes downcast with guilt.

"But you told me you were sorry," Rebecca reminded him softly. "You were honest with me about the entire matter. And most importantly, you corrected your mistakes as best you could. Publicly, even."

He hunkered down beside her chair, somewhat awed by the tenderness resonating from her voice, the glow of understanding glinting from her eyes. But he was even more astonished when she reached out and skimmed the tips of her fingers across the firm line of his jaw.

"And all of those things tell me that you know what love is, Grady." Her voice was as soft as the touch of her hand on his face. "As a matter of fact, I think you know more about love than anyone I've ever known."

He wanted to believe her, desperately so, but a residue of hurt was still lingering in his heart. Only a few nights ago, she'd declared that he knew nothing of love. "What changed your mind?"

"Lots of things." Her fingers slid across his cheek, then brushed across the curls of hair around his temples. "I remembered the expression on your face when you were holding the Fords' new baby. I remembered the way you look at my daughter, the way you look at me." A smile whispered across her lips. "And the auxiliary ladies reminded me of your chivalry, too."

"My chivalry?" he echoed in disbelief. "What have I done that was so chivalrous?"

"When you withdrew from the wager, you gained the respect of every woman in town, including the auxiliary ladies." Her smile was shy and warm. "But what everyone else in this town thinks about you doesn't matter anymore to me. What you did for Jessica and the way you backed off from the bet made me realize the kind of man you are, Grady Cunningham. And I'm proud to be associated with you."

Grady felt like the weight of the world had been lifted from his shoulders. Ecstatic, he wanted nothing more than to scoop this woman into his arms and whirl her around the room until she was dizzy and breathless and begging for more.

But this was neither the time nor the place, he knew. Instead, he settled for brushing his knuckles against the velvety softness of her cheek. "So does this mean I have your approval to play two more rounds of poker with Jessica after lunch?"

A smile sparkled from her lips and eyes. "As long as you deal her another winning hand."

"Just one more hand, Mama!" Propped up in bed, Jessica splayed five playing cards between her little fingers. "If I can win one more time tonight, I'll be the champion for the day. And that'll make three days in a row that I've won more hands than Mr. Cunn'ham!" She glanced over at Grady and giggled. "Isn't that right, Mr. Cunn'ham?"

Leaning forward in a chair beside the bed, Grady grunted. "That's right, Miss Jess."

Standing at the door, watching the unlikely pair as they studied the cards in their hands, Rebecca had to bite her cheek to keep from laughing out loud. Since Jessica had learned the basic skills of the card game on Tuesday morning, playing poker with Grady had become her favorite pastime.

"I'd better not hear about the two of you wagering any bets while you're playing poker," she teased, stepping into the room.

Jessica giggled again. "We wouldn't make bets, Mama! We're just playing for fun!"

"Don't be so certain about that," Grady cautioned, winking at Rebecca, looking as if he might choke on his laughter at any second.

Observing the affectionate bantering between the card-shuffling duo, Rebecca suddenly doubted that Jessica could be as fascinated with playing poker as she was pretending to be. Every instinct she possessed told her the child was much more enchanted with all the attention she was receiving from Grady than the prospect of winning at cards.

Of course, she fully understood the reasons why Jessica was so captivated with the man. After all, Grady Cunningham was difficult for any female to resist. Merely looking at him sent her blood racing through her veins.

"You know, my brother and I used to wager chores against our poker hands." Grady gathered up the deck of cards and stacked them into a neat pile. "And we'd sneak out of bed at night, after our parents were asleep, and play poker until the wee hours of the morning."

"Having a brother sounds like fun." Jessica smiled dreamily. "I wish I could have a brother someday."

"Brothers are real nice to have around," Grady mused, his voice dropping to a low, husky timbre.

Rebecca wanted to agree, but she was too overwhelmed from the rush of memories sweeping through her to utter a sound. All too well, she could remember the joy of having a brother of her own. Though she'd been younger than Jessica when Tyler had been snatched out of her life, she'd never forgotten how much she'd adored him.

Trying to set aside the haunting memories, Rebecca forced a smile onto her lips. "Time to get to sleep, Miss Jess. It's way past your bedtime. Why, you've stayed up later than Grandpa! He went to sleep over an hour ago."

"I know." Jessica grinned. "He kissed me good-night before he went to bed."

Grady leaned over and kissed the child on the cheek. "Good night, Poker Princess."

Jessica giggled. "Good night, Mr. Cunn'ham."

After Grady left the room, Rebecca listened to Jessica's prayers and tucked her into bed for the night. "Remember, Grandpa and I will be calling on our patients tomorrow," she reminded the child. "Samantha will be here in the morning when you wake up."

"Do you think Samantha knows how to play poker?"

"If she doesn't, I'm sure you can teach her tomorrow." Laughing softly, Rebecca brushed her lips across her daughter's forehead and quietly slipped out of the room.

Grady was waiting for her in the parlor, slumped into the settee. When she entered the room, she was surprised by the remorseful expression tainting the chiseled features of his face.

"I hope I didn't stir up any trouble by bringing up the subject of brothers with Jessica," he said in an apologetic tone.

"You didn't," Rebecca assured him, settling down beside him on the settee. "It's the first time she's ever mentioned wanting a brother, but I'm sure it won't be the last, either. Besides, I think it's only natural for a child to want a brother or sister."

"Probably so," he mused, his eyes clouding with distant memories. "Odd, but it's been years since I've thought about the times when Paxton and I snuck out of bed to play poker in the middle of the night. I suppose shuffling cards with Jessica in her room tonight dredged up all those memories for me." He paused and shook his head as if to shove aside the recollections.

"I only have a few memories about growing up with my brother." A sense of wistful longing suffused her as hazy images of her dark-haired brother flickered through her mind. "But I distinctly remember how much I adored him. I was constantly tagging after him around the farm, hanging onto every word he said, mimicking everything he did."

"But you haven't seen him in a long time, have you?"

"I'm afraid not." She sighed. "I'd give anything in the world to know what's happened to him. Hardly a day goes by when I don't think about him, wonder where he's living or if he's safe and happy." A lump swelled in her throat. "Of course, I try to remind myself that he might not be alive any longer, especially considering how many men were casualties of the war. So many things could have happened to him since we were children ..."

"Fearful of what you might find if you tried to locate him?" Grady guessed perceptively.

"I suppose so," she conceded. "Of course, I moved so many times when I was living with the Breckinridges, it would have been almost impossible for us to catch up with each other. But now, I think if I ever met anyone who hails from Tennessee, I wouldn't hesitate to ask if the name of Tyler McRae sounded familiar."

"McRae, you say?" When Rebecca nodded, Grady combed his memory. "You know, I once stayed in a real nice hotel in Tennessee called The McRae. I've never forgotten the place because it was one of the nicest hotels I'd ever seen."

Rebecca's brows narrowed. "Exactly where was this hotel located?"

"Chattanooga," he answered. "When I went to Boston for my mother's funeral a few years ago, I wasn't crazy about the idea of coming straight home. So I traveled down the east coast and stopped at several cities in the

South, working my way back to Kansas. Chattanooga was one of the places I visited."

"I remember some talk about Chattanooga when I was little. It seems like our farm was located near there." A touch of sadness flickered across her delicate features. "But I seriously doubt my brother could be the owner of a lavish hotel."

"There's always that one chance," he reminded her, aching inside, feeling her pain as deeply as if it had been his own.

"True, but it's only a remote possibility." Sighing, she kneaded the nape of her neck. "I suppose I should be getting to sleep. Tomorrow will be a long day, and I need to get my rest. I'm planning to visit two of my patients. Both women are due to give birth within the next month, and I—"

"When do you plan to leave?" he asked, more sharply than he'd intended.

Her head snapped up. "Around daybreak."

He bristled, furious she hadn't mentioned the journey to him before now, wounded she'd never asked him to accompany her. "I'll have the buggy waiting by the time you're ready to go."

"But—"

"No arguments, Rebecca." He glowered at her. "I'm going with you. Don't you remember what happened the last time you ventured out alone?"

"Yes, but—"

"Can you honestly say you'd feel comfortable traveling by yourself?"

"No." She lifted her gaze to his face and

whispered, "Actually, I'm glad you want to go."

Her eyes were shimmering with so much warmth and sincerity that Grady's heart rolled over. Struggling to keep his emotions in check, he ripped his gaze away from her. But even as he stared at the bookcase in front of him, he was still aching to kiss those rosy-tinted lips, burning to feel the silky softness of her skin, longing to capture her in his arms and crush her against him.

She couldn't possibly know how much he wanted her, how many times he'd fantasized about claiming her as his own. And with each passing day, the desire simmering in his loins burned deeper, hotter, than the day before.

Now, passion, raw and unyielding, coursed through him with such intensity that he couldn't prevent a strangled groan from rising in his throat. Never had he wanted a woman like this. And never before had a woman set him afire merely by gazing at him.

Unable to resist touching her, he reached over, tilted her chin up ever so slightly, and brushed his lips across the sensuous curves of her mouth. He struggled to keep from demanding more, knew he shouldn't force himself on her. But with that first soul-jarring contact between them, all reason vanished from his mind. As his tongue slipped past her parted lips and probed her mouth, shafts of stark need pierced through him.

"God, you're sweet," he murmured into her mouth as he kissed her, plunging his hands through her hair. "And I can't stop myself from wanting more . . ."

He eased her down across the settee, splaying hot, open-mouthed kisses over the curve of her jaw and neck. Rebecca shuddered from the flood of desire washing through her, too overwhelmed by emotion to voice any protests, uncertain if she possessed the strength to stop him even if she'd wanted to.

His fingers moved to the buttons on the bodice of her dress, nimbly unclasping them. She heard his sharp intake of breath when the last button fell free, saw the passion glinting from his eyes when he gazed down at the swollen tips of her naked breasts.

"You can't imagine ... how long ... I've been dreaming about this, Rebecca." He swooped his mouth over one swollen mound, running his tongue over the hardened, rosy peak.

A slow, simmering heat erupted between her legs, then spread through her body like wildfire. The seductive movements of his tongue left her breathless, dizzy, begging for more. Moaning, she moved one hand to the back of his head, pressing him more tightly against her breast. The sensations soaring through her were more incredible than she could have ever fathomed. "Don't stop," she whispered, gasping for breath.

Edging back slightly, he gazed down at her. "Let me make love to you, Rebecca. Let me show you more ..."

Hearing his tender plea, Rebecca suddenly realized what was happening between them. Reality, coupled with fear, abruptly overwhelmed her desires. "We can't, Grady. Jacob and Jessica are upstairs, and—"

"But they're asleep," he countered. "And you want this as much as I do, I know. Don't deny us—"

"Stop, Grady." Wincing, she splayed trembling fingers across the wide expanse of his chest and pushed him away from her. "We shouldn't have let things get so out of hand. We shouldn't have—"

"And why the hell not? We're both adults. We know what we're doing."

She struggled to button her dress. "Which is precisely why we should have maintained control of our emotions."

"Fine, then," he snapped. He clenched his jaw with steely resolve and stalked to the door.

Just as he placed his hand on the knob, Rebecca slipped up behind him. "Good night, Grady." Her voice, whispered as softly as a caress, eased the turbulent emotions racing through him.

Bending down, he brushed his mouth over her swollen, red lips. Then, summoning every ounce of strength he could muster, he turned and walked away.

An evening breeze slapped against his face as he stepped outside. Heading back to the Grand Central, Grady forced himself to forget about what might have transpired between them if Rebecca had not yielded to her fears. But he couldn't stop thinking about the longing that had shimmered from her eyes when she'd talked about her brother.

All too well, he could identify with her yearnings to see her brother again. And he desperately wanted more for her relationship

with Tyler than he'd managed to have with
Paxton.

As soon as he arrived at the Grand Central,
he could no longer resist the temptation of
investigating a possible connection between
Tyler McRae and a hotel in Tennessee.
Though he was acutely aware the odds were
against him, he knew he'd never forgive himself if he didn't attempt to locate the man.

He raced into his room, located a piece of
paper, and sat down at the small desk near
the window.

And then he dipped a pen into the inkwell
and began to write.

True to his word, Grady was waiting for
Rebecca beside the barn when she emerged
from the house the next morning. Something
akin to joy rushed through her as soon as she
saw him. She scurried across the yard, clutching a basket of medicinal herbs in one hand
and a larger, heavier basket in the other.

"Let me give you a hand," he insisted,
bounding up to greet her. As he grasped the
larger of the two baskets, surprise flitted
across his face. "There must be a ton of bricks
in here."

Rebecca laughed. "It's only food, Grady. I
thought we might want something to eat
around noon." Whirling, she darted toward
the back of the house. "There's a jug of water
on the back porch for us, too."

Grady had just finished packing the baskets
into the back of the buggy when Rebecca returned with the water jug. Within a few moments, they were ready to leave.

A brilliant sunrise shimmered across the horizon as they pulled out of town. Enjoying the splendor of the lavender and rose hues streaming across the sky, Rebecca sighed with contentment. "You know, there was a beautiful sunrise, similar to this one, not too long ago. I saw it on the morning I went to ..." She faltered, stung by the sudden realization that she'd never told Grady about her visit to the Cunningham estate. "Oh, my."

Turning, Grady lifted one eyebrow in surprise. "What's wrong?"

"Nothing is wrong," she quickly assured him. "It's just that I've been wanting to tell you about my conversation with your father last week. But so much has happened in the last few days, I haven't had the chance to talk with you about it."

His mouth thinned, and the line of his jaw hardened. "You talked to King Cunningham?"

She nodded. "Jacob was taking care of some emergencies in town last Friday, and he asked me to call on the mayor for him. While I was visiting the Cunningham estate, your father and I talked about you."

"And?"

"And I sensed he still cares deeply for you, Grady." She gazed into the distance, struggling to find the right words. "I didn't know Mayor Cunningham before his stroke, but something tells me that he's always been a very proud, very stubborn man."

"Keep on trustin' those instincts of yours, darlin'," Grady muttered. "The man is more obstinate than a mule."

"Then that explains why he wouldn't concede to a reunion with you. His pride is standing in the way, Grady. He doesn't want you to see him confined to a wheelchair. He can't bear the thought of you seeing him as less than he once was." A sigh escaped from her lips. "Physically, he's not the man you once knew."

"I suspect he thinks I'm after his money, too." His voice was clipped, strained.

"Initially, he voiced those thoughts. But he seemed surprised when I told him that you had no need for his money." When Grady lapsed into a stony silence, she added, "I hope you don't think I'm trying to meddle in your affairs. I was merely hoping I could open a door that might lead the way to a reconciliation between the two of you."

"I appreciate what you've tried to do, Rebecca." A shadow of darkness flickered across the ruggedly hewn planes of his face. "But it's hard to imagine my father welcoming me home like the prodigal son. I don't expect any miracles, you know."

"But he could have a change of heart, Grady. Especially when he hears about the success of your efforts to restrain the use of—"

"Don't, Rebecca." He scowled. "You'll have to remember, I'm the son who has never been able to do anything right. Mark my words, the old man will find something wrong with my tactics to reduce the violence in Hope."

"But surely he'll see—"

"I don't give a damn what the old man thinks, Rebecca. I didn't establish the deadline to impress him. Everything I did was for Jessica." His blisterings of outrage suddenly diffused, and he managed a wry grin. "I couldn't bear the thought of anything happening to my best poker buddy, you know."

Images of the poker-playing six-year-old danced through her mind. She shared a smile with Grady, and a warm, wondrous feeling suffused her. "I'm awfully glad you wanted to make this trip with me today."

The heat of his gaze spoke volumes. "And I'm glad I'm here with you."

They settled into a comfortable silence as the Kansas sun soared higher into the sky. From time to time, Grady noticed clumps of buffalo bones scattered along the side of the trail. Each time he caught a glimpse of the massive skeletons, he remembered the huge mound of bones piled near the creek at Owen Ford's homestead.

A senseless waste, it was. But what could be done with a pile of bones?

Trying to erase the nagging question from his mind, he focused his attention on the woman beside him. "So tell me about the family we'll be visiting soon," he urged.

"You'll like the Kirkmans," she predicted confidently. "Irene and Kenneth Kirkman already have two boys, so they're hoping for a daughter this time. The baby isn't due until next month, but I wanted to call on Irene today and make certain everything is still progressing normally."

A few moments later, Rebecca pointed to a sod shanty. "That's the Kirkmans' homestead."

They traveled over a bumpy path leading
up to the shanty. When they rolled to a stop
in front of the dwelling, an empty, desolate
silence greeted them. Grady gazed around the
claim, searching for some sign of life. "Are
you certain this is the right place?"

"I'm positive," she said. "I've called on
Irene at least a half dozen times."

"Then I'll see if anyone is here." Grady
leaped down from the buggy and strode to
the door. "Mr. Kirkman?" he called out.

The door, warped and faded from the summer sun, was slightly ajar. Nudging it open a
few more inches, Grady peered inside the
shanty. As soon as his eyes adjusted to the
dim light, he was able to confirm what he
had suspected all along. The place was empty,
void of all life.

Whipping around, he returned to the
buggy. "The place has been stripped clean,
Rebecca. The Kirkmans are gone."

Disappointment clouded the vivid blue of
her eyes. "I knew they were having a difficult
time this summer, but I never dreamed they
would abandon their homestead."

"They may not have had another choice.
With this blasted heat, it's tough for anyone
to survive out here for long." He paused,
skimming a callused finger across her cheek,
wishing he could erase the disappointment
shimmering from her gaze. "Makes a man
mighty happy to know he's travelin' with a
lady who's got enough sense to bring along
some food for the both of them."

A soft laugh escaped from her throat.

"There's a creek not too far from here. We could stop there for lunch, if you'd like."

"Sounds good to me," he agreed, grasping the reins.

A half hour later, Grady leaned back against the trunk of a scrawny cottonwood and groaned. Never before had he eaten such a tasty feast on the trail. Fried chicken, biscuits, and cheese had been topped off with a huge slab of the tastiest chocolate cake he'd ever put into his mouth. "I don't think I've ever eaten so much in my life," he muttered. "What are you tryin' to do to me, darlin'?"

Packing up the remains of their lunch, Rebecca looked over at Grady and smiled. "I was just tryin' to make sure you wouldn't starve to death before we got back to Hope."

She returned to her task, her face shining with a beauty so mind-boggling he could barely breathe. Studying her, Grady felt the jagged edges of desire pierce through him. He longed to tell her that he was still starving, but not for food. He was ravenous for the taste of her, the feel of her against him.

Her skirts rustled as she bent over to retrieve something. But Grady never knew what that something was. He was too busy staring at her, transfixed at the indentation of a waist so narrow he could span it with his hands, mesmerized by the gentle swell of breasts so tantalizing that sweat beaded his upper lip.

He was still gawking when the soft purr of her voice broke into his thoughts. "I suppose we should be heading out to the Yessicks' homestead now," she suggested. "It's about a half hour away from here."

Ripping his gaze away from her, he leaped to his feet. "I'll load up the buggy, then."

They'd traveled less than a mile when the prairie winds picked up, whipping around them. Grady squinted, peering up at the cloudless sky. "Winds are pickin' up, for certain, but I don't know why. No sign of a storm is headin' our way."

Though the winds were still billowing across the prairie when they arrived at the Yessicks' homestead, Grady's concern over the weather vanished as soon as Rebecca introduced him to Landon and Kathleen Yessick. Judging by the appearance of the young couple, Grady suspected they hadn't eaten a decent meal in months. Landon's clothes hung loosely over his thin, scrawny frame, and Kathleen seemed frail in spite of her protruding, round belly. Her eyes were shadowed with dark circles, and her face was pale and drawn.

More disturbed by the couple's plight than he cared to admit, Grady tended to the black gelding while Rebecca scurried inside the shanty to examine her patient. Gazing at the desolate surroundings, he had no doubt about the reasons for the Yessicks' fragile physiques.

Grady was silently cursing the injustices of life when Rebecca emerged from the shanty. As she retrieved her basket of herbs from the buggy, lines of worry furrowed her brow.

He stepped up beside her. "It's Kathleen, isn't it?"

"I'm afraid so. I fear she's not getting enough to eat. And she's working herself into an early grave, too, struggling to survive out here." Sadness shadowed her face. "I suppose I should be glad the Kirkmans pulled up stakes when they did. Maybe they've moved to a place where they won't have to be grappling for food any longer."

"Mrs. Summers?" Landon emerged from the shanty. "Kathleen and I were hoping you and Mr. Cunningham can join us for an early dinner before you return to Hope. It's the least we can do, considering you've come all this way to check on Kathleen."

Grady's gut wrenched with turmoil. Every morsel of food was as valuable as a nugget of gold to this young couple, and they couldn't afford to share what little they had. But turning down the invitation would be a blow to Landon's pride. And considering the man's barren claim and sickly wife, Grady suspected that pride was one of Landon's few remaining possessions.

He offered no protest when Rebecca accepted the dinner invitation for both of them. Still, dining on bland potato soup and stale cornbread, Grady became acutely aware of the reasons for the Yessicks' unhealthy state.

And it was obvious that the desolate living conditions were disturbing to Rebecca, as well. Her shoulders were sagging, he noticed, and the furrows in her brow told him that she was troubled by her patient's lack of stamina and energy.

As they prepared to leave the homestead, Rebecca turned to the young woman and grasped her hand. "I'm concerned about you, Kathleen. You should have gained a bit more weight by now, and I'd like to keep an eye on your condition until the baby is born. Is it possible for you and Landon to room in town for a month or so? I've heard the monthly rates at Hope Cottage are quite reasonable."

Landon spoke up for his wife. "I'm afraid we can't even afford a room for one night, Mrs. Summers."

"Then Kathleen can stay at my house," Rebecca offered. "I have plenty of room, and I'd love for—"

"We can't accept no charity, ma'am." Landon shook his head emphatically. "But thank you for the offer."

"I understand," Rebecca returned quietly. "But if you should change your mind, the offer still stands."

At that instant, a gust of wind blasted over the prairie, rustling the women's skirts and hurling bits of dust through the air. Grady gently nudged Rebecca toward the buggy. "We should be headin' back," he urged.

After Rebecca hastily bid good-bye to the Yessicks, promising to return within a few weeks, Grady gently boosted her into the buggy seat. Within a few moments, they were pulling onto the main road.

Though Grady sensed the winds were nippier than usual, he wasn't particularly alarmed by the strong gusts that occasionally slapped against them. But as the winds picked up momentum, a tiny pulse of fear began to throb through his veins. Was this the beginning of a Kansas dust storm?

Grady tugged at the bandanna around his neck, pulled the fabric over his nose and mouth, then motioned for Rebecca to imitate him. "Use a hanky," he shouted over the roar of the wind.

With each passing mile, the winds continued to strengthen, showering dust and grime over them. Grady pressed on, but traveling against the force of the blasts slowed their pace along the rugged trail. "At this rate, we can't make it back into town before dark," he conceded.

"Then where can we go?"

"I know just the place," he bellowed, charging through the clouds of dust swarming around them.

Chapter 15

The dust swirling across the plains was so thick and blinding that Rebecca had no idea how Grady was managing to keep the buggy from veering off the trail. She could barely discern the dark outline of the black gelding in front of her, even though the horse was only a few feet away. The wind was slapping fine particles of dirt into her face, stinging her skin like the tips of a thousand needles, blinding her eyes with hot tears of pain.

Rebecca clamped her hanky more tightly over her nose and mouth, dismayed that the dust was still seeping through the fine weave of the lace-trimmed linen, clogging her nostrils and choking her. The buggy lurched and swayed from the force of another gust of wind.

Cold shivers of fear raced through her. Terrorized beyond words, she clutched the edge of the seat and squeezed her eyes shut, breathing a silent prayer for their safety, hoping Grady could find shelter before the wind could sweep them away.

Her fingers were still curled around the rim of the seat when Grady slowed the buggy to a halt. She blinked, struggling to open her eyes, just as the house that had once belonged to Grady's brother came into view through the fog of dust.

Grady worked quickly, leaping to the ground, hurling open the barn doors, and guiding the buggy into the frame building. After hastily tending to the black gelding, he draped an arm around Rebecca's shoulders and led her across the yard.

She was still trembling from the horror of the ordeal as they raced into the house. Suddenly drained of all energy, she sagged against Grady. Leaning against that hard, strong shoulder, feeling his inner strength melt into hers, she felt her fears subsiding. "And to think I'd entertained the notion of calling on my patients by myself," she mumbled into the folds of his vest. "I don't know how I would have survived this journey without you, Grady."

"I'm glad you didn't try to make the trip all alone," he admitted, his voice husky and low. He lifted her chin with a callused finger, forcing her to meet his steady gaze. "I don't even want to think about what could have happened to you."

His eyes raked over her face, studying each feature with an alarming intensity. Disconcerted by the heat of his gaze scorching through her, Rebecca became vividly conscious of her rumpled appearance. Cringing at the thought of how she must look to him, she slithered out of his arms. "If you don't mind, I'd like to clean up." Feeling a slight tinge of embarrassment staining her cheeks, she grinned shyly. "For some strange reason, I feel like I have dust in my hair and on my clothes."

"I wonder why." His lips twitched with the hint of a smile. "I'll get some water for your bath."

Rebecca wandered up to the second floor, finding a copper tub in the first bedroom to the right of the stairs. Decorated in becoming hues of blue and white, the room was elegantly furnished with a dresser and matching bed, wash stand, wardrobe, and night table. She was admiring the furnishings and color scheme when Grady appeared at the door, buckets of water in hand.

"If my housekeeper has been doing her job, you should find some towels and soap in the washstand cabinet," he said, hauling the buckets into the room.

"Your housekeeper?" Rebecca echoed in surprise.

He shrugged. "I didn't want the place to run down while I was gone, so I hired a woman to come by here about once a week. Her husband comes with her and takes care of the grounds." He paused. "Actually, since you've been calling on King Cunningham, you've probably met Helen and Frank."

"No wonder everything is so clean and orderly," Rebecca remarked, gazing around the room. "The Taylors seem like a very honest, dependable couple. And they've been working for your family for a long time, haven't they?"

"For as long as I can remember." Grady emptied the buckets of water into the tub.

Anxious to wash the dust from her hair, Rebecca tugged the pins from her chignon. "You're fortunate to have someone as reliable and trustworthy as the Taylors looking after the place for you."

Grady nodded in agreement as he drained the last drop of water from the buckets. But as he edged back from the tub, Rebecca had the strange feeling that the Taylors were not the primary focus of his thoughts. She could tell by the way his gaze was sweeping over the strands of hair spilling over her shoulders, sensing that he was longing to reach out and brush his fingers through the dark waves.

Then, without warning, he stiffened, pulling back his shoulders and clenching his jaw. "I'll be right back with the rest of the water for your bath. One more trip and the tub should be full."

Buckets clanging, he wheeled and stalked down the stairs. When he returned a few moments later, he swept past Rebecca without a glance in her direction and unceremoniously dumped the water into the tub. Then he jerked open the doors to the wardrobe and tossed a man's shirt onto the bed. "Just in case you need something to wear while you're airing out your clothes," he muttered.

With that, he stormed into the hall and slammed the door behind him. Rebecca winced, wondering what was bothering him.

"He's probably just tired," she murmured,

stripping off her gown and undergarments, leaving the clothes in a heap on the floor.

She lowered herself into the tub, relishing the warmth of the water swirling around her. Then she leaned back and smiled, splashing a handful of water over her face, grateful she could wash away the dust clinging to her skin.

Grady lunged down the stairs and hurled open the back door. Stepping outside, he sucked in a deep, shuddering breath. Grateful the covered porch offered protection from the gusty weather, he gazed into the distance.

Darkness had settled over the plains. The winds were still roaring, though not as violently now. He suspected the worst of the storm had passed through the area, moving eastward at a rapid clip, heading toward Hope and places beyond, coating everything in sight with a blanket of dust.

He shrugged off his vest and shirt. Eager to get rid of the grime clinging to him, he stepped over to the pump and splashed water over his hair and face.

But not even the refreshing feel of the water could wipe away his inner turmoil. He'd been rude to Rebecca upstairs, he knew, but he couldn't seem to help himself. As soon as he'd seen that glorious mane of hair tumbling away from the restricting confines of her tight chignon, he'd been tempted to plunge his hands through those dark waves and crush her against him. Overwhelmed by the flames of desire surging through his loins, he'd summoned up every ounce of willpower he could muster and forced himself to turn and walk away.

But removing himself from her presence had only made matters worse. Now, forbidden fantasies were dancing through his mind, complete with detailed images of the activities that were taking place upstairs at this very moment.

He washed the dust from his hair, trickling water over his face and neck and chest, trying to rinse away the provocative thoughts flooding through him. But no matter how hard he tried, he couldn't purge the tempting images from his mind. He shuddered, knowing she was bathing, fully unclothed . . .

Behind him, the door creaked open. "Grady?"

He whipped around and froze, startled by what he saw. Rebecca was padding across the porch in her bare feet, wearing nothing but his shirt around her slender frame. The hem of the garment dangled around her knees, showing off the sleek line of her legs.

"I'd like to air out these clothes on the porch." She draped her gown and undergarments over the railing, never once meeting his gaze.

"I suppose you realize . . ." He struggled for words. Why did he feel as awkward as a schoolboy? "The storm is heading east, in the direction of Hope, and I don't want to risk the chance of venturing back into town tonight. Besides, it's already too dark to see the roads clearly."

She heaved a sigh. "I suppose that means

I'm stuck here with you for the rest of the night."

Was that a glimmer of amusement shimmering from her eyes? He couldn't be certain. "Will Jacob be worried about you?"

Dark strands of hair tumbled around her face as she shook her head. "He wasn't expecting us to return until tomorrow. He's aware that it's too tiring to drive out to the homesteads and return to town in the same day."

"Well, it's good to know that Jacob won't be worried." He cleared his throat. "So did you find everything that you needed upstairs?"

"Everything but a brush."

"A brush?" He retreated into the house. "I should be able to find one for you."

He didn't even realize that she had followed him up the stairs until he plucked a brush from the dresser and pivoted around. She was standing at the door, arms folded across her chest, studying her bare toes, appearing painfully, awkwardly aware of her inappropriate dress. "I don't mean to be such a bother," she said.

"You're no bother, believe me." Just as he edged toward her, clutching the handle of the brush, a tempting thought occurred to him. What would happen if he offered to brush her hair?

He stumbled to a halt. Would the soothing strokes of the brush calm her fears? Ease the tension sizzling between them? Satisfy his need to touch her?

"I can brush your hair, if you'd like," he volunteered.

Her head snapped up, and her eyes widened in surprise. "You want to brush my hair?" she echoed, her voice just above a whisper.

"No one will ever know except you and me." His mouth curled into a teasing grin. "And I won't tell if you won't."

That brought a smile to her lips. "Then you'd better be a man of your word, Grady Cunningham."

In spite of her lighthearted remark, her shoulders were stiff with tension as she slipped into the room. She perched herself on a corner of the bed, holding her back ramrod straight.

"I've never brushed a woman's hair," he admitted with reluctance, "so let me know if I get too rough with you."

"Don't worry. I'm sure you'll do just fine."

He set the brush on the crown of her head and inhaled a deep breath. Then he worked the bristles through the damp curls, edging down to her shoulders, with as much tenderness as he could muster. After repeating the process several times, he paused. "So how am I doing?"

"Incredibly well," she murmured. Her lashes fluttered to a close, and the tightness vanished from her neck and shoulders. "It feels wonderful, Grady. Please don't stop."

His mouth went dry. Not bothering to mention that he'd already smoothed out most of the tangles, he ran the bristles through the dark waves once again. He wasn't even certain he could have pulled away, even if she'd insisted on it. He was becoming addicted to threading his hands through that silky mane, relishing the velvety feel of those glorious waves against his fingers.

Hoping to extinguish the flames of desire searing through him by offering to brush her hair had been the craziest notion he'd ever had. Each stroke aroused his passions even more, heightening his senses to a dizzying degree. He moistened his lips, longing to press his mouth over that creamy neckline of hers, yearning to nibble on those delicate little ears, burning to spin her around and devour every part of her.

His hands began to tremble, and he felt a slight sheen of sweat glistening along his brow just as the soft purr of her voice filled the air.

"You know, I'm still hoping Landon will allow Kathleen to move into town as her time draws closer," she murmured. "I'm terribly worried about her."

"I can understand why." His hand stilled in her hair. "Still, inviting her to stay in your home was quite generous of you. Not many people would open their homes to a virtual stranger."

"It wasn't such a noble invitation," she insisted. "It just seemed like the right thing to do, considering the circumstances. Besides ..." She shifted her weight, turning to face him. "Besides, I know what Kathleen is going through, Grady. I know what it's like to be living in isolation on the plains, carrying a child, terrified no one will be there to hold your hand when your baby arrives."

"I never realized ..." Bewildered, he sat down beside her. Sensing her need to talk, he draped a comforting arm around her narrow shoulders. She nuzzled her cheek against his bare chest.

"I met David—Jessica's father—during the war. He was on leave from the Union Army, visiting his parents. At the time, I was still living on the Breckinridges' homestead. Unfortunately, their shanty was similar to the Yessicks'." She sucked in a shuddering breath. "About six weeks after David returned to his brigade, Jacob received word that his son had been killed on the battlefield. A few days later, I realized I was carrying David's child."

Grady grimaced, aching for her. "Were you still living with the Breckinridges?"

"Yes, but they promptly banished me from sight when I told them about my baby. I wouldn't be able to earn my keep any longer, they said." She choked back a sob. "I didn't know what to do, where to turn. I had no place to go, and I didn't know what would happen to my baby."

"So how did you end up with Jacob?" he asked, genuinely curious.

"As soon as I told Jacob and his wife about my circumstances, they welcomed me into their home—and into their hearts. I suppose that's why I invited Kathleen to stay with me until the baby arrives. I understand what she's going through, more than she'll ever know, and opening my home to her seemed like the only thing for me to do."

He sighed, resting his chin on the soft crown of her head, instinctively tightening his arms around her. She burrowed her face deeper into his chest, and Grady felt something stirring in the depths of his soul.

He'd never known a woman who possessed so much compassion and understanding. Never known anyone who could provoke so many emotions in him. Wishing he could wipe away all of the anguish of her past, he peered down at her. "And what about now, Rebecca? Does being here seem as right to you as it does to me?"

She edged back, gliding her fingers over his chest, curving them around his nape. The soft touch of her hand skittering over his bare skin jolted him to the core.

She didn't respond to his question with a verbal reply. But she didn't have to. She told Grady all he needed to know by the passion shimmering from her eyes, the slight parting of her lips, the seductive movements of her fingers curling through his hair.

He bent his head and brushed his lips across hers, terrified she might pull away, unable to bear the thought of letting her slip away from his grasp. But his doubts vanished when he heard a soft whimper escape from the depths of her throat, and he realized she was as deeply shaken as he.

She parted her lips, allowing his tongue entry into her mouth. He closed his eyes, deepening the pressure of the kiss, exploring, searching, savoring the taste of her. "Ah, Rebecca . . ." he murmured, tracing the crease of her lips with the tip of his tongue.

Still kissing her, he eased them both down on the bed. His loins flamed from the feel of her breasts crushed against his chest, from the touch of her hands roving over his shoulders and back. Waves of passion swept through him, swift and hard.

He wedged his hand between them, fumbling for the buttons on her shirt, burning to touch and taste and explore all those delectable curves and swells hidden beneath the fabric. But just as the first button fell free, Rebecca's fingers clamped over his hand, preventing him from plunging ahead. "I've had a baby, you know, and my body isn't as—"

"I've already seen part of you, Rebecca. And I saw nothing but perfection, beauty . . ."

Too impatient to contend with one more button, he yanked on the folds of her shirt, popping the buttons free. Then he slid the fabric aside, easing the shirt over the pale curve of her shoulders.

As his gaze trailed down the length of her slender, naked form, his heart thundered in his chest. He'd been fantasizing about this moment for weeks, but never in his wildest dreams could he have fathomed such flawlessness. Her breasts were full and high, crowned with rosy nipples, swollen with passion. Her stomach was taut and flat, her waist small, her legs slender. And the nest of dark hair curling over the juncture of her thighs almost seemed to be beckoning to him . . .

"You're the most gorgeous creature I've ever seen," he murmured, cupping her breasts in his hands. Then he swooped down and captured one rosy nipple with his mouth, flitting his tongue over the hardened peak.

She arched her back, moaning with desire. "Oh, Grady . . ."

She was trembling now, and he covered her body with his own. "Don't be frightened, Rebecca. The last thing I would ever do is hurt you," he murmured, raining a shower of hot, hungry kisses over her neck and shoulders.

She lifted her eyes to his face, and he saw glimmers of trepidation there. "But it's been so long for me, Grady. Before Jessica was born—"

"You'll know what to do, I'm certain. You're already driving me out of my mind, darlin'."

"But I'm not as experienced as you think I am." Her bottom lip was trembling, he noticed. "I've only been with one man . . . only one time."

He stilled. "You and your husband only made love once?" He didn't understand. If he were married to this ravishing creature, he would be devouring her night and day.

She gulped. "He had to report back to his unit, you see, and . . ."

Her voice faded away, and Grady knew something wasn't quite right. There was more to the story than she was willing to admit, he sensed. But he didn't press her for more information, didn't want her dredging up any more painful memories at the moment. "It's all right, Rebecca," he whispered, pulling her back into his arms. "You don't have to explain anything to me. Just give me the chance to love you like you've never been loved . . .''

The rest of his words remained unspoken as he captured that excruciatingly sweet mouth of hers with his own. She coiled her arms around his neck, pulling him deeper into the kiss. Grady moaned as the tips of her fingers skittered over his shoulders and roved across his back. Ripping his mouth away from hers, he blazed a trail of fiery kisses over the fragile cords of her throat and across the delicate sweep of her jaw. "God help me, I can't get enough of you," he rasped.

His loins were flaming, his heart was thundering, his hands were trembling with need. With lightning-swift movements, he rose from the bed and rid himself of his trousers.

Her gaze slithered down the length of his body, and he was pleased to see a mixture of admiration and astonishment glinting from her eyes when she caught sight of his arousal. But as he eased down beside her once again, he detected another expression flickering across her face. He stilled, suddenly alarmed by what he saw. He'd seen that look once before, and now he was seeing it again.

She was afraid.

But he wasn't the source of her fears, he sensed. She was afraid of something far greater than his passion-drenched gazes. She wasn't an innocent young virgin, after all. She had been married once, had even borne a child. But, nonetheless, she was afraid of something, something he couldn't name or define.

Burning to replace her fears with more

pleasure than she'd ever known, he moved his fingers over the flat plane of her belly, across the soft wisp of dark curls, and into the moist juncture between her thighs. Stroking that delicate, secret opening, he discovered she was moist and pliant, ready to accept more of him.

In one swift movement, he moved across her, covering her body with his own, crushing her breasts against his chest, grinding his lips against hers. Then he staked his arms on either side of her, staring deep into blue eyes smoldering with passion as he thrust his hips forward and plunged inside of her.

Sweet agony jolted through him. He wanted to be everything she needed, wanted to be more than she'd ever dreamed. But he wasn't certain how long his body could sustain the jolting sensations pulsing through him. Her deep-throated moans were rocking him to the core. And the touch of her hands, roving across his back and digging into the curve of his buttocks, were urging him to plunge deeper, harder, faster, inside of her.

"Grady, I can't wait . . ."

"I'm with you, darlin'," he rasped.

Just as shudders coursed through her, his whole body convulsed. Tremors quaked through him as he spilled his seed deep within her. Then he buried his face in the tumbled waves of her hair, sated beyond all reason.

The pressure of a strong arm curled around her bare torso and the touch of a firm hand skittering across her tummy roused Rebecca from a deep slumber the next morning. Never having experienced the delight of awakening with the warmth of a masculine body curled up behind her, she moved closer into the curve of Grady's embrace, wanting to savor the moment forever.

Stirring, she felt his breath whispering across her shoulder. "Good mornin', darlin'."

Her lashes fluttered open. Morning sunlight was streaming through the windows. "Looks like it's going to be a beautiful day," she murmured.

"It's startin' off mighty fine," he agreed meaningfully, nuzzling his mouth over her ear. "Of course, yesterday ended mighty fine, too."

The soft laughter emerging from her throat faded away as the husky timbre of his voice took on a more serious tone. "I realize last night wasn't the first time for either of us, Rebecca. But I've never known anything as wonderful as what we shared."

Shame seeped through her, dissolving the joy of the moment. Though her virginity wasn't the issue here, Grady's softly spoken words forced Rebecca to face reality. For the second time in her life, she'd given herself to a man without any guarantees or promises for the future.

Still, she couldn't deny that those fiery moments of passion had been more glorious than she could have ever fathomed. "Last night was ... was indescribable," she confessed, wishing she could find the right words to express her tumultuous emotions.

"It was more perfect than my wildest fantasies." His arm tightened around her. "There has never been another woman like you in my life, Rebecca."

But how many more woman will there be after me? Try as she might, she couldn't prevent a myriad of doubts and fears from assaulting her. Grady had never indicated he wanted to settle down with one woman for the rest of his life.

"I wish we didn't have to go back to Hope," he mumbled. "I wish we could stay right here all day. . . ."

His hand drifted over her ribs, then paused to linger on the gentle swell of her abdomen. But the touch of his fingers splayed across her belly brought another unsettling thought to Rebecca. New life could have been spawned during the passion-drenched pinnacle of their lovemaking, she realized. She could be carrying his child at this very moment.

"I wish we could stay here, too," she whispered back, burrowing her head deeper into the pillow, not daring to admit she wanted far more than just another day with him.

She squeezed her eyes shut, grateful he couldn't see her face. She had the strange feeling she was aglow with love for a man who had never once mentioned the subject of marriage to her.

Chapter 16

⌒～◯◯～⌒

Forcing herself to set aside her worries and fears about the future, Rebecca planted a bright smile on her lips during the ride back to Hope with Grady. Try as she might, she couldn't begrudge the man for making love to her. And since she truly enjoyed his company, she made every effort to be pleasant and cheerful during their time together.

But as soon as they pulled into town, Grady's brows narrowed with concern. "Seems mighty quiet around here for a Saturday afternoon," he observed.

Following his gaze, Rebecca understood the reason for his puzzled frown. Though the main street of Hope was far from deserted, there was a noticeable absence of the usual throng of cowboys. On a typical Saturday, scores of young men could be seen in the heart of town, invading stores and businesses, purchasing clothes, and spending their hard-earned wages before wandering into the Red Dog for the remainder of the evening.

Today, however, Rebecca noticed that most of the people ambling over the boardwalk were permanent residents of Hope. "Strange," she murmured as they rolled through the main street of town.

"Maybe I should check with the volunteers who are manning the deadline this afternoon," Grady suggested as they arrived at the house. He leaped down from the buggy, then bounded over to Rebecca, offering his hand for support as she stepped down from the vehicle. "It's a little too quiet in town, it seems, and I want to find out what's been happening around here since we've been gone."

"Can you spare just a minute before you leave?" Rebecca asked, retrieving her basket of medicinal herbs while Grady unloaded the rest of their belongings from the buggy. "I'm sure Jessica is anxious to see you."

He grinned. "I never intended to leave without seeing Miss Jess."

Jessica squealed in delight when they entered the house, hobbling up to greet them. "You're home!" She buried her face into the folds of her mother's skirt, giving her an affectionate squeeze before turning to Grady and hurling her arms around his legs.

Grady set aside the basket of supplies, then hunkered down and planted a kiss on the child's cheek. "Looks like you're on the mend, Miss Jess."

She beamed at him. "My leg doesn't hurt much at all now."

"And she's been on her best behavior since you've been gone, too," Samantha interjected, stepping up to join them.

"That's nice to hear." Rebecca smiled at the young girl. "Has Jacob been busy today?"

"He hasn't had any emergencies, if that's what you mean. But he said he wanted to check on some of his regular patients this afternoon." Samantha shifted her gaze to Grady, fluttering her lashes. "Did you enjoy the trip?"

"As a matter of fact, we encountered several surprises along the way." He straightened, peering over at Rebecca. "But it turned out to be one of the most enjoyable trips I've ever had. Wouldn't you agree, Rebecca?"

She nodded, too distracted by Samantha's fluttering lashes to contribute anything more to the discussion.

"Can you stay and play poker with me, Mr. Cunn'ham?" Jessica pleaded.

"I'm afraid not, Miss Jess." He patted the dark crown of her head. "At the moment, I need to take care of some business in town. But I promise I'll be back tomorrow."

"Promise?"

"Promise."

Rebecca stepped outside with Grady, closing the door behind them. "Can you join us for Sunday dinner after church tomorrow?"

"You can count on it, darlin'." He slipped his hands around her waist, drawing her close to him, grinning down at her.

But as he bent his head to kiss her, the front door rattled open. Rebecca jerked away from Grady's hold just as Samantha came out of the house. "I guess I should be getting home now," the girl announced.

"I'm heading that way, too." Grady motioned toward the street. "May I see you home safely?"

A blush rose to her cheeks. "That would be wonderful, Mr. Cunningham."

Grady winked at Rebecca before he fell into step behind the young girl, obviously amused by her flirtations. But Samantha's infatuation with Grady was no laughing matter to Rebecca.

An uneasy feeling rolled through her as she retreated into the house. She sighed, hoping the girl's crush on the man would not escalate into anything more.

"I truly appreciate you seeing me home, Mr. Cunningham."

"It's not any bother." Grady smiled down at the girl as they sauntered toward the main street of Hope. "Besides, a pretty young lady like yourself shouldn't be roamin' through town all alone."

"Do you really think I'm . . . pretty?"

"Yes, I really do," he admitted, admiring the long sweep of blond hair tumbling over her shoulders. "In fact, the other girls around here can't hold a candle to you."

Samantha blushed. "You're just teasing . . . aren't you?"

"I'm as serious as a judge." Grady's smile faded as they approached the boardwalk. "You're pretty enough to catch a man's eye, darlin'. And there are lots of men around here with rovin' eyes, anxious to take advantage of a young girl as pretty as you. That's why I don't think you should be venturin' through town by yourself all the time."

"But I've never run into any problems."

"Still, you can't be too careful these days." Grady's boots halted in front of the Collinses' store. Winking devilishly, he tilted the brim of his hat in Samantha's direction. "Of course, you can always count on me if you see trouble headin' your way."

"I'm sure I'll be just fine, Mr. Cunningham," Samantha said, giggling with delight as Grady turned and walked away.

The sound of familiar voices lured Rebecca into the parlor when she returned home from Sunday morning worship services. As she slipped into the room, she discovered that Grady was reading a story to Jessica. The child was curled up in his lap, leaning her head on his chest as he read aloud from the pages of a book.

Grady glanced up as Rebecca approached. "So how was church this morning?"

"Crowded and warm." She grinned down at her daughter. "Looks like you're having fun."

Jessica nodded. "Mr. Cunn'ham can read books almost as good as he can play poker."

Biting back a smile, Rebecca headed for the kitchen. "Maybe he'll finish reading the book to you while I'm getting dinner on the table."

Grateful she'd fixed most of the meal before leaving for church, Rebecca draped a bibbed apron over her Sunday gown. Then she set to work, preparing gravy to serve with the roast beef, carrots, and potatoes simmering on the stove.

It wasn't until she was seated at the table,

enjoying the meal, that she remembered to ask Grady about the mysterious lull in Hope's business activity on Saturday afternoon. "Was there any particular reason why the business district was so quiet yesterday?"

"I'm afraid so." His lips thinned as he pushed aside his empty plate. "Word has spread among the cattlemen about the success of our restriction on weapons in Hope. Apparently, cattle drivers have been opting for the railroad shipping facilities in Abilene and Ellsworth. Instead of using Hope's terminals for shipping out their livestock, they've been heading for places where their rowdy behavior is more acceptable."

"For cripes' sake," Jacob grumbled, heaving a disgusted sigh just as a rap sounded at the door.

Rebecca rose, wiping her hands on the skirt of her apron, and scurried to greet the caller. As soon as she opened the door, Frank Taylor tipped the brim of his hat. "Sorry for disturbing you on a Sunday afternoon, ma'am."

She motioned for him to enter the house. "You're not disturbing me at all," she insisted. "As a matter of fact, we're just getting ready to have a slice of pound cake for dessert. Would you care to join us?"

"I'll have to pass." Frank removed his hat as he stepped inside. "Actually, I'm not here on a social call."

Her heart lurched. "Has Mayor Cunningham—"

"No, no, the mayor is fine," he interrupted hastily. "I didn't mean to alarm you. I'm just wondering if you know where I can find the mayor's son, Grady. I checked at the Grand Central, and they said—"

"Well, I'll be damned." Grinning like the devil himself, Grady came into the parlor.

Frank smiled broadly. Rushing forward, he clapped Grady on the shoulder. "You're lookin' good, son."

"You're not lookin' so bad yourself," Grady returned, still grinning. "So what brings you here today?"

Frank's smile died. He fiddled with the brim of his hat. "It's your father, Grady."

Sheer terror ripped across Grady's rugged features. "The old man?"

Frank nodded grimly. "It's not his health, mind you. But he wants to see you this afternoon. Seems his business has been droppin' off somethin' fierce the last few days. His holding pens for livestock are almost empty. He figures it's got somethin' to do with this deadline in town, and he wants to discuss the matter with you."

Every muscle in Grady's body went whipcord taut. "You can tell the old buzzard to go straight to—"

"Grady." Rebecca reached out, placing a cautioning hand on his arm. "It's not the best of circumstances, I'll admit. But it's a chance to see your father again, face-to-face."

He remained silent for a long moment. Then he pulled back his shoulders and clenched his jaw. Determination and steely resolve glinted from the depths of his eyes as he turned to Frank. "Tell the old man I'll be there at three."

*   *   *

As Grady prepared to leave for the Cunningham estate, Rebecca retrieved her basket of herbs from Jacob's office. "I'd like to go with you to visit your father, Grady."

He jammed his white Stetson over his head, staring at her in disbelief. "Why in the hell do you want to get involved in a family dispute?"

"Because I'm already involved. I care about you and your father. I'd like to be there for you. And I'd like to be there for the mayor, too. He isn't in the best of health, you know."

Something akin to gratitude flashed across his face, and the tautness eased along the line of his jaw. "Then we best be leaving if we intend to be there by three," he said quietly, opening the door.

Though Grady greeted Helen with an affectionate embrace when they arrived at the Cunningham mansion, he resumed a defensive stance as he approached the mayor's private living quarters. His back was erect, his chin held high, as he entered the room. Rebecca quietly trailed behind him.

The air sizzled with unspoken tension when the two men faced each other for the first time in three years. Rebecca thought she detected a slight wince of pain flickering across Grady's features at his first glimpse of his father. But he quickly regained his stalwart demeanor as he focused a steely gaze on the invalid seated behind a large desk at the opposite end of the room. "Frank said you wanted to see me," he bit out.

The old man nodded, narrowing his eyes. His gaze wandered over the length of Grady's muscular frame, then lingered for a moment on the angular grooves of his face. It almost seemed as if he were struggling to find a point of common ground, searching for something to bridge the gap of division between them. "It's been a while, hasn't it?" he finally asked.

"It was my understanding that I was no longer welcome here," Grady said flatly.

"Circumstances often dictate the need for change." Malcolm leaned back in his chair. "I'm interested in hearing about this weapons ban of yours. The town council tells me that you're the one responsible for establishing it."

"Something had to be done to curb the violence," Grady returned, bristling defensively. "Too many innocent people were getting hurt. Even Rebecca's own daughter—a six-year-old child, mind you—got caught in the line of fire. We're damn lucky she wasn't seriously injured."

Malcolm peered at Rebecca. "I'm sorry to hear about your daughter, Mrs. Summers."

"Thankfully, she's doing much better now," Rebecca returned.

"It's a pity when an innocent child becomes the victim of violence." He shook his head in dismay. "Of course, it's a pity when a ban on weapons discourages new business from patronizing our town, too."

"I hope you're not implying that the deadline is driving off your business," Grady began. "Because if you are—"

"I'm not accusing you of anything," Malcolm denied. "Restricting weapons to assure the safety of innocent women and children is a good idea. But cattlemen don't like the notion of surrendering their firearms to anyone. They'd rather do business where they can keep their guns in their holsters."

Frustration lined Grady's face. "What's going on here?" he demanded, stalking across the room, approaching the older man. "Are you asking me to drop the ban on firearms so you won't lose any more customers at the stockyards? Is that why you've summoned me here today?"

Malcolm boldly met his son's heated gaze. "I wanted us to reach an agreement, Grady. I wanted us to discuss another option, to find a way to keep the peace in town while keeping the cattlemen happy."

Surprise and sudden understanding replaced the sparks of anger glinting from Grady's eyes. Sighing, he wearily leaned against the edge of the desk. "You know, for a minute there, I thought you were trying to find fault with me again. I thought you'd called me here to point out all my mistakes in restoring order to the town that you practically built with your own two hands."

Malcolm stared at his son in disbelief. "Why would I want to do that?"

"Because I've never been able to do a damn thing right in your eyes. Paxton was the only one who could ever meet your standards." Old resentments, simmering for years, flared in Grady's voice. "I don't deny that I've made some stupid mistakes in my life, especially when I was younger. But I've never understood why you couldn't believe in me, believe in my ideas, in spite of my shortcomings." He paused. "If you'd bothered to ask me about what happened on the night of Ned Sikes's death, you might have learned that I never disgraced the family name."

Malcolm winced. "Then I'm asking now. What happened on that night?"

Grady trudged toward the window and stared aimlessly through the glass panes. "I tried to warn Mary Anne about Ned before she ever married him. I knew he drank too much, and I'd seen his volatile temper. But Mary Anne wouldn't listen to me. She was crazy in love with Ned, and she insisted their marriage would be a good one."

A shadow of darkness crossed his face as the memories came rushing back. "The first time I noticed the bruises on her face, she claimed she'd tripped over a rug and fallen, facedown, on the floor. When she was sporting a black eye, she insisted she'd been standing in the way of some books that had mysteriously fallen from a shelf. Then she started running out of excuses, and I knew she'd been trying to cover up for Ned."

He grimaced, continuing to recall the painful memories. "I couldn't stop worrying about Mary Anne after she and Ned moved to Kansas City, so I decided to see how she was doing. Unfortunately, I caught Ned in the act of damn near choking her to death when I arrived at their house. When I jerked him away from her, he lunged at me with a knife. I reached for my gun and killed him—before he had the chance to kill Mary Anne and me."

He whipped around, facing his father once again. "But nobody bothered to find out the truth about that night. Everyone—you, Priscilla, the whole damn town—chose to believe the worst about me, jumping to conclusions and reaching a verdict without knowing any of the facts."

Lines of regret deepened the wrinkles in the old man's face. "Everyone assumed you were smitten with the girl, son."

"But I'd known her for most of my life, for cripes' sake!" Grady bellowed. "Yes, I treasured her friendship, but we weren't having an affair. We were childhood friends, and nothing more! Why is that so difficult for everyone to believe?"

The deep roar of his own voice echoed in his ears, alerting Grady that his temper was flaring out of control. Some inner sense warned him that he was being unreasonable, but the tumultuous emotions careening through him were too powerful to restrain. Seething with fury, he lunged toward the door. "I should've known it would be senseless to come here," he muttered, storming out of the room.

Malcolm massaged the bridge of his nose and sighed. "So what do you think about my wayward son, Mrs. Summers?"

"I think he's the finest man I've ever known, Mayor," she answered without a moment's hesitation.

His bushy brows narrowed. "Why?"

"Because he's a giving, caring person. He may pretend not to care about anyone or anything at times, but that's because he's discovered that caring too much about other people often brings problems his way."

When Malcolm remained silent, Rebecca continued on. "He cared enough about one of his crew members to seek medical treatment for him. He cared enough about my daughter's safety to restore peace to Hope. And he obviously cared enough about a woman's life to save her from further harm."

Malcolm was gazing through the window, lost in his thoughts. Without further ado, Rebecca quietly slipped out of the room.

When she emerged from the mansion, Grady was waiting in the buggy for her. As they pulled onto the main road leading into town, he remained silent and pensive. Trying to think of something that might bolster his sagging spirits, Rebecca wondered if he would agree to a short trip.

"Would you like to visit the Fords tomorrow?" she blurted out on impulse. "If we leave early, we could make the trip in one day."

"I wouldn't mind seeing Owen and Hattie again." He glanced over at her and smiled. "Not a bad idea, darlin'. Not a bad idea at all."

Rebecca cleared the soiled dishes from the table shortly after daybreak the next morning, pleased Grady and Jacob had enjoyed the fried eggs, bacon, biscuits, and gravy that she'd prepared for breakfast. Now, as the men retreated to the barn to hitch up the buggy for the trip to the Ford homestead, Rebecca hastily placed the dirty plates into a tub of soapy water, anxious to finish with her chores.

She had just wiped the crumbs from the table when Jacob's voice drifted through the open kitchen window. "Rebecca will be glad to know you're here so early, Samantha. If you'll go through the back door, you'll find her in the kitchen."

Rebecca scurried across the room to greet Samantha, grateful the girl had agreed to watch Jessica for the day. But as soon as she opened the door, Rebecca noticed that Samantha seemed pale and distraught. "Good morning, Rebecca," she murmured in a flat, lifeless tone.

"Good morning, Samantha." Rebecca quickly ushered the girl into the kitchen. "Jessica isn't awake yet, but she should be getting up soon. There's enough bacon and biscuits here for both of you, if you'd like to join her for breakfast."

Samantha grimaced. "For some reason, the thought of eating breakfast doesn't appeal to me at all." She inhaled a deep shaky breath, then wrinkled her nose in disdain. "Just the smell of that bacon is making me—"

She halted, her face turning ashen. Gagging, she clamped a trembling hand over her mouth. Then she whirled around and bolted through the door.

As Samantha leaned over the porch railing, retching uncontrollably, Rebecca hastily dampened a cloth in the wash basin. Rushing to the girl's side, she pressed the wet cloth over her brow. "This should make you feel better, Sam," she soothed gently.

"I'll be back to normal in a few minutes," Samantha insisted, struggling to hold up her head. "The queasiness always passes by midmorning."

Rebecca's hand stilled. "How long have you been feeling like this?"

"Just a few days."

Rebecca pressed the back of her hand against the girl's cheek. "You're not running a fever," she murmured, becoming more troubled by the moment. "Tell me, Sam. Do your breasts feel swollen and tender?"

Samantha sagged against the railing. "Yeah, they've been hurting really bad lately."

A tiny pulse of fear pounded through Rebecca's veins. "And when was your last monthly?"

"About six weeks ago, I think." A horrified expression suddenly flashed across her pale face. "Surely you don't think . . ."

"I can't make any definite predictions until I examine you, Samantha." Rebecca placed a comforting hand on the girl's shoulder. "But it appears you're contending with some morning sickness."

A lone tear trickled down Samantha's cheek. "What am I going to do, Rebecca?"

Seeing the distress on the girl's face, Rebecca felt something tight and restricting grip her chest. All too well, she could remember the anguish of coping with the tumultuous emotions of being unwed and pregnant.

At that instant, Grady's voice bellowed through the air. "Ready to go, Rebecca?"

"I'm on my way," she called out. Turning

back to Samantha, she added, "Grady and I will see you home, dear. I'm sure you don't feel like staying with Jessica today."

Samantha lifted her chin. "I'll be fine, Rebecca, truly I will. By the time Jessica gets up, I'm sure I'll be feeling normal again."

"Very well," she conceded. "But if you'd like, I can stop by the store and talk with your mother about—"

"No!" Samantha's eyes widened in alarm. "Please don't say anything about this to my mother, Rebecca. I need some time to sort things out for myself."

"I understand, Samantha." *More than you realize*, she added silently, slipping back into the house to gather up her belongings for the journey across the plains.

"Just wait till Hattie finds out you've come callin'!" Owen greeted Grady and Rebecca with a broad smile. "She'll be the happiest woman in Kansas when she sees the two of you."

Rebecca laughed. "So everything has been going well for the new mother and her baby?"

"Couldn't be better." Owen motioned toward the shanty. "Come see for yourself."

Just as Owen had predicted, Hattie shrieked with delight when they entered the shanty. "What a wonderful surprise!" she exclaimed.

While the women launched into a lengthy discussion about Blake's eating and sleeping habits, Owen proudly displayed his new son to Grady. "He's lookin' a little bit more like his pa everyday, wouldn't you say?"

Grady grinned. "Once his beard gets as thick as yours, no one will be able to tell the two of you apart."

Chuckling, Owen returned the baby to his cradle. "Let's get some water for that gelding of yours before the poor creature dies of thirst."

A few moments later, the two men were ambling through the dry fields, water buckets in hand. Halfway to the creek, Owen paused. He pointed toward several buffalo bones that were partially buried in the ground. "Take a look at this, Grady."

"If I didn't know better, I might think you'd actually planted those skeletons," Grady observed, chuckling at the thought. "If you're tryin' to grow a crop of buffalo, my friend, you're gonna be mighty disappointed with your yield."

"To be honest, I'm not quite sure what to think. A couple of weeks ago, I noticed somethin' different about the soil around that big mound of buffalo bones down by the creek. It looked richer, more fertile, than any other spot of ground on this claim. Thinkin' those skeletons must be feedin' the soil somehow, I put some bones here in the fields to see what would happen."

Kneeling, Grady pulled a bone from the dirt, then plunged his fingers through the soil that had surrounded it. In spite of the lack of rain, the soil appeared rich and fertile. "You might have something here, Owen," he assessed, sifting the dirt between his fingers.

Owen hunkered down beside him. "What do you think I have?"

"A source of fertilizer that you can sell for cold, hard cash." Grady grinned. "Looks like you may have a good yield from this crop of bones, after all."

Chapter 17

A golden glow was shimmering over the prairie as the buggy sped along the trail toward Hope. Enjoying the splendor of the colorful sunset splashed along the horizon, Rebecca sighed contentedly. "It's been a wonderful day, hasn't it?"

Nodding, Grady glanced over at Rebecca and smiled. "I'm glad you suggested this trip. Getting away from town for the day has been a boost to my spirits."

"It's good to see you smiling again." She laughed. "Of course, it's not hard to smile after spending the day with Owen and Hattie."

"And Owen and I stumbled across an idea this afternoon that has the potential of putting a lot more smiles on their faces."

When he offered nothing more, Rebecca frowned. "Is this some sort of big secret?"

"Not really." He shrugged. "Owen has a few things that he would like to sell, and I'm going to see if I can find a buyer."

How considerate, Rebecca thought. Not many men in this world would seek a buyer for another man's merchandise without expecting anything in return. "Do you already have someone in mind?" she asked.

"I'm planning to send some wires to a few business contacts of mine in Chicago and Boston. But I might even sweeten the deal with a personal sales pitch."

Rebecca's heart skipped a beat. "You may be leaving town?"

"Possibly." A lazy smile sprouted on his lips. "It's never been easy for me to stay in one place for very long. Taking in some new sights every once in a while breaks the monotony for me."

"I didn't realize Hope had become so boring to you," she observed crisply, prickling from the implication of his words, wondering if she could be part of the reason for his growing discontentment with life in Hope.

"Boring? Hardly." He chuckled. "I haven't had the chance to get bored lately. No, I'm just getting restless, I suppose. I'm not the type of man who enjoys a routine life. I'm too anxious to sample everything the world has to offer."

Were women included in the list of activities he intended to pursue? She cringed at the thought. "If I ever have the chance to travel, I'm sure I would enjoy it. But I couldn't stand the thought of never having one special place to call home."

"Settling down in one place is good for the soul," he agreed. "But occasionally getting away from familiar places and faces is good for the soul, too."

"As long as you aren't running away to avoid resolving the problems you've left behind," she added thoughtfully.

His eyes narrowed. "What do you mean?"

"I'm talking about the business trip that you're considering. Leaving town now means you could miss the chance to make amends with your father, Grady. Can't you see why he asked you to meet with him yesterday? In his own way, he was reaching out to you, trying to open the door for a reconciliation."

"The old man's intentions might have been honorable, but we didn't come close to solving our problems." He scowled. "And I'm not gonna spend the rest of my life waiting around here, holding my breath, expecting him to change."

"Leaving Hope won't bring you any closer to making amends with him," she pointed out.

"Staying doesn't guarantee any resolutions, either," he grated.

"But you can't expect to settle any unfinished business in your life if you walk away from the problems!" she blurted out.

Taken aback by her emotional outburst, Grady halted the buggy at the side of the trail. "What's gotten into you, darlin'? I'm not planning to leave Hope for good. I'm only thinking about taking a business trip for a month or so."

"Fine, then," she snapped. "Go ahead and make your trip. I don't care what you do. Obviously, you're too stubborn to regard anyone else's feelings about the matter."

Her feelings in particular, he realized, jarred by a sudden flash of understanding. How could he have been so thoughtless? He'd been babbling like a mindless fool, never once considering her feelings.

Wanting to soothe her fears, he slipped an arm around her shoulders. "I doubt I'll be travelin' anywhere, darlin'. I just got carried away, thinkin' out loud. More than likely, I can sell Owen's goods by sending some wires back East. I won't even have to leave town."

"Don't let me keep you from doing what you want, Grady." She stiffened beneath his touch. "Obviously, the thought of being apart from me isn't of any concern to you."

"Oh, but it is." His fingers glided to the base of her neck, stroking and massaging the tense muscles there. "I feel empty inside when we're not together, almost like part of me is missing. Nothing in my life seems right without you beside me. My feelings for you are hard to explain, but they're inside me, just the same, growing stronger everyday. And being apart from you is the last thing I want."

The rigid set of her shoulders relaxed beneath the soothing touch of his fingers. "I don't want to be apart from you, either, Grady. I'm so much in love with you that I can't bear the thought of you leaving . . ."

The softly spoken admission moved Grady beyond words. An overwhelming sense of love surged through him, love so potent and powerful that he trembled from the intensity of it. He wanted this woman to share his life, his home, his bed. Never had he wanted anything more.

But this was neither the time nor the place to ask for her hand in marriage, he sensed. A woman as special and rare as Rebecca Summers deserved a proper proposal, one whispered beneath a sultry moon and a sky full of twinkling stars after an evening of intimacy and romance.

In the meantime, sitting here on the side of the dusty trail, he could show her how much he loved her. Desire ripped through him like a searing flame. Emitting a low groan, he pulled her into his embrace, mindless of anything other than touching her, kissing her, loving her.

His eyes darkened with passion, stealing Rebecca's breath away just before his lips clamped down over hers. Her mouth opened beneath the grinding pressure of his, sensing the urgent hunger, the desperation. His breathing became heavy and ragged, and she could feel the beat of 'his heart thundering against her breast.

His Stetson slipped to one side as he crushed her against him. Reaching behind him, she removed the hat from his head, then delved her fingers into the dark waves of his hair. All the while, his hands were roaming over her, searching, groping, seeking.

She shuddered when he grasped her breasts, trembled as his fingers kneaded the swollen mounds. "God, I'll never stop wanting you, Rebecca," he whispered. "Never in a million years . . ."

"I'll never stop wanting you, either,

Grady," she whispered back just before his mouth claimed hers once again. But even as she uttered the words, Rebecca sensed he couldn't possibly comprehend the depths of her love for him, realize how much she wanted to become his wife.

Longing for a commitment from him, a promise for the future, she tightened her arms over the broad expanse of his shoulders and thrust her breasts against his chest.

Responding with a low groan of desire, he pressed fiery kisses along the curve of her jaw and neck, unaware of her desperate need to hear the words that he failed to say.

Rebecca dutifully attended the auxiliary meeting the next morning, though she opted for driving the buggy to church instead of walking into town. By the time she returned home, Jacob was preparing to leave for the Cunningham estate.

"I thought I should check on Malcolm again today," Jacob explained as he packed some supplies into his medical bag.

"I hope he's doing well." Rebecca sighed. "His meeting with Grady on Sunday was an emotional one, I'm afraid."

She was still thinking about the encounter between Grady and Malcolm long after Jacob had departed for the mayor's home. Though the divisions between the Cunningham men were painful and deep, Rebecca thought their stormy relationship would have a better chance of succeeding if they could set aside their stubbornness and pride long enough to make amends.

Still, she suspected Grady was still too distressed over the meeting with Malcolm to discuss the matter again. And he confirmed her suspicions when he dropped by the house later in the day.

"Where's Jacob this afternoon?" he asked.

"He's paying a call on your father. Just a routine visit, I believe."

"I see." Promptly dismissing the subject, he turned to Jessica and grinned. "How about a hand of poker, Princess?"

Squealing with delight, Jessica raced to fetch a deck of playing cards from her room. Within a few moments, the pair were sprawled out on the parlor floor, absorbed in their game.

"You're the champ again for the day, Miss Jess," he praised at the end of the second hand, kissing the child on the cheek. He turned toward Rebecca. "Sorry I can't stay, but it's almost time to report for my deadline shift. And I need to stop by the telegraph office to see if I've gotten any responses to the wires I sent back East this morning, as well."

"Maybe you can stay longer tomorrow," Rebecca returned optimistically.

But spending more than a few minutes with Grady proved to be difficult for Rebecca throughout the remainder of the week. Though he faithfully dropped by the house each afternoon for a brief visit, tending to business matters and manning the deadline occupied the majority of his waking hours.

More than a week passed without any moments of privacy between them. By the following Thursday, Rebecca was longing to snatch some time alone with him. Soon after he arrived at the house for his daily visit, she ushered him through the kitchen and out the back door.

As soon as they stepped onto the small porch, she heaved a troubled sigh. "I've been missing you lately," she admitted frankly.

"I've been missing you, too." Grimacing, he raked a hand through his hair in frustration. "It's been hectic, to say the least."

"I know you've been busy." She tilted her head to one side, studying him intently. "Can you spare the time to come to dinner tomorrow evening?"

"I'm afraid not, Rebecca. I'm leaving for the Ford homestead in the morning. I heard from my contacts back East today, and I'm anxious to discuss their offers with Owen. If all goes well, I should be back in town by Saturday night."

Though the news sounded promising for Owen, Rebecca couldn't ignore the feeling of loneliness growing inside her. She was already missing him, and he hadn't even left. "You'll be careful, won't you?"

"You're the one who needs to be careful while I'm gone." He slid his hands around her waist, pulling her close to him. "I hope you haven't been venturing into town by yourself lately."

She placed her hands on his shoulders, welcoming his closeness, savoring the scent of him, relishing his touch. "I've been driving the buggy instead of walking," she assured him.

"Good." His mouth swooped down on

hers, capturing her lips in a kiss so mind-
boggling and breathtaking that her heart
slammed against her ribs.

Rebecca clung to him, losing herself in the
hard, lean-muscled feel of his shoulders and
chest, the heady, masculine scent surrounding
her. She shivered, every nerve ending of her
body raging with need.

"It's been almost two weeks since . . . we've
been together," she whispered on a breathless
sigh. "And now that you're leaving . . ."

Taking her hand into his, he led her across
the yard. "I'm not leaving until tomorrow,"
he reminded her in a low, provocative tone
as he guided her into the barn.

He closed the doors, then pulled her into
his arms. He covered her lips with a hot, hungry kiss, his body moving urgently against
hers. She felt his hands at her breasts, the
pulse of his manhood against her stomach.
Rebecca moaned into his mouth, consumed
by a savage warmth that she'd never known.

He lowered her onto the hay, still kissing
her. "I'm aching to be inside you, Rebecca,"
he whispered, his hand plunging beneath
her skirts.

Mindless of anything other than the touch
of his fingers sliding between her thighs, she
writhed against him. "I want you, too," she
confessed. "I want you more than anything . . ."

She arched her hips, aiding him as he
stripped away her drawers, welcoming him
as he entered her with one swift, firm plunge.
She reveled in the feel of him buried deep
within her, the way their bodies fit together so

perfectly, so completely. They moved together with a frenzied urgency, each bringing the other to the brink of passion, each finding fulfillment in the union of their love.

Rebecca was checking her herbal supplies in Jacob's office on Saturday morning when she heard a frantic knock at the door. Hoping Grady had returned early from his journey, she swept across the room and swung open the door.

Frank Taylor stood on the porch, fingering the rim of his tattered hat. "Is Doc Summers here?"

"Why, yes, he is." Rebecca opened the door wider, disturbed by the frown marring Frank's weathered face. "Is something wrong?"

The man nodded grimly. "It's the mayor. He's taken a turn for the worse, I'm afraid."

At that moment, Jacob shuffled down the steps. "What's all this, now?"

"Mayor Cunningham isn't feeling. well, Doc," Frank explained. "Helen and I thought you should take a look at him right away. I ain't no doctor, but I'm afraid he's suffered another stroke. His entire left side is drooping now, even his face."

Jacob sprang into action, hurrying into his office and grabbing his black leather satchel from the desk. "I'll be right behind you, Frank." Turning to Rebecca, he added grimly, "I'm not sure how long I'll be gone. It might be several days before I can get home, depending on Malcolm's condition."

"Then take care," Rebecca whispered, breathing a silent prayer for both the physician and his patient as Jacob scurried out the door.

Rebecca sauntered through her herb garden after an early dinner with Jessica, trying to sort through the chaotic thoughts whirling through her mind. The last two weeks had been filled with challenges that were far from ordinary, she thought.

Though she had not seen Samantha since returning from the Ford homestead, she hoped the girl had found the courage to confide in her parents about her dilemma. It would be difficult for Samantha, she knew, but what other choice did the girl have? Obviously, she couldn't confide in Hank Murdock.

To make matters worse, she'd seen little of Grady in recent days. Though Rebecca was well aware that he'd been distracted by his secretive dealings with Owen and distressed about the recent encounter with his father, she couldn't help but feel a bit slighted by him. And she couldn't stop wishing that he would ask her to marry him. Was it so wrong to long for a lifetime of happiness with one, special man?

And now, Malcolm Cunningham's health was deteriorating rapidly, she feared. She only hoped the man and his son would have another chance to put their problems to rest.

The merry sound of Jessica's voice sang through the air, jarring Rebecca from her wayward thoughts. "Look at Uly, Mama!" The girl giggled with delight. "He's glad I can play outside with him again, isn't he?"

"He sure is, Jess. And I'm glad, too."

Watching her daughter scamper across the
yard with the family's beloved pet, Rebecca
felt a lump swell in her throat. Jessica's rapid
recovery was a true blessing, she thought.

She was still admiring the child's pink
cheeks and energetic steps when a commotion
erupted from the street. Wagon wheels were
churning, horses were galloping, and men
were shouting with glee. Startled and curious,
Rebecca grabbed Jessica's hand and raced
across the yard. Uly hobbled behind them,
nipping at their heels.

As they rounded the corner of the house,
Rebecca stumbled to a halt, amazed by what
she saw. "What in heaven's name . . ."

She edged forward, gaping in stunned disbelief. Riding on horseback, Grady was leading a caravan of two wagons into town. Hattie
and Owen Ford and their baby were the occu-
pants of the first wagon. In the rear vehicle
were Kathleen and Landon Yessick.

But the most surprising sight of all was the
unusual cargo. Both wagons were loaded
with buffalo bones. Was this the merchandise
that Owen wanted to sell?

Jessica squeezed her mother's hand, capturing Rebecca's attention, when they reached
the edge of the road. "Why are they hauling
all those awful bones to town?" the child
asked.

"I'm not sure," Rebecca admitted just as
Uly barked a greeting to Grady.

"Evenin', ladies." Grinning devilishly,
Grady tipped the brim of his hat toward Rebecca and Jessica. He guided his horse to a

halt, motioning for the wagons to come to a stop behind him. "Well, what do you think?"

"I'm not sure what to think," Rebecca admitted, returning his smile.

"Grady here found us a buyer for all these bones," Owen called out. "We're shippin' them to a company in Chicago that's gonna make fertilizer from these skeletons."

"Fertilizer?" Rebecca echoed in surprise.

Grady chuckled. "Owen and I noticed the bones on his claim were fertilizing the soil."

"And Grady's contact in Chicago said he would buy as many bones as we could send him!" Hattie exclaimed. "Isn't it wonderful? We'll have enough money to tide us through till next plantin' season!"

"But bones have been the easiest cash crop we've ever raised," Landon joked.

"And now we'll be staying in town until the baby is born," Kathleen added shyly. "Hope Cottage will be our home for the next month or so."

"I'm gonna treat my wife to a new dress while we're in town," Owen boasted. "And we might even stay at Hope Cottage for a week or so, too!"

"Then I suggest we get this cargo down to the railroad yards." Grady hurled his arm into the air, signaling for the caravan to press forward. "See you in the mornin', ladies."

Rebecca watched in silence as Grady led the little procession toward the depot, her heart swelling with pride.

Something wasn't quite right.

Grady noticed the glimmer of apprehension

flickering from Rebecca's eyes as soon as she greeted him at the door the next morning. Though she responded to his kiss with more passion and warmth than he could have fathomed, the anxiety was still present in her gaze after the heat of their kiss had faded away.

Tugging at his hand, she led him into the parlor. "What you did for the Yessicks and the Fords was quite remarkable, Grady. I never dreamed those bones would be good for fertilizer!"

"Apparently, they're good for other things, too." Grady grinned. "Another buyer has ordered four shipments to produce bone china."

"China?" Rebecca laughed, a bit louder than normal. "That's wonderful! The homesteaders will be thrilled with the news. And they'll have enough money to make it through the winter and—"

"You're babbling, Rebecca." Grady grasped her shoulders, peering down into her flushed face. "You're avoiding something, something you don't want to tell me. Am I right?"

Her eyelids drifted shut, and a pained expression flickered across her delicate features. "It's your father, Grady. I fear he might have suffered another stroke."

His fingers tightened over her shoulders. "When?"

"Yesterday morning. Jacob has been with him ever since."

A sickening feeling swept through Grady. "God help me, I don't want to feel anything for that old man." Frustrated, he pulled away from Rebecca. "But in spite of everything, he's still my father."

"I know this must be difficult for you, Grady." Her eyes were pools of understanding and compassion. "But if you have something you'd like to discuss with your father, I think you should seriously consider talking to him today. None of us knows what tomorrow might hold."

He shrugged. "I doubt anything I have to say would change the situation."

"You never know." She inhaled a shaky breath, and he sensed she was struggling to find the right words. "You've told me about your regrets for not making amends with Paxton and your mother before they died. And I'd hate for the same thing to happen all over again with your father."

"But it takes two to make amends," he snapped, more harshly than he'd intended.

"You can't control your father's behavior," she agreed readily. "But you can take charge of your own."

"What do you mean?"

"You may not have another chance to say all those things that have been left unsaid. Even if your father doesn't respond with the words you'd like to hear, at least you'll have the contentment of knowing you said all you can say, did all you could do."

Hearing the heart-wrenching tremble in her voice, Grady felt something stirring in the depths of his soul. Never in his life had anyone expressed so much concern for him. And witnessing her compassion for his problems moved him like nothing ever had.

Emotions, rough and raw, seared through him. His fingers were trembling as he lifted them to her face, stroked the soft velvety skin of her cheek. How could he not love this woman?

She'd found the courage to express what he hadn't been able to put into words, reminding him of what he'd known all along. And she was standing beside him, helping him face the most difficult challenge of his life by nudging him in the right direction with her words of encouragement.

He pulled her into his arms, crushing her against him, never wanting to let her go. He stood there for a long moment, resting his chin on the soft crown of her head, savoring the feel of her softness pressed against him. "I suppose I should be leaving now," he finally dragged out.

"I'd like to go with you, if you don't mind." She leaned back in the cradle of his arms. "I'd like to be with you, Grady."

Shouldn't he have known she would see him through to the end? "Can you leave right away?"

A troubled frown marred her brow. "I'm afraid not. I'd forgotten Jacob has the buggy with him. And I have to consider Jessica, too."

"I can rent a buggy from the livery," he offered. "Do you think Samantha can watch Jessica?"

"I'm not sure. It's Sunday morning, so she's probably getting ready to leave for church with her family."

"Then maybe the Collinses could take Jessica to church with them."

"You might have something there." Her

frown vanished. "I don't think anyone would object if we dropped off Jessica at the Collinses' place before they leave for church. After services are over, Samantha can stay here with Jessica for the rest of the afternoon."

Nodding, Grady headed for the door. "I'll be right back with the buggy."

They arrived in town just as the Collins family emerged from the building that served as both their home and business. Rebecca waved, snaring their attention.

Charlotte bustled over to the buggy. "Heading to church?"

"I'm afraid not," Rebecca said. "We fear the mayor has taken a turn for the worse, and Grady and I would like to spend the day with him at the Cunningham estate. But I don't want Jessica to miss church this morning, and—"

"You go right ahead," Charlotte insisted with a wave of her hand. "We're on our way to church right now, and we'd be glad for Jessica to join us."

"Thanks, Charlotte." Rebecca's gaze shifted to Samantha. "Can you watch Jessica this afternoon? I don't think I'll be able to get home until later in the day."

"Of course, Rebecca," Samantha agreed.

Jessica scampered down from the buggy, squealing with delight. Just as Grady picked up the reins, Virgil added, "Give our best wishes to your father, Grady. He's done a lot for this town, and I hope he'll recover quickly."

Taken aback, Grady felt a rush of gratitude sear through him. "Thanks, Virgil."

* * *

Riding along the familiar route leading to
the Cunningham estate, Grady became
acutely aware of the multitude of emotions
churning inside him. He didn't want to see
Malcolm Cunningham again, didn't want to
face another rejection from him. And he certainly didn't want to expose himself to the
pain and anguish that was certain to accompany another turbulent encounter with the
old man.

Yet, he couldn't bear the thought of living
the rest of his life filled with regret. After coping with the heartache and guilt of not making amends with Paxton and his mother,
Grady knew he had no other choice except to
approach his father one last time. And he also
knew he would be eternally grateful to
Rebecca for standing beside him.

Steeling himself, Grady entered the Cunningham mansion with Rebecca. Helen somberly escorted them to Malcolm's room,
where Jacob was waiting at the door. The
physician gripped Grady's shoulder with a
warm hand. "He's had a close call, I'm afraid.
But he's a fighter, and I predict he'll get
through this."

Still, Jacob's subtle warnings couldn't have
prepared Grady for the shock of his father's
condition. As he approached the man's bed-
side, he felt as though someone had knocked
the wind from his lungs. In the span of two
weeks, Malcolm Cunningham looked as
though he had aged by two decades. The left
side of his face was sagging, deepening the

chiseled lines and grooves, and his color was pallid and lifeless.

Malcolm struggled to open his eyes. "Just the man I wanted to see," he mumbled in a slurred voice. One corner of his mouth curled into something resembling a grin. "'Course, I thought you might be too busy hauling buffalo bones into town to stop by and see me."

Grady frowned in confusion. "Where did you hear about that?"

Malcolm actually chuckled. "Word gets 'round in this town faster than lightnin', son."

Son. Grady savored the sound of the word.

"Damn smart thinkin' on your part about sellin' those bones for fertilizer," Malcolm rattled on. "Made me wish I'd thought of it myself."

Grady stilled, unable to believe what he was hearing. Was King Cunningham actually praising him for something he'd done?

"'Course, I always did see a lot of myself in you." Malcolm paused, his voice becoming gruff and strained. "And that may be why I always favored Paxton. I saw things in you that I didn't like in myself. And I never took time to see all the good things in you . . . all the things that Rebecca here pointed out to me."

Grady whipped around, his eyes locking on Rebecca, his heart swelling with love.

Malcolm's slurred voice snared his attention once again. "This little lady here told me about all the things you've been doin' to help other folks—your crew, her daughter, the whole damn town." Malcolm swallowed with difficulty. "Told me about the things I've been too blind to see, too stubborn to hear."

"I appreciate what you're saying." Grady felt an ache swell in his chest. "More than you know."

The old man boldly met his son's gaze. "You're a fine man, son. I'm just sorry I've had to stare death in the face to realize it. I've had a lot of successes in my time, and I haven't liked to admit my shortcomings. But doubting you, never believing in you, were the greatest mistakes I've ever made."

Grady closed his eyes, too overcome with emotion to speak. When he summoned up the courage to meet his father's gaze once again, he extended his hand.

Malcolm reached out, his gnarled fingers entwining with his son's.

The brief exchange of words had not mended every broken fence between them, could not compensate for the years that had been lost. But the simple gesture of an extended, weathered hand rekindled the flame of hope that had been buried deep within Grady's heart, lighting the way for brighter days ahead.

Grady draped an arm around Rebecca's shoulder as they left the mansion. Overwhelmed by the unexpected turn of events, he remained silent until they reached the main road. "Instead of heading straight back to Hope, I think I need to unwind for a bit," he admitted. "Would you mind if we stopped by my house for a while?"

"I think that sounds like a wonderful idea," Rebecca agreed.

When they arrived at the house a few moments later, Grady paused before approaching the porch. Standing in the yard, narrowing his eyes, he admired the beauty of the dwelling for a long moment. "You know, this is the first time I've truly felt that this place belongs to me."

Rebecca stepped up beside him, coiling her hand around his arm, leaning her head on his shoulder. "I think your brother—and your father—realized from the start that this land and house rightfully belonged to you."

"Maybe so." He peered down at her, somewhat awed by the changes in his life, even more astonished by this woman's unflinching belief in him. "But I don't think I could've ever understood that by myself. It took the wisdom of one very wise woman to help me comprehend the feelings of my brother and father."

"But you were the one who took the initiative to resolve all the unsettled matters from your past," she insisted, refusing to accept any credit for the incredible sense of peace flooding through him. "And what I witnessed between you and your father this afternoon was one of the most touching moments I've ever known."

They sauntered onto the porch, arms entwined. "It was incredible," Grady agreed. "In fact, my whole life has been incredible lately. And I think you're partially to blame."

"Me?" A hint of amusement sparkled from her eyes.

"Yes, you." He whirled her around, pressing her against him. "You're the one who encouraged me to do what I think is right, and to let the rest fall into place."

"But you were the one who convinced an entire town that weapons should be restricted in Hope. And you were the one who stumbled across the crazy idea of selling buffalo bones for fertilizer. Goodness knows, I'm not going to take credit for that one."

He grinned, running his fingers over the soft curve of her cheek. "You're one incredible lady, Rebecca Summers. You're the only woman in the world who has ever made me feel this way."

Doubts suddenly clouded the blue of her eyes. "But what about . . . Priscilla?"

His smile died. "I never truly loved Priscilla. And it became obvious that she never truly loved me. She wanted to marry the Cunningham name, not a Cunningham man." He sucked in a deep breath. "You've never mentioned much about Jessica's father, either."

Shrugging away from his hold, she ambled into the house. He fell into step beside her, disturbed by the shadow of darkness flickering across her face.

"There's not a lot to tell, actually," she began. "We didn't know each other for very long. We met while he was visiting his parents, on leave from the Union Army. I was seventeen years old, and I fell madly in love with him at first sight." Her bottom lip trembled, and he could have sworn that he heard a catch in her voice. "Now, I can barely remember what he looked like. Everything we had together seems like a hazy dream. So much has happened since that summer ..."

Her voice faded away, as if she were lost in her thoughts. Grady's heart stilled. Something deep inside of him said she was holding back some painful memories, blocking out parts of her life that she didn't care to share with anyone just yet.

He reached out, tucking a wayward strand of dark hair behind her ear. "This isn't a hazy dream, Rebecca. What we have together, right now, at this very moment, is real. Nothing in the past, nothing in the future, can change how we feel about each other today."

Today. Rebecca ached inside, wanting to express all the love surging through her for this incredibly wonderful man. She needed him to know how deeply he had touched her heart, how he had filled her with longings so fierce that she was trembling inside. If only for one afternoon, she wanted to set aside her doubts and fears and worries and simply show this man just how much she loved him.

Stretching up on her toes, she curled her arms around his neck and lifted her lips to his. Within the next breath, her entire world became centered around loving this wondrous man. She felt the frantic thundering of his heart against her breasts, heard the deep groan of pleasure escaping from his throat, tasted the hungry pressure of his mouth grinding against hers, relished the enticing scent of him filling her senses.

"You don't know what you're doin' to me, darlin'," he rasped into her mouth, sliding his hands over her back, pressing her against his arousal.

"If it's anything like you're doin' to me, you must be having a hard time catching your breath," she reasoned with a hint of a smile, sucking in a shuddering gasp before offering her lips to him once again.

In the next instant, he was scooping her into his arms, cradling her head on his shoulder, tucking one arm beneath her knees, and sweeping her up the staircase. He kicked open the door to the room they had once shared together, then gently set her feet on the floor.

"Let's get you out of these damn Sunday clothes before I rip them off you," he insisted impatiently, fumbling with the buttons on her gown.

Clothes cast aside, he eased her onto the bed. She pressed the full length of her naked body against his bare skin, abandoning all reason, relinquishing every inhibition she'd ever known, shuddering from the wonder of it all. She was mesmerized by the touch of his hair-roughened skin against her fingers, tantalized by the desire ripping through her from the touch of his lips on her breasts, fascinated by the hardness of his arousal pressing against her, tormented by the waves of longing rushing through her.

"Please," she pleaded, gasping for breath. "Please love me, Grady."

"There's nothin' I'd rather do, darlin'." His fingers worked their way through the delicate petals that shielded the most private part of her, exploring that sweet inner core. Finding her moist and ready, he slid on top of her trembling frame.

As if wanting this loving to last forever, he entered her slowly, seductively. She arched her back, longing for him to fill that aching emptiness inside of her, urging him forward by clamping her hands over the firm muscles of his buttocks.

The rhythmic motions of their bodies soon became one as he plunged deeper, faster, harder. She closed her eyes as tremors rocked them both, shuddering from the sensations exploding inside of her, crying out Grady's name.

He collapsed against her, sated with passion. Nuzzling his mouth along the curve of her neck, he sighed with contentment. "I love you, Rebecca. I've never known anything like this in my life."

"I love you, Grady." She snuggled against him, wishing the moment would never end. "I wish we could stay here forever."

"I wish we could, too. But since we can't stay here forever ..." His mouth captured hers in a slow, lingering kiss that sent the blood rushing through her veins all over again. ". . . I say we should stay here for another hour or two."

Lifting her lips to his, Rebecca willingly agreed.

Shortly before six o'clock, Rebecca hurled open the front door, anxious to see her daughter. "Jessica, I'm home!"

She stepped inside the house, wondering why the child wasn't responding to her call.

She wandered into the kitchen and peered through the window. Though she was hoping to see Jessica and Samantha in the backyard with Uly, she could find no sign of the girls.

She whirled around, sighing in frustration just as she spotted a note on the kitchen table.

Rebecca,

Jessica is staying with me at my house until you get home.

Samantha

Though Rebecca was relieved to know Jessica was safe and sound, a troubled frown creased her brow. Grady had already left for the evening, and the buggy remained with Jacob at the Cunningham estate, which meant she had no alternative except to walk into town and pick up Jessica at the Collinses' home.

Trying to avoid any negative thoughts, Rebecca reviewed all the reasons why she shouldn't be frightened as she headed into town. She had plenty of time to pick up Jessica and get back to the house safely before dark, she reasoned. And very little violence had occurred since Grady had established the deadline.

Absorbed in her thoughts, Rebecca didn't realize she was the only person on the street until she reached the railroad tracks. She was reminding herself that Sunday afternoons were usually calm and quiet in Hope when she heard the thud of boots rushing up behind her.

Her heart pounded with fear. She glanced behind her just as a foul-smelling hand clamped over her mouth. "Finally, I've found you," a deep voice bellowed into her ear.

She screamed in terror, but his hand muffled her cry. A thick arm coiled around her midriff, yanking her off the ground, knocking her feet from beneath her. Then the man dragged her into a narrow alley lodged between two buildings.

Panic ripped through her. Chaotic, disjointed thoughts clicked through her mind. Her worst nightmares were coming true . . . her stalker had found her . . . no one would hear her cries for help . . . the street was deserted . . .

"First the preacher and now Cunningham!" the man sneered. "When are you gonna learn your lesson, 'Becca?"

That voice. Terror sliced through her. Somewhere in the past, she'd heard that voice. But she couldn't recall a specific name or face.

"When are you gonna learn your lesson?" he repeated thickly, jerking her around, removing his hand from her mouth.

He slammed her against the wall of the building. Rebecca gazed up into the face of her assailant and froze. "Alfred," she rasped in disbelief.

"Don't call me that," he snapped, glowering at her. "I'm not the dirt-poor son of a Breckinridge homesteader anymore. They call me Big Al now."

Rebecca gaped at the man, assaulted by

sudden understanding. Big Al, the trouble-maker who'd wounded two men from the Red Dog, Alfred Breckinridge, who'd terrorized her as a young girl, and her stalker—all three were one and the same.

"Why are you doing this?" she demanded. "Why have you been stalking me?"

"Why?" He cackled. "Because you keep runnin' away from me. First, you ran off with that Yankee soldier, the doctor's son. You thought I wasn't good enough for you."

"That's not true," she insisted, quaking with fear.

"Don't lie to me!" he snarled. "I thought you'd come back to me after that soldier boy upped and died on you. But you're still lettin' other men kiss those purty little lips of yours ... when those purty lips should be mine." He grabbed her hair, tugging at it until tears sprang to her eyes.

Rebecca shuddered, repulsed beyond words. "Please don't torture me like this, Alfred."

"I can do anything I want," he hissed. "You're mine, darlin', and I don't want anyone messin' with my woman. Especially that damn Cunningham fella."

He yanked harder on her hair. Tears of pain streamed down her cheeks. She hated being at the mercy of this horrible, despicable man. "What do you want from me?" she pleaded.

"I don't want you seein' Cunningham anymore!" His eyes took on an evil gleam. "Mark my words, little lady, if you see that man again, I'll make certain you'll regret it."

He fumbled for something strapped around

the thick expanse of his waist. In the next instant, he was holding the edge of a sharp knife against her neck. "Don't even think about lettin' that man touch you again," he threatened, pressing the tip of the blade across the tender cords of her throat. "You don't want that purty little gal of yours to get her throat slashed, do you?"

"No!" she cried. Rebecca squeezed her eyes shut, seized by an inner pain more intense and violent than any she had ever known. "Not my Jessica . . ."

A low, menacing growl suddenly erupted in the alley. Startled, Alfred turned his head just as Uly let out a ferocious bark and lunged at him.

The dog rammed its full weight against the man's legs, knocking him off balance and breaking his hold on Rebecca. The knife clattered to the ground. "Goddam you, mutt!" Alfred roared, howling in pain as Uly clamped his teeth over his leg.

Rebecca whirled, bolting through the alley on trembling legs, seizing the chance to escape.

Chapter 18

Early on Monday morning, Grady strode into the telegraph office. Intending to confirm plans for a second shipment of buffalo bones with his business contact in Chicago, he handed a scribbled note to the telegraph operator behind the counter. "I'd like you to wire this message as soon as you can," he instructed.

"I'll take care of it right away, Mr. Cunningham." After accepting Grady's payment, the man plucked a piece of paper from the desk. "This message arrived for you a few minutes ago. All the way from Georgia, I believe."

Georgia? Grady's eyes narrowed skeptically as the man handed the paper to him. He didn't know anyone in Georgia.

Or so he'd thought.

"Well, I'll be damned," he mumbled, staring in disbelief at the name of the sender. *Tyler McRae.*

He quickly scanned the wire. Tyler would

be arriving in Hope next week for a reunion with his sister, Rebecca McRae. And his wife and children would be accompanying him to Kansas, the message said.

Elated with the results of his letter to The McRae Hotel in Tennessee, Grady had to restrain himself from letting out a whoop of joy in the middle of the telegraph office. But as he bolted through the door, he couldn't resist kicking the heels of his boots together. Some things in life deserved to be celebrated, after all. He sprinted toward Rebecca's house, unable to contain his excitement.

But when Rebecca opened the door, his heart plummeted to his toes. Dark circles shadowed her eyes, and her face was pale and drawn. Judging by her haggard appearance, Grady suspected she hadn't slept at all.

Hoping his news would brighten her spirits, he flashed a grin in her direction. "You look like you could use some cheerin' up, darlin'." He plunged his fingers into his vest pocket to retrieve the telegram. "And I've got some news that will—"

"Don't, Grady." She pursed her lips together. "I'm afraid you'll have to leave. I'm not feeling well today."

His heart lurched. "What's wrong?"

"Lots of things are wrong." Her gaze skittered past him, scanning over the street. Her eyes darted to the right, then the left, as if she were frantically searching for someone. Or afraid of what she might see.

Grady steeled himself. "What in the hell is going on?"

She sagged against the door. "You have to

leave, Grady." Her voice was weak and strained. "And you can't come back."

He stared at her, unable to believe what he was hearing. Was this the same woman who'd so passionately shared herself with him yesterday afternoon? The woman who'd declared her love for him? *"What?"*

She lifted her chin, but Grady could have sworn her bottom lip was trembling. "Don't come back. And don't make this any harder on me than it already is. I won't let you inside the house, no matter what you say or do. It's too dangerous to have you here . . . for Jessica and for me."

Grady was still standing on the porch in stunned disbelief long after Rebecca had closed the door. What—or who—had frightened her so? Led her to the point that she wouldn't even see him?

Distraught and confused, he vaulted across the porch and cornered the house. The buggy was still missing, he noticed. More than likely, Jacob was still at the Cunningham estate, caring for his father.

Unable to consult Jacob about Rebecca's unsettling behavior, he paused. Who else would know what was going on with Rebecca?

Samantha. Charlotte.

Five minutes later, he stormed into the Collinses' store. But never in his wildest dreams could he have imagined what was awaiting him there. As soon as he set foot into the establishment, Virgil Collins grabbed his vest and shoved him against the counter.

"Just the man I wanted to see," Virgil

hissed, fury lining his face. "I was on my way out the door to come huntin' you down."

"And to think I'd believe you'd turned into a fine, upstanding citizen!" Charlotte shrieked. She bustled through the store, dragging Samantha behind her. Coming to an abrupt halt in front of Grady, Charlotte shoved her daughter toward him. "What do you have to say for yourself, young man?"

Grady blinked in confusion. "What in the hell are you talkin' about?"

"You know what I'm talkin' about." Charlotte lifted her chin a notch. "You and Samantha."

"Me and Samantha?" Grady echoed in disbelief.

"Don't act so surprised," Virgil snapped irritably, releasing his hold on Grady's vest with a rough shove.

Samantha stepped forward. Her red-rimmed, swollen eyes avoided Grady's stormy gaze. "I told them the truth about you and me, Grady. And they know I'm carryin' your baby."

"*What?*" he roared.

Virgil clamped a hand over Grady's shoulder. "Quit actin' like you don't know what's goin' on around here, Cunningham. For Pete's sake, you deserve to be shot for takin' advantage of my daughter the way you have!"

Grady ripped Virgil's hand away from his vest, seething with fury. "And you deserve to be shot for making accusations against an innocent man. I haven't laid a hand on Samantha, Virgil, and I'm not the father of her child."

Wheeling, he stalked away from the store.

Jacob returned home from the Cunningham estate shortly after noon, pleased to report that the mayor was steadily improving. "But I decided to come home when Grady arrived to visit his father," he explained, joining Rebecca in the parlor. "He insisted he could keep an eye on Malcolm until tomorrow afternoon."

"I'm glad he could relieve you." Rebecca managed a weak smile. "You need to get your rest, you know."

"You look like you could use some rest yourself, 'Becca," Jacob observed, a frown creasing his brow.

"I'm just a little tired, I suppose." She dismissed his concern with an airy shrug, praying he wouldn't press the matter any further. She wasn't entirely certain she possessed the strength to relive the horror of yesterday's encounter with Alfred.

Despite the trauma of recent days, Rebecca found herself looking forward to attending the weekly auxiliary meeting the next morning. Though she offered no protest when Jacob hitched up the buggy for her short ride to the church, she promised she would come straight home from the meeting so he could return to the Cunningham estate soon after lunch.

Arriving at the church, Rebecca swept into the assembly room. But she'd taken only a few steps when she stumbled to a halt, surprised by what she saw. Why was Samantha here?

She slowly approached the group of ladies, noticing that Samantha's eyes were red and swollen. Charlotte stood rigidly behind her daughter, while Agnes, Lydia, and several other ladies were clamoring around the pair.

Rebecca's heart sank. Obviously, Samantha's condition was no longer a secret, she was surmising just as Charlotte confronted her with an accusatory glare. "Samantha tells me that you've known about her condition for several days now."

"Yes, I have," she admitted. "But she asked me to refrain from saying anything until she had the chance to talk to you about the matter herself."

"I see." Charlotte heaved a troubled sigh. "Well, I shouldn't be angry with you, I suppose. But all of us—especially you, Rebecca—should be furious with Grady Cunningham for what he has done."

Rebecca's pulse throbbed with fear. "Why should I be angry with Grady?"

"For making a fool out of you, dear. The man tried to make everyone believe he was interested in pursuing you, while he was secretly seeing my daughter. And I would have never praised him to high heavens if I'd known what he was doing behind my back!" Charlotte moaned.

"What a scoundrel," Lydia agreed sorrowfully. "Of course, even when everyone was praising him for all his good deeds, I wasn't entirely convinced that he was as wonderful as everyone claimed. Once a scoundrel, always a scoundrel, I say."

Stunned beyond words, Rebecca sagged against the edge of a table before her trembling legs could give way beneath her. For a long moment, she stared at Samantha in disbelief.

All along, she'd suspected Samantha had been infatuated with Grady. But in spite of the girl's flair for the dramatic, Rebecca never dreamed she would accuse Grady of fathering her child, never fathomed she would make him a scapegoat for her wanton behavior. Worse yet, the stinging accusation was stirring up old memories of Grady's scandalous past, lending credibility to Samantha's claim.

Grady. Rebecca's heart twisted at the thought of another unjust scandal ruining his name. But how could she prevent a foolish young girl from destroying the reputation of the man she loved?

A surge of anger abruptly replaced all of her shock and dismay. No longer willing to tolerate the unbearable thought of anyone— especially a desperate young girl—trying to smear the good name that Grady had worked so hard to establish in Hope, Rebecca lifted her chin with resolve.

She approached the group of ladies, knowing what she had to do. Concerns about her own reputation faded away, overshadowed by the strength and depth of her love for Grady Cunningham.

"Samantha's claim couldn't possibly be true, ladies," she announced quietly. "Grady Cunningham is one of the finest men I've ever known. I love him with all my heart, and he loves me, as well."

She lifted her chin another notch, summoning up every ounce of courage she could muster. "There is no way Grady would do something like this to me. I'm certain he would never betray our love by fathering a child with another woman. He has been my lover for weeks now, and I'm convinced he hasn't been intimate with anyone else but me."

A unified gasp swept through the crowd, followed by a stunned silence. Feeling the women's condemning stares pressing down on her like heavy weights, Rebecca became acutely aware of what she had just done. She felt a sickening sensation rolling through her, knowing she'd tarnished her own good name by defending Grady.

Charlotte cast a stern glance at her daughter. "You have some explaining to do, young lady. Why would you accuse Grady of fathering your baby if it isn't true?"

"Because Hank left me!" Samantha blurted out, bursting into tears. "He left without a word. I don't know where he is, and I don't know if he's ever coming back! And I th-th-thought he loved m-m-me. I th-th-thought he wanted to m-m-marry m-me . . ." Her voice died, drowned out by sobs.

Charlotte paled. "You and . . . Hank Murdock?"

Nodding, Samantha gulped. "But I blamed Grady," she admitted, regret tainting her voice. "He seemed like a good man. I thought he might be willing to take care of me if he realized how desperate I was. . . ."

Relieved Samantha's confession had cleared Grady of any wrongdoing, Rebecca quietly slipped out of the room. But as she ventured home, she couldn't ignore the painful ache swelling in her chest. Now, everyone in town would know Rebecca Summers wasn't the respectable lady that she'd pretended to be.

And Jessica would suffer for her mother's sins, just as Rebecca had endured the heartache of her own parents' mistakes.

"Your father's condition is improving, Grady," Jacob assessed soon after arriving at the Cunningham mansion. "His color looks much better this afternoon."

"He's eating better, too," Grady noted. "And he rested comfortably during the night."

"That's good to hear." Turning, the physician headed back to the mayor's room. "I'll take over from here, son. You go on about your business, and enjoy the rest of the day."

Once he left the mansion, Grady mounted his horse. Though he genuinely cherished the moments that he'd spent with his father, he wished they'd been able to iron out the rest of their differences. Between his fury over Samantha's allegations and his distress over Rebecca's behavior, he'd been too befuddled to fully enjoy his father's company.

During the night, sitting beside his father's bed, Grady had tried to sort out the events of the day. Just before dawn, a startling revelation had assaulted him. Rebecca must have known about Samantha's accusation. Worse yet, she must have *believed* the sordid tale. Why else would she have turned him away from her door?

Now, returning to Hope, Grady felt a knot coil in his stomach. Why had Samantha accused him of fathering her child? And why hadn't Rebecca dismissed the girl's allegations?

Determined to set the record straight, Grady tightened his grip on the reins. Long ago, he'd sworn never to allow anyone to falsely condemn him again. Heading into town, he vowed to prove his innocence by forcing a confession from Samantha in front of her parents.

He stalked into the store, clenching his jaw with steely resolve. But as he stormed up to the counter, he was astonished to see an embarrassed flush creeping over Virgil's face.

"I believe we owe you an apology, Grady." Virgil raked a hand through his hair in frustration.

"Samantha admitted she lied about your involvement with her," Charlotte confessed sheepishly.

"Well, that's the best news I've heard all week," Grady mumbled. Slightly dazed, tremendously relieved, and suddenly puzzled, he frowned. "What made her tell the truth?"

Charlotte heaved a troubled sigh. "It was all Rebecca's doing. At the auxiliary meeting this morning, Rebecca was appalled when Samantha accused you of fathering her baby. She insisted you couldn't be the father because the two of you had been ..." She paused, floundering for words, as a flush rose to her cheeks. "Rebecca said the two of you had been intimate for some time now. When she leaped to your defense, Samantha broke down and confessed her former suitor is the baby's real father."

"And the scoundrel can't be found," Virgil added in disgust. "He's somewhere between here and Mexico, workin' on a cattle drive."

A myriad of emotions swamped Grady. He was surprised Samantha had retracted her charges against him, relieved he was no longer being unjustly accused. But an incredible sense of joy was also flooding through him. Rebecca had defended him, believed in him, without once considering the possibility that Samantha's accusation could be true.

She had *believed* in him.

Wrought with emotion, Grady stilled. Rebecca had defended him, never once considering the consequences of her actions.

And in the process, she'd tainted her own name.

The revelation hit him as forcefully as if an iron fist had rammed into his gut. Above all else, Rebecca treasured control of her good name. And she'd tarnished her honor by defending his.

He couldn't allow her to relinquish her most treasured possession for his sake, couldn't permit her to lose the honorable standing in the community that she'd worked so hard to attain for herself and for Jessica.

But what could he do?

Gripped by a sudden thought, Grady curled his lips into a smile. "I suppose, then, that Rebecca told you about our marriage, as well."

Charlotte blinked in confusion. "You and Rebecca are . . . husband and wife?"

He nodded. "It wasn't planned, mind you. It was a spur-of-the-moment decision for both of us. But coming to terms with my father made me realize that life is too fleeting to waste a single day. And I knew I didn't want to wait another moment for Rebecca to become my bride."

"But when . . . and how?"

"We got married on Sunday afternoon," he answered as smoothly as he could, hoping an air of assurance would lend some credibility to the fabrication. "An old friend of the family—a justice of the peace—was paying his respects to my father when Rebecca and I arrived at the estate. And I convinced him to marry us, right then and there."

"Oh, my. How romantic! You must truly, truly love her." Charlotte clutched her throat and sighed.

"That I do," Grady admitted, suddenly overwhelmed by the intensity of his emotions. Yes, he loved Rebecca Summers, loved her more than words could express. And he truly wanted her to become his wife.

Bewilderment abruptly replaced Charlotte's wistful expression. "Why didn't Rebecca tell us the good news?"

"Well, she . . ." Grady hedged for a brief instant as he groped to find a plausible reason for Rebecca's silence. "She insisted on waiting a few days before telling anyone so the entire town can celebrate with us at the same time," he finally offered. "She's planning for us to exchange vows again, in front of all her friends and family, and she wanted the chance to plan a satin and lace affair for everyone to enjoy."

He politely tipped the brim of his hat, promptly ending the discussion, before Charlotte could ask anything more. Leaving the store, he headed straight for the Summerses' residence, intent on asking Rebecca to become his wife. But the joy and excitement soaring through him vanished when he arrived at the house. Rebecca was hesitant to open the door, and the woeful expression on her face ripped his heart into shreds.

Troubled by the lines of defeat marring her beautiful features, he shoved his way into the house. "You've got to tell me what's going on with you, Rebecca," he insisted, barging into the parlor.

"It's no use, Grady." She sagged with defeat.

He grasped her shoulders. "The strength of our love can overcome anything, Rebecca, even gossip. I've just talked with the Collinses, and they told me how you defended my name this morning. And I told them—"

"Don't, Grady." She squeezed her eyes shut, as if to block out the pain. "Nothing you could say will change anything. Even if I hadn't told everyone about us, I couldn't possibly continue to see you."

"And why the hell not?" he snapped.

"Alfred—the oldest Breckinridge son, the one who terrorized me while I was growing up—is here in Hope. Except no one calls him by the name of Alfred anymore. Everyone knows him as Big Al. And he's the one who has been stalking me. He cornered me in an alley, and he threatened to hurt Jessica if I continue to see you."

"What in the hell is that son-of-a-bitch trying to prove?" he roared.

A shadow of darkness crossed her face. "He has always been angry with me. He hated me for rejecting him, for falling in love with David that summer." A tear of sorrow cascaded over her cheek. "I never married Jessica's father, Grady. He died in the war shortly after we met, and we never married. He never even knew I was carrying his child. When Jacob and Emma took me into their home, they insisted I assume the name of Summers. Looking back on it now, I suppose the situation didn't fall into place like Alfred wanted it to. He and the rest of the Breckinridges were aware that I'd never become David's wife, and I suspect he thought I would turn to him for help out of desperation as an unwed mother."

"And now, Alfred is threatening to harm Jessica unless you stop seeing me . . . because he wants you for himself," he surmised, seething with fury.

"I'm afraid so." Tears shimmered on her lashes. "And I can't bear the thought of anything happening to Jessica. I've never wanted her to suffer on account of me. I've always tried to protect her, always tried to live a good life so she wouldn't have to be ashamed . . ."

Sudden understanding assaulted him, swift

and hard. All along, he'd sensed she was harboring a secret, shielding her past from scrutiny. Now, she'd broken through the last barrier standing between them, revealing her deepest secret.

Silently resolving to put an end to her worries, Grady lunged for the door. "Big Al won't be bothering you any longer," he vowed, silently promising to find the culprit before the night was over.

Rebecca was trudging up the stairs, feeling more despondent than she'd ever felt in her life, when a knock sounded at the door.

She was surprised to find Charlotte standing on the porch. Dangling from her hand was a large basket. "May I come inside for a moment, dear?" she asked pleasantly.

"Of course, Charlotte." Opening the door wider, Rebecca ushered the woman into the parlor.

"I came to apologize to you, Rebecca," Charlotte explained, lowering her thin frame to the settee. "I wasn't very pleasant to you this morning, I'm afraid."

"You don't have to apologize for anything," Rebecca contended. "I'm well aware that you and Samantha are going through a difficult period right now."

"We'll survive." Charlotte forced a bleak smile onto her lips. "Hopefully, Hank Murdock will find his way back to Hope and do right by my daughter when he finds out she's carrying his child."

"I hope so." Rebecca sighed. "Weddings are wonderful occasions."

"And speaking of weddings ..." Amusement and joy suddenly twinkled from Charlotte's eyes. "Grady came by the store this afternoon and told us about the good news. Congratulations on your marriage, dear!"

"M-M-My m-m-marriage?" Rebecca sputtered.

Charlotte laughed. "You don't have to keep your secret any longer, Rebecca. Half the town has already heard that you and Grady were married at his father's estate on Sunday. And everyone is thrilled for the two of you!"

Rebecca stilled, stunned by what she was hearing. Realizing why Grady had voiced the falsehood, she was moved beyond words. His valiant efforts to preserve the honor of her name in the community touched her heart in a way that nothing ever had.

"This isn't much in the way of a wedding gift, dear," Charlotte said, presenting the large basket to her. "But Virgil and I—and Samantha, too—wanted you and Grady to know just how happy we are for the both of you."

"Thank you," Rebecca whispered hoarsely, unable to utter another word as she quietly escorted Charlotte to the door, too choked with emotion to deny Grady's claims about their marriage.

Just as she pried open the wooden lid to the basket, another rap sounded at the door. Setting aside the gift, Rebecca scurried to greet the unexpected callers.

Owen and Hattie Ford were smiling broadly as Rebecca opened the door. "Congratulations!" Owen bellowed. "We just heard the news!"

"I've been savin' this for someone special," Hattie said, presenting Rebecca with a wedding ring quilt stitched in delicate shades of blue and white. "This is for you and Grady, in honor of your marriage."

A steady stream of callers flowed into the house throughout the afternoon. Agnes, Lydia, and other members of the auxiliary brought wedding gifts, as well as the Yessicks.

When Jacob returned from the Cunningham mansion, he gaped in disbelief at the gifts strewn across the parlor. "What's going on here?"

Rebecca managed a weak smile. "Have a seat, Jacob." She motioned toward his favorite chair. "I believe you'll need to sit down."

During the next half hour, Rebecca related the events of the past few days to Jacob, covering everything from her frightening encounter with Alfred to Grady's defensive efforts to protect her honor.

When she finished, hot tears were stinging her eyes. "When Grady left this afternoon, he swore Alfred Breckinridge wouldn't bother me again." She choked back a sob. "But I'm afraid I'll never see Grady again, either."

Too distraught to continue, she picked up her skirts and retreated into the privacy of her room. And not even the dawn of a new day brightened her dismal spirits.

Though troubled and disheartened, Rebecca tried to concentrate on her chores the next morning. She was sweeping the dust from the front porch when the sound of hooves galloping over the road caught her attention.

She glanced up and froze. *Grady*.

Her heart leaped into her throat as he dismounted. With quick, long strides, he bounded up to the porch. Pushing back the brim of his hat with a callused finger, he grinned down at her. "It's all over now, Rebecca. Big Al is behind bars, where he belongs, and he's gonna stay there for a long, long time."

"But—but where did you find him?"

"Carl and I caught up with him a few miles out of town. As it turned out, most every sheriff in Kansas has been lookin' for him. Seems he's wanted for several robberies and a couple of shootings." His eyes were warm and loving as he gazed down at her. "Big Al isn't a threat to you or Jessica anymore, Rebecca."

"Thank God. It's comforting to know he won't be coming around here again." She peered up at him. "And it's a relief to know you're back, safe and sound. I wasn't certain if I would be seeing you again."

"A man would have to be a fool to walk away from a woman like you." He slid his hands around her waist, pulling her close to him. "And I may have done some foolish things in my life, but I'm not a damn fool."

Confusion fluttered through her. "What do you mean?"

"I mean I want to marry you, Rebecca, if you'll have me." His eyes darkened with passion as he brushed his lips across hers. "Will you be my wife?"

"Of course I will, Grady." She returned his kiss with all of the longing and urgency rushing through her. "Besides, I couldn't possibly refuse," she added, a smile whispering across her lips. She tugged at his hand, guiding him into the parlor, motioning to the baskets and crates, the quilts and linens, the pottery and china, spread across the room.

"What's all this?" he asked, his gaze sweeping across the assortment of items with stunned disbelief.

"They're wedding gifts, Grady. After you told the Collinses that we'd been married everyone in town started bringing wedding gifts to us." She twinkled up at him. "So I'm terribly glad you asked me to marry you. Otherwise, I'd have to do the proper thing and return all these presents."

He laughed, pulling her back into his arms, sealing their vows of love with a long, leisurely kiss. "So when do you want to get married?"

"Tomorrow couldn't be soon enough for me." A frown suddenly creased her brow. "But everyone thinks we're already married . . ."

"We'll just tell everyone that we're exchanging vows for a second time because we want the entire town to celebrate our happiness with us." He paused. "Plus one very special person from Georgia."

"Georgia?" Her brow narrowed in confusion. "I don't know anyone from Georgia."

"Oh, I believe you do." Smiling mysteriously, he retrieved a piece of paper from his vest pocket. "Ever heard of a man by the name of Tyler McRae?"

Her eyes widened incredulously. "You found ... Tyler?"

Nodding, he handed the wire to her. "I couldn't resist writing to The McRae Hotel in Chattanooga after I saw how much your brother meant to you. Apparently, someone from the hotel forwarded my letter to Tyler's home in Georgia."

Rebecca's eyes swelled with tears as she read the message from her brother. "And he's going to be here next week ..."

"... Just in time for the biggest wedding this town has ever seen," Grady finished, grinning as he stole a kiss from his wife to be.

Epilogue

"Do you think I'll recognize him? Do you think he'll recognize me? Do you think we'll—"

"Calm down, Rebecca." Grady draped a steadying arm over her trembling shoulders as the train chugged to a stop at the depot. "Everything will be just fine, I'm certain."

"I hope so." Rebecca nibbled on her lower lip, scanning the faces of the passengers as they stepped down from the train.

For some reason, an attractive woman wearing a stylish traveling suit caught Rebecca's eye. A little girl with dark hair was standing beside the woman, and she was holding a baby in her arms.

At that moment, a tall man with dark hair came up behind the woman and children, a man with blue eyes and an olive complexion . . .

Rebecca's heart leaped into her throat. "Tyler?"

He whipped around. As their eyes met and

374

locked for the first time in more than two decades, an expression of joy flooded his handsome features. With quick, long strides, he bridged the gap between them. "I can't believe I've finally found you, Rebecca!" he exclaimed, hugging her tightly.

The next few minutes buzzed with excitement. Rebecca was delighted to learn that the attractive woman was Tyler's wife, Julia. She was equally thrilled to be introduced to her infant nephew, Jeremiah Tyler McRae. And she was moved to tears when she met her namesake, Rebecca, Tyler and Julia's older child.

Two days later, moisture was still brimming in Rebecca's eyes as she stood at the door of the church, her hand linked over Jacob's arm. As she swept her gaze over the crowd of guests, she was touched by the sight of friends and family who were waiting for her to march down the aisle and declare her love and devotion to Grady Cunningham.

At that moment, sweet chords of organ music flowed through the sanctuary. Rebecca focused her gaze on the man standing beside the altar, and love swelled in her heart. Eager to declare her vows of commitment to Grady Cunningham, she stepped forward, anxious to begin their new life together as husband and wife.

Avon Romantic Treasures

Unforgettable, enthralling love stories,
sparkling with passion and adventure
from Romance's bestselling authors

LADY OF SUMMER *by Emma Merritt*
77984-6/$5.50 US/$7.50 Can

TIMESWEPT BRIDE *by Eugenia Riley*
77157-8/$5.50 US/$7.50 Can

A KISS IN THE NIGHT *by Jennifer Horsman*
77597-2/$5.50 US/$7.50 Can

SHAWNEE MOON *by Judith E. French*
77705-3/$5.50 US/$7.50 Can

PROMISE ME *by Kathleen Harrington*
77833-5/ $5.50 US/ $7.50 Can

COMANCHE RAIN *by Genell Dellin*
77525-5/ $4.99 US/ $5.99 Can

MY LORD CONQUEROR *by Samantha James*
77548-4/ $4.99 US/ $5.99 Can

ONCE UPON A KISS *by Tanya Anne Crosby*
77680-4/$4.99 US/$5.99 Can

Avon Romances—
the best in exceptional authors and unforgettable novels!

THE HEART AND THE ROSE Nancy Richards-Akers
78001-1/ $4.99 US/ $6.99 Can

LAKOTA PRINCESS Karen Kay
77996-X/ $4.99 US/ $6.99 Can

TAKEN BY STORM Danelle Harmon
78003-8/ $4.99 US/ $6.99 Can

CONQUER THE NIGHT Selina MacPherson
77252-3/ $4.99 US/ $6.99 Can

CAPTURED Victoria Lynne
78044-5/ $4.99 US/ $6.99 Can

AWAKEN, MY LOVE Robin Schone
78230-8/ $4.99 US/ $6.99 Can

TEMPT ME NOT Eve Byron
77624-3/ $4.99 US/ $6.99 Can

MAGGIE AND THE GAMBLER Ann Carberry
77880-7/ $4.99 US/ $6.99 Can

WILDFIRE Donna Stephens
77579-4/ $4.99 US/ $6.99 Can

SPLENDID Julia Quinn
78074-7/ $4.99 US/ $6.99 Can